What's a lady to do when her heart
refuses to make a proper match...?

... How I choose to comport myself with a suitor is none of your business."

His hand snaked up to capture her finger in its punishing grip. "Isn't it?"

And then his lips descended on hers.

Surprise was a funny human emotion.

It could trigger a range of reflexes, from desperate flight to violent resistance, depending on the patient in question. In Clare, it appeared to pin her frozen, helpless as a fledgling bird upon its first, unplanned exit from a nest.

The unforeseen kiss had surprised Daniel, as well. He could own this as a mistake he should not have made. The oath he'd taken—the oath he lived by—forbade this degree of interaction with his patients, in no uncertain terms.

But once his tenuous control had snapped, there was no going back.

It was clear she'd never been kissed before. No doubt her mouth had opened to lodge a protest, not to invite him in, but his own roiling emotions drove him on. Dimly, he realized his kiss was too fierce, too possessive, for someone so inexperienced.

Then again, it hadn't been planned, and he was damned if he knew how to script it better.

By Jennifer McQuiston

DIARY OF AN ACCIDENTAL WALLFLOWER
HER HIGHLAND FLING: A NOVELLA
MOONLIGHT ON MY MIND
SUMMER IS FOR LOVERS
WHAT HAPPENS IN SCOTLAND

JENNIFER McQUISTON

Diary of an Accidental Wallflower

AVON

An Imprint of HarperCollins*Publishers*

AVON BOOKS
An Imprint of HarperCollins*Publishers*
195 Broadway
New York, New York 10007

Copyright © 2015 by Jennifer McQuiston
ISBN 978-0-06-233501-2
www.avonromance.com

First Avon Books mass market printing: March 2015

Avon Trademark Reg. U.S. Pat. Off. and in Other Countries, Marca Registrada, Hecho en U.S.A.

HarperCollins® is a registered trademark of HarperCollins Publishers.

Printed in the U.S.A.

10 9 8 7 6 5 4 3 2 1

*To my mother, Joy Hensley, who taught me to
always appreciate a good book, a good horse, and
a good husband, not necessarily in that order*

Acknowledgments

As always, a big shout of thanks goes out to writing friends and partners in crime Alyssa Alexander, Romily Bernard, Tracy Brogan, Sally Kilpatrick, and Kimberly Kincaid. You ladies make it a pleasure to sometimes bang my head against this writing wall, mainly because you always provide willing company. A special shout-out is owed Noelle Pierce, who gives beta reads that rock, and to Nicki Salcedo, who is just plain awesomeness in a skirt. Special thanks to Georgia Romance Writers, an organization that helps authors realize their potential and that provides a continuous source of new and amazing friends.

The life of an author-with-a-day-job can be downright annoying at times. My family probably deserves better, but for now they seem to be sticking with me and I am grateful for their support and enthusiasm. To my amazing agent Kevon Lyon, my wonderful editor Tessa Woodward and her assistant Gabrielle Keck, and Avon publicity rock star Caroline Perny: I could never thank you enough, but I promise to keep trying. To the entire team at Avon and Harper Collins, from the art department, to marketing, to the wonderful staff who convince stores to stock me on their shelves: thank you so very much! You always pretend I know what I am doing.

Keep on pretending, and I'll keep writing.

Diary of an
Accidental
Wallflower

May 2, 1848

Dear Diary,

If a man's worth is measured in pounds, a woman's is measured in dance steps. And if those dance steps are with a future duke, surely they are worth all the more. Mr. Alban, the future Duke of Harrington, asked me to dance again last night, the third time since the start of the Season. My friends are abuzz with what he might ask next, and I confess, I hope it is something more significant than a dance. I know the Season has just begun, but surely a proposal cannot be far from his mind?

When I feel the sting of jealousy from the less fortunate girls lining the walls, I remind myself some casualties are inevitable if I am to dance all the way to a ducal mansion. Any girl who feels tempted to accept the first offer that comes their way would do well to comfort themselves on the arm of a mere marquess.

Miss Clare Westmore
The Future Duchess of Harrington

Chapter 1

Miss Clare Westmore wasn't the only young woman to fall head-over-heels for Mr. Charles Alban, the newly named heir to the Duke of Harrington.

Though, she was probably the only one to fall quite so literally.

He appeared out of nowhere, broad-shouldered and perfect, trotting his horse down one of the winding paths near the Serpentine. His timing was dreadful. For one, it was three o'clock on a Friday afternoon, hardly a fashionable hour for anyone to be in Hyde Park. For another, she'd come down to the water with her siblings in tow, and the ducks and geese they'd come to feed were already rushing toward them like a great screeching mob.

Her sister, Lucy, poked an elbow into her ribs. "Isn't that your duke?"

Clare's heart galloped well into her throat as the sound of hoofbeats grew closer. What was Mr. Alban *doing* here? Riders tended to contain themselves to Rotten Row, not this inauspicious path near the water. If he saw her now it would be an unmitigated disaster. She was wearing last Season's walking habit—fashionable enough for the ducks, but scarcely the modish image she wished to project to the man who could well be her future husband. Worst of all, she was with Lucy, who brushed her hair approximately once a week, and her brother Geoffrey, who ought to have been finishing his first year at Eton but was expelled just last week for something more than the usual youthful hijinks.

Clare froze in the center of the milling mass of birds, trying to decide if it would be wiser to lift her skirts and run or step behind the cover of a nearby rhododendron bush. One of the geese took advantage of her indecision and its beak jabbed at her calf through layers of silk and cotton. Before she knew what was happening—or even gather her wits into something resembling a plan—her thin-soled slipper twisted out from under her and she pitched over onto the ground with an unladylike *oomph*. She lay there, momentarily stunned.

Well then. The rhododendron it was.

She tucked her head and rolled into the shadow of the bush, ignoring low-hanging branches that reached out for her. The ducks, being intelligent fowl, followed along. They seized the crumpled bag of bread still clutched in her hand and began gulping down its contents. The geese—being, of course, quite the opposite of ducks—shrieked in protest and flapped their wings, stirring up eddies of down and dust.

Clare tucked deeper into the protection of the bush, straining to hear over the avian onslaught. Had she been seen? She didn't think so. Then again, her instincts had also told her no one of importance would be on this path in Hyde Park at three o'clock on a Friday afternoon, and look how well those thoughts had served.

"Oh, what fun!" Lucy laughed, every bit as loud as the geese. "Are you playing the damsel in distress?"

"Perhaps she is studying the mating habits of water fowl," quipped Geoffrey, whose mind always seemed to be on the mating habits of *something* these days. He tossed a forelock of blond hair out of his eyes as he offered her a hand, but Clare shook her head. She didn't trust her brother a wit. At thirteen years old and five and a half feet, he was as tall as some grown men, but he retained an adolescent streak of mischief as wide as the Serpentine itself.

He was as likely to toss her into Alban's path as help her escape.

Lucy cocked her head. Wisps of tangled blond hair rimmed her face like dandelion fluff and made her appear far younger than her seventeen years, though her tall frame and evident curves left no doubt that she was old enough to show more care with her appearance. "Shall I call Mr. Alban over to request his assistance, then?" she asked, none too innocently.

"Shhhh," Clare hissed. Because the only thing worse than meeting the future Duke of Harrington while dressed in last year's walking habit was meeting him while wallowing in the dirt. Oh, but she should never have worn such inappropriate shoes to go walking in Hyde Park. Then again, such hindsight came close to philosophical brilliance when offered up from the unforgiving ground.

She held her breath until the sound of hoofbeats began to recede into the distance. Dimly, she realized something hurt. In fact, something hurt dreadfully. But she couldn't quite put her finger on the source when her mind was spinning in more pertinent directions.

"Why are you hiding from Mr. Alban?" Lucy asked pointedly.

"I am not hiding." Clare struggled to a sitting position

and blew a wayward brown curl from her eyes. "I am . . . er . . . feeding the ducks."

Geoffrey laughed. "Unless I am mistaken, the ducks have just fed themselves, and that pair over there had a jolly good tup while the rest of them were tussling over the scraps. You should have invited your duke to join us."

"He's not yet a duke," Clare corrected crossly. Much less *her* duke.

But oh, how she wanted him to be.

"Pity to let him go by without saying anything. You could have shown him your overhanded throw, the one you use for Cook's oldest biscuits." Geoffrey pantomimed a great arching throw out into the lake. "*That* would impress him, I'm sure."

The horror of such a scene— and such a brother—made Clare's heart thump in her chest. To be fair, feeding the ducks was something of a family tradition, a ritual born during a time when she hadn't cared whether she was wearing least year's frock. These days, with their house locked in a cold, stilted silence and their parents nearly estranged, they retreated here almost every day. And she *could* throw Cook's biscuits farther than either Lucy or Geoffrey, who took after their father in both coloring and clumsiness. It was almost as if they had been cut from a different bolt of cloth, coarse wool to Clare's smooth velvet.

But these were not facts one ought to share with a future duke—particularly when that future duke was the gentleman you hoped would offer a proposal tonight. No, better to wait and greet Mr. Alban properly this evening at Lady Austerley's annual ball, when Lucy and Geoffrey were stashed safely at home and she would be dressed in tulle and diamonds.

"I don't understand." Lucy stretched out her hand, and this time Clare took it. "Why wouldn't you wish to greet him? He came to call yesterday, after all, and I was given the impression you liked him very much."

Clare pulled herself to standing and winced as a fresh bolt of pain snatched the breath from her lungs. "How do you know about that?" she panted. "I didn't tell anyone." In fact, she'd cajoled their butler, Wilson, to silence. It was imperative word of the visit be kept from their mother, who—if last Season's experience with potential suitors was any indication—would have immediately launched a campaign to put Waterloo to shame.

"I know because I spied on you from the tree outside the picture window." Lucy shrugged. "And didn't you say that he asked you to dance last week?"

"Yes," Clare agreed between gritted teeth. Mr. Alban *had* asked her to dance last week, a breathless waltz that sent the room spinning and held all eyes upon them. It was the third waltz they had shared since the start of the Season—though not all on the same night, more's the pity. But the glory of that dance paled in comparison to the dread exacted by Lucy's confession.

Had her sister really hung apelike from a limb and leered at the man through the window? Except . . . hadn't Alban sat with his back to the window?

She breathed a sigh of relief. Yes, she was almost sure of it. He'd spent the entire quarter hour with his gaze firmly anchored on her face, their conversation easy. But despite the levity of their exchange, he'd seemed cautious, as though he were hovering on the edge of some question that never materialized but that she fervently wished he'd just *hurry up and ask*.

Given his unswerving focus, there was no way he would have seen her clumsy heathen of a sister swinging through the branches, though she shuddered to think that Lucy could have easily lost her balance and come crashing through the window in a shower of broken glass and

curse words. But thankfully nothing of the sort had happened. No awkward siblings had intruded on the flushed
pleasure of the moment. Her mother had remained oblivious, distracted by her increasing irritation with their
father and her shopping on Bond Street.

And to Clare's mind, Mr. Alban had all but declared his
intentions out loud.

Tonight, she thought fiercely. Tonight would be the
night when he asked for more than just a dance. And that
was why it was very important for her to tread carefully,
until he was so irrevocably smitten she could risk the introduction of her family.

"I *do* admire him," she admitted, her mind returning reluctantly to the present. "I just do not want him to see me
looking like . . ." Clare glanced down at her grass-stained
skirts and picked at a twig that had become lodged in the
fabric. "Well, like this."

Lucy frowned. "I scarcely think his admiration should
be swayed by a little dirt."

"And you didn't look like that before you dove behind
that bush," Geoffrey pointed out. "Stunning bit of acro-
batics, though. You ought to apply to the circus, sis."

"I didn't dive behind the bush." Clare battled an exasperated sigh. She couldn't expect either of them to understand. Lucy still flitted through life not caring if her hair
was falling down. Such obliviousness was sure to give
her trouble when she came out next year. Clare herself
couldn't remember a time when she hadn't been acutely
aware of every hair in its place, every laugh carefully cultivated.

And Geoffrey was . . . well . . . *Geoffrey.*

Loud, male, and far too crude for polite company.

As a child, the pronounced differences between herself
and her siblings had often made her wonder if perhaps she
had been a foundling, discovered in a basket on the front

steps of her parents' Mayfair home. She loved her brother and sister, but who wouldn't sometimes squirm in embarrassment over such a family?

And what young woman wouldn't dream of a dashing duke, destined to take her away from it all and install her within the walls of his country estate?

Clare took a step, but as her toe connected with the ground, the pain in her right ankle punched through the annoyance of her brother's banter. "Oh," she breathed. And then, as she tried another step, "*Ow!* I . . . I must have twisted my ankle when I fell."

"I still say you dove," Geoffrey smirked.

Lucy looked down with a frown. "Why didn't you say something?" she scolded. "Can you put any weight on it at all?"

"I didn't realize at first." Indeed, Clare's mind had been too much on the threat of her looming social ruin to consider what damage had been done to her person. "And I am sure I can walk on it. Just give me a moment to catch my breath."

She somehow made her way to a nearby bench, ducks and geese scattering like ninepins. By the time she sat down, she was gasping in pain and battling tears. As she slid her dainty silk slipper off, all three of them peered down at her stocking-encased foot with collective indrawn breaths. Geoffrey loosened an impressed whistle. "Good God, sis. That thing is swelling faster than a prick at a bawdy show."

"*Geoffrey!*" Clare's ears stung in embarrassment, though she had to imagine it was an apt description for the swollen contours of her foot. "This is not Eton, we are not your friends, and that will be *quite* enough."

"Don't you have Lady Austerley's ball tonight?" Lucy asked, her blue eyes sympathetic. "I can't imagine you can attend like this. In fact, I feel quite sure we ought to carry you home and call for the doctor, straight away."

But Clare's mind was already tilting in a far different direction. This evening's ball hadn't even crossed her mind when she had been thinking of the pain, but now she glared down at her disloyal ankle. *No, no, no.* This could not be happening. Not when she was convinced Mr. Alban would seek her out for more than just a single dance tonight.

It didn't hurt so much when she was sitting.

Surely it would be better in an hour or so.

"Of course I can go." She struggled to slip her shoe back on, determined to let neither doubts nor bodily deficiency dissuade her. "Just help me home, and don't tell Mother," she added, "and everything will be fine."

Chapter 2

*Y*ou belong in bed, not in a ballroom."

Dr. Daniel Merial chased this medical opinion with his most impressive glower and prayed his patient would see reason. He'd been summoned to 36 Berkeley Square by a furtive note, delivered to the morgue at St. Bartholomew's Hospital. He'd come immediately, no matter that he'd been forced to abandon a body lying half dissected on the theater table. The deceased was of unusual height and abnormal bone density, and a cataloging of the body's physical findings would have lent itself well to a paper on the subject.

But it was an opportunity now lost.

The physician who'd taken over the case had seemed far more interested in helping the students position the corpse into grotesque, suggestive poses than locating a pencil to record his findings. It annoyed Daniel to turn a perfectly interesting cadaver over to a fool like that, but St. Bart's was full of pompous young doctors whose positions had been secured by wealthy fathers willing to contribute to a new hospital wing, rather than any clear demonstration of intelligence. Unlike them, *he* needed to supplement his meager instructor's salary by serving as a personal physician to the wealthy and cantankerous, at the beck and call of London's elite.

Though this patient, in particular, was proving a very troublesome case.

Lady Austerley's lips thinned— if indeed an aging dowager countess's lip could thin any more than nature already commanded. "Cancelling my annual ball is not an option, Dr. Merial. It is seven o'clock already. Half of London will be summoning their coaches, and the other half will be lamenting their lack of an invitation." She rubbed her gnarled hands together. "Now, surely you have some more of that marvelous medication. It helped so much the last time you gave it to me."

Daniel sighed, suspecting this irksome venture could be explained by little more than an old lady's lonely pride. It had not escaped his notice that he was one of Lady Austerley's most frequent—indeed, one of her only—visitors. Her husband was long dead, and their forty year union had not been blessed with children. The cousin who had inherited her husband's title never came to call. She'd outlived her friends, and now she seemed determined to outlive her heart.

"The belladonna extract is a temporary fix, at best," he warned, "and may well do more damage to your heart in the long term. What you *need* is rest, and plenty of it."

"But I *am* resting." Lady Austerley offered him a smile, one that showed her false ivory teeth in all their preternatural glory. "You see, I am lying down on the bed while my maid curls my hair." As if offering testimony to this nonsensical thought, the pink-cheeked maid—who'd been casting him dream-filled glances since his arrival—pulled the curling tongs from her mistress's thinning gray hair with an audible hiss.

"And I promise not to dance," the countess continued, "if you would but leave a draught or two, enough to get me through this evening."

Daniel was sorely tempted to leave her laudanum instead, but he wasn't sure he had the heart to deceive her into sleep. Lady Austerley could be difficult, but she had also been his first substantial client in London. Her remarkable and unexpected patronage had opened the doors of his fledgling practice, and he was only now beginning to attract the occasional notice of other well-connected clients.

But that didn't mean she actually *listened* to him.

His client might be lying down in bed, but she was also already dressed for her ball, swaddled in a gown of gold brocade that at turns threatened to asphyxiate and dazzle. The room should have smelled of camphor, but instead it smelled of French perfume and the faint, acrid scent of burning hair. "I told you weeks ago you were making yourself ill, Lady Austerley." He ran a frustrated hand through his hair. "You ought to have cancelled the event then. Instead, you've exhausted yourself with preparations."

"You did tell me my remaining time fell on the side of months, rather than years, did you not?" At his nod, she shrugged her thin shoulders—unapologetically, to Daniel's mind. "I am determined to make my last days memorable, and give them all something they won't soon forget. What was that bit of Latin you quoted for me?"

Her expectant pause made him want to fidget. *"Quam bene vivas referre, non quam diu,"* he admitted reluctantly.

It is how well you live that matters, not how long.

He'd offered her the phrase soon after it became clear her condition was carrying her surely and steadily toward the grave. But he'd meant to encourage her to reflect on the life she had led. He'd certainly not intended it to be a dictum for how she should go on.

Her frown shifted to a wrinkled smile. "There, you see?" she beamed, quite pleased with herself. "I am just following my doctor's orders."

"Lady Austerley, you must know you are shortening the time you have left by the very choices you make now. You could easily suffer another fainting spell tonight, even with the medication," he warned. "You were fortunate your maid was attending you during your bath this afternoon when the latest one struck, or you might have drowned. This is the second attack you've experienced this week, is it not?"

The dowager countess nodded innocently.

"My lady is perhaps forgetting several spells," the maid piped up. "By my count, it is the fourth such episode since Monday."

Lady Austerley turned her gimlet glare on the younger woman. "Am I to count higher mathematics among your skills as my ladies' maid now? I cannot believe you bothered our beleaguered doctor with that note. I imagine it had as much to do with *you* wishing to see him again as any need for me to. You've been mooning over him for months."

The poor maid blushed, but not before her eyes darted tellingly in Daniel's direction. "I was thinking only of your health, my lady."

"Hrmmph." Lady Austerley's gaze shifted back. She lifted the quizzing glass she always kept around her neck, and he felt the sting of the older woman's visual dissection. "Not that I blame you," she added, a wrinkled smile playing about her lips. "He's a stunning specimen, with all that thick, dark hair and those soulful brown eyes.

Makes an old woman's heart flutter, even one whose heart is just barely ticking along. Truth be told, he puts these new London bucks to shame."

Daniel raised a brow, determined to circle this conversation away from the issue of whether or not he was considered attractive to the female species and back around to the medical issue at hand. "Lady Austerley—" he said sternly.

But she was not yet through. She lowered her lens and struggled to a sitting position as the maid plumped her pillow. "It's his heart that makes him different, though. Heart of gold, to come rushing to an old lady's aid like this. These young men today can't be bothered to look further than their phaetons for entertainment."

Daniel fought the urge to roll his eyes.

"I would have you come to the ball tonight and put my theory to the test, Dr. Merial." Lady Austerley lifted her quizzing glass again. "Yes, yes, my personal physician in attendance. That would be just the thing to show them all."

Daniel breathed out through his nose. Show them what, precisely? Her loss of sanity? He was tempted to dismiss her nattering as the beginnings of dementia. But alas, he knew there was nothing at all wrong with Lady Austerley's head. She was as lucid as a lark.

He might have stood a better chance at changing her mind if she wasn't.

"It sounds as though your attacks are increasing in frequency, as I predicted they would. Your heart is failing. You should be confined to your bed, if not to ward off these periods of syncope, to at least ensure when they occur you do not risk falling and causing more serious injury." He took in the dowager countess's impossibly straight back. "And didn't I advise against wearing a corset? You cannot afford to restrict your breathing further."

Lady Austerley waved a fist, the ropy veins crisscrossing the backs of her hands like twisted paths to truth. "I cannot have a ball without a corset, and as I've already said, I refuse to entertain the notion of cancelling the event. I must carry on, at least until tonight is behind me. Which is why I need you there, in case I suffer another spell."

"I cannot prevent these attacks," he informed her gravely. "I can only advise you on what you must do to reduce their frequency."

"Perhaps you cannot prevent them, but I will feel better knowing you are there." She tossed a bemused look at her maid, who was still star-gazing in Daniel's direction. "And if I should be so unfortunate as to feel off-balance again, surely if you are already present we can manage another episode with far less drama than this afternoon's little spell has entailed."

The maid blushed further, and tucked her head.

Daniel hesitated. He enjoyed spending time with the dowager countess, but he already had plans for this evening, plans that involved patients who didn't disagree with his diagnoses—namely, the unfinished cadaver he'd left lying prone on the theater table. If he agreed to this farce of an idea, he would need to slip back to his rooms now to bathe and dress instead of returning to the morgue. He'd also planned another phase of his experiment for later this evening, testing varying doses of a promising new compound called chloroform with the anesthetic regulator he was developing. Losing valuable hours at a ball was not high on his list of priorities.

Although, if he were brutally honest, tonight's event might benefit him in the long run. He was very afraid Lady Austerley might not live to see Christmas. He would regret the eventual loss of that income, though not as much as he would regret the loss of her sometimes prickly friendship. Tonight would be an opportunity for introductions to future clients, if nothing else.

The countess leaned back against her mountain of plush pillows, and her hand crept out to grab his own. Her frail touch was a shock. He could feel her thready pulse, beating faintly through her bones, hinting at coming trouble. "I would ask this of you, Dr. Merial. As a favor to a scared old lady whose heart needs to last through at least one more ball."

Daniel swallowed his misgivings. How could he say no to such a request?

She had no family to speak of, no remaining close friends. She was lonely and ailing and he'd been unable to refuse the dowager countess anything since their first chance meeting, when she'd fainted dead away in St. Paul's Cathedral and he'd been the only one with enough sense to come to her aid. He squeezed her hand. "If it would ease your mind."

"Excellent." Lady Austerley smiled. "I'll have an invitation penned for you, posthaste."

Chapter 3

Clare's ankle wasn't better in an hour or so.

Neither had it improved by the time the coach was brought around to the front door, nor by the time she stepped into Lady Austerley's vaulted foyer. If anything, it was worse, sporting whimsical new shades of red and purple and stealing her breath with every step.

"Do try to keep up, dear." Her mother frowned over her shoulder, the red feather on her headdress bobbing with discontent. "I declare, you dawdle more like your father every day."

Clare gritted her teeth. She could not admit to her mother the real reason for her hesitation, or else risk being whisked home to bed. And any comparisons to Father were to be avoided if her mother was to remain in an ebullient mood this evening. She hobbled faster, her mismatched shoes clunking ominously on the marble tile.

Step, thump. Step, thump.

Her mother didn't seem to notice, but Clare's cheeks heated at the disparate sounds. She ought to be grateful Lucy was possessed of overlarge feet and, moreover, had been willing to donate an old shoe to the nearly lost cause of getting her foot into something approximating a slipper. At least she hadn't needed to resort to wearing *Geoffrey's* shoe.

But gratitude was not foremost on Clare's mind as her mother gave their name to the footman. She lifted her chin, knowing that aside from the travesty of her mismatched shoes, she had never looked better. Her maid had taken hours with her hair, and her new green gown was an absolute wonder, clinging to her shoulders with what appeared to be nothing more than hasty prayer. But though the gown's voluminous skirts hid her feet from public view, they could not change the fact her ankle still felt like a sausage shoved in a too-tight casing.

She looked out on the glittering swirl of London's most beautiful people, her stomach twitching in anticipation. The ballroom was awash with colors and scents, by now familiar after the triumph of her first Season. She knew what to expect, whom to greet, and whom to cut. And somewhere in the crowd Mr. Alban waited, a proposal surely simmering on his tongue.

Almost immediately she was set upon by her usual pack of friends, and her mother drifted off. "Where have you *been*?" Lady Sophie's fan snapped open and shut in agitation, though her eyes sparkled with mischief.

"Mr. Alban arrived nearly a half hour ago," Rose supplied helpfully.

Clare fit a careful half smile to her face as she greeted her friends. Lady Sophie Durston always stood out like a dark hothouse flower amidst the crowd, though this evening she stood out more because of her vivid pink gown. Miss Rose Evans was a classic English beauty, blond and blue-eyed. Tonight she was dressed in virginal white— though Sophie had snidely confided to Clare just last week that perhaps Rose should avoid that color, and not only because it was a miserable complement to the girl's too-pale complexion.

They were the young women all the men watched and the less fortunate girls envied. Together they had captured the hearts and imaginations of half the eligible men in the room. But since the start of this Season, Clare had been interested in only one of those hearts, and her friends knew it all too well.

She risked a veiled peek in Mr. Alban's direction. He was speaking with Sophie's father, a pompous windbag of an earl who had recently helped secure Parliament's new ban on public meetings. Intended to hobble supporters of the growing Chartist movement, the news had been splashed across all the papers and bandied about polite Society in hushed, worried tones. She briefly wondered which side of the debate Alban claimed, though it was something she could never ask during the space of a waltz.

But as the overhead chandelier caught the white flash of his teeth, those distracting thoughts fell away. Oh, but he looked resplendent tonight in a dark jacket and emerald waistcoat, his chestnut hair gleaming. She could almost see him looking just so across a morning breakfast table, polished to a shine by her careful attentions, the *Times* spread out amicably between them.

"Has Mr. Alban asked anyone to dance?" she asked, turning away from the heart-stopping sight of him so she could not be accused of mooning overlong.

"Not just yet," Rose piped up from Sophie's elbow, where she almost always hovered like a pale, blond shadow.

"He's been speaking with Father since he arrived," Sophie confirmed, her voice a low purr. "Business over pleasure, you know."

Clare was relieved to hear he had not been busy with other girls' dance cards, though she wasn't worried. Mr.

Alban had been remarkably persistent in asking her to dance the first waltz each evening. She harbored no doubts that this evening would go the same way.

As the musicians began to take their seats behind the screen of potted greenery that had been erected to hide them from view, a young man approached their group with the sort of enthusiasm usually displayed by unruly puppies—or, barring that, their eight-year-old owners.

"Good evening, Miss Westmore!"

Clare sighed, knowing she must acknowledge him. "Good evening, Mr. Meeks."

He beamed at her, though she'd gifted him with the barest of greetings. "I was honored last week when you said you would grant me the first dance this evening."

Clare gripped her dance card. Had she really done something so rash? He was a perfectly unthreatening specimen of a young man, but he was also one of the gentlemen Mother had encouraged far too enthusiastically last year. Still, Clare was predisposed to be kind. He meant well, even if he didn't make her heart stir with anything other sympathy.

And she liked to think she *would* have honored her agreement to dance with the young man, had things been different. But the conversation with Meeks had occurred one week and one turned ankle ago. She could scarcely be expected to honor such a promise given her current circumstances.

"I am afraid you must have misunderstood." She shook her head, knowing her ankle was unlikely to last more than a dance or two. "I am otherwise engaged."

He deflated before her eyes. "Oh. I see." His feet shuffled as he turned to Sophie and Rose, a nervous sheen on his high forehead. "Perhaps, then, if either of you are free?"

Sophie shook her head in mock regret. "I am afraid you

are far too tardy in asking, Mr. Meeks. Our cards are already full." She pointed her fan toward a line of restless young ladies sitting against the far wall of the ballroom. "You might aim your sights over there. I feel sure someone in the wallflower line will still have a few open spots remaining for a gentleman of your punctuality."

Mr. Meeks's cheeks flared with color as Rose tittered behind a gloved hand. As he turned away and began to trudge toward the wallflower line, Clare sighed. "Honestly, Sophie, was it necessary to be so cruel? He's done naught to earn our ire."

"Oh, don't look so glum," Sophie chided. She flicked her fan open and fluttered it lazily below her green eyes. "Truly, the occasional set-down is the best thing all around for him. Have you forgotten about that debacle last year, when he had the gall to think you might consider his proposal?" The air rang with her light laughter. "It isn't as though he should harbor hopes for anything beyond the occasional dance where *we* are concerned."

Clare held her tongue. It was true she had set her sights higher than a proposal from Meeks, but that did not mean she thought it was all right to snub him. There were some in the crowd who thought she *should* have accepted his proposal, her mother among them. After all, Mr. Meeks had an annual income of two thousand pounds and would one day be a viscount, the same title as her own father. There was potential there, to be sure.

But Sophie had decided, based on some unfathomable criteria only she knew, that Mr. Meeks was not within their sphere.

In contrast, though he was only the heir presumptive to a dukedom, Mr. Alban had been immediately welcomed into Sophie's circle. Of course, he was handsome as sin, something Mr. Meeks had no hope of claiming. Furthermore, the elderly Duke of Harrington was clearly consumptive, and, rumor had it, none too interested in females, so Alban was as good as the heir apparent in many eyes.

Still, it frightened Clare sometimes to see how unpredictable the tide of public opinion could be. Next year Lucy would be out among this harsh crowd, and in a few short years Geoffrey would also be navigating this same social gauntlet. She didn't like to think that her siblings—embarrassing though they may be—might be similarly sized up and dismissed.

So tonight she offered her friends nothing more questionable than an agreeable nod. Because being included in Sophie's gilded circle was far better than being shoved outside it, and she'd worked too hard to get here to ruin it tonight in a fit of misplaced kindness.

As the opening strains of the first set of the evening rang out, Sophie's lips curved upward. "Not that I would ever question your desire to wait for a better offer than was afforded by Mr. Meeks, but you've just arrived."

"Yes," Rose added, suspicion adding a half octave to her voice. "What was that nonsense about being otherwise engaged? You can't have a single name on your dance card yet."

"I . . . I might sit out the first set." At their looks of horror, Clare tried to smile, though she suspected it came out more as a grimace. "I'm a little fatigued this evening. I might prefer to save my strength to dance with Mr. Alban."

"You do look a trifle pale." Sophie's hand reached out to gently squeeze Clare's arm. "Heavens, what are we thinking, chattering away like magpies when you look close to swooning? You need to sit down and rest." She inclined her head toward the row of chairs she had earlier pointed out to Meeks. "There's a prime seat, just there. Now, which dance were you hoping for from Alban? Maybe I can help hurry him along."

Clare contemplated the vicious throbbing of her foot. The wallflower line was the furthest thing from a refuge, but it was also becoming increasingly obvious her ankle would be unlikely to tolerate more than a turn or two around the dance floor. "I think I should be recovered by the first waltz of the evening," she replied, eyeing an empty chair as if it might have teeth. "If you speak with Mr. Alban, you might offer him such a hint."

Sophie's smile deepened as her own partner arrived to collect her for the first dance. "Of course," she tossed over one shoulder, already gliding toward the dance floor. "You know I would do anything for a friend."

DEATH WAS RARELY —IF ever—a laughing matter.

Pity, that.

Daniel supposed it took a man with a sense of humor to prefer to stay with a decomposing corpse and a room full of eager young medical students rather than attend a ball. Still, he had promised Lady Austerley he would come tonight, and a promise made to a lonely, ailing countess was one you oughtn't break, unless the death you contemplated was your own.

Newly scrubbed and dressed in his best jacket, he greeted the dowager countess with a clinical eye, noting the pale fragility of her skin and the way her hands shook slightly through her gloves. Though the overhead chandeliers blazed with light, her pupils were dilated, providing some reassuring evidence the atropine he had given her earlier was still working.

"You look well tonight," Daniel lied, lifting her hand to his lips. "I see you have chosen to partially heed my advice and greet your guests while seated. Still, I would be negligent in my duties if I did not advise you that lying down would be the preferred course of action."

Lady Austerley's lips twitched. "If I were forty years

younger I would blush to hear such a thing from a handsome gentleman, Dr. Merial." She squeezed his hand. "Now. You may have come out of medical necessity, but I very much hope you will enjoy yourself this evening, because I have no intention of embarrassing myself with anything so gauche as a fainting spell. Perhaps you would do me the honor of a dance later?"

Daniel smiled down at the older woman. "Of course," he agreed, though they both knew the countess would not be dancing tonight, and probably never again.

As he moved on, searching for a space along the wall that would permit him a good view of his patient, he recognized a peer he had recently treated, a man whose various health woes he could catalog down to a resting heart rate. "Good evening, Lord Hastings," Daniel nodded.

The gentleman stiffened and turned away. For a moment Daniel was perplexed. Had he been incorrect in his address? Somehow rude in his delivery? But then he overheard another person greet the man, and he knew he'd had the right of it.

Ah, so *that's* how it was going to be.

When he was summoned to their homes to deal with a medical complaint, he was greeted with the sort of desperation reserved of a savior. But let him step among their ranks with an invitation in his pocket, and such niceties were lost.

The ladies in attendance, however, were a decidedly different story. Several among the painted and perfumed crowd ducked their heads behind their fans, then came back for a second, surreptitious look. Daniel had been in London only six months now, but already he understood why *these* women—women who had husbands and wealth and boredom to burn—looked at him with hooded eyes, fluttering fans, and undisguised interest. It was not comfort they were seeking.

He was young. He was handsome. He was *here*.

And those were apparently the only criteria to be considered.

He'd sidestepped their bold offers until now, but perhaps he'd been going about this all wrong, courting the male heads of these households in his bid to win more clients. He didn't doubt he could leave tonight with several new female patrons, if he applied a modicum of charm.

Or—given the way several smiled invitingly—an eager new bed partner or two.

Though he was tempted to test this theory by smiling back at them, Daniel aimed for the east side of the ballroom instead, where the crowd opened up and a row of chairs lined the wall. As he threaded his way there, he realized that Lady Austerley had been right to be concerned she might suffer one of her increasingly frequent dizzy spells tonight. The heat from the overhead chandeliers was stifling, and the mingling scents of beeswax and floral perfume made his own stomach feel off-kilter.

Worse, however, was the noise. All around him nonsensical conversations swirled like eddies of dust caught in the wind. This blond-haired chit felt another's gown was a simply *awful* shade of puce. That one shuddered to hear such a third-rate cellist sawing on the strings. One graying matron loudly bemoaned the fact the heads had been left on the prawns, no doubt to mock those guests possessed of more delicate sensibilities.

Though on the surface everyone was smiling, the undercurrent of female malcontent caught him by surprise. He could not help but feel there was something unhealthy about smiling to one's hostess in one moment and disparaging her in the next. Hadn't they come here tonight to honor the dowager countess, who, in her day, had been a widely admired figure? Though he knew she preferred to keep the details of her diagnosis private, anyone with a pair of functioning eyes could see the signs of the countess's declining health and realize this was Lady Austerley's last annual ball.

He wedged himself against a wall and scowled out at the crowd. Though it was difficult to credit the emotion, given that he was at a bloody ball, boredom began to creep in. Lady Austerley, bless her bones, was holding her own from her chair near the entrance to the ballroom, and looked to require no immediate assistance. He had no desire to dance, and refused to consider the horrors of puce or prawns, one way or the other.

Indeed, he had no desire to sample any of the diversions on offer here tonight.

Step, thump. Step, thump.

A sound cut through the drivel of small talk, and Daniel turned his head to search for its source. In the midst of such glitter and polish, that incongruous sound seemed his greatest hope to encounter something more thought-provoking tonight than third-rate cellists. He suffered an almost irrational disappointment to see nothing more interesting than a young lady approaching. A brunette, slim, and exceptionally attractive young lady, to be sure, but really no different than any of the other tittering flora and fauna on display tonight.

Step, thump. Step, thump.

Well, except for *that.*

His clinical skills flared to life. A few inches over five feet, but probably less than seven stone. She was within a year or two of twenty, though on which side she fell was little more than an educated guess. He had always been an ardent student of the human form, favoring symmetry over chaos, and his eye was drawn as much to the finely wrought curve of this girl's bones as the rich brown hair piled on top of her head. Her neck alone was an anatomist's dream, long and elegant, drawing the eye to the prominent line of her shoulders.

She flashed a half smile at someone who passed and he caught a glimpse of not-quite-perfect teeth, though the minor misalignment of her left cuspid did little to lessen the impression of general loveliness. If anything, it heightened his sense that she was real, rather than a porcelain doll waiting to be broken.

His eyes lingered a moment on the stark prominence of her clavicles, there above her neckline. She could stand to gain a few pounds, he supposed.

Then again, couldn't they all?

Step, thump. Step, thump.

That part was deucedly odd. She didn't appear outwardly lame, though her shuffling gait lacked the smooth refinement he expected in young ladies of the fashionable set. She settled herself into an empty seat along the wall and carefully arranged her skirts, but not before he caught the edge of one hideously ugly shoe, peeking out from beneath the hem of her gown.

Now that she was sitting still, her symptoms told him a far different story than the one delivered by her fixed half smile. Her gloved hands sat on her lap, the picture of feminine innocence, but as he watched, they knotted and unknotted in the shimmering green of her skirts, seeking traction against some unseen force. Her forehead was creased in concentration, and beads of perspiration had formed above her upper lip.

He well knew the signs. Either the chit was constipated or in severe pain.

He was betting on the latter.

And just like that the evening's entertainment shifted toward something far more promising than Lady Austerley's staunch refusal to faint.

Or even, God help him, the corpse.

Chapter 4

What was taking Alban so long?
Clare could see that he'd moved on from his earlier conversation. Now he was picking his way around the periphery of the ballroom, stopping here, smiling there.

He shimmered like a wish, but he was a wish that would not be realized, however much she willed him to glance in her direction. As the orchestra embarked on the third song of the evening, she knew a moment's panic. If her future duke was going to claim the first waltz, shouldn't he have already placed his name on her dance card?

She leaned back against her seat in frustration. Someone really ought to say something to Lady Austerley about this chair. Oh, there was nothing objectionable about the embroidered cushion or the gently curving back, but the view it offered of the dance floor was a matter of acute discomfort. She could see Sophie and Rose laughing in their partners' arms, spinning and shining like the view at the end of a kaleidoscope toy.

Envy burned a hot trail down the back of Clare's throat.

No one was approaching her to ask for a space on her dance card. Not even poor Mr. Meeks was offering her a second glance, choosing instead to dance with a horse-faced heiress from Lincolnshire.

By the opening strains of the fourth song, Clare's palms had started to sweat beneath her gloves. It seemed her position along the wall screamed out her unavailability to the crowd.

Either that, or her undesirability.

Good heavens, she hoped it wasn't *permanent*.

Why was she even here? No matter her friends' encouragement to sit and rest, there'd been mischief in Sophie's smile, and perhaps a bit of malice. She eyed the girls sitting on either side of her, a veritable herd of young ladies with unfortunate chins and thick waists. She ought to move. Leave the wallflowers to their misery and lurch back into the fray. But even as she contemplated it, her ankle throbbed a violent protest. If she couldn't even think about standing without cringing, how on earth was she going to dance?

Clare fingered one diamond ear bob, even as she scanned the crowd for her mother. Surely going home and being put to bed with a hot brick and a tisane would be better than abject humiliation, which was the only thing looming on her present horizon.

"Might I be of some assistance?"

Clare jumped. The motion made her injured ankle knock against the leg of her chair, and she gasped out loud from the shock of pain.

"Steady on," the masculine voice said next. "I didn't mean to startle you."

"Didn't you?" She glared up at the commenter. He was startlingly attractive—enough so that her limbs wanted to soften, for no reason other than feminine instinct. Refusing to give in to the impulse, she forced her gaze downward from his dark hair and eyes, only to realize the rest of him was every bit as befuddling as his face. Trim waist, well-proportioned limbs, and none of the softness inherent to most gentlemen of the ton.

The man's clothing, at least, provided an easier landing spot for her disdain. He was wearing a necktie far more appropriate for an office than a ballroom, suggesting he spent his days bent over books or ledgers. Clare narrowly suppressed a shudder as she cataloged the coarseness of his cheap wool jacket.

"I do not know you, sir. It is improper for you to speak to me." She fixed her gaze straight ahead again.

The stranger stepped closer—too close, really, for someone who had not been properly introduced. No matter his pleasing features, he was what Sophie and Rose laughingly called a "lurker." And according to Sophie, one did not encourage a lurker's interest, not if you wished to retain the title of "incomparable." She cut another glance in his direction. She was caught in this chair like an insect in amber, and he appeared to know it by the way his gaze still scraped across her skin. "You are staring, sir."

"That is because you ought to be home resting your turned ankle, rather than contemplating your next dance."

Clare peered up at her tormentor in horrified surprise. How had he known? Not even Sophie had guessed the reason for her discomfort this evening, and Sophie saw *everything*. The night's success with Mr. Alban depended on her to be sound—or, at the very least, to appear so for the length of a waltz. "There is nothing wrong with my ankle," she lied.

"I would wager a month's income to the contrary."

Clare's mouth rounded in indignation. "And that would be the shocking sum of three, perhaps *four* pounds?" she said tartly.

The man's lips twitched upward, making him appear

even more attractive, if such a thing were even possible. He crossed his arms. "You are wearing mismatched shoes, and your breathing is labored, though you have been sitting quite still for some ten minutes. The cumulative evidence suggests otherwise, Miss . . . ?"

"Westmore," she snapped. Her vision wobbled, even as she tucked her traitorous shoes farther beneath her skirts. "My father is Viscount Cardwell," she added, "so I am sure you can agree that it most improper for me to be speaking with you." She pulled her shoulders back to a position which ought to have screamed "untouchable," but the motion had the misfortune of pressing her breasts against her corset and stifling her ability to draw a full breath.

Worse, it made his gaze drop alarmingly to her neckline.

Clare imagined she could see an unhealthy speculation grinding to life in his dark eyes— whether due to expanse of flesh visible above her low neckline or the mention of a wealthy, titled father, it was difficult to be sure. "Well, then," he said easily, "let us find a quieter spot, Miss Westmore. In my experience, most fathers want their daughters well cared for. There could be no impropriety in permitting an examination by a physician."

She smothered a snort of disbelief. How dare this stranger speak to her this way?

For that matter how dare he *look* at her this way, as if he could peel back her layers and poke about in search of hidden secrets? She generally tried to avoid men who displayed an improper interest in her bosom or her dowry— not that she wouldn't mercilessly use either attribute to snare the right gentleman. Why, when Alban asked her to dance tonight, she'd willingly tug her bodice an inch lower and do her best to remind him that she was an investment guaranteed a return of five thousand pounds.

But not for this man. Though she granted the occasional sympathetic dance to the Mr. Meekses of the world, she was not obligated to indulge *this* type of gentleman, men who talked innocent, dowered young ladies into darkened corners, even as they slouched about in cheap wool jackets.

"If you wish to impress the less astute young ladies here tonight, and convince one of *them* to lift their skirts for your so-called examination, I've a word of advice," she said archly. "You might want to pretend a more admirable sort of profession, one that doesn't involve snatching corpses from their graves and carving people up with knives."

Dark brows rose high. "There is a legal trade in bodies now, you know. And I am a physician, not a common surgeon."

But Clare was committed to her path now. "Barrister should do, given your stated interest in weighing the evidence put before you. Clergyman, in a pinch, though I suspect it may not get you as far as you wish, given the limits it might place on your persuasive techniques." She canted her head. "Truly, claiming to be a fishmonger might be your best bet, given your careless attire. Most clergyman can afford a decent tailor."

He blinked. "You believe I am lying because of how I am dressed?"

She smiled wickedly, unable to help herself. "Evidence, and all."

Unexpectedly, he laughed, and Clare found herself unable to look away from the resulting flash of white teeth. Surely the man had *some* physical flaw? But no, there was not a scar to be seen on that smoothly shaven cheek, nor a single misaligned tooth to fix the eye and ease the mind. She was struck by the disloyal notion that, lurker or no, the man was objectively as handsome as her future duke.

Possibly even more so

He uncrossed his arms, though his smile lingered. "I have failed to properly introduce myself, I see. Perhaps we should start again."

"I believe you already have my name," she replied coolly, though his continued smile kept her traitorous heart thumping away in her chest. Almost as if it were enjoying this scandalous exchange and was urging her on to greater folly.

"Dr. Daniel Merial. Fellow of the Royal Medical and Chirurgical Society, and lecturer of forensic medicine at St. Bartholomew's teaching hospital." He bowed from the waist. "As well as serving, on occasion, as Lady Auster-ley's personal physician."

She scoffed, though the first strains of unease began to scratch at her conscience. "You expect me to believe the dowager countess would invite her physician to her own ball?"

"I was not invited as a guest."

Clare licked lips gone suddenly dry. "What ails the countess, that she would have need of her physician to-night?"

He shook his head. "I cannot divulge matters of such a personal nature. A physician is sworn to keep his patients' secrets in strictest confidence. But rest assured, you have sorely misinterpreted my interest, Miss Westmore. I am suggesting a medical evaluation for your obviously in-jured ankle, not a sordid tryst in the library. I presume you have a chaperone here tonight who could ensure nothing untoward happens?"

Clare flushed, as unmoored by his smooth speech as the reminder of her own ill manners. "My mother is here," she admitted. She scanned the crowd again, seeking her mother's feathered headdress. When a sighting remained elusive, her gaze fell instead on their hostess, who was seated in a chair near the entrance to the ballroom.

For the first time, she realized that Lady Austerley *did* look rather ill.

Her stomach tilted.

"If you require a reference beyond Lady Austerley, Lord Hastings is in attendance tonight, and he has also recently employed my services," he continued. "But if you have not yet seen a physician, I would suggest you do so before indulging in the extravagance of the dance you appear to be waiting for. You wouldn't want to cause further damage."

Clare found herself battling a far different sort of panic than her initial distress over her empty dance card. Was the gentleman telling the truth? Had she just accused Lady Austerley's physician of trying to toss up her skirts in a public ballroom? She had insulted this man's profession, his morals, *and* his clothing.

Worse, no lurker's smile had ever affected her so viscerally.

Could this night get any worse?

The first notes of a waltz rang out. Her gaze fell like a loosened arrow on Mr. Alban, walking along the edge of the ballroom. Her heart fluttered in its cage.

And then froze as her future duke stopped in front of Lady Sophie.

For a moment she could only stare in disbelief as Sophie extended her hand. Surely she *wouldn't*. Sophie knew her confessed hopes for Mr. Alban, hopes that went far beyond the first waltz of the evening. But as Sophie placed her hand in Alban's and tossed a telling smile in her direction, it became very clear that such things mattered not a whit.

Sophie's claws had just come out beneath her kidskin gloves.

Tears pricked Clare's eyes, hot and unwelcome. She should have known Sophie was up to something. But could she blame Mr. Alban for choosing to dance with a graceful beauty over a lame wallflower? She was wearing mismatched shoes and lingering with a lurker.

If the situation had been reversed, she wouldn't dance with someone like her, either.

WHAT IN THE deuces had just happened?

One moment he had been feeling his way toward a potential new patron.

The next, tears were spilling out of Miss Westmore's wide, hazel eyes, dampening a dangerous degree of décolletage.

She stood up without even a word of polite apology, though they'd been locked in something that went a degree or two beyond casual conversation. Daniel caught the faint scent of roses on the air, and then she turned on an unbalanced heel and lurched her way through the crowd. *Step-thump-step-thump-step-thump-step-thump.*

He watched her retreating form with an inexplicable urge to follow. Whatever ailed the girl, he was no longer sure it was within his capacity to help. Did lunacy run in Cardwell's bloodline? She'd gone pale as new milk, and toward the end of their exchange, her labored breathing had become more of a pant. Of course, some of those symptoms might be laid at the hands of her corset, the boning clearly visible against the delicate green silk of her dress.

Unfortunately, there was no clear cure for stupidity in the name of fashion.

"Miss Westmore," he called out. "Wait!"

If she could be credited with any sort of reaction, it was speed.

He set off after her, though he questioned his own motives in doing so. The girl had eschewed his offer of assistance and insulted him in the process. There were at least a hundred other peers he might pursue tonight as potential clients. He ought to be going in the *opposite* direction of the bewildering Miss Westmore.

Instead, he followed her through the large double doors that marked the rear boundary of the ballroom and led toward the deeper recesses of the house. Here, scattered couples lingered in corners, and the shadows stretched longer. There were no overhead chandeliers to light the way, just a series of wall sconces that flickered in the wake of her headlong path.

She turned left down a hallway, one hand braced against the wall for support. Even the last scattering of people had fallen away now, and the hall echoed with naught but her comically uneven steps. It was the absolute fringe of propriety for a girl without a chaperone, and she had just leaped clean across it in her mad dash from the ballroom.

"Miss Westmore," he warned. "You risk doing your ankle irrevocable harm if you do not have a care—"

She glanced back over her shoulder. He had the merest glimpse of reddened eyes as she reached a hand for the nearest door. And then she wrenched it open and plunged through, her green skirts billowing out behind her.

Daniel stopped stock-still. She'd entered Lady Austerley's library, a room he knew well from his regular visits. Did Miss Westmore mean for him to follow, then? He'd been quite serious when he suggested a chaperone accompany them. His financial future depended on the continued trust of the ton, and he had no desire to be caught in an indelicate situation with *any* young lady, much less one who might or might not be a half-wit.

Perhaps she was trying to trap him, flaunting her injury

like a lure, drawing him into her web before she struck like a venomous spider.

A faint scream rent the air.

His feet propelled him forward, sanity and spiders be damned.

He pushed through the door and skidded to a stop amidst the smells of aging paper and leather-bound spines. Miss Westmore stood frozen, one hand clapped over her mouth. Daniel followed her startled gaze to the room's other occupants, even as his mind sought to catalog his various means of defense. In his left pocket lay a wooden auscultating device that could be hefted as a bludgeon, should circumstances come to that. A book would work equally well, given that they were in a library, for Christ's sake.

But just *who* he was to bludgeon remained a bit of a mystery.

The scene was the furthest thing from threatening. There were books, of course. Thousands of them, more than a body could hope to read in a dozen lifetimes, lined with military precision along the walls. He'd even read one or two of them, at Lady Austerley's invitation. A fire burned in the grate, the orange flames recently stirred to life.

A couple was disentangling themselves in front of the fireplace, where they had clearly been locked in an embrace. The man's jacket had been removed and tossed aside.

The reality of the situation snapped into place.

"My apologies," Daniel offered curtly. "We did not mean to intrude."

Far from being embarrassed, the gentleman—if indeed, such a title could be claimed—laughed. "We'll only be another moment, old chap. Happy to quit the room when we're done. Unless you're here for a turn yourself?"

Distaste for the proceedings made Daniel's stomach churn. Not that he objected to a bit of consensual bed sport if both partners were unencumbered, free of syphilis, and willing.

But he'd never been one for an audience.

"Miss Westmore," he said, turning away from the scene and keeping his voice low. "We should go." He took her by the arm. Her skin felt strong and alive beneath his gloved fingers, and he knew a moment's surprise as she planted her feet and resisted his gentle tug.

Not so frail after all, then.

He leaned in close to her ear, drawing in a rose-scented breath in the process. "It is not appropriate for you to be here. I did not intend for us to come without your mother as chaperone."

She came to life, blinking rapidly. Whatever tears had possessed her moments ago had fled, chased into the shadows by the bright wash of color on her cheeks.

"Then how fortuitous," she hissed, jerking away from his hold, "to find her already here."

Chapter 5

Oh God, oh God, oh God.

Blasphemous, perhaps, but if ever a situation called for her eternal damnation, this was it. At least in hell she could escape the nightmare of this evening.

Clare's ankle throbbed in violent protest to the treatment it had just suffered during her headlong rush from the ballroom, but the sick, empty feeling in her stomach did a fair job of pushing the pain from her mind. She had naively presumed her mother came to these events to gossip with the other matrons and to sip lemonade from the shadows.

She'd never before stopped to consider what occupied her mother's attention every evening while she flitted about the dance floor.

This, then, was the physical embodiment of why she lived in terror of introducing Mr. Alban to her family. It wasn't just Geoffrey, with his crude language and questionable manners, or Lucy, with her fly-away hair and two left feet. It was not even the fear of being seen in last Season's walking habit, or being caught tossing stale biscuits to water fowl.

It was because her very life was a house of cards, threatening to come down with a single stiff wind.

Clare glared at the gentleman standing before the fire. He was young. Impossibly so, perhaps even her own age. She had no notion of the stranger's name, and had never danced with him, thank goodness. Then again, why would she have? With his tousled brown hair and hooded eyes, he was possessed of the sort of Byronic good looks her mother had always warned her against.

"I've been looking for you, Mother." She was surprised to discover her voice was steady. She felt as though the very floor were vibrating beneath her.

"Is something amiss, dear?" Her mother seemed distracted. Distant. Perhaps she was embarrassed, though her face was oddly blank, as though she were having trouble staying upright. But Clare discovered she wasn't in a very forgiving state of mind, particularly when her mother drifted toward her and said, "It isn't like you to come in search of me."

She battled a moment's dark disbelief. Shouldn't it be her chaperone's responsibility to come in search of *her*?

The nameless gentleman snatched up his coat and gave them all a smart salute as he stalked from the room. As the door pulled shut behind him, Clare settled on the first logical excuse she could find, though it was one she had been running from mere moments before. "I have twisted my ankle. This is Dr. Merial, Lady Austerley's personal physician. He has offered to examine it for me."

If the doctor was ruffled by the strange situation, he didn't show it. "We had thought to conduct the examination in the library," Dr. Merial confirmed.

Clare's cheeks heated at that. In truth, she hadn't known her mother was in the library. She hadn't even known the room *was* the library, only that it offered a door that promised escape. But she was ill-inclined to defend her actions, given the circumstances. She gathered her wits into a tight ball and took aim at her mother with an acidity that should have shamed her. "Provided, of course, I can locate a *reasonable* chaperone."

But her words fell on deaf ears, because her mother's bleary eyes were focused on Dr. Merial. "I confess, I am surprised to hear she has injured herself. Clare has always been the most athletic of my children. Now her sister, Lucy, perhaps. We've given up any hope for grace with that one, and begun to pray for a miracle instead."

"Mother," Claire groaned. Had the word "athletic" really just fallen from her mother's lips as a suitable description for her eldest daughter? And shouldn't they be speaking well of Lucy, building a sense of refinement in people's minds that would help counteract the terrible physical impression her sister was bound to make next year?

Now was not the time to spill such family secrets.

Though, on the scale of calamities, her sibling's clumsiness paled in comparison to the disaster Clare feared may have just been uncovered in this very room.

She glanced away, and caught sight of her reflection in the mirror hanging over the mantel. Though her world had just been upended and forcefully shaken, she looked the same as she had earlier in the evening, albeit a trifle paler: same dress, same hair. The same clenched smile, with the slightly crooked front tooth she always tried to hide.

But she felt like a fraud.

From the start of her first Season, she had wrapped her self-doubts in tissue paper, carefully cultivating the image she wished to project. She'd draped herself in silk from London's most sought-after modiste and aligned herself with the most beautiful girls from the most influential families. Through a combination of good fortune and careful choices, she'd reached a pinnacle of popularity most only dreamed of, and had dared to set her sights on a future duke.

And yet, now that she had arrived, she felt that delicate paper slipping away to reveal the tarnished surface below. She battled the constant peril to be found in every potential slight, every snide comment.

Every new, dark secret.

"Sit down on the settee, dear," her mother said, "so Dr. Merial can examine your leg."

"It is my ankle, not my leg. And I shall sit where I please." Clare turned and began to lumber instead toward an enormous leather chair.

A touch on her arm halted her small rebellion. "You do not have to do this, Miss Westmore," Dr. Merial said, his voice low. "If you aren't planning on dancing, you could just return home and call on your regular doctor tomorrow."

Clare cut a glance toward her mother, who was settling herself on the eschewed settee in a froth of red skirts. The doctor was giving her a welcome choice, but the secrets of this room could not be so easily bundled into the coach and sent home. A ghost of an idea swirled, poorly formed but gaining teeth. Merial had said himself that a doctor was required to keep a patient's confidence. He'd even proven himself trustworthy, refusing to divulge Lady Austerley's secrets.

Perhaps, if she suffered through this examination, he would be forced to overlook what he had seen here.

"You've suffered a shock," he was saying now. His voice pitched low so her mother could not hear, and his hand fell away from her arm. "Did you even mean to come into the library? I was given the impression that you were fleeing something."

Someone. Clare swallowed the word into silence.

She refused to admit she'd stumbled in here tonight to escape the image of Sophie waltzing in Mr. Alban's arms. Her flight from the ballroom had been a careless indulgence. She could not afford such folly, not with so much at stake. And her escape from the ballroom had not *only* been about Sophie and Mr. Alban. There had been that simmering attraction she'd felt toward the doctor to push her along, and a good dose of fear that he was able to see right through her skin to the secrets she kept well buried.

But her initial reaction to the man no longer mattered. His knowledge of her mother's seeming infidelity was a threat to her family's reputation that needed to be defused.

MISS WESTMORE TURNED away.

For a moment Daniel was relieved. She had decided to be sensible, to retreat home and call on her own physician tomorrow. Truth be told, he was no longer sure he wanted to proceed with his earlier offer of an examination. No matter his need to acquire the trust and support of additional well-placed patrons, the entire situation was deucedly strange.

For one thing, Lady Cardwell was swaying on her feet. The woman looked ill. No, that wasn't quite right. She looked inebriated. He could see it now, echoes of similar souls he encountered on a daily basis, both in the casualty ward at St. Bart's and again along the route home when his shift at the hospital was over.

Worse, the clock ticking on the mantel served as a harsh reminder of the passage of time. Lady Austerley could be in need of his care at this very moment. But just as he was about to lodge an objection, the slip of a girl who had lured him here with nothing more tempting than her tears limped toward a high-backed leather chair and flung herself down, hiking a frothy confection of skirts and underpinnings up to her knees.

Well then. Apparently she meant to go on.

As far as examinations went, this one already qualified as the most bizarre in his memory. But there was a chaperone—of sorts—in place, clothing being shifted around, and a patient awaiting his clinical assessment.

Might as well see it done.

"Did you choose the chair instead of the settee for a particular reason?" he asked, striding toward her and removing his gloves.

She shrugged. "It is closer to the fire. I thought the light might help."

"It will," Daniel agreed as he bent down on one knee. But it also meant they were sitting an unfortunate distance from their agreed-upon chaperone, and that if voices were kept low, their conversation would remain largely private. Worse, the fire bathed this corner of the library in a delicious degree of warmth, and cast flickering shadows across Miss Westmore's already arresting face.

She bent over her legs, fumbling about her feet. "I don't suppose you would consider averting your eyes for this part of it?" she asked, her words infused with a hint of the earlier haughtiness she had displayed in the ballroom.

He sat back on his heels and shrugged out of his jacket. "I assure you, I've seen the odd ankle before, Miss Westmore. You've no need to be shy."

She peered up at him, and a slim, dark brow arched upward. "I am resigned to showing you my ankle, Dr. Merial. I simply have not yet come to terms with showing you my shoes."

Her words pulled a chuckle from his chest. "I might remind you that I've already seen them in the ballroom.

One brown leather, one beaded silk, I believe?" But his amusement bled into concern as she struggled with the buckle of her right shoe and a hiss of pain escaped her lips. "Would you like assistance?"

"No," she said, her voice tight. "I will manage at least *one* thing right this evening."

Finally the shoe was wrenched free, though she'd sacrificed some color to the effort. She straightened and handed it over to him. Daniel turned it over in his hand, the serviceable brown leather still warm from her skin. He had seen the merest glimpse of it in the ballroom, of course, but now realized that his first impression was a bit simplistic.

His ancestors might have worn such a shoe. No, his ancestor's *ancestors* might have, two hundred years ago in their Gypsy wagons. Nothing about this unwieldy shoe, with its scratched silver buckle and scuffed toes, matched the smooth, collected image Miss Westmore projected to the world. "Your father's, I presume?" he asked, louder than he had intended.

A cough of amusement shattered the silence behind them, reminding Daniel that no matter the manufactured intimacy of this corner, with the crackling fire and the promising shadows, they entertained an audience. "Lord Cardwell has his faults, to be sure, but even he would never wear anything so hideous," the girl's mother called out, her words slurring in places. "That is her sister's shoe, the one who is always tripping over her feet. Clare, what were you *thinking*, wearing Lucy's shoes to a ball?"

Miss Westmore's hands gripped the arms of her chair. "I suppose I had thought tonight was too important to miss," she muttered, far too low for her mother to hear.

Daniel put the shoe to one side and eyed an impressive length of stocking-clad leg. He could understand a need to suffer something distasteful in order to advance one's cause. Wasn't that, in a way, why he was here this evening? But what could be so important as to make a girl like this succumb to such a fashion atrocity?

As he rolled up his sleeves and contemplated his next step in this examination from hell, it occurred to him that the bit of silk still blocking his view was no ordinary set of stockings. Though they were surely not meant to see daylight, Miss Westmore's stockings were of the clocked variety, pale ivory and embroidered with an intricate pattern of black swirls and loops. The cost of such stockings, he knew, would keep his small bachelor's flat in coal for a month. Such extravagance was enough to focus him back on the task at hand.

"Do you feel comfortable removing your stocking?" he asked.

She hesitated only a moment before pulling her skirts up higher. She untied her stocking from a garter that flashed a tempting green ribbon and began to roll it down. He averted his eyes, as any physician must in this situation, but could not quite keep his eyes safely anchored to the Abyssinian carpet as pale, gleaming skin began to emerge in the wake of her attentions.

She eased the silk garment from her injured foot and then handed it to him with a flourish. The motion seemed uncalculated, but it held a dangerous edge of flirtation. "Shall I remove the other as well?"

"No," he choked out, his voice strangled. *Christ above*, no. As long as the skin emerging from beneath those stockings required a professional assessment, he might maintain a hold on his sanity. But toss in a perfectly uninjured leg and he would be done for.

"May I?" He held out his hand, palm up. When she nodded, Daniel placed his fingers on her bare knee, then cursed his body's reaction to the feel of her. Her skin was warm and soft, and the taut stretch of her limb trembled slightly against his palm. It was disconcerting to realize his interest in these proceedings was running toward something less seemly than a physician's simple appreciation for human anatomy.

He forced his hands lower, toward her ankle, feeling like a bloody bounder for leering after her with her mother sitting twenty feet away. He could easily tell the limb was swollen—hell, a half-blind butcher could have made *that* diagnosis. The distortion was visible from across the room, and he had noticed it even before she removed her stocking. But a shadow lay across the area he needed to examine, making it hard to see just what sort of damage he was dealing with. He heard her breath catch in her throat just as his fingers grazed the top of her foot. "I am sorry," he murmured. "This may hurt a bit."

He placed a flattened palm against her instep and lifted the limb closer to the firelight, gauging the stopping point by her sudden gasp of pain. The dancing light of the fire played over a nightmarish beauty of a sprain. As he'd expected, this was no mild swelling or a bit of discolored skin. The inflammation was so pronounced it quite obliterated the delicate lines of bones that should have been visible.

A hesitant vein of respect threatened to intrude. Miss Westmore had initially struck him as the sort of girl who would be quite happy to have others dance attendance on her, but this suggested a hidden core of steel.

How was she even walking, much less contemplating dancing?

He pressed experimentally against the top of her foot, bracing himself against her resulting hiss of pain. He observed the deep indentation left by his fingers and the accentuated refill time of her damaged vessels.

"I do not believe you mentioned how you injured it," he observed.

"No." She fidgeted above him, her voice as taut as the skin on her injured foot.

"This looks a bit more serious than the usual turned ankle on the dance floor." And judging by the degree of discoloration, it had happened far earlier in the day. "I'll need the details if I am to ascertain the degree of damage."

She rolled her eyes to the ceiling. "If you must know, I twisted it in Hyde Park, around three o'clock this afternoon." Her voice dropped to a whisper. "I was . . . attacked."

"Attacked?" Daniel ill-expected the punch of anger that possessed him at her admission. It was none of his business. And yet, his fingers tightened against the damaged limb. "In broad daylight? By whom?"

She hesitated. "Geese, if you must know."

Relief flooded in, all the more disturbing for how ill he still felt to think of her suffering a more dangerous sort of assault. His fingers ran upward, to a reddened, crescent-shaped mark on her right calf. "That would explain this spot, I presume. Impertinent beasts, were they?"

"I would have been fine if it had only been the ducks," she responded with a wrinkled nose. "But geese are another matter entirely."

Daniel stifled a laugh. "I think Hyde Park's ducks might have had a decent shot at felling you as well. You could stand to put a few pounds on your frame, Miss Westmore. I would recommend a blood-building diet if you plan to venture out among their ranks again."

Her shapely lips firmed. "You, sir, are not being paid to consider anything beyond the state of my ankle."

"I wasn't aware I was being paid at all."

At least not yet. He did not add that he hoped this bit of altruism might lead to more. In the near term, Miss Westmore was likely to need medical care for several weeks. And in the longer term, adding Lord Cardwell's family to his meager list of patrons could help fill out his almost-empty pockets. He lowered her foot. "I don't think anything is broken, but it is difficult to assess once this degree of swelling sets in. At a minimum, you've suffered a significant degree of tendon damage. But I would not rule out the possibility that the metatarsal or cuboid bones in your foot might be displaced internally."

Her eyes widened. "There's more than one bone?"

Daniel almost snorted. Had she never taken a good, close look at her body beyond the prettier parts that stared back from a mirror? Or even *opened* a basic textbook on science?

"There are twenty-six in all." He glanced over his shoulder, seized with what was probably a very bad idea. The girl's mother was still sitting upright on the settee, but her eyes were half shut and her head was beginning to droop. Satisfied the moment was as private as it could be, he reached a hand toward Miss Westmore's other foot, the one still ensconced in its glass-beaded slipper. "May I show you?" he asked.

She nodded her assent, but otherwise stayed as still as a mouse in a trap.

He removed the dainty silk slipper—a useless thing, with its sole as thin as paper—and ran his fingers feather-light across the surface of her stocking, careful to avoid the embroidered areas so he would not snag the delicate silk threads. Her uninjured foot felt small and alive in his hands, and he was struck by the notion that perhaps he'd been in the company of cadavers far too much of late. "The metatarsals run just here. There are five." He touched each one in turn, the beauty of her noninjured foot's shape evident even through the thin layer of silk. He ran his fingers appreciatively down the length of her toes, and heard her sharply indrawn breath. "Phalanges make up the tips, the part a layman calls the toes. There are fourteen of those."

"Not fifteen?" she asked, almost breathlessly.

He looked up, surprised that she had so neatly understood. "No, though it is a good guess there would be three for each digit. Nature favors symmetry, but the largest toe lacks its third." He cupped her pert heel and recited the rest as though she were one of his students. "Here you've several cuneiform bones, the cuboid, navicular, talus, and calcaneous."

The moment ended on a drawn-out note of silence, the air thick with something he cared not to think about. He rocked back on his heels and looked up. She was peering down at him in frozen surprise, as if captured by some Gypsy spell. And perhaps she was. There was more than a drop of Roma in him, as anyone with eyes could fair see. She would not be the first female to succumb to strange behavior in his presence, only to later resent him for inciting it.

He set her left foot down and cleared his throat. "With respect to your injury, it would have been far better to see a doctor before it reached this point. Why did you wait?"

Her eyes darted over his shoulder toward her mother, who by now had started to snore softly. "I do not care to discuss it."

Daniel pushed himself to standing. Clearly no further explanation would be forthcoming on *that* point. He picked up his jacket as he considered what sort of prognosis to deliver. He'd seen worse, of course. Just this morning he'd seen a carter's foot with gangrene, the toes blackened and dying. That inspection had ended in an amputation. Miss Westmore, thank goodness, appeared in little immediate danger beyond a looming disruption to her social calendar.

"I'm afraid you've extended your convalescence by

several weeks by walking on it so much this evening. I recommend a month's rest —strict rest, mind you, sitting still with your foot elevated. No flitting about ballrooms or excursions to galleries."

"A *month*?" She gaped at him. No lowered voice now, and no ascetic show of courage. Behind him, he could hear the rustle of fabric that signaled her mother's waking.

Daniel raised his voice so Lady Cardwell would hear the worst of it. "No standing. No walking. And most *certainly* no dancing, for at least four weeks."

Her outrage simmered across the foot or so that separated them. "You are deranged, Doctor. It is the start of the Season. I cannot afford to—"

"Qui totum vult totum perdit, Miss Westmore," he interrupted. "That means he who wants everything loses everything."

"I know what it means, Dr. Merial." Her eyes narrowed. *"Sicut palmes non facit philosophus."*

A quote does not make one a philosopher.

He grinned at the sheer unexpectedness of hearing Latin fall from her lips. Half the medical students he taught lacked even a basic command of the ancient language, and here he'd just been insulted by a young woman who looked as though she studied little other than fashion plates. But despite being intrigued enough to chuckle, on this matter he would not bend. "You cannot afford to ignore solid medical advice."

Though, she was probably correct to call him out on the length of her convalescence—she might be up and about within a fortnight if she'd escaped a more serious break and if she took care to properly rest her ankle. But he was in the habit of erring on the side of caution, and he was hardly doing something unethical by stretching the possibility of a required period of rest.

"If you exacerbate the injury," he warned, "you will

likely be facing a convalescence that could last well into autumn."

"Autumn?" Her mouth opened. Closed. Opened again. Her earlier pallor had by now given way to flushed outrage. "I scarcely think more than two weeks' rest is necessary for something so minor as a turned ankle."

Daniel grinned, despite himself. She was a spirited handful, and more intelligent than he'd first credited her. "I admit it can be difficult to know with any degree of certainty, as we need to wait for the swelling to go down to know if anything is broken. But don't you think that is more a matter for your physician and parents to decide?"

She lurched to her feet, already ignoring his advice. "I rather think it depends on the physician," she snapped. "Dr. Bashings would never—"

"Bashings?" Daniel interrupted, even as a rustle of nearby skirts signaled the girl's mother had risen and was heading toward the fray. "Is he still engaged in practice?" To hear the rumors, the man still carried vials of leeches and cobwebs about in his pockets. At twenty-eight, Daniel might be young, but at least he had the benefit of a modern education.

That, and a firm appreciation for hand-washing.

"He's our usual family physician." She hesitated. "But that does not mean . . . that is . . . I imagine you could still . . ."

At her clear discomfort, Daniel's hopes for procuring Lord Cardwell's patronage withered like fruit on a frost-ridden vine. "Miss Westmore. I believe clients should feel comfortable with their physicians, given the enormity of trust such relationships require." He inclined his head in a gracious recusal, though his fingers clenched at the likely loss of this client. "If you wish to use Dr. Bashings, by all means that should be your choice."

Miss Westmore's panicked eyes darted to her mother,

who was emerging beside him in a waterfall of red skirts.

Lady Cardwell blinked unfocused blue eyes that looked nothing like her daughter's heated flash of hazel. "Dr. Bashings has been our family's physician for over twenty years, but I see no harm in employing your services until my daughter's ankle is properly healed." She fumbled in her beaded reticule and clumsily produced a card, which he accepted with more caution than not. "Do stop by Cardwell House tomorrow, around noon, if you would."

Daniel fingered the edge of the card. It was made of fine linen, and was as much a testament to Lord Cardwell's wealth and influence as the Grosvenor Square address printed upon it. "Regretfully, I'm to deliver a noon lecture to the first year students at St. Bartholomew's tomorrow."

Why was he hesitating?

This was what he had been hoping for, wasn't it?

"Ten will do as well. Clare rises with the pigeons." Lady Cardwell fluttered her fingers, as if such a notion pained her. "And I insist on paying for the kind assistance you have provided us tonight."

Payment. God knew he could use it, when all was said and done.

It was one thing to have Lady Cardwell's drunken invitation, but her daughter's willingness to play along seemed far less assured. He risked a glance at Miss Westmore, whose lips were pressed together in stubborn silence. The desire to extricate himself from this prickly situation warred indelicately with the need to further his acquaintance with someone as potentially influential as Lord Cardwell.

Need won out, as it was always bound to do.

Dearest Diary,

I have faced the worst evening of my life . . . and lived.

Some would be grateful for the fact of their continued survival, but as I write this tonight, I am not sure it was the most favorable outcome. I still cannot believe the scope of Sophie's betrayal. She encouraged me to sit in the wallflower line, and then danced with Mr. Alban as if he was a prize she was well on her way to winning. Well, she will find I do not relinquish my dreams so quickly. The minute I am able, I will be out on the dance floor again, and she will soon realize I've claws every bit as sharp as hers.

But Mother . . . oh, that is a betrayal I cannot yet wrap my thoughts around. She didn't even apologize during the coach ride home, just fell asleep on the seat. Perhaps she is embarrassed, but my feelings run a bit deeper than that. This is a secret that has the power to destroy my family, and I refuse to wreck the people I love with something so callous as the truth.

Although I am grateful no one of importance followed me into the library, Dr. Merial's knowledge of what transpired there is a problem I am now left to sort out. I am to rest my foot (all twenty-six bones,

drat the man's impudence) for at least a month. Well,
I may be forced to tolerate his attentions to ensure his
confidence, but I am determined to prove him wrong
on the matter of my healing. There can be no other
option.

A month's absence would give Sophie an advantage
I cannot bring myself to contemplate.

Chapter 6

Daniel came awake to the sound of firm rapping on his door.

His head ached like the very devil—a nasty little side effect of the chloroform, he was coming to understand—and his neck felt as though he'd spent the evening crammed into a two-by-two box. He opened his eyes, only to encounter a raucous beam of sunlight that punched its way through the room's single window and took aim at his protesting pupils.

Christ, but he'd fallen asleep at his work again.

And was it any wonder? Up until all hours at Lady Austerley's ball, his experiments delayed into the wee hours of the morning. He must have dozed off as he recorded his findings. God's teeth, but what he wouldn't give for a normal schedule.

That, and the comfort of a normal bed, every now and again.

He lifted a hand to rub his eyes, only to discover that a piece of paper had somehow become stuck to his cheek during the night. Had he drooled onto his notes? Given that an image of Miss Westmore's lovely lips was still seared into his brain, there was no mistaking the direction his dreams had taken him.

And in his dreams, she had removed far more than clocked silk stockings

Grimly, he extracted the scrap of paper from his cheek and shifted on the hard seat of the chair. He supposed, given the nature of his dreams and his body's stiff morning salute, he ought to be glad that drooling was all he'd done.

The knocking came again. "Dr. Merial!" a determined female voice called out. "Are you home?" It was impossible to mistake his landlady's unspoken suspicion: *And are you alone?*

Daniel pushed himself to his feet. Yes, he was alone. The rules of the boardinghouse aside, he was *always* alone. What self-respecting female would consent to spend the night in a place like this? The rooms were close to St. Bartholomew's, and he had his own private entrance that opened to the street, but in terms of basic comforts, the flat was sorely lacking.

"One moment!" He swept his sleep-crushed notes into his satchel. In the six months he'd been lodging here, Mrs. Calbert had generally respected his privacy. But based on this morning's unannounced visit, it seemed she was increasingly prone to test it.

"Is everything all right?" she all but shouted.

"Yes, yes, just grabbing my trousers!" He grabbed a blanket off his bed and tossed it over the flotsam of the previous evening's experiments, still scattered about his dining table. The frogs fell quiet in their algae-stained glass bowl, but the crickets in their wire cages were less circumspect. They chirped ominously beneath their woolen shroud, no doubt berating him for his plans to feed them to the frogs.

The latch rattled on the door, and Daniel belatedly glanced down to make sure he was decently dressed. Fortunately—or perhaps unfortunately, given the bedraggled state of his shirt—he was still wearing the same clothing from last night. He'd been dressed in his finest jacket then, but best was apparently relative. A fishmonger, Miss Westmore had called him. The memory made him smile. Had it been more the jacket or the necktie that caused her to sniff in such haughty disapproval?

Though, he supposed it scarcely mattered which bits of clothing Miss Westmore found most offensive when she had also objected to the person *in* them.

He shrugged away those snarls of memory, turned the key in the lock, and yanked open the door to confront the more pressing issue at hand.

"Mrs. Calbert." He leaned one shoulder against the door frame, partly to block her view inside and partly because the sun outside his door made him want curl into a ball and beg for mercy. The sunlight bounced off the occasional silver strand in his landlady's dark hair, making her appear older than her thirty-odd years. Smithfield's streets had a way of aging a body before its time, as the daily flood of patients at St. Bartholomew's charity ward could testify. "What an unexpected surprise."

He waited for her to gather her wits about her and ask him for advice on whatever malady must have brought her to his door at such an early hour. He'd already observed she was plagued by consumptive lungs and limped a bit on cool mornings. The poor woman's husband had kicked off soon after Daniel arrived, leaving her with little more than a somber wardrobe and the running of this five-room tenement house. It occurred to him, as he waited for Mrs. Calbert to find her courage, that today she was dressed in bright, sunny yellow.

That was certainly new.

"Were you wanting something of me?" he prompted.

Instead of launching into the expected bodily complaint, Mrs. Calbert gave a breathless sigh. "You . . . ah . . . needed to put on your trousers?"

Bloody hell. Why hadn't he chosen a different excuse for his delay in answering the door? Now the woman would be imagining he slept in the nude. It would be just his ill fortune to be awakened by her knock every morning, hoping to catch a peek. He was fastidious enough to want to choose his own bed partners, and Mrs. Calbert was not at the top of that list.

He ran a hand through his sleep-mussed hair, and that at least brought her eyes back around to his face. "How may I help you this fine morning?"

Her ruddy cheeks plumped up, and she pushed a basket covered with a checkered cloth into his hands. Daniel caught the scent of fresh bread. "You came in quite late last night. Heard you outside my door." She smiled, revealing a gap where a tooth had gone freshly missing. "I've brought you some breakfast, figuring you might be running behind this morning."

Daniel accepted the basket with a silent groan. She'd waited up for him last night and now was bringing him breakfast? Just what did she expect him to offer in exchange for such a kind but unnecessary gift? He could certainly offer some guidance in the area of improved dental hygiene, but he doubted she would consider his recommendation for tooth powder a worthwhile expense, given the fact she charged her tenants scarcely fourteen shillings for weekly rent.

"Now Mrs. Calbert," he said, even as his stomach emitted a ferocious growl, "there is no need for such kindness. I am to provide my own meals, according to the house rules you've set yourself."

"Oh, posh. By the hours you keep, I imagine you're too

busy by half to think of your stomach. You need a wife, Dr. Merial, if you don't mind me saying." She gestured to the basket. "There's a bit of jam in there as well, my own recipe. I remember you once said you enjoyed your sweets." She peered around his shoulder, stretching to catch a peek inside. "I'd be happy to lay it out on your table, and dust off some things, besides." She sniffed the air. "There's a peculiar odor, and there seems to be an infestation of some sort. I think a solid cleaning would do you well."

Daniel's hands clenched around the handle of the basket. He wasn't doing anything wrong, per se. A constable would find no legal fault with his nightly activities. But Mrs. Calbert had a list of house rules the length of Aldersgate Street, and it was hard to refute the sweet, pungent scent of chloroform that hung thick in the air and permeated every porous surface in the room. "Cleaning is the tenant's own responsibility," he reasoned, recalling the rules he had been forced to agree to some six months prior.

She sniffed again, this time in greater suspicion. "It isn't opium, is it? I don't approve of such things. I try to run a respectable establishment."

"No, no, nothing like that," he soothed quickly.

Not opium. But perhaps, given the direction of his experiments, something far more promising. Opiates numbed the mind to insensibility, while chloroform possessed solid anesthetic properties. But while the liquid form of the drug was every bit as dangerous as opium, it was proving safe in small, aerosolized doses, at least in his experiments with frogs. He'd been testing different concentrations and delivery mechanisms since arriving in London this past December, working late at night after his hours at St. Bart's were finished. His painstaking work had led to the creation of a device with the potential to deliver precise dosages of the drug, based on a patient's size and state of health.

But Daniel was not convinced his landlady cared enough about the advancement of medical science to overlook the odd menagerie he used in the course of his experiments. He'd be out on his bum if she saw the frogs, of that he was quite sure.

Either that or be invited into her bed, encouraged to help her forget what she had seen.

He cast about for an alternative that would violate neither the house rules nor his landlady's sensibilities. "'Tis only a bit of turpentine, Mrs. Calbert," he offered. "For my . . . er . . . paintings."

She lifted a dark bushy brow. Out of nowhere, he was reminded of Miss Westmore's fastidiously groomed arches, which had been hefted to far more potent effect the previous evening. He needed to clear his head of the troublesome girl.

And his doorstep of his troublesome landlady.

"A doctor *and* an artist?" Mrs. Calbert's eyes swept his face in open appreciation. "How is it you aren't already married, then, Dr. Merial? A woman appreciates a man of many talents." She went up on her toes, trying to peer over his shoulder. "My late husband had an eye for a nice painting. Dabbled a bit in oils, he did."

Daniel moved to block her view. "I am afraid my latest work is covered, at the moment."

Her eyes narrowed back on him. "Are they not proper sorts of paintings, then?"

"Proper?" he echoed. No, they weren't proper. They weren't *real*.

The ruddiness of Mrs. Calbert's cheeks deepened. "I don't approve of that either. A girl's a girl, and it's against the rules to bring one in, even if she's only sitting to model." But despite her clear censure, one hand crept up to fiddle with a button at her throat. "Although, I suppose *I* could sit a spell for you. Wouldn't break the rules that way. And Mr. Calbert once said I ought to be painted in the morning light, as naught but nature intended."

Daniel smothered a laugh, imagining his landlady sitting in his flat, nude and outraged, swatting at escaped crickets. "I . . . ah . . . I don't think you'll do. 'Tis a likeness of a dead man, the body opened for examination. It is needed to teach the new students."

"A cadaver?" Her eyes widened, but a hint of macabre fascination infused her words. "Mr. Calbert liked a good funeral, God rest his soul. Mayhap I could take a look?"

Daniel cursed beneath his breath. By the stars, was there no way to dislodge her? He began to inch the door shut. "I'm afraid it's too much. Chest flayed open, intestines strewn about. Most unpleasant. I wouldn't want to subject you to such a thing, particularly considering Mr. Calbert's untimely passing."

A euphemism, perhaps. To hear the other tenants talk, the man had been gutted in a nearby alley. Yet another side effect of Smithfield's mean streets.

Mrs. Calbert's face paled, and he felt like a bounder for it, but short of inviting her in for tea, there was naught for it. "But thank you for your kindness." The door hovered, nearly flush against the jamb now. "I shall enjoy my breakfast."

The door clicked shut. Daniel stood still, holding his breath. Finally, through the thin-walled door, he heard the sounds of his landlady shuffling away, and his lungs loosened. He turned to the table and placed the basket down. Pulling the blankets away, he warily eyed the device that was causing all his problems.

"Damn it all," he muttered. Six months, he'd been here, working on his experiments without interruption, and *now* Mrs. Calbert was growing suspicious?

Or was it only that she was growing lonely?

His landlady was proving a danger he had not anticipated. There was no doubt he was close to a breakthrough. He was tempted to stay here this morning and keep working. But he had a noon lecture to give the first year students, and while his instructor's salary from St. Bart's was meager, it was still his most predictable means of income at the present, next to Lady Austerley's payments.

He picked up the chloroform regulator, running his fingers across the surface of the tin body and linen-wrapped tubing, reassuring himself that there were no cracks that might permit the vapor to escape and impact the results. Last night's results had been highly promising—on frogs, at least. If things continued to go well, he felt certain it would result in a groundbreaking paper, one he could possibly even publish in London's leading medical journal, the *Lancet*.

But he anticipated several more weeks of work before he was ready, and the completion of his experiments depended on a healthy population of amphibians. It had taken him weeks to grow the fragile creatures to an age that would suit the purposes of the experiment, and at times he felt as though he lived and breathed according to the whims of their delicate constitution.

If he was forced to pack up and move now, he risked losing the lot of them and having to start over.

His fingers hovered over the mask, which was shaped to fit over the nose and mouth of a patient. He fished a hand in his coat pocket, seeking to clean it with the handkerchief he always kept here. His fingers closed unexpectedly over the edge of a card. Drawing it out, he saw Lady Cardwell's name and direction on it.

A flooding memory returned—the sound of Miss Westmore's voice, and the feel of her skin, quivering against his hand. The way her brows had formed an unexpected wrinkle between her eyes as she'd concentrated on his words, and the way her lips had rounded in protest when he'd prescribed a month's rest.

Bloody, bloody hell. He couldn't stay here this morning and work on the regulator. He had an appointment to keep, and he refused to contemplate the small rush of eagerness he felt at the thought. There was naught for it but to gulp down his breakfast of bread and jam and catch the omnibus toward Mayfair.

That, and pray Mrs. Calbert didn't return to pick the lock.

Chapter 7

*N*ormally, Clare quite enjoyed a nice family breakfast.

Before Geoffrey left for Eton, the entire family had often taken the meal together, Mother included. More recently, with her parents' inexplicable estrangement so keenly felt, breakfast had become a jealously protected sliver of time, that hour before Mother woke up and set the household scrambling, the only part of the day where she could sit with her father in an unguarded fashion and not worry about whether one parent felt slighted or the other annoyed.

Of course, there was nothing normal about the way *this* family breakfast was shaping up. For a start, it was far too bright. Sunlight streamed through the lace curtains, an ominous harbinger of one of those uncommon London Saturdays so sunny and clear it practically begged one to plan outdoor pursuits. The swelling in her foot was more severe this morning, and the pain reminded her that she would not—under any circumstances—be permitted to enjoy such a day.

Then there was the additional oddity of having Geoffrey present at the breakfast table again. He appeared not the slightest bit chagrined over the fact that he ought to be nose-to-the-books at Eton. Grimly, Clare considered whether he might have been expelled from school on account of his table manners. Instead he was here, uncouth and uneducated, shoving sausages into his mouth and slurping his tea like a costermonger.

But far worse than the minor irritation of the morning was the bone-weary knowledge of her mother's indiscretion last night. Clare looked across the table at her father and swallowed the lump that rose in her throat at the sight of his thinning blond hair, just visible across the top of his morning paper. No matter the difficulties between her parents, she imagined her father would still be hurt by the knowledge of such a betrayal.

She was determined to keep the truth from him, if possible.

Would Dr. Merial keep her family's confidence? She'd almost destroyed the possibility last night when she unwittingly implied Dr. Bashings would be a better choice for her continued care. Thank goodness she hadn't offended Dr. Merial to the point he'd refused her mother's request. But she hadn't specifically asked him about confidentiality, either. She liked to imagine that perhaps his physician's oath would be enough to ensure this secret was kept, but fear had kept her awake and tossing in her sheets.

Clare picked up her cup of coffee—a vice Mother would have objected to had she the gall to rise before noon—and studied the headlines that hid their father from view. "It looks as though the Chartists have suffered another set-down," she offered by way of making conversation. The headlines she could see certainly shouted their opinion on the matter. So did many in the ton, who objected to those commoner upstarts who had the audacity to gather in public rooms and demand a say in their country's disposal. Her fingers itched to have their own chance to peruse the printed pages.

"Hmm," came her father's noncommittal response.

Clare thought of saying more, but hesitated. She always read the *London Times* from front to back when her father finally put it down and tucked himself away to his club. Not to prepare herself for the shallow drawing room conversations so common during the Season. No, those events required nothing more taxing than elbowing her way through delicate discussions without actually expressing anything so gauche as an opinion. She read the *Times* because she enjoyed it, and because private pleasures were otherwise rare during the height of the Season.

But having opinions on political matters was one thing. Expressing them was clearly another.

A flash of movement caught her eye. She intuited its source, even before she turned her head. "Geoffrey," she warned.

Her brother froze, his twitching fingers just inches from Lucy's hair, which had been tied back this morning in a masculine queue at the nape of her neck, an old strip of leather holding it in place. They owned an entire department store's worth of ribbons and any number of hair combs, but Lucy insisted on these eccentric touches, as if she could ward off the march of time and her looming Season by playing the heathen instead.

"Yes?" Geoffrey asked, his blue eyes the very picture of the devil.

"It is customary to finish one's breakfast before moving on to other distractions, is it not? And aren't you a little old to be pulling hair?"

"You sound just like Mother." Geoffrey grinned. "And *I'm* not the one who isn't eating this morning." He pointed at Lucy with an accusing finger. "If you want to play mother hen, shouldn't you be squawking at her, too?"

Clare bit back a retort. She hated being compared to their mother. But Geoffrey was right about one thing. The conundrum of her hair aside, Lucy's latest obsessive rebellion was on full display this morning. A plate of wilted watercress had been served up by the kitchen staff, apparently intended as an accompaniment to the unbuttered toast Lucy lived on now that she was refusing to eat meat.

"The smell of your sausage is turning my stomach," Lucy declared, matching her brother's volume. "It is barbaric to eat the flesh of animals."

Privately, Clare considered that this most recent eccentricity might have been better timed to ensure her sister remained a respectable—and marriageable—height. A little malnutrition, properly timed to best effect, could only help matters.

But no, Lucy had to decide on this moral course of action only *after* she'd obtained the rough proportions of an Amazon.

"How can you object to eating animals, but not to wearing strips of them in your hair?" Geoffrey countered.

A rustling of paper froze them all in their seats. Father frowned over the top edge of the paper and adjusted the wire rims of his spectacles. "Geoffrey, stop pulling your sister's hair. You should have matured past such nonsense. Clare, stop pestering your brother. He's too old to need a nursemaid." His gaze fell on the disgusting lump of watercress, shimmering in the middle of the table. "And Lucy, eat your . . . er . . . grass."

The paper lifted again.

They all exchanged bemused glances, although no one looked surprised that Father had been aware of their brewing row from behind his newsprint facade. Even in the midst of their worst family squabbles, their father remained calm and unflappable.

"You know, I think the Chartists have the right of it," Geoffrey proclaimed, proving he had actually been listening during his assault on the sausages. "It seems unfair to limit their ability to even meet to discuss their options, or plan a peaceful protest. They caused no real trouble in April, during the march from Kennington."

"True." Lucy stirred her watercress with a dubious fork. "And at least they marched on foot, instead of riding their poor horses."

Clare pressed her lips together to keep from tossing her own opinion into the mix. She thought it was rather doubtful the sort of men who had marched from Kennington could even *afford* a horse, much less one used primarily for riding. After all, it was a cause for commoners, working men who wished to have a say in their own destiny in the form of voting rights and the ability to serve in Parliament. But while the crowd of a hundred thousand had certainly been impressive, it was also a little frightening, and the talk in London's drawing rooms had been ringing with an undercurrent of anxiety ever since.

Clare had hidden her instinctive sympathy behind a well-placed smile, even as Parliament had scrambled to find a way to silence them.

"*I* think the new rules limiting public assembly are a load of horse piss. Why, those same rules could be presumed to apply to church, or even school." Geoffrey brightened, punctuating the air with his fork. "In fact, maybe I should refuse to return to classes at Eton. It could be treasonous to assemble in such a fashion, after all."

The paper lowered again. Their father frowned. "You are aware, are you not, that your latest capers have earned you an expulsion? This is different than last November's suspension. You won't be returning, at least not to Eton, though God knows who will take you now. And horse piss is hardly a phrase appropriate for the breakfast table."

Geoffrey looked down at his plate. "I know what an expulsion is, Father," he grumbled.

Their father lifted the paper again. "Then perhaps you should have considered that before you irrevocably angered the headmaster with your latest escapade."

Though she secretly agreed, Clare felt Geoffrey's acute discomfort. Lucy must have felt a similar solidarity for their beleaguered sibling, because she pushed her plate away and cleared her throat loudly. "Well, *I*, for one, know all about horse piss. And I am thinking of taking up a new cause. The way Londoners treat their animals is appalling. Did you know the average life of an omnibus horse is only four years?"

Clare groaned. "Lucy, don't you think your time would be better spent focusing on matters more pertinent to your immediate future?" *Such as your hair?* "You are coming out next year," she continued, "but one would never know it to look at you. Don't you want a Season? A husband? A *life*?"

"Oh, yes, this grand scheming for a handsome, titled husband, as if that alone should be enough to fulfill my hopes and dreams." Lucy's blue eyes narrowed. "Do tell us about *your* adventures in attempted matrimony, dear sister. Did your twisted ankle hold up well enough to dance with Mr. Alban last night?"

Clare made a shushing motion with her hand, but it was too late.

"Mr. Alban?" This time her father laid the paper firmly down. "Isn't this the same gentleman who came to call, the one we are keeping secret from your mother?"

Clare winced as she met her father's blue eyes through

the lens of his spectacles. "You ... ah ... knew about Mr. Alban's visit?"

And more importantly, what did this knowledge mean?

It was too soon to force Alban to a formal introduction with her family, of that she was sure. Until she sorted out how to mend the damage rendered by her ill-fated decision to sit in the wallflower line last night, she needed to be more careful than ever with her future duke.

"Of course." Father folded the *Times* calmly, then straightened his jacket. The gesture sent the faint scent of pipe tobacco and peppermint wafting across the table, a comforting smell Clare had always associated with her father. "Wilson would never admit a gentleman caller without informing me of the fact. Mr. Alban was recently declared Harrington's heir, wasn't he? To hear the talk, he is a respectable young man."

"Yes." Clare leaned forward, her hands splayed against the table. "Please, oh *please* don't tell Mother," she begged. "She will devise some embarrassing scheme to throw me at him, much as she did with Mr. Meeks last year." She still bore the mental scars from that encounter.

No doubt Meeks felt similarly.

"Given that I scarcely ever see your mother these days, I can't imagine it will be a difficult confidence to keep." Her father offered her a thin smile and handed the paper across the table to her. "Now, what is this about twisting your ankle?"

Clare's fingers clenched around the delicate edges of the newsprint. "'Tis nothing of consequence." Nothing, that was, except four weeks of misery and a threat to her future.

"Should I summon Dr. Bashings to have a look at you?"

"No." Clare choked on the word. Despite her near misstep last night, Dr. Bashings was dreadfully old and smelled of cabbage. She lived in abject fear of his affinity for leeches. "Mother has arranged for another doctor to come by and check on me this morning." She felt a curious flare of anticipation at the thought. Why would she look forward to seeing a man she was quite sure she disliked? "We met Dr. Merial last night, at Lady Austerley's ball. He's the countess's personal physician." She tossed a glare at Lucy. "And no, I did not enjoy an opportunity to dance with Mr. Alban last night."

But Sophie certainly had, hadn't she?

"I am sorry," Lucy offered, and seemed to mean it.

Clare took a determined sip of her coffee, contemplating how to turn the conversation back around to Lucy's peculiar ideas on animals and Geoffrey's recent expulsion.

Anything to deflect the attention from her own sad state of affairs.

Her father, however, was finished. He rose, and with another tug on his waistcoat, announced, "Well, I suppose I'm off, then. Let me know how it goes with the new doctor. Dr. Bashings isn't getting any younger, and we'll probably need to consider a proper replacement soon."

Geoffrey and Lucy scrambled to their feet, eager to see Father to the door, according to family tradition. Clare, of course, was in no condition to scramble anywhere, much less see him off. Instead, she offered her cheek for a quick kiss, knowing that once Father left for his club, he would be gone for the entire day. Not that she blamed him for doing what he must to avoid a forced conversation with Mother.

As the dining room fell quiet, she stared down at the mystery of her coffee, as bitter as the secrets of her parents' marriage. The beverage, at least, would be improved with a hefty dose of sugar, but she was afraid that after her discovery last night, her parents' near-estrangement might soon become an even more unpleasant thing to swallow.

Clare reached for the sugar bowl, but hesitated at the point of dumping the contents into her cup. She had a dreadful sweet tooth and usually didn't worry about such things, given that her figure fell more on the slight side. But she also had an entire wardrobe full of new gowns already made, awaiting their own debut this Season and carefully cut to her current measurements. In the thick of the Season, there would no time for further alterations.

She thought back to last night's conversation with Dr. Merial, and how he'd accused her of being too thin. *Blasted man.*

What did he know?

An image returned, of Sophie's malicious smile just before she placed her hand in Mr. Alban's. That was enough to make Clare shove the sugar bowl aside and place her napkin down over her half-eaten plate. She had four potential weeks of inactivity stretching before her, and she refused to emerge from this penance with a healed ankle but clothing that no longer fit.

Even if her waistline wasn't in jeopardy, her future clearly was.

She had not achieved her stunning social success by being willing to smile while others grabbed at the treasure she wanted. She could afford to give her ankle one week to heal, two at the most. And then her foot was going back in a slipper, and she was going back on the dance floor.

Chapter 8

aniel was directed to the drawing room by a stone-faced butler who had clearly been instructed to expect him. Aside from the orchestrated exchange of money, presumably to cover today's visit and last night's services, this felt far more like a social visit than an examination, and the sun-soaked room papered in gold and blue did little to dispel the notion.

The faint smell of lemon oil niggled at his memory, reminding him of a time when he lived in a house where someone had cared enough to polish the furniture. But that was where the domestic association ended. This parlor was nothing like the small but well-kept cottage where he'd spent the first ten years of his life. Gilt-framed watercolors hung on the wall, and the thick carpet beneath his feet muffled even the most determined of footfalls. After the austerity of his rented rooms and the squalor of the Bow and Stratford omnibus, the comfort and opulence of Lord Cardwell's drawing room felt a bit like someone had tossed sand in his eye.

Much like Miss Westmore herself.

This morning she was sitting on an overstuffed sofa, clad in a day dress of deep blue silk, her head bent over a bit of embroidery. Without the distraction of a flounced ball gown, she seemed even prettier than he remembered. Perhaps it was the way this particular shade of blue brightened her rich, chestnut-brown hair and made her skin glow like polished marble. Or perhaps that was merely the fanciful brightness of the sun, bouncing off the wallpaper and shimmering like a halo against her head.

"Dr. Merial has arrived, Lady Clare," the butler announced in a grand, stiff fashion.

She looked up and frowned. "Thank you, Wilson."

As the butler departed, she looked down again, the needlework in her hand clearly a more interesting prospect than the coming appointment. Presumably she did not feel the same keen edge of anticipation that had consumed him the past half hour. Daniel tamped down his rising irritation—damnably inconvenient thing that it was—and forced himself to take more clinical stock of the situation. She had her right foot elevated on a stool.

He wasn't sure what he'd expected, but after her near-tantrum the night before, it hadn't been this docile creature, sitting still as a church mouse.

He looked around the room as he waited to be noticed. Behind the sofa, beneath the arch of a picture window, two young men were sitting cross-legged on the floor, their blond heads bent over a chessboard. Lady Cardwell, notably, was nowhere to be seen.

Not that her presence last night had served as anything close to a proper chaperone.

"Were you going to come in?" Miss Westmore's voice sounded clipped. She still wasn't looking at him, but it was a small improvement over being ignored.

He obligingly stepped toward her, his leather satchel clasped in both hands. "I see you've chosen to heed my advice and keep off your ankle. Obedient little thing, aren't you?"

"*Obedient?*" Her head jerked up and the needlework slipped from her lap. "Bother it all!" She lifted an index finger to her mouth and glared up at him. "You've made me stab myself."

Daniel chuckled. "And here I was given to believe you were the graceful one."

Her frown deepened. "My mother should not have said that last night." She cast an uneasy glance behind her, toward the two young men. They could only be family, sitting as they were on the floor, chins on their hands, staring at the board.

Daniel set his bag down on a nearby table but didn't open it. He'd brought a draught of laudanum, thinking that perhaps she would be in pain. He had further considered the drug might lull her into acquiescence if she'd decided to be unruly about it all, but it seemed she was resolved to be more level-headed than he'd imagined. "Well, I am sorry if I have startled you with my choice of words. I confess to being startled myself. After your exuberant arguments of last night, I'd expected calisthenics from your quarter," he teased. "Or at the least, a petulant walk in Hyde Park."

Hazel eyes widened, a hair *too* innocently. "Why, however would I outrun the geese?" Daniel choked back a snort of laughter as she turned her head toward the figures on the floor. "Lucy, be a dear and go and fetch Mother," she called out. "Dr. Merial is here."

One of those blond heads popped up from the chess-board. "But I've nearly got Geoffrey in checkmate, and I don't trust him alone with the pieces," a feminine voice protested. "And isn't Mother still asleep? It's scarcely ten o'clock."

Daniel blinked in surprise. This, then, was Lucy.

The clumsy one who owned a pair of shoes that would make a Quaker proud.

With her hair pulled back in a masculine queue and her shoulders hunched over, he'd made an incorrect presumption she'd been male. First impressions of gender aside, his second impression did little better to convince him of a familial connection to the delicately fashioned Miss Westmore. This girl's bones were broad, her nose slightly upturned. Her hair was a pale blond, the color of sun-baked straw, whereas Miss Westmore's rich brown tresses scattered the light. But despite those differences, something in the tilt of the girl's chin reminded him very much of the woman who had sparred with him from the wallflower line last night.

The second head came up to regard him curiously, a young man of perhaps twelve or thirteen, just growing into his skin. "*You're* the new doctor?" He inclined his golden head. "Fecking handsome sod, aren't you?"

"*Geoffrey!*" exclaimed Miss Westmore, blushing furiously.

Daniel regarded the young man with a raised brow. It wasn't as if his appearance wasn't already a bit of a lodestone around his neck, attracting constant female attention, no matter how poorly deserved. But he'd not come here today and sacrificed the shilling for omnibus fare to suffer such ribbing at the hands of Miss Westmore's spot-faced brother.

"Bit of a bully trap for you, I'd imagine, having a face like that." The young man stood up, knocking over the chessboard and earning a cry of protest from his sister. "The prettier boys at Eton tend to get their mettle tested." He grinned as he walked toward Daniel, a jaunty bounce to his step. "You sure don't look like old Dr. Bashings."

"Er . . . thank you." Daniel turned back to his patient,

hoping to proceed with the more pertinent matters at hand, but Miss Westmore refused to meet his eye.

In fact, she had buried her face in her hands.

"I bet you know the proper names for all sorts of things," young Geoffrey went on. He grabbed Daniel's arm and pulled him to one side. "I've been hoping to probe the mind of a more educated man," he whispered. "Not that *I* engage in such activities, but I am asking for a friend, you know." He chanced a look behind them, no doubt checking for spies in their ranks. "Will you really go blind?"

"Blind?" Daniel echoed.

The boy's ears were turning a bit pink now. "You know. For doing . . . *that*."

"Er . . . what is that, exactly?"

Geoffrey squirmed. His voice lowered to a whisper probably meant only for Daniel's ears but which still carried far too loudly "I know the common names for it, of course. Pulling the pudding. Tossing off. But maybe you've got something more polished? A phrase to impress my friends?"

The unfortunate light dawned. Not that Daniel believed current medical opinions on the practice, which claimed such things led to a variety of volatile complaints, from stomach ills to cancerous humors. Speaking as a scientist, nothing untoward had ever happened to *him* as a result. But they were in mixed company, no matter how quietly the boy whispered.

He fished about in his mind for a more acceptable alternative to the word "masturbation," one the present company was unlikely to know. "Ah . . . perhaps onania would serve?"

A strangled gasp came from Miss Westmore's quarter. She clearly had better hearing—and a more impressive vocabulary—than he'd imagined.

"Onania." Geoffrey canted his head. "Carries a nice, phonetic ring, that does."

"Better still, it encompasses any range of delinquencies." Daniel patted the young man on the shoulder. After all, he remembered what it was like to be such an age, and possessed of unwieldy urges and no common sense. "And for what it's worth, you may tell your friend that I believe the rumors of blindness are greatly overexaggerated."

Not that he should be encouraging the scamp to greater curiosity. He had a feeling a bit of knowledge could be a dangerous thing in this one's hands.

CLARE RAISED HER head, sorting through the flood of unwelcome emotions unleashed by Dr. Merial's deft handling of the situation with her degenerate brother.

Respect, embarrassment, and anger collided at the top of the list.

"Geoffrey, I am sure Dr. Merial has more important things to worry about than your vocabulary," she snapped.

But now it was Lucy's turn to elbow her way into the fray. "I understand you provided some assistance to my sister last night, Dr. Merial," she exclaimed. "I *told* her she ought to see a physician yesterday at the park, but she insisted on going to the ball anyway. She's quite stubborn when she sets her mind to something."

"I'd noticed." The doctor grinned. "I'd wager she didn't even thank you for the loan of your helpful shoe, did she?"

Lucy's cheeks reddened. "You saw my shoe?" Her fingers reached up, self-consciously pulling several strands of hair down from the old-fashioned queue. "I . . . ah . . . it was not my normal shoe, of course. I only wear those when I am tromping about in the stables."

Far from inspiring hope for her sister's future, Lucy's fumbling attempts to tame her hair and explain her choice of footwear made Clare's patience snap clean in two.

For heaven's sake. He was only a doctor.

"Lucy and Geoffrey, if you will loosen your hold on Dr. Merial for a moment, he's come here for a different reason than to be pestered by either of you." She glared at the man and pointed to her propped ankle. "Or is this delay part of your devious plan to charge by the hour, Doctor?"

He smiled, at *her* this time, and the gesture made her insides flip in an alarming fashion.

As her siblings charged back to the chessboard and started bickering over who had turned over the pieces, Dr. Merial sat down on the sofa beside her. "I did not realize you were so anxious to get started," he said, "or I would not have humored them."

"Somehow, I doubt that," Clare muttered, her gaze falling to his hands. He wasn't wearing gloves today, and her eyes lingered on the long bones of his fingers. There was a scar along the edge of one thumb, neat and clean as the swipe of a kitchen knife. *Finally*, a physical flaw in this otherwise perfect specimen of a man. She wondered at the cause, only to be jerked from her wandering thoughts by the intrusion of his rumbling voice.

"Would you like to show me the progress you've made toward mending, then?"

Clare pulled up her skirts and held her breath against the spear of pain that came as she repositioned her foot on its stool. "You were very good with them," she admitted grudgingly. "I must apologize. They know better manners, I assure you. Although, that was the first time I've seen Lucy attempt to comb her hair in a month. And as for Geoffrey . . . we never know what is going to come out of his mouth."

Dr. Merial's eyes swept her bared ankle. Oddly, it made the skin along the back of her neck burn, though his gaze was directed quite a bit lower. "His behavior may simply be a call for attention," he murmured. He reached out a hand, running the fingers she had just ogled across the surface of her foot. "Still rather swollen this morning, isn't it? Can you turn it to the left?"

She tried, though the effort left her panting.

"Now the right?"

That way was harder still, and the sweat broke out across the top of Clare's forehead.

"Hmmm. Let's have a better look." He lifted her foot into his lap and pressed his fingers more forcefully into the discolored skin. "Not to be indelicate, but boys at his age often need a male figure they can talk to. Is your father around to answer some of his questions?"

Clare gritted her teeth, as much against the probing question as the pain. Geoffrey's growing fascination with his . . . well, his *pudding* . . . was scarcely this man's business. But she could not deny the doctor's words echoed some of her own fears for her brother's future.

"Our father is gone a lot," she admitted, her instincts muddled enough to let her usual reticence regarding family secrets slip. "He's always at his club, probably because Mother scarcely speaks to him anymore. And Geoffrey's spent the past year at Eton in the company of ruffians, it seems. He was still a sweet boy of twelve when he left, so this particular homecoming has been a bit of a shock."

She hesitated before meeting the doctor's dark eyes. "I admit to being worried for him. Not only this matter of . . . er . . . blindness. He's going to have to manage the title someday, and to look at him now I see nothing but dissolution in his future." She knotted her hands in her lap, embarrassed to be sharing such details, and yet reassured that this man was at least bound by the tenants of his profession to tell her the truth. "Do you think he requires a medical intervention?" she asked bluntly, visions of asylums looming in her mind.

Dr. Merial assuaged her fears by laughing out loud. "No matter the opinions of some experts, I believe 'tis perfectly natural in a boy of his age, Miss Westmore. It will pass in a year or so, I promise. But if he has questions in the near term, you can always send him to me."

Clare nodded, comforted by his response. The conversation had tipped into overly intimate territory, but the doctor's expression remained open and nonjudgmental, even as his fingers continued to probe her injured ankle. He had given much the same impression last night, betraying not even an ounce of disapproval over her mother's clear indiscretion.

She was beginning to understand why Lady Austerley thought so highly of this man. He had a way of listening that made one feel as though they were the most important thing in the room. Certainly, Dr. Bashings had never inspired her to share such a confidence.

She exhaled the breath she hadn't realized she was holding as he placed her foot back down on the stool. Though his fingers had caused a good deal of pain with their nudging and prodding, the loss of his touch against her skin felt wrong, somehow. Her eyes drifted over his straightening back, and it occurred to her he was wearing the same jacket as last evening. This morning the fabric seemed less offensive than it had last night, and the rumpled nature gave him little more than an air of mild disreputability.

Or perhaps it was more that today she shouldn't help but notice it covered a set of appealingly broad shoulders?

Good heavens. Where had *that* thought come from?

She shook herself from the clutches of such inappropriate musings, ashamed of the wandering direction of her thoughts and the inexorable softening of her opinion on cheap wool coats. "Well," she said, almost too brightly, "What is your verdict regarding my ankle?"

"It is more swollen than I had expected. More so than even last night, and still too distended to provide a proper assessment of whether any of the bones have been broken." He pulled a length of cloth from his pocket and began to unwind it in his hands.

Clare eyed it dubiously. "What do I need a bandage for? There's no bleeding."

"There is bleeding on the inside, which is why your ankle continues to swell. This may help." He began to wrap the long strip of cloth around her ankle. "Keep it wrapped, until my next visit. It will remind you to keep off it, more than anything else." He looked up from his task. His grin was a sharp, sudden thing. "I cannot help but presume you need the reminder."

Clare couldn't help it. She laughed out loud. Oh, if this man had any notion of her plans to heal faster than anyone ever in the history of the world.

He secured the ends of the bandage with a pin, then leaned back, resting his hands on this thighs. "I can return Tuesday and have another look. Unless you'd rather use Dr. Bashings, of course." His lips twitched. "Why, I imagine the man has any number of barbaric treatments he could recommend for young Geoffrey."

Clare shook her head. "Tuesday would be acceptable." She didn't want the frankly terrifying Dr. Bashings anywhere near her brother—who knew where the man would put his leeches? And with respect to her ankle, she supposed a reassessment in three days' time was better than the four weeks of convalescence Dr. Merial had threatened last night.

Of course, he'd not yet said she *wouldn't* be forced to the full month.

But he had no idea the depths of her tenacity.

As he rose from the sofa, she gathered her wits about her. Dr. Merial was displaying a remarkable sensitivity, and not only in the matter of her difficulties with Geoffrey. There had been no specific mention of her mother's indiscretion last night. No snide remark, no cutting wit wielded like a sword of Damocles.

It was far more than she could have expected from any in her circle of friends.

But still, assurances needed to be gathered, especially as her family's secrets were not of the usual medical variety. "And given that we are retaining your services, you'll keep our conversation about my brother—and the matter of events in the library last night—private?" she asked cautiously.

He picked up his bag. "All that may come to my knowledge in the exercise of my profession or in daily commerce with men, which ought not to be spread abroad, I will keep secret and will never reveal." A perfect, straight smile claimed his mouth as he finished. "That is the oath I took upon entering this profession, Miss Westmore. So you see, you've no need to worry on either quarter. Everything we share will be kept in the strictest confidence."

Clare exhaled in relief. She had hoped for just such a pledge of privacy, but she found herself grateful enough to smile. "Meaning you *still* won't tell me what ails Lady Austerley?"

His smile faltered. "I'm afraid only the countess herself can provide those details."

"I am sorry. I didn't mean . . ." Clare's voice trailed off as she realized the inadequacy of the apology rising to her lips. Well, yes, she *had* meant.

She was embarrassed enough to acknowledge the double standard, at least to herself.

Gossip was the stock in trade of her social circle, and

Sophie had cultivated it to a proper art form. Clare was admittedly curious about the sort of ailment that might cause the dowager countess to invite her personal physician to last night's ball. "It's just that your association with her is rather strange," she blurted out. "And you must admit, you aren't the usual sort of physician employed by members of the ton."

For a start, most wore better coats.

"I would argue that Lady Austerley is not a usual member of the ton." His jaw worked a wordless moment before he added, "I met her through odd circumstances, which I suppose I am at liberty to share, given that half of London saw them. She fainted during services at St. Paul's Cathedral, and I was the only one who noticed and came to her aid."

"Surely not." Clare was appalled. She tried to envision it, and rejected the notion on the grounds of logic. "Why, she's a countess. Half of London attends her annual ball. How could no one feel compelled to help her?"

He shrugged. "She would be the first to tell you that titles and balls are meaningless where such things are concerned. She was childless in her marriage to Lord Austerley, and the title went to a cousin who has quite abandoned her. She has no remaining family and no close friends. I have been fortunate to win Lady Austerley's patronage, and her recommendation has encouraged several other clients to request my services, but I do not attend her merely for the money. I count the dowager countess as a friend."

Clare felt as stunned by the thought that a wealthy, well-known countess could pitch over in her church pew and go unnoticed by the ton as the notion that such a presumably powerful woman could befriend a young, struggling physician. "You are right, of course. I should not have inquired about her circumstances." She twisted her fingers in her skirts. "And I thank you for your discretion with my own family."

He headed for the door, only to pause on the threshold. His eyes met hers, dark and probing. "I imagine that Lady Austerley would be happy enough to share details of her health and her life with friends who may care to ask. Perhaps you might take an hour or so to visit her next month, when your ankle is healed. She would welcome the company, I think."

His words lingered, even as he disappeared from view. Despite the warmth she'd detected in his voice when he spoke of Lady Austerley, and the oddity of a physician who seemed to actually care for his patients as people, she had difficulty looking beyond his declaration that a visit with the dowager countess might take place in a month.

A month. She glared at the empty doorway, even as his heels echoed a retreat down the tiled hallway. Drat it all, she'd been as still as death itself all morning long, and he had declared her ankle worse, not better.

And who was he to lecture her on who to visit? *He* got to leave, blast the man. No doubt he had an interesting day planned, a day full of sunlight and walks and doddering old countesses as patients, while she was stuck here with an embroidery frame and bickering siblings.

Clare slumped back against the couch, her blood already humming with the sort of boredom hatched of forced and unwelcome inactivity. She wasn't sure how long she could manage such meekness.

And Tuesday couldn't come soon enough.

Chapter 9

Daniel arrived at half past nine on Tuesday to find Lucy and Geoffrey engaged in a raucous game of whist, despite the early hour. Their raised voices drowned out the faint drumming of rain against the windowpanes.

"You're cheating!" Lucy accused.

"Well, you didn't say I *couldn't* cheat," came Geoffrey's retort. When the boy spied him, he waved. "Ho, Dr. Handsome is here!"

Lucy smiled over the top of her cards. "It is nice to see you again, Dr. Merial." She made an unladylike face as Geoffrey craned his neck to see her hand. "Geoffrey, I swear, if you don't quit trying to peek at my cards I am going to gouge you in the eye with a fireplace poker."

Daniel smiled as he shook the drops from his umbrella. It was a household steeped in noise, far different from his own upbringing. Though he had been well-loved and happy enough as an only child, there was something about the rowdiness of this particular family that made him feel vaguely regretful of that past, as if he'd been happy only because he hadn't known a better alternative existed. He'd looked forward to returning this morning more than he cared to admit.

A crisper sort of greeting was offered by his actual patient. Miss Westmore was sitting on the sofa again, her bandaged foot propped up on the stool, but this morning she was gripping the *London Times* instead of an embroidery frame. She made an awkward attempt to stow the paper beneath the sofa at his approach but was hampered by her foot's odd position on the stool. "It is not yet ten o'clock. You are early," she accused, glaring up at him.

"And you are reading the newspaper," he responded, setting down his bag. "The editorial section, at that, unless my eyes deceive me. An interesting discovery. And here I thought sordid novels were the rage among your set."

She flushed a marvelous shade of pink, hinting at a lovely and well-functioning circulatory system. "Those dreadful things?" She lifted two hands, as though to smooth down her perfectly coiled hair. "A well-bred lady would never read such drivel."

Daniel's gaze followed the trajectory of her busy hands, then skipped further afield, over the swell of her pert breasts, down through the waterfall of her skirts, to the remnants of the crumpled newspaper, discarded upon the floor. He made his living through close observations, reading the signs and symptoms a patient didn't want to confess.

And damned if this particular patient didn't look embarrassed to have been caught reading the paper.

"You never read them?" He lifted his gaze back to center, to the refreshing color of her cheeks. He withdrew the book he'd brought from his bag. "Such a shame, given that I've brought you one of those dreadful things to pass the time."

Her lips firmed, though her fingers stretched out in a

telling fashion. "And here I thought only medical tomes were the rage among your set."

He stifled a chuckle, absurdly pleased by her quick wit. "It is not my book." He held out the book but kept it just out of her hand's reach. "And clearly ladies *do* read such drivel, because it is one of Lady Austerley's favorites. She asked me to bring it, thinking it might be welcome during your recovery. She was very sorry to hear about your ankle, particularly as it happened at her ball."

Miss Westmore's eyes narrowed. "I thought matters between a patient and their doctor were to be kept confidential."

"*I* did not tell her, of course, but the gossip of other guests is another thing entirely. Apparently, others noticed your infirmity the night of the ball, no doubt during your lumbering flight from the ballroom. And as I promised you my discretion, I was not able to correct Lady Austerley's misimpression that you twisted your ankle on her dance floor. When I checked in on her yesterday, she asked me to deliver de Balzac's *Cousin Bette* by way of an apology."

Her lips firmed, but she held out her hand for the book.

He was discovering that teasing this woman gave him a perverse pleasure, and so he only held it higher and grinned down at her. "Of course, if ladies refuse to read such drivel in English, I can scarcely imagine you will enjoy the French—"

"I didn't say I *refused* to." Miraculously, the corners of her mouth began to lift, as if she, too, was enjoying the banter but was determined not to acknowledge it. "And I do appreciate Lady Austerley's kind gesture." She wiggled her fingers, and her smile widened until that crooked tooth he had glimpsed the first night slid into view. "Although I will never be able to give her my thanks if I am not able to actually read it, Dr. Merial."

He relinquished the prize, though he was not above leaning in to bedevil her further. "I think you might call me Daniel," he said softly. "After all, if I am to be held on retainer to answer your brother's questions, it seems we should be on more familiar terms."

She settled the book onto her lap, and her hand swirled a circle across the cover. For a moment he thought she would be sensible and tell him precisely what she thought of his fumbling attempt at familiarity.

But then she looked up at him through dark sooty lashes. "Then I suppose you must call me Clare. After all you've seen of my family, I suppose you have earned the right of informality." Her gaze settled briefly on the clock on the mantel, an ornately carved thing that no doubt had an entire staff of servants whose sole job was to see to its winding. "You failed to mention why you are here so early."

He grinned. "Perhaps I am a busy man."

"That is a better argument for being late, I should think."

Touché. And busy or no, the sight of his patient this morning sorely tempted him to linger. Though the day was a haze of rain and drizzle, the soft gray light filtering through the window made her skin glow like a polished pearl. Unlike the day dress she'd worn Saturday, today she was wearing a lovely walking gown of deep rich mauve, the heavy skirts styled in the latest fashion. He could see the defining shape of a corset stiffening her spine. "Were you planning on going out today?"

She shrugged, though a pretty challenge flashed in her eyes. "That depends on how your examination goes, I would imagine."

"I doubt my prognosis will include a recommendation for a vigorous walk."

"Well, perhaps someone of note might come to visit *me*." She paused. "And you still haven't answered my question."

Despite the stirrings of concern at her clear plans for defiance, Daniel smiled at the censure in her voice. He knew he didn't qualify as anyone of note in her mind. She'd made that quite clear the evening they met, though he felt her frosty disdain had thawed a significant degree or two. "I've come early because I've brought a proposition for Master Geoffrey, and we'll need a quick start for it if I'm to get him to St. Bart's and back before my noon lecture to the medical students."

Geoffrey's blond head popped up from the whist table. "A proposition? For *me*?"

Daniel grinned, knowing the young man was about to dissolve into a quivering mass of youthful excitement. "I've a colleague at St. Bartholomew's who collects odd anatomical artifacts. Two-headed infants, that sort of thing. He keeps them in his office."

"Gor!" Geoffrey nearly knocked over his chair in his effort to reach Daniel's side. "You are taking me to see a two-headed baby?"

"Among other things. You see, this particular doctor assisted during Napoleon's postmortem at Saint Helena, and he retained a pertinent . . . er . . . piece of the man's anatomy, so to speak." He cleared his throat. "The ladies of the French court were rumored to think it most impressive, but perhaps you could be the judge of that."

Geoffrey's blue eyes widened. "He's got Napoleon's prick? In a *jar*?"

"Geoffrey." Clare's voice was little better than a tangled knot. "I scarcely think—"

"Actually," Daniel said, breaking off her protest with an apologetic grin, "young Geoffrey is nearly correct. It isn't in a jar, though. It's more of a mummified piece. My colleague invited us to come and have a look. You'll need your mother's permission, of course."

Clare shook her head. "She's still asleep."

"But, a chance for me to see Napoleon's pizzle is *surely* worth waking her," Geoffrey protested, bouncing up and down with excitement.

Lucy sauntered up, a surprising flash of blue ribbon visible amidst the blond tangle of her hair. "You know as well as I do that waking Mother before noon is never a good idea," she said matter-of-factly. "I'm afraid it's impossible." She smirked, and waved Geoffrey's abandoned cards. "Much like your chances of winning this trick, I'm afraid."

Geoffrey turned to Clare, almost pleading now. "Then *you* can give me permission. Father always says you are in charge when he's off to the club and mother is indisposed. Oh, please. Don't say no. I want to go, ever so much."

Daniel could see the hesitation in her hazel eyes. "But what if something should happen to you?" she protested.

Geoffrey threw up his hands. "Well then, he's a doctor. And we're going to a *hospital*. He'll know how to patch me up, won't he?"

The room waited with expectant breath. Clare glanced from her brother, to Daniel, back to her brother again. "If you promise to be back before Mother wakes," she said reluctantly. "And only if you promise to wear a coat, and *not* to tell me all the inglorious details."

"Oh, thank you, thank you!" He kissed his sister on the cheek and then bounded off to fetch his coat.

"I want to go too," Lucy's voice rang out.

An objection rose to Daniel's lips, given his own ulterior motives in asking Geoffrey on this outing, but Clare had the good sense to beat him to it. "Absolutely not. It is not at all an appropriate venture for a young lady of good breeding."

Lucy glared at her sister. "But if Geoffrey is permitted to go, I ought to be able to as well." She crossed her arms, the cards forgotten. "I can wear a pair of Geoffrey's old pants. I do it all the time, and no one ever guesses I am female."

"Lucy," Clare said, sternly now. "You are almost eighteen, and it is time to start acting it. You can dress your hair like a boy's. You can even act like a boy, climbing trees and playing cards. But you cannot *be* a boy."

The younger woman's color flared, and she threw her cards down on the floor with an angry flourish. "Just because I am a girl, I am not permitted to have any fun?" She whirled and stomped out of the room with clenched fists. Her voice echoed down the hallway. "Someday I will show you. Someday I will show *everyone*."

And then the room fell quiet to all but Daniel's own faint chuckle, and Miss Westmore's nearly audible displeasure.

As HE SAT down on the sofa and pulled her injured ankle into his lap, Clare sucked in a breath in anticipation of the pain. She was surprised to find the sting of it had lessened since her last encounter with the doctor. "Well, *that* didn't go well," she mumbled.

"Better than I expected, truth be told." He began to unwind the cloth. "Your siblings have abandoned us, it seems. Would you like to ring for a maid, to ensure some propriety?"

"*Now* you're worried about propriety?" Clare felt herself flush, given that her injured foot was lodged dangerously close to *his* pertinent piece of anatomy, her bare toes pointing like an arrow toward the center of his lap.

But from her position on the couch, she couldn't reach the bellpull. Besides, she preferred to take this rare moment of privacy to unsheathe her frustration. "You really shouldn't encourage Geoffrey like this. And Lucy will sulk for the rest of the day."

Daniel laid the bandage to one side and took a long, assessing look at her ankle. "Your sister is old enough to handle the disappointment, I should think. And Geoffrey would scarcely be the first person on earth to see this particular artifact. The doctor in possession of it shows it to anyone with the stomach for it."

"If it was only Napoleon's stomach, I wouldn't have the same objections," Clare retorted. She tossed her chin toward the window, where rivulets of water streamed down. "And it's raining. You couldn't have waited for a nicer day?"

She feared her unspoken accusation was clear in the hurt pitch of her voice.

And how can you leave me here?

He probed her foot, testing the integrity of the many bones he claimed lurked beneath the surface. Even she could see the swelling was markedly reduced, and the color had shifted from an angry red to more of a mixed purple and yellow. "I imagine you've noticed your brother is no longer a child, Clare."

She suffered the twinge of conscience that came as her name fell from his lips, no matter the fact she'd given him permission to use it. She should not have done so. He was a doctor, paid by her family. She was the daughter of a viscount, and she'd not yet even invited Mr. Alban to use her given name, though *he* was a future duke.

But it was a little too late to go back to a place where such things made sense.

"He's a young man, and growing rapidly," Daniel went on, his fingers against her skin a painful reminder of his proximity. "You mentioned the other day that your father was frequently absent, and that Geoffrey might have a need of a proper gentleman to speak to. I thought this might provide an opportunity for that conversation, and a good reminder of how to conduct himself in public."

Clare glanced down at the book still sitting in her lap, mollified by his logic. "I see." Her fingers knotted over the embossed lettering. "Then I suppose I should thank you. You are going to a good deal of trouble on my brother's behalf."

"It's no trouble." He shrugged. "A little distraction, a little instruction, and I predict young Geoffrey will soon be on his way to something more promising than New-gate." He set her foot back down on the stool. "You are fortunate in that I don't think anything is broken. Is the pain improved?"

"A bit," she admitted.

"A consequence of resting it properly and keeping it bandaged, I should imagine. I think we can adjust your sentence down to a total of three weeks of strict rest. A little care, and I predict you'll be back out on the dance floor in no time."

"Three weeks?" Clare wallowed in an instinctive denial. She'd barely survived the three days since his last visit. It was a lifetime sentence, particularly at the start of such a promising Season. Not even the *London Times* had been able to buoy her spirits this morning, mocking her with news of the city she was being denied.

Three weeks wasn't just a poor idea: it was nigh on impossible.

She would go mad with boredom first.

Her mind raced through various alternatives as Daniel began to rewrap her foot, his hands strong and swift as they wound the cloth around and around. Every circle of the bandage felt like a noose tightening about her sanity.

"Is there nothing I can do that may speed healing?" she asked, almost desperate enough to call in Dr. Bashings. "The bandage seems to have helped. Surely there is more I could do."

He pinned the binding back in place. "Time is your friend, in this case. You want to be sure you've healed properly, or else you'll risk injuring it again. It's vulnerable in the weeks after the initial injury, and you're likely to reinjure it, to worse effect."

He placed her foot carefully back on the stool. "I'll return to check on you, of course. Say, next Tuesday again? Until then, all you can do is keep it elevated, and keep your mind off of things with *Cousin Bette*." He rose from the sofa and fished a hand in his pocket, drawing out a paper-wrapped item. He passed it solemnly to her. "And this may help pass the time as well."

Clare accepted the package, still stunned by the man's declaration of three weeks of purgatory. The waxed paper edges fell away to reveal a paper box, and inside, a delicate bit of marzipan, whimsical fruit shapes in shades of red and purple nearly the same color as her foot.

She stared down at them, frozen in want and horror. "Are these from Lady Austerley as well?"

"No." His smile was slow and spreading, and not the least bit doctorly. "These are a gift from me."

Clare looked up at him, aghast. It was a stroke of culinary cruelty. If sweets were her general weakness, marzipan, in particular, was her Achilles' heel. "I don't understand what you expect me to do with this."

Though of course she did.

She held *marzipan* in her hand, and her mouth was already halfway to watering.

He shrugged. "Eat it, of course."

"*Eat* it?"

"For medicinal purposes. I've seen the way you care for

your siblings. Geoffrey is fortunate to have you, and there is no doubt in my mind that Lucy will one day appreciate your meddling, however much she may resist now. But you need to care for yourself as well. You're too thin by half. If nothing else, you should use these three weeks of rest to fill out your frame to a more healthful size." He smiled, the flash of white teeth probably meant to be reassuring. "You could stand to gain a stone, at least."

Clare was consumed by a twitching irritation in his powers of observation, even as her insecurities scratched to be let off their lead. She felt enough doubt in her slight figure's ability to capture Mr. Alban's attention without this man pointing it out. "It is not appropriate for you to comment on my frame," was all she could think to say, though her brain certainly screamed a more robust denial.

"As your doctor, it is entirely appropriate. It astounds me that young ladies of good breeding starve themselves on purpose, when there are many in England's rookeries who have no idea where their next meal may come from."

Clare was struck by the unsettling notion that he was not merely relating something he had read about in a textbook: he had seen these souls. Touched them.

Healed them, perchance. She felt a hesitant stirring of respect.

But then his eyes settled alarmingly on her chest, and narrowed in grim humor instead of admiration. "And it is my firm opinion—my medical opinion, mind you—that you should not be wearing a corset, either. It's a most unhealthful practice. Hampers the breathing, sometimes to a lethal degree. Worse, it squeezes the organs and contorts the spine. I've seen the ill effects on any number of cadavers."

She gaped up at him, all thoughts of rookeries and respect forgotten. Now the man was comparing her to *cadavers*? "Have you considered that those patients likely wore the corset to improve an intrinsic deficiency in their posture?" she demanded, fishing about for some sort of logical argument that would keep her corset firmly in place, thank you very much.

A dark brow rose, faintly mocking. His eyes trailed down her torso, then back again, making the fine hairs along the back of her neck prick to rigid attention and her skin ripple with anticipation. Worse, as her body responded to his long, slow slide of a perusal, she felt the answering expansion of her lungs, pressing against the unyielding cage of her corset.

Blast the man to Hades and back, he might be right about the breathing part.

"I see no deficiency in *your* posture," he drawled, coming back to her face and settling squarely—inappropriately—on her lips. His teasing eyes danced over hers. *"Yet."*

He was deranged. An absolute, raving lunatic. Had the man no notion at all that the very construction of every gown she owned required a corset as a base undergarment?

"Be that as it may, Dr. Merial—"

"Daniel." He grinned. "As we agreed."

"Daniel." Her breath was coming in hard pants now. She pushed the box of marzipan back at him, though her fingers clutched an involuntary protest. She refused to think about what the sweets must have cost him—he had no right to bring her such an extravagant gift, even for *medicinal* purposes. "While I appreciate the gesture, I cannot accept these."

He held up a hand, refusing their return. "Well, I cannot accept them back."

"Oh, you are positively *mad*," she huffed in indignation. "I've an entire wardrobe of lovely new ball gowns hanging upstairs, currently unused, thanks to your dire prognosis. And I assure you, the future usefulness of those gowns depends on both the retention of my corset and a stern resolve *not* to eat marzipan!"

That mocking brow rose to a high salute once more. "You would choose to be fashionable over healthful?"

She drew a deep breath, praying for patience.

Only an idiot—or a man— would ask that question.

Chapter 10

A flurry of activity at the drawing room door saved Clare from having to deliver a well-deserved tongue-lashing.

Geoffrey bounded in, his coat hanging half off his shoulders. "You have some visitors, sis. Wilson was going to bring them in, but I told him I would do it." He wiggled his hands, pantomiming the act of milking a cow. "Lovely bubbies, the dark-haired one has. Top notch." He laughed, even as two familiar faces filled the doorway behind him.

"Geoffrey!" Clare gasped. "That is *not* an appropriate way to announce a guest."

And how, oh *how* had she earned the misfortune of being born into this family?

"Oh, I think we can forgo the pleasantries," Sophie said haughtily as she swept into the room, trailed—as always—by Rose. She briefly eyed Daniel as if he might be a dish of cream before apparently deciding he was a servant and handing her reticule and gloves over to him. "After all, these are scarcely official calling hours."

With her good foot, Clare kicked the remnants of the

newspaper deeper beneath the sofa, then shoved the book Daniel had given her into the crease of the cushion. As an afterthought, she tucked the box of marzipan in her skirt pocket. No, these *weren't* calling hours, and it was difficult not to resent the intrusion, especially when she'd had no time to prepare.

Now she would be forced greet her friends properly— although, perhaps "friend" was a bit of a stretch, at least as far as Sophie was concerned.

Yet, despite being outside of regular calling hours, wasn't their arrival more a blessing than a curse? Even the sight of Sophie's treacherous smile promised a more interesting day than the one she'd been facing moments before.

"Why have you come so early in the day?" she asked, forcing a smile on her face.

Sophie sat down in the chair opposite the sofa and untied the ribbons of her pink bonnet. "We heard the news about your ankle, of course, and simply had to come and see for ourselves."

Rose settled on the sofa beside Clare in a sympathetic froth of white lace, though she kept sneaking none-too-subtle peeks in Daniel's direction. "Is it dreadfully painful?"

Clare willed herself to show no obvious surprise. She'd sent no note to either Sophie or Rose regarding her forced incapacitation. How would they have heard of her ankle? In this circle, lack of knowledge was a definite weakness, and she needed to remember to not bare her throat. Indeed, if only she'd had enough sense to not reveal her hopes for Mr. Alban, her friends wouldn't have that knife to twist in her side, either.

"It is improving every day," she said evasively. From the corner of her eye she watched as Daniel smirked and then tossed Sophie's reticule to Geoffrey like a ball. Geoffrey, of course, promptly threw it back. She pulled her eyes away from the spectacle and gave Sophie a terse smile. "I should be up and about shortly."

"I do hope it doesn't keep you from attending the opening of the Royal Gallery this Friday," Sophie purred. Her voice floated on the air, as sweet as marzipan and just as dangerous. She and Rose exchanged amused glances. "Mr. Alban is planning to attend, you know."

Clare refocused her attention on Sophie. "Am I to presume he mentioned this during the waltz you shared?" she asked, none too sweetly herself.

But Sophie only laughed, fluttering dismissive fingers. "Honestly, it wasn't as if you were in any condition to dance. I was doing you a favor, dancing with Alban. Why, we talked about you the entire time. He is hoping to see you at the gallery's opening, you know."

Hope—that most exhausting of emotions—leaped to attention once more. Clare no longer quite knew what to believe. But no matter the direction of Sophie's loyalties, the Royal Gallery was an impossibility, given that the opening was in only three days' time.

She looked up, catching Daniel's eye. "I'm afraid Dr. Merial says I must have another week of rest," she sighed dramatically, "but then I should be fine to resume my normal activities." She met his gaze over Sophie's head, daring him to contradict her. He glowered at her from across the room, clearly eavesdropping and disapproving of her shortened sentence.

"Another week? And at the start of the Season? Oh, dear, that *is* a blow." Sophie patted a gloved hand to her gleaming curls, which, despite the rain outside, had somehow resisted the puff of humidity. "Dr. Merial, did you say? Who is he? I've not heard of him."

"Oh, you've not met Lady Austerley's personal physician?" Clare leaned forward, knowing that for once she had a delicious drop of gossip that Sophie did not. "He was kind enough to assist me when I sustained my injury during Lady Austerley's ball." No sense mentioning the geese, really. Better for Sophie to believe the less colorful version being handied about. "My family has retained his services during my convalescence." Clare gestured in Daniel's direction. "Dr. Merial, may I present my friends, Lady Sophie Durston, and Miss Rose Evans."

They shifted in their seats to stare at him with wide eyes.

"*That's* your doctor?" Sophie frowned. "I thought he was your footman."

"Your very *handsome* footman," Rose added in an unladylike whisper. A flush crept up her neck as she peeked back at him, and then she cupped a hand to Clare's ear and giggled. "Although I am beginning to see why you sprained an ankle. I feel a swoon coming on myself."

Clare fought the urge to roll her eyes. This bold interest in Daniel felt remarkably similar to how she had felt watching Sophie waltz with Mr. Alban, and it was an emotion she didn't care to examine or revisit.

"It is a pleasure to meet you both, ladies." He put down Sophie's things and picked up his bag and umbrella. "But I fear our introductions are bound to brief. I have an . . . er . . . appointment to keep." He winked at Geoffrey and gestured to the door. "Are you ready, Mr. Westmore?"

They took their leave, their voices growing fainter down the hallway. For an impulsive moment Clare stared at the open door, wishing she could just go with them.

But it was impossible, and not only because of her ankle.

"*Well.*" Sophie turned her speculative gaze back to Clare. "I suppose there are worse ways to spend one's time." She raised a brow, her meaning all too clear. "Still, it's already been four days. It is a terribly long time to be absent, is it not? I thought you had your hopes pinned on an excellent match this year." She smiled, the gesture feline and mildly threatening. "A good deal can happen in such a period of time, especially during the height of the Season."

Clare fidgeted in her seat, wondering what Sophie was up to. It was clear she was leading her *somewhere* with this conversation. "Surely you haven't come to talk only about my ankle," she said, trying to turn things around. "I was rather hoping to catch up on the news I missed when I was forced to leave the ball so early." News she had already gleaned from the *Times*, of course, but would now be forced to pretend she didn't know.

Sophie's lips returned to their usual curving ribbon of mischief. "Oh, didn't you know? *You're* the news. Why, Lady Halsey said she saw you limp from the ballroom, dragging your maimed foot behind you. We decided we must come and get all the details."

Clare covered her nervousness with a dismissive laugh. "It was not as bad as that, surely? I simply twisted my ankle." And Sophie had just admitted she'd known about the turned ankle for four entire days, and was only now coming to check on her welfare.

Lovely friends, they were.

"Not maimed, then?" Rose sounded almost disappointed.

Clare shook her head. "No." She needed to shift this conversation in a new direction, one that led squarely away from her. The one vital bit of education she'd received at the hands of the ton was that it was always better to be the bearer of unfortunate gossip than the subject of it. She leaned forward from her perch on the sofa. "Now, tell me about Lady Halsey. She has the most hideous taste in fashion. What was she wearing?"

Her question effectively dissuaded the malicious interest

in her ankle and encouraged Rose and Sophie to chatter on about other things. But she found it difficult to concentrate. No doubt Daniel and Geoffrey were halfway to their grand adventure by now. Though a part of her itched to go with them and leave Rose and Sophie to their gossip, she felt an odd reassurance that with respect to her brother, at least, the doctor appeared to have things well in hand.

And so would she, once she returned her head—and her body—to the game.

MAYFAIR EVEN MANAGES to make a dreary London rain appealing, Daniel thought as he opened his umbrella on the front steps.

He breathed in deeply, enjoying the rare, clean scent of rain on spring leaves. Only a few blocks away the trees of Hyde Park shimmered, an almost violent gasp of green against the gray clouds and white stone town houses.

Unlike the streets of Smithfield, the alleys off Grosvenor Square boasted garden courtyards, instead of drunken souls sleeping off a bender. Here there were no belligerent carters, their voices raised in angry shouts, and no manure-clogged sewers, blocking the outflow of rainwater. No, Mayfair's inebriated residents laid their heads on feather beds instead of cold paving stones. The streets in this part of the city—and the strange, titled creatures who inhabited it—were a world away from his own humble flat and the bustling charity ward at St. Bartholomew's.

As they stepped down to the sidewalk, he regarded his companion, wondering if the boy realized how rare it was to live in a place of such privilege and safety. While he didn't begrudge the young man his wealth, he *did* begrudge him his naiveté. Between Mayfair and Eton, it was doubtful Geoffrey had seen much of the world, and Daniel hoped to show him something more enduring today than Napoleon's privates.

Once Geoffrey saw the charity ward at St. Bart's, the young viscount-in-training might even realize there was more to life than lewd jokes and bubbies.

But at the moment, the boy appeared far more distracted by puddles than life lessons. He took a flying leap and jumped into one, splashing mud and water before grinning impishly up at Daniel. "I *never* get to do that," he crowed through the drizzle.

"Well, you might want to limit the experience to the one," Daniel advised, turning north. "The bus driver will make us ride outside if he thinks we are too wet."

Geoffrey ducked under Daniel's oilskin umbrella. "We're going to ride the omnibus?" he asked incredulously. "Gor, this *is* the day to end all days! Clare will be sorry she missed it."

Daniel thought back on Clare's hesitant agreement to let Geoffrey go. "I doubt very much your prim and proper sister would think riding on a public omnibus to see a Frenchman's shriveled penis is a worthwhile way to spend her day."

Geoffrey scoffed as they walked slowly northward. "Oh, she's not so prim, nor proper, either. I'll admit, you couldn't have bounced a quarter off that tight smile she put on when her visitors arrived, but that's not Clare." He tapped a conspiratorial finger against his nose. "At least, that's not the real Clare."

"Ah," Daniel said, intrigued by this alternate picture of her. *"Non sum qualis eram."*

"What does that mean?" Geoffrey asked, cocking his head.

"It is a quote, from Horace. *I was not what I once was.*" Daniel lifted a brow. "Didn't they teach you Latin at this mythical place they call Eton?"

"They taught us Latin. And I'm not stupid," Geoffrey

protested, the tips of his ears turning pink. "It just wasn't my favorite class."

Daniel stopped, forcing Geoffrey to stop as well to continue enjoying the protection of the umbrella. "I do not think you are stupid. In fact, I suspect you are quite sharp, and that is partly what gets you into trouble. While I can see why a boy with your energy might consider conjugating Latin verbs the height of tedium, if you pay a bit more attention you can say things like *'Quidquid Latine dictum sit altum videtur.'*" He grinned. "That means whatever is said in Latin sounds profound. You'll find there is little more satisfying than delivering a sound set-down to your detractors using a language they don't understand."

"Oh." Geoffrey blinked. "Well, I'll admit I wasn't much of a student in any of my classes at Eton. But that's not why they turned me out. Clare is as mad as a wet hen over it, and fusses over me to the point of madness. She says I don't care about my future, but she's wrong, you know. It was *because* of my future I did it. And hers, too."

Daniel guarded his response, given that he didn't know what "it" was.

The boy would reveal all when he was ready.

"Anyone can see she cares about you," Daniel said solemnly as the rain dripped down on the spread surface of his umbrella. He knew they needed to move on quickly if they were to make the next bus, but somehow this conversation seemed important enough to take a moment, and so they continued to stand in place, talking as the rain pattered down. "You are fortunate to have a sister that fusses over you. I myself was an only child, and both my parents are now gone."

"Oh. I am sorry," the lad mumbled. The faint pink on the tips of his ears spread to his cheeks. "For your loss, I mean."

Daniel nodded. Christ, but these Westmores were a fair-skinned lot, wearing their emotions on the surface of their skin. It was perhaps the only obvious physical trait Clare shared with her siblings. "Thank you," he said gently. "But I didn't tell you such a personal thing to make you feel uncomfortable, or to embarrass you. I told you so that you might realize how important it is to appreciate the family you have."

Geoffrey threw his hands up in a universal gesture of adolescent frustration. "I know you're right. It's just when Clare's sniping at me, I get a devilish urge to vex her. You know, before she started going to parties and such, she used to be a lot more fun. She can throw a ball better than any boy I know. She's stubborn to a fault, although she smiles at you while she refuses to listen." He met Daniel's eyes, nearly man-to-man. "She's smarter than she pretends. Reads like a demon, and she can give me a thrashing on the chessboard. She knows Latin, too. Better than I ever will."

The stubborn part Daniel had already gathered. The Latin as well. He recalled how Clare had tossed that stinging barb back in his face in Lady Austerley's library. Yet, today she had dispatched her newspaper with a speed that would have put a burning mail coach to shame.

"She pretends she lacks intelligence?" he asked, perplexed.

Geoffrey shrugged. "It's more that she takes pains to hide things she used to enjoy. Although, you may be right about the omnibus. She hates to get wet, unless it's soaking in a tub, which she does for hours when she's getting ready for one of those fancy balls." An indelicate shudder possessed the boy, whether at the thought of a bath or a ball, it was difficult to tell. "But then, we've Father's coach at our disposal, so there is never a need for us to take a bus or a cab."

Daniel considered that a moment as the rain began to pick up, drumming on the slick surface of his umbrella. Riding everywhere by coach was easier—and drier—than taking public transportation or walking, but it was also an unhealthy way for a vigorous, active young man to spend his days. There was a downside to always being cosseted on velvet seats, and he wondered if some of Geoffrey's social difficulties might not stem from a lack of wholesome diversions. Daniel's own childhood had been rather more remarkable for its *lack* of bus fare, but he'd at least been permitted to run and jump in all the puddles he'd wanted.

"We'll catch the bus two blocks north on Oxford Street," he said, motioning up ahead. "And you can tell your sister all about it when we return. Perhaps I'll even teach you some Latin, to surprise her."

But as they once again started to walk, his thoughts wanted to stay behind. All the talk of Clare—and Geoffrey's claim that his sister hid her true inclinations from the world—bothered him. Why did she feel the need to hide what might arguably be the most interesting aspects of her character? He thought back on Clare's behavior after her friends had arrived, trying to dissect some hidden meaning behind her brittle smile. There had been a brief moment in the drawing room when it seemed like she regretted not coming along.

It had surprised him, that glimpse of acute uneasiness he'd detected when she greeted her friends. He'd have thought their arrival would be a welcome distraction, especially given the bleakness of the weather and her stated hope that someone of note might come to visit her.

But despite his curiosity, it was none of his business. Geoffrey was his main concern at the moment. She'd given the charge of her brother over to him, and he'd see the lad safely to Smithfield and back again.

As they turned north toward Oxford, a mass of brown wool tumbled out of a large oak tree in front of Lord Cardwell's town house, sending up a wall of dirty water to engulf them both.

"Ooomph!" the figure gasped. Two arms flailed about, splashing more muck.

Daniel shook the water from his eyes, even as he stretched out a hand. The youth who had soaked them clambered to his feet, a grin stretched widely across his mud-splattered face.

Correction. *Her* mud-splattered face.

"For heaven's sake," he growled, taking in Lucy's damp wool trousers and shapeless brown coat. Her blond hair was bundled up beneath an old felt hat, which, judging by the bits of straw clinging to it, must have been snatched from one of Cardwell's grooms.

Now that he'd seen evidence of her clumsiness first-hand, he could see why Clare worried over the girl. "You might have been killed if you'd landed on your head," he pointed out. "I doubt it's worth risking life and limb, all for a bit of eavesdropping."

"I wasn't eavesdropping." A slight flush stained her cheeks. "I had planned to follow you, once you set out. But then I lost my balance and . . ." She shrugged, and swiped a hand across her dirty face. "So now I shall go *with* you. Besides, I want to see the horses on the bus line, and judge for myself how they are being treated."

"Horses?" Daniel echoed, trying to sort it all out.

"Lucy fancies herself a bit of a savior where London's animals are concerned," Geoffrey broke in. "But she's mad, if you ask me. There's thousands of them, everywhere you look. More than people, even."

Bloody hell. Lucy wanted to go with them because of horses?

"Are you trying to get me drawn and quartered?" Daniel

demanded, visions of kidnapping charges and prison dancing in his head. It occurred to him, as he glared down at the girl, that she was quite adept at this particular brand of subterfuge. If he hadn't already known her as female, he wouldn't have looked twice. He readjusted his grip on his umbrella. "Your sister has already made her opinion on this matter quite clear."

Lucy's eyes narrowed in a fashion that reminded him remarkably of Clare, though in truth they shared few physical traits that bespoke a familial connection. "I am seventeen years old. Clare can't tell me what to do."

"Well, *I* can." He transferred his bag to the hand holding the umbrella, then clasped her arm and tried to steer her back to the safety of the town house. "Back you go, then. Through the front door, where I can see you safely delivered."

"No!" both siblings cried out, identical horrified expressions on their faces.

Daniel was startled enough to drop his hold on the miscreant's arm.

"Are you daft, man?" Geoffrey demanded.

"The drawing room window is *right there*." Lucy pointed to the large picture window fronting the street.

Daniel followed the direction of the girl's finger to an unassuming picture window—unassuming, that was, until he realized it overlooked the street. Lucy had cleverly staged her appearance to fall on the opposite side of the tree, out of view of anyone inside the house.

"Well, you should have considered the risk to your hide before you chose to dress like this," he told her. He had plans for educating young Geoffrey on this outing, and the presence of a woman—even one dressed like a boy— would make the coming conversation difficult.

"If you take me back dressed like this," Lucy warned, "Clare will be the one to suffer."

"How will your sister be the one to suffer," Daniel asked, growing exasperated now, "when *you* are the one falling out of the tree?"

"Lucy's right," Geoffrey protested. "Did you see the way her friends turned their noses up when they marched into the drawing room? I saw that expression on a good number of bullies' faces at Eton, usually right before they attacked someone. They'll be looking for an excuse to pounce on her while she's down."

Lucy nodded her agreement, sending a handful of blond hair cascading down from the cover of her cap. "I heard them whispering to each other on the front porch steps while I was in the tree. The blond girl said Clare was a terrible dancer anyway, and that she had probably twisted her ankle on purpose to avoid further embarrassment. And the dark-haired one said that with a family like Clare's, Mr. Alban would be mad to offer for her."

"Mr. Alban?" Daniel echoed stupidly.

"The presumptive heir to the Duke of Harrington, and the gentleman Clare hopes to marry, though I can't help but question her sanity in wanting to marry at all."

Daniel blinked. Clare wished to marry a duke? The pronouncement shouldn't have surprised him, but there was no denying his body's reaction to the thought. Bloody hell, his fist was clenching around the slick handle of his umbrella.

Lucy lifted her chin. "I know Clare is concerned about appearances, but I suppose I didn't realize before *why* it was so important to her. Now that I've seen her friends, I have a better sense of why she's been so worried of late. So, while *I* don't care what they think or say about me, I imagine Clare does."

Daniel eyed the window again, still distracted by the thought of Clare marrying anyone, much less a bloody duke. He could see the logic in Lucy's arguments, he supposed, but he refused to be manipulated by this scrap of a girl. "You shall return through the back door, then." He turned back to her with a frown and plucked a piece of straw from her cap, holding it accusingly in front of her face. "Or take yourself to the mews, where it looks like you spend a good deal of time anyway. But you can't come with us. Not without a chaperone, and not lacking your sister's permission."

"But that's not fair!" Her face scrunched up in something close to a pout. "Geoffrey isn't being forced to have a chaperone."

"I don't want you to come either, Lucy," Geoffrey broke in. "You'll just ruin things. Probably the doctor would refuse to show us Napoleon's doodle with a silly *girl* in tow."

"No one would have to know I'm a girl," Lucy retorted, her fists balling up.

At this, Daniel chuckled. "Miss Westmore, I regret to be the one to inform you of this, but anyone with an ounce of sense and two functioning eyes can see you are a girl. A very *lovely* girl, no matter what manner of men's clothing you put on or how many trees you tumble from."

She went still. "They can?"

"My advice to you, should you care to take it, is to just be yourself." At her resulting sour face, he plowed on. "You do not have to pretend to be someone you aren't, be it a boy or a young woman of high fashion."

"Don't I?" she protested. "Next year I am expected to be presented at court, whether I want to or not." She rolled her eyes, then added vehemently, "Judging by Clare's experience, I will turn into someone I scarcely recognize. I don't *want* to change. I'd rather be a spinster."

Daniel hid a smile. "But can't you see? You *are* changing yourself, in reaction to fear. Do you have some specific objection to women's clothing, or is it only that you reject it to make a point?" He could tell he'd hit close to the truth when she glared at her shoes and kicked out at a pebble on the cobblestone street. "Surely there is some middle ground," he said, more easily now, "where you can be comfortable in your skin *and* pursue your own dreams."

"And save all the cart horses in London," her brother added unhelpfully.

"Stuff it, Geoffrey," Lucy mumbled, but she seemed less belligerent about it.

Daniel lifted an eye from the simmering family squabble to the sky, hoping to get a sense of time, but the sun was quite obliterated by low-hanging clouds. There was only one way he could see out of this, though it was going to land him in a good deal of trouble with their sister.

"Flectere si nequeo superos, acheronta movebo," he muttered.

Lucy glared at him. "I don't understand what that means."

"If I cannot move heaven, I will raise hell." Daniel gritted his teeth. "Listen, both of you. I am under a tight schedule today, and don't have time to argue further. Lucy, what if I promise to take you on an adventure as well, once Clare's ankle is healed and she can come with us for propriety's sake. Would that help get you back in the house, in some form or fashion?"

Her nose wrinkled in consideration. "It might."

"I give you my word," he said solemnly, placing a hand across his heart. "When Clare can walk again, we shall go on an outing. I shall even give you the choice of venue."

After a moment she huffed, "Fine." She turned and shoved her hands in her pockets, head bent down in rejection. Two steps had her calling back over her shoulder. "But if my adventure doesn't include Napoleon's privates, it had better at *least* involve an omnibus!"

Dearest Diary,

I used to think Sophie and Rose had a remarkably sharp wit, but listening to them today, it was hard to remember why I once found them amusing.

Or perhaps it is only that their banter seems increasingly at my own expense?

If there was one good thing to come of today's visit, it was that Sophie wore pink, and her dress cast a ridiculous iced-cake shadow across her face. A better friend would tactfully steer her toward deeper hues, given the way she suffers in it.

No matter her claim of innocence, I am not completely inclined toward civility where Sophie and Mr. Alban are concerned. If she has my best interests at heart, time will tell. And if she doesn't, surely there is no shame in permitting an opponent to disarm herself with an injudicious bit of color.

When they left, there was no recourse but the marzipan. If the box was truly intended for medicinal purposes, I should soon be feeling much better, because I ate the entire thing in one sitting. I only hope Daniel doesn't bring more when he comes to visit next Tuesday, or I shall be the size of one of Lucy's *omnibus horses by the end of this. And if I cannot attend the gallery opening this Friday, I must pray that Sophie chooses to wear pink there.*

I should like Mr. Alban to see her in that.

Chapter 11

A lady was expected to greet her day with a graceful smile and good humor, but Clare had to imagine such sentiments applied to the healthy and marginally sane.

By the second Tuesday of her convalescence, she was regrettably neither.

Her ankle was improving but was still not quite sound. Every day, the pain became a little less severe. She could hobble from her bed to the water closet without limping now, and had even dared take a lap or two around the drawing room that had become her prison, but the dire threat of reinjury kept her exertions to a minimum. Her mending basket boasted a half-dozen false starts on embroidery projects that served no purpose beyond inciting homicidal levels of boredom. Like an exiled political scholar, she read the *Times* every day, studying the news for glimpses of the life she was missing. *Cousin Bette* proved a welcome diversion, but it was scarcely an intellectual tome and she finished it in only two days.

And through it all, the clock on the mantel ticked on.

She thought of her new doctor more than was sensible. And not only in irritation, which would have been understandable, given the circumstances. No, *she* had to think of him in ways that made her cheeks flush and her heart race and her eyes drift distractedly toward the picture window. She would have liked to place him firmly out of mind, but how could she, when Geoffrey could speak of no one else? The boy had developed a serious case of hero worship, chattering on as much about his eye-opening visit to the hospital charity ward as Napoleon's privates. Lucy was little better, expressing her excitement to see the doctor again on an almost hourly basis. So when ten o'clock Tuesday morning came and went with no sign or word from Daniel, a gnawing irritation settled in her stomach.

It was his fault she was sitting here, drat the man.

The *least* he could do was put in a promised appearance.

"Where is he?" Lucy groaned sometime after luncheon, flopping into a chair with a dramatic sigh. "I asked Wilson to send him straight in. I expected we'd see Dr. Merial hours ago."

Clare looked up over the top of her wooden embroidery frame. "He's a physician with a busy schedule. I am sure he has other patients to see," she admonished, though her own thoughts tripped in much the same direction as her sister's.

Lucy lifted a hand to smooth back the wisps of blond hair that fluttered about her temple. "It's a shame Geoffrey will have to miss Dr. Merial now because of his afternoon studies. You must admit, last week's outing has proved remarkable in tempering his behavior. He's been close to pleasant all week, tolerating his books and quoting Latin at the oddest moments." She laughed, but it was unexpectedly a ladylike sound. "Who would have ever expected a shriveled organ to accomplish so much?"

Clare hid a smile. She suspected the changes they were seeing in Geoffrey had more to do with the miraculous Dr. Merial himself than the condition of Napoleon's manly parts. Indeed, it seemed the doctor's presence had affected more than just her brother's behavior this week. Lucy had unconsciously adopted a softer and surprising new vein of maturity as well.

Today she was wearing a dress.

A *clean* dress.

She had even brushed her hair and permitted her belea-guered ladies' maid to put it up in a loose topknot. Clare didn't know whether to laugh at her sister's antics or have a miniature made to commemorate the occasion.

"You know as well as I that Geoffrey's studies must come first," Clare stated, though privately she thought Daniel stood a better chance of improving her brother's character than the boy's sour-faced instructor who came every day after luncheon. "Afternoons are to be spent with his tutor until Father can arrange for another school to take him."

"I still can't believe he needs another school, when I've never even been permitted to attend one." Lucy scowled. "He's only thirteen. What did he do that was terrible, anyway?"

"I do not know." Clare pushed her reluctant needle through the linen. "He won't speak of the details, and nei-ther will Father."

"Have you asked Mother?"

"You know as well as I that Mother is either always sleeping or shopping." Clare stabbed at her embroidery in frustration. "And truly, I don't think she knows, either."

Lucy tapped a finger against her lips. "Perhaps Dr. Merial can get it out of him. Geoffrey clearly talks to him." She eyed Clare's propped ankle. "You'll have to feign injury a bit longer, though, so Dr. Merial has a reason to keep coming back."

Clare glared at her sister. "I am *not* feigning my injury."

But Lucy's words reminded her that these visits were finite. Someday soon, possibly even today, she would be declared fully healed. Daniel would return to his usual patients, and her family would return to Dr. Bashings's dubious care.

And the anticipation she felt over seeing him again would cease to be a problem.

Footsteps echoed in the outside hallway. Clare tossed aside her needlework and straightened her skirts as a curious jolt of energy thumped in her chest.

But it was Wilson who appeared, stiff and formal, holding a silver tray bearing a card. "You've a visitor, Lady Clare."

That was odd. Daniel had a tendency to just emerge in the door frame, like a dream or a nightmare, depending on your perspective. To her knowledge he'd never once left a card.

Lucy leaped to her feet as Clare reached out a hand. She felt oddly deflated when she saw the name was not that of the deliciously dark doctor who haunted her spare thoughts.

Oh God, oh God, oh God.

What was Mr. Alban *doing* here?

Lucy sauntered closer and stared down at the card, her eyes widening with what could have been either excitement or mischief. "Oh, good," she said, one side of her mouth quirking up. "It looks as though I will finally get to meet your future duke." She gestured to her dress. "After all, I'm scarcely dressed for climbing trees."

Clare sighed. There was no way around it she could see. Geoffrey was upstairs at his books, thank goodness, and Mother was surely shopping on Bond Street by now, but it was far too late to properly dispose of Lucy, especially now that she had seen the name on the card.

"Please show him in, Wilson." As the butler turned, Clare risked another glance at her little sister. Astonishingly, Lucy was settling herself primly in her chair again, and had even picked up an embroidery frame.

Perhaps it would be all right. Lucy *had* been showing signs of improvement lately. To someone who didn't know her, she might even appear— *gasp*—ladylike, sitting placidly with her embroidery in her lap.

But looking presentable and *acting* presentable were not nearly the same thing.

"Wilson," she called out, remembering nearly too late her intent to keep Mr. Alban's visits a secret from her mother. Her words halted the butler's retreat. "Do you remember our agreement regarding Lady Cardwell?" Her father and Lucy might be necessary co-conspirators in this plot, but she was still convinced of the need to keep her mother out of it, at least until Alban was more firmly on the hook.

The servant inclined his head. "Yes, miss. It shall be as you wish."

Clare sighed in relief as the butler left, vowing to speak to her father about increasing the poor man's wages. All this subterfuge might force Wilson to an early retirement.

And *then* who would help keep her secrets?

All too soon Mr. Alban was standing before her. She drew a steadying breath and prayed for her sister's best behavior. "I cannot tell you what a lovely surprise this is." She gestured to Lucy. "May I present my sister, Miss Lucy Westmore."

Lucy lifted her hand. "A pleasure to meet you, Mr. Alban," she said, affecting the droll tone of voice she often employed when teasing Geoffrey.

Worry rippled down Clare's spine as Alban bent over Lucy's hand. She clearly hadn't thought this through. Lucy's face might be clean, but were her hands? Good

Lord, what if Mr. Alban saw the dirt that so often lay beneath her sister's ragged nails?

But she couldn't very well order Lucy from the room now.

She was left with no recourse but to cast up a silent prayer to whichever God presided over family squabbles that her sister would stay on her best behavior.

Alban settled onto the sofa beside her. "It's a pleasure to spend time in the company of two lovely ladies." He smiled. "But I must say, I wasn't aware you had a sister, Miss Westmore. Hiding her at home, are we?"

Clare's stomach clenched. How to craft an appropriate explanation for why Lucy had no interest in social outings beyond things involving Napoleon's mummified appendage? "She . . . ah . . . isn't out yet. She'll be presented next year."

"Perhaps." Lucy waved a vague hand. "The details are still being sorted out."

Clare suppressed a groan. *Please, please not now, Lucy.* Not now. Not here.

Not *him.*

She would have made a deal with the very devil in that moment, had Satan cared to make an appearance and promised to silence her sister.

Mr. Alban's careful gaze moved from Lucy, to Clare, back to Lucy again, causing the fine hairs on Clare's arms to prick to attention. Was his unwavering focus that of a besotted gentleman, wanting to make a good impression, or that of a man assessing her family's attributes and finding them lacking? His curious expression made her feel breathless, but it was not the same sort of breathlessness she was coming to associate with the exasperating Dr. Merial.

The current emotion felt more worrisome than not.

"It's really rather remarkable," he finally said, his gaze

returning to meet hers. "You and your sister share little physical resemblance."

Clare blinked. She would have thought—would have *liked*—to hear him say how attractive she looked today. After all, she had dressed with care this morning, knowing she would see Daniel. Her day dress was a bright primrose, and the color had been carefully chosen because she knew it brought out the natural flush in her skin. Moreover, she'd instructed her maid to arrange her hair in a flattering style, with soft curls left loose to frame her cheeks.

Although, perhaps Alban was simply remarking on the lack of family resemblance, as one would the weather. It was a difficult point to refute, after all.

"I take after Father," Lucy broke in helpfully. "Clare was fortunate to escape such a sentence. But don't worry. I've quite resigned myself to being the plain Westmore sister, Mr. Alban."

Clare cringed. How could Lucy consider herself plain? Awkward, yes. Stubborn—almost certainly. But with her blue eyes and blond hair, there was a waiting prettiness to her that even her staunchest attempts to hide couldn't quite squelch.

Particularly today, when she was actually wearing a dress and sitting up straight.

"Lucy likes to tease," Clare said quickly. "We have every faith she will be brilliant next Season." She glanced sideways at the gentleman sitting next to her. She was struck again by his hesitancy, the sense that an all-important question hovered, just out of reach.

Perhaps she should just *ask* him to marry her.

That had been the way of Queen Victoria's betrothal, after all. Surely she could be forgiven for such brazenness, if it meant she could secure a future duke in hand.

But with Lucy watching, her nerve quite failed her, and

so—though inside she was screaming for Mr. Alban to get on with things—she smiled placidly instead. "Speaking of Seasons, I confess my injury has made me rather starved for news. Pray tell, did the Queen attend the opening of the Royal Gallery this year?"

Though of course, Clare already knew the Queen hadn't. According to the *Times*, the Royal Family was away at Osborne house, retreating from the civil unrest that was permeating the city. But confessing her knowledge of such events would prove she read more than gossip sheets, and so she guarded her tongue.

Alban settled himself back against the sofa, his eyes drifting again across her face in a way that made Clare's stomach tighten. She'd never been comfortable with close scrutiny, and she was coming to realize Alban had a way of indulging in it that made her fidget.

What did he see in her face this moment? A pretty, empty-headed girl? Possibly he was fixated on her crooked tooth, or the flush she could feel stealing over her cheeks.

"No," he finally answered, shaking his head gently. "The Queen did not put in an appearance this year. Nearly everyone else was there, though. It was a shame you were forced to miss it. I had hoped to see you there."

"Oh?" Clare breathed stupidly. It was hard to think of anything more gracious to say when Lucy was watching them, her gaze bouncing between them like a tossed ball.

"Lady Sophie attended the opening, and she implied you had recently suffered a grievous injury that removed you from the Season. I came to offer you my wishes for a speedy recovery." Alban leaned in. "But clearly, she must have been mistaken about the nature of this mythical injury, because I must say, you appear close to perfect, Miss Westmore."

A giggle escaped Lucy, but Clare refused to look in her sister's direction.

"*Oh.*" She buried her clammy palms in the safety of her primrose skirts and peeked up at Alban through half-lowered lashes. His light brown hair had been freshly combed and his hair pomade reflected the room's gentle sunlight, just the way she'd once imagined it looking across the breakfast table. She willed her stomach to flip over in interest instead of dread.

Perhaps it didn't matter what Sophie was plotting.

Alban was here, in *her* drawing room, saying she was close to perfect.

And if only Lucy would play along for the next quarter hour and she could convince her heart to agree with her head, this man could be her future.

BY NOW DANIEL knew his way to the Cardwells' drawing room, and the butler, Wilson, waved him along.

He paused in the doorway, greedily gulping down the sight of her. Normally, this first, unguarded view of Clare was enough to knock the wind from him, a response he still didn't quite understand and couldn't decide whether or not he enjoyed. No other woman had ever affected him so viscerally. When he wasn't dissecting the emotion she engendered—and attempting to dismiss it as nothing more than a biologic reflex to a beautiful, maddening female—he was miserably counting the moments until he could see her again.

She was sitting on the sofa, her ankle properly wrapped and elevated. But instead of waiting for him, as he had wretchedly hoped, she was seated next to a well-dressed gentleman. Her long, pretty neck was tilted up to the man's admiring gaze, and the sight made Daniel's hands clench around the handle of his bag.

He cleared his throat, angry at himself for reacting this way, and refusing to come closer without acknowledgement. "Excuse me. The butler directed me to come straight in."

Across the room, Clare did not look his way. In fact, he would have sworn she was refusing to acknowledge him.

Lucy, however, leaped up from her chair. "Dr Merial!" She bounded toward him, but just as she reached him, her foot caught on her skirts and she tripped into a nearby table.

"Steady on." Daniel reached out a hand to right a vase she'd knocked over in her collision. "I think one patient per family is enough on any given day, don't you?"

Lucy's lip stuck out in a gesture that approximated a pout, but it was clear she had too little experience with the notion for proper execution. "We expected you earlier, you know," she said to Daniel. "I had hoped you might take me on the outing you promised me today, but the day is too far gone. Geoffrey waited as long as he could, but he's been sent to his books, I'm afraid."

Daniel took a step away from the door. He did not want to disappoint this family, but in a doctor's world—in *his* world—priorities required constant reordering. He'd been roused from his bed—well, from his desk, really—by a frantic knock at his door before dawn. He'd opened it half expecting to find his landlady standing there in the all-together.

Instead, he'd found a messenger bearing the news that Lady Austerley had suffered another fainting spell. He'd rushed to the dowager countess's bedside anticipating that, once again, she would be awake and scoffing at the significance of her attack, though it had scared her servants enough to go dashing off to Smithfield in the dregs of the night.

But this time she'd still been unconscious when he arrived.

Daniel had stayed with her until she returned to lucidness, which took far too long for comfort. "My apologies," he said gruffly to Lucy. "I was detained with another patient." He eyed the couple on the couch. "I'm already late for my afternoon rounds at St. Bart's, and I've no wish to interrupt. Should I come back another time?"

Lucy shook her head. "You should wait. I imagine Mr. Alban won't stay longer than a few more minutes." She lowered her voice even further, to a conspiratorial whisper. "See how he's watching the clock, when he's not staring at Clare? I would guess he's another appointment to keep after this one."

Daniel stared in Clare's direction. So *this* was Mr. Alban, the gentleman she hoped to marry. His chest tightened at the thought, and he eyed the man more carefully. Alban was a loose-limbed fellow, well made and handsome enough. But Daniel could scarcely spare the man a proper perusal when his eyes insisted on pulling toward Clare.

Christ, but she looked lovely today. Like a literal blow to his bruised heart. Her red gown was cut to perfection and her eyes sparkled with interest—though unfortunately not at him. They were fixed tight on the gentleman sitting next to her, and Daniel felt a kick of envy at the sight.

"Should you tell her I'm here?" he asked.

"Oh, she knows. See how her head is cocked a little to the left?" Lucy whispered. "That means she's angry with you. You made her wait, and now in her mind turnabout's only fair."

Daniel looked again. Clare gave every appearance of being riveted by her caller's conversation, but Lucy was right. Those chestnut curls *were* tilted in his direction, even if she wasn't looking at him. So the patient wished him to wait, did she?

Odd how that only made him want to wrestle a bit of control from her hands.

"Might I beg a favor?" Daniel pulled a paper box from his pocket and handed it to Lucy. "I'd like you to give this to your sister later, after I leave."

Lucy glanced down at the package he pressed into her hands. "What is it?"

Daniel hid a grin. He was late, to be sure. And short on this month's rent. But not so late or destitute that he hadn't taken the time to stop by the confectioner's shop again. "Just a prescription she is proving reticent to accept."

Lucy tucked the box unquestioningly into her pocket. "Now, about our outing—"

"Next week. I promise."

"But—"

Daniel placed a finger on his lips, and trained his ears in his patient's direction. Sometimes, just listening to someone speak could tell him as much about their state of health as their words, and something in Clare's demeanor sounded . . . *off.* It was hard to put his finger on exactly what it was. Mr. Alban seemed only marginally interested in the conversation, engaging in the same sort of polite chatter Daniel often resorted to with new patients. And while Clare was listening intently to her guest and murmuring occasional encouragements that made Daniel's collar feel far too tight, she wasn't *contributing* to the conversation.

"Have you been passing the time reading?" he heard Mr. Alban ask. The man gestured to the rumpled newspaper, which lay scattered across a nearby table.

"Oh, not very much." Clare offered Alban that vague, half smile she sometimes affected. Daniel didn't know whether to be glad or offended she so carelessly granted him the full imperfection of her crooked tooth, when she was now so clearly trying to hide it from Mr. Alban. "The *Times* can be intellectually taxing, don't you agree?"

Lucy whispered in Daniel's ear again. "What rubbish. She's been ripping through the paper every day, and she finished that book you left by Thursday. You really ought to bring her a few more novels, if you ask me. When her reading material for the day is gone, she terrorizes the household with her boredom."

"Now, is it your foot or your ankle that's been injured?" Mr. Alban asked politely.

"Oh, I couldn't say." Clare giggled, and her hands flapped like small epileptic birds. "I declare, the bones get all jumbled up in my head."

Daniel couldn't help it. He laughed.

Out loud.

The choked amusement escaped his throat before he could stop it, earning him a jab in the ribs from Lucy and a perceptible stiffening of Clare's slim shoulders. But this was a woman who had quickly grasped the concept of anatomical symmetry when he'd shown her the bones in her foot. Did she really think she was fooling anyone with her claims of ignorance?

"Well, whichever it is," Mr. Alban said, "I hope you will be recovered enough to attend Lady Austerley's musicale this Saturday."

Daniel froze, his earlier amusement dying in his lungs.

Surely he'd just heard wrong.

He'd left Lady Austerley pale and wan in her bed not a half hour ago, a bevy of servants hovering around her. Once she recovered her capacity to speak, the dowager countess had not said anything to him about hosting a musicale. In fact, she had promised him she would take the time to rest and recover in the aftermath of her *last* event. Exhaustion was one of the dowager countess's triggers, and if she was planning another gathering this Season, it could very well send her health spiraling in the wrong direction.

"Yes, I think I *will* try to attend," came Clare's answer. "I think a musicale would be just the thing to ease me back into the Season, no matter my doctor's opinion on the matter."

Daniel gritted his teeth. *For the love of all that was holy.*

Did *none* of his patients listen to his advice?

The clock chose that moment to strike the half hour. True to Lucy's prediction, Alban rose. "I've no wish to fatigue you any further, Miss Westmore. It has been a pleasure visiting with you, and I do hope I will see you at Lady Austerley's musicale." Alban bent over Clare's proffered hand. Though there was little in the motion that suggested anything beyond gentlemanly manners, the gesture unleashed an unexpected groundswell of jealousy that threatened to take Daniel by the throat.

He stepped aside as Alban made his exit, then turned to glare at the man's retreating form. What did Clare see in him, aside from the obvious? Physically, they were a well-matched couple, though Alban seemed far too easily distracted for a man with amorous intentions. Besides, in Daniel's opinion physical appearances were a poor basis for a marriage. Shared interests and a healthy respect for each other had proven the keys to his own parents' short but loving marriage. What else held her attention in this man? There was no shortage of money in Alban's coffers, if the man's gleaming boots and embroidered waistcoat were any indication.

But money couldn't make up for a lack of intellectual capacity.

And if leaving Clare on the stroke of the half hour was foremost on the gentleman's mind, Alban was the village idiot.

Chapter 12

When Alban had left, Clare stood up, ignoring her ankle's mild twinge of protest. She'd been achingly aware of Daniel from the moment he'd stepped into the room, and it had been torturous to know he was standing there listening to—and judging— every word she'd said.

She'd been forced to sit smiling, trapped in a conversation with a man who *should* have held her full attention but couldn't quite measure up. Now she was feeling reckless, and the set-down she was itching to deliver required a bit of privacy.

"Lucy, please go and fetch Geoffrey."

Lucy's eyes widened. "But . . . he is in the west wing, studying. That will take a good ten minutes," she protested. "You cannot be left that long without a chaperone."

Her sister's objection might have been encouraging under different circumstances, but given that Lucy had stomped off in a snit and left her alone with the doctor for a good deal longer than ten minutes last week, the reaction seemed misplaced, at best. "Geoffrey wished to speak with Dr. Merial this afternoon, did he not?" Clare was surprised to hear her voice tremble, and readjusted her grip on her emotions.

Lucy nodded. "Yes, but—"

"He's about to miss his opportunity."

"Can't we have Wilson do it?"

"Please don't argue, Lucy. Not now," Clare said between clenched teeth. "I would like a moment alone with Dr. Merial."

Lucy's eyes narrowed, but she slouched toward the door, her skirts twitching an added protest about her ankles. Clare made a mental note to remind her sister that young women of breeding did not walk like hobbled monkeys. Lucy would need to shorten and refine her steps before her debut next Season, but that could come later.

For now, she had a doctor to berate.

She fixed her gaze on Daniel. "Shut the door please, Dr. Merial."

"I thought we had agreed on given names," he said, though he dutifully reached out a hand. The door closed with a soft click.

"That implies the sort of friendship that would warrant a note of explanation when one is going to be delayed. You'll forgive me for presuming we had regressed to a more formal state."

Outwardly, she was proud of how calm she sounded now. But on the inside she was still seething. She'd tried very hard to play the proper hostess during Mr. Alban's visit, but it had been impossible to focus on her future duke while it was clear Daniel was judging everything she said and laughing behind her back. She couldn't scold him for *that*, because there was no strain of logic she could find where his opinion of her should matter.

So instead she gave vent to the more obvious complaint.

"Why are you late?" she demanded.

Rather than answering her question, Daniel set his bag down on a side table. "Why are *you* pretending to be a dimwit?"

Clare gasped. "I beg your pardon?"

He took a deliberate step toward her. "To clarify," he drawled, "*I* don't think you are a dimwit. I think you're rather an enigma." His dark eyes pinned her in place, even as his body continued its forward trajectory with what now seemed an almost predatory intent. "But I suspect your suitor might be convinced of it, and I can't help but think that is by your own design. Why? Is it considered fashionable to belittle your own intellect?" He showed no signs of stopping at a respectable distance, and her treach erous pulse thumped in eager anticipation. "You'll forgive me if I fail to recognize the appeal."

She pulled in a resentful breath as he stopped square in front of her. Her bid for air had the misfortune of filling her nose with a distinctive fragrance of soap and starch and an odd, sweet-smelling chemical fragrance. It annoyed her that she should recognize the scent as belonging uniquely to him. "You haven't the slightest idea of which you speak."

"Don't I?" he replied softly.

Clare eyed him warily. He looked tired today, though it did little to detract from his physical perfection. He sported an unshaven jaw and a wrinkled coat, but even disheveled, he struck her as being far more attractive than Alban. The disloyalty of that thought made her feel off-balance. It was one thing to compare the two men and have the scale tip toward even. It was quite another to imagine this man might hold a greater appeal.

"No. You don't. And we are not speaking of me," she added. "We are speaking of *you*, and how you might have sent a note—"

"I had no opportunity, Clare." His expression hardened. "Lady Austerley had a medical emergency this morning, and I was called to her house before dawn."

His explanation doused the heat of her anger. What was wrong with her? She was acting like a ninny, snapping at him over a few hours' delay when she'd not stopped to consider that someone else may have had a greater need. She wasn't even sure why she was so upset. She knew only that she wanted to strike out and make him feel as small as he'd made her feel when he'd laughed at her.

She bit her lip. "I am sorry, Daniel. Is she all right?"

"The countess was resting when I left, although Mr. Alban's claim that she is hosting a musicale has me worried. Her health is fragile. And you aren't the only patient who refuses to listen to solid medical advice."

Though she was still irritated with the man, Clare's lips wanted to twitch at that. Despite plainly considering the older woman a bit of a trial, the respect Daniel held for Lady Austerley was clear. "Well then, perhaps you should attend the musicale as well," she suggested. "To ensure her health." But even as she said it, she wondered whether the suggestion sprang more from a desire to help or an illogical need to see Daniel outside the confines of her drawing room.

He leaned in until no more than a few inches separated them. "I do not wish to talk about Lady Austerley in this moment. I wish to talk about *you*. Why are you pretending to be a flighty young miss for Lord Perfect, when we both know you aren't anything of the sort?"

Clare glared at him. "His name is *Mr. Alban*. And he is not a lord yet."

"Ah, you'll have to forgive me." He treated her to a slow, spreading smile. "I declare these titles get all jumbled up in my head. It is *so* academically taxing to remember them all."

His teasing bumped her right back up to the keen edge of anger. Had she really started to forget why she ought to be mad at him? How kind of him to open his mouth and remind her.

"Perhaps you can be excused for your ignorance, given that you do not move in these circles," she snapped, "but Mr. Alban is a gentleman. Soon to be a *titled* gentleman, the presumptive heir to a dukedom. I did nothing more than listen to and support his interests, as any well-bred lady might."

"Come now, Clare. I know you a bit better than this by now." His voice became a sharply seductive tool, boring a hole through her confidence. "Better than Mr. Alban does, at any rate. You are a far more interesting person than your performance supports."

Her heart leaped at the faint praise, but she refused to give in to the pleasure his words wanted to kindle. "You don't know me at all," she ground out.

How could he, when she didn't even know herself in this moment?

"I know you can name every bone in your foot." A smirk still hovered on his lips. "I'll wager you never forget a fact, once it's lodged in your head."

He was wrong. She was hard-pressed to recall her middle name at the moment.

But while his derision of Alban—or was it of her?—had hobbled her ability to think, her tongue was miraculously free of such a curse. "You are mistaken, sir." But a series of traitorous words swirled in her thoughts, words and bones that had no business being in a fashionable young lady's head.

Cuneiform, cuboid, calcaneous.

She rattled the syllables back into submission with a brief shake of her head. "I forgot that ridiculous lesson as soon as you imparted it."

His smile began to fade. "As your doctor, I can promise you discretion in my dealings, but I refuse to promise you falsehoods. I would hope you would offer me the same." His dark eyes flickered. "Mr. Alban is a poor intellectual match for you."

"How *dare* you?" She poked her finger into his chest, but the gesture did little more than prove that a coiled, muscled body lurked beneath the cheap wool coat. "Mr. Alban is handsome, and brilliant, and . . . and . . ."

"Wealthy?"

"*Important*. When he speaks, men listen."

Daniel scowled. "Is it because they respect the man, or merely his future title?"

"There is very little difference, in the world in which I live."

"Well, in the world in which *I* live, respect is earned by a man's contributions. I choose to respect men whose work has the potential to change the lives of thousands of people for the better. *That* is the sort of man I would be."

She tossed her head in disbelief, though an unforeseen part of her stirred in admiration. What would it be like to so passionately express an opinion about something other than a stern dislike of the color pink? But she was seized by the moment now, and there was no slowing her tongue. "You flit from town house to town house, carrying a leather bag, Daniel," she pointed out. "How is that changing the lives of thousands?"

He stilled, and to Clare's mind it was a dangerous sort of stillness, an unsheathing of claws before the spring of a predator. "There is more to me than you know. And I promise you, there are more rewarding and scintillating aspects to my life than wrapping the ankles of spoiled, fashionable young ladies."

She gasped at the insult, even as she threw herself into the pleasure of a well-voiced argument, the sort she was prohibited from indulging in on a ballroom floor. Heaven knew she hadn't felt this wild thrumming in her veins during Mr. Alban's placid visit, and it was unnerving to realize how satisfying her reckless pulse felt.

"Well, scintillating or no, you have no right to belittle my interest in anyone, much less someone who could secure my future the way Mr. Alban can." She pressed her point home through the tip of a nail, tapping it against his distracting chest. "You are my doctor, Dr. Merial, not my judge and jury. How I choose to comport myself with a suitor is none of your business."

His hand snaked up to capture her finger in its punishing grip. "Isn't it?" He hovered above her, something undefinable radiating off him like heat from the sun.

And then his lips descended on hers.

SURPRISE WAS A funny human emotion.

It could trigger a range of reflexes, from desperate flight to violent resistance, depending on the patient in question. In Clare, it appeared to pin her frozen, helpless as a fledgling bird upon its first, unplanned exit from a nest.

The unforeseen kiss had surprised him as well. He could own this as a mistake he should not have made. The oath he'd taken—the oath he lived by—forbade this degree of interaction with his patients, in no uncertain terms.

But once his tenuous control had snapped, there was no going back.

It was clear she'd never been kissed before. She had no idea what to do with lips or tongues. No doubt her mouth had opened to lodge a protest, not to invite him in, but his own roiling emotions drove him on.

He took disgraceful advantage of her vulnerability, diving into her open mouth in a manner that should have appalled them both. He gave her no room for air, no room for thought. Dimly, he realized his kiss was too fierce, too possessive, to be inflicted on someone so inexperienced. He held her fast in his grip, her fingers twisting a mute protest beneath the strength in his hands. He'd not even examined her ankle before succumbing to madness.

Then again, it hadn't been planned, and he was damned if he knew how to script it better.

She was a jarring contrast in tastes and textures: tart mouth and sweet breath, soft curves and rigid spine. He forced himself to loosen his grip on her hand, but once it was free, his palm displayed a mind of its own and wandered down the whale-bone-sculpted length of her torso, following its own compass until it reached the curve of her hip.

If he still held any claim to the title of gentleman, he'd end this. Step back, apologize, and hand her back her dignity with a fumbled apology. He reluctantly lifted his hands from her body to cup her face, a far safer prospect than where they wanted to go.

But as if a string had snapped in mid-pluck, she began to struggle against him. She untangled herself with a hard shove, and then she stood heaving, her eyes flashing.

He spread his hands. "Clare—"

The slap caught him out of nowhere. It was a powerful blow, impossible to have come from such a small, frail creature. "Don't apologize," she hissed, eyes flashing. She took a step away. "There is nothing you can say to make this right."

Daniel blinked against the sting on his cheek. *Apologize?* He hadn't been about to do anything of the sort. Because while he could regret the snapping anger in her eyes, he could not bring himself to regret the lingering taste of her on his lips. An apology would be one of the very falsehoods he'd told her he wouldn't give her.

Instead, he gave her the truth. "I would wager Alban doesn't kiss you like that."

She cringed.

He knew it wasn't fair. He didn't specifically dislike Alban—he didn't know him well enough to inform an opinion. Outwardly, there was nothing at all objectionable about him, except that Daniel saw no spark of chemistry at all between Clare and her wealthy beau. He'd observed mild, superficial banter. A passionless exchange.

And he foresaw a predictable, unhappy marriage.

"My association with Mr. Alban is none of your business." She pressed two fingers against her kiss-swollen lips, and then turned and sat down heavily on the sofa, refusing to look at him. There was no hope of a ladylike blush in the aftermath of such a kiss: her face was close to crimson, nearly the color of her dress. "I think you'd better take your leave now, Dr. Merial."

He regarded her a long, silent moment. "He doesn't make you happy, Clare. That, more than anything else, should tell you why he's a poor match for you."

She lifted her chin, though her red cheeks still screamed an inner embarrassment. "He is a duke's heir. I could certainly find myself *less* happy."

Daniel's gaze landed on the delicate hollow at the base of her throat where he imagined a pulse beat steadily. Possibly frantically, if his own was used as a reasonable comparison. He felt off-balance, as though his vertebrae had come unhinged. It wasn't only the thought that Clare might warm the bed and home of another man, that she would belong to someone else, body and soul.

It was that she wouldn't belong to *him*.

He had no right to think of her this way. She was supposed to be nothing more than a patient, a source of potential income, though he'd struggled from the first to separate his emotions from his professional actions where this woman was concerned. He should have turned her over to the inept care of Dr. Bashings from the start and saved them both the trouble of this conversation, which he could see now had been practically preordained.

He'd thought, in the early days of their acquaintance, his inexplicable attraction to her was mere biology, but it wasn't only his reproductive urges telling him to gather her in his arms again and do whatever it took to convince her of his regard. His bloody *heart* wanted this woman, and that was an organ he couldn't dismiss so easily.

"Clare. You must know that titles and fortunes do not define happiness," he said gruffly, knowing it was the truth.

But she only lifted her chin higher. "Neither do unwelcome kisses."

Daniel picked up his bag. "Don't you realize what you'd be giving up by marrying Mr. Alban?" he asked quietly, a last parting shot. "What about love? Affection?"

"What do you know of love?" she scoffed, though he imagined he heard a tremor in her words. "You steal kisses from practical strangers. That isn't affection, it's theft. Love is something that grows between two people with time."

Daniel shook his head, thinking back on his own parents' example. He knew something of love, what it could give, what it could cost. "I am afraid your potential for happiness will be sorely tried with those expectations. Think of your parents, Clare. If your mother was happy in her own marriage, would she arrange liaisons with strangers in darkened libraries?"

She choked on a protest, and he knew then he'd crossed an irrevocable line—possibly one more far-reaching than the kiss.

"Go." Her hazel eyes were now wide with fury, and something that might have been fear. "I neither require your guidance nor welcome your opinion on any matter related to my future or my family." She gestured fiercely to the door. "Good day, Dr. Merial. We won't be needing your services again."

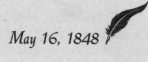

May 16, 1848

Dear Diary,

I cannot believe I ever thought ~~Daniel~~ Dr. Merial a gentleman.

Geoffrey and Lucy were sorely put out to have missed him, although I confess, I could not find the courage to tell them why he left so quickly, or that he would not be returning. But what else was I to have done? I have entrusted my brother's moral character to the care of a scoundrel, and heaven only knows how much damage has been done. The gall of the man is endless, lecturing me on what makes a proper marriage and then kissing me in so barbaric a fashion. It was an unconscionable breach of trust.

And worse, it is a scene I cannot stop replaying in my mind.

Try as I might, I cannot imagine suffering such a disturbing kiss from Mr. Alban.

Which, of course, only proves why he is the right choice.

Chapter 13

"You've scarcely touched your plate tonight, Clare. Is anything amiss?"

Clare stared down at her rosemary lamb, perfectly rare and delicately seasoned. Her stomach growled at the sight, but she refused to reach for her fork.

"I am just a bit tired, Mother." It was not a complete untruth. She *was* tired, though she'd done nothing more strenuous than fume in the two days since Daniel's departure. The tenderness of her lips had disappeared, but her mind kept reeling in new and dangerous directions.

She'd never imagined her first kiss would be so memorable.

Or so disturbing.

Despite her full plate, there was also the gnawing ache of her growing hunger to contend with, although her corset was helpfully attempting to counter the discomfort by burrowing into her ribs. It was a reminder that the nearly two weeks of inactivity—as well as the lamentable marzipan "prescription"—had endangered her wardrobe's carefully measured fit. She needed to dazzle Mr. Alban at

Saturday's musicale, and necessity was keeping her fork a safe distance from her mouth. She feared it was already too late, though, and had already suffered through one humiliating visit from the modiste's assistant.

"Well, do stop frowning, dear." Her mother lifted her glass of Madeira and took a long draught. "'Tis bad for your complexion."

Clare shifted in her chair, as much against the persistent pinch of her corset as her mother's admonishment. She hadn't realized she *was* frowning, but given that yesterday's unwelcome kiss was occupying an insistent place in her mind, she supposed it was inevitable.

Her gaze snagged on her mother's glass. A thought scraped against the distraction of the kiss. When had Mother started having her glass of Madeira *during* dinner, instead of after, as was her usual habit? And was the evening meal usually this uncomfortable? Or was it only that she was more aware of it tonight? Unlike their family breakfasts with Father, which were easy, informal affairs, Mother always insisted they dress for dinner. The nightly ritual was imbued with an almost painful amount of formality, requiring Clare and her siblings to sit through at least five courses. She had long wondered whom her mother insisted they dress for. Was it an attempt to persuade their father to return home?

If so, it seemed her methods were poorly placed, because increasingly, Father took his meals at his club, claiming such ceremony worsened his dyspepsia.

"You look a bit flushed." Her mother inclined her head as she took another sip. "Are you feverish? Is your ankle festering? Perhaps we should ask Dr. Merial to have a more thorough look at you."

"*No.*" Clare jumped guiltily, knocking her fork from the plate to the floor. She waved away the footman who attempted to bring her another.

Her waistline was far safer with her fork on the carpet.

"I told Dr. Merial on Tuesday that we will no longer require his services."

Her pronouncement sent a ripple of silence down the long table. Cutlery ceased to clink against the gilt-edged china. The rustling of uncomfortable fabric stilled. It was the sort of silence that demanded an explanation. But Clare couldn't give full voice to the myriad reasons why never seeing the man again was an excellent idea for all of them. Explaining the kiss to her family would be disastrous.

Not because anyone could possibly condone such behavior in a physician, but because she'd risk revealing her own conflicted feelings on the matter.

"Shouldn't that have been *my* decision?" Her mother frowned, setting her glass down on the table.

Clare's fingers curled over her napkin. "My ankle is now quite healed," she insisted. "I am wearing my own shoes again, and walking without a limp. In fact, I'd thought to attend Lady Austerley's musicale on Saturday. There is no reason to remain under a doctor's continued care if I am well enough to go out."

"You've sent him away for good, then?" Lucy accused, her voice ominously low. "You told us Dr. Merial had only gone on to his next appointment."

Geoffrey gave more volume to his displeasure. "You've ruined everything!"

Clare looked between her siblings. "I don't see how I can be accused of ruining anything," she protested. "Dr. Merial was not hired as a playmate for either of you."

Though, she could grudgingly admit he had made good headway in the matter of influencing some important changes in her siblings. Geoffrey was devoting every afternoon to vigorous study, and Lucy had even ordered a bath before dinner tonight. "I understand you like Dr. Merial a good deal," she said haltingly, "but—"

"We *all* like him a good deal." Geoffrey's voice took on an adolescent whine. "He's fun to talk to, and he's doing the most admirable work at St. Bart's. He's got me thinking that we all should be doing more to help others who are less fortunate. He's encouraged me to study my Latin, in the event I decide to attend university."

"Please lower your voices," their mother broke in. "You cannot attend university, Geoffrey." She hiccuped, and raised a hand to her lips. "You will be a viscount, dear. Your future is already decided."

"I don't recall being asked my opinion on the matter of whether I wished to be viscount," Geoffrey retorted. His face turned red, though it had been over a week now since he'd reverted to such a juvenile display of temper. *"Astra inclinant, sed non obligant."*

The stars incline us, they do not bind us.

Clare's fingers clenched the edge of her seat. Normally, she would have been pleased to hear proof of her brother's improving studies. But the phrasing smacked of an outside influence, and she felt a twinge of irritation. Such axioms—while encouraging from an academic standpoint—were crossing over into seditious territory for an eldest son.

"I don't know what that means," Mother said, lifting her glass once again to her lips, "but if your father deigned to grace us with his presence once in a while, he might remind you of the fact that inheriting the title is scarcely something you can choose to ignore." She drained her glass, then motioned for the footman to refill it.

"Geoffrey . . ." Clare soothed, her thoughts pulled in ten directions, not the least of which was her mother's interest in Madeira. "No one is saying you shouldn't study Latin."

"You've just proven my point!" He leaped to his feet. "It isn't about bloody Latin! Dr. Merial *listens* to me. He understands what I am saying when no one else in this house does."

Their mother frowned. "I blame your father for this outburst. He should be here, disciplining you, and instead he's always . . ." Her voice wobbled. " . . . with *her*."

"Her?" Clare sucked in a startled breath. "Don't you mean his club, Mother?"

But her mother was now staring down at her lamb, as if it might somehow come to life and walk off her plate. Clare had no idea what to believe. She could not believe her father was the sort of man to take a mistress. But *something* was wrong. She'd never seen her mother so detached and self-absorbed.

Although . . . perhaps she had. A certain dull edge in her mother's voice reminded Clare all too well of the way she had acted the night of Lady Austerley's ball.

Lucy threw her napkin down over her lamb. "This is a bloody mess."

"Did you say something, dear?" Mother barked.

"The lamb." Lucy smiled tightly. "It's a bloody mess. I can't eat it."

"Oh." Another sip. "Perhaps you can ask the cook to send out some chicken, then."

Lucy rolled her eyes. "Geoffrey has legitimate reasons to resent Dr. Merial's undiscussed departure. As do I, quite frankly. Dr. Merial promised to take me on an outing of my choice, and I do not think it is fair of you to dismiss him before he keeps that promise."

"He did *what*?" Clare asked, incredulous.

But Lucy was already turning to face their mother. "And as for chicken, I don't eat meat, Mother. I haven't for at least a month. If you'd rise before noon and take breakfast once in a while with us, you'd have been part of those conversations and realize it." She paused, filling her lungs. "And *perhaps*, if you didn't make us dress like dancing bears every night, Father would stay home long enough to take an occasional dinner with us."

Their mother swayed in her chair. Then she set down her half-emptied glass of Madeira and leaned forward across her plate, dragging her silk bodice through the remnants of her lamb. "I think you should both leave the table immediately. Without dessert," she added, as if her children were still five years old with a sweet tooth that could be swayed by such threats.

Geoffrey's hand slammed down on the table, upending his plate and the remnants of his lamb in a soggy red mess on the white tablecloth. "Stuff the dessert!"

"Geoffrey, please sit down," Clare hissed beneath her breath. "And don't shout at Mother. She's . . . she's not well."

But Geoffrey was too far gone to see that their normally immaculate mother was covered in lamb. "You should be threatening Clare, not us," he declared hotly. "*She's* the one who sent Dr. Merial away, for no other reason than the fact that she's so stubborn. She's lying, you know. She still limps when she thinks no one is watching. I'd like to see her waltz on that ankle. I bet she can't make it more than halfway around a dance floor."

And then he stormed from the dining room, his too-large body radiating a boy's disappointment. Clare suffered a pang of guilt as she watched his angry retreat. She wanted to call him back, to better explain her motives.

But that would require a confession she didn't know how to give.

"Well, *that* didn't go very well," she muttered to her lamb.

"Did you imagine it would?" Lucy stood up with an angry scrape of her chair, then pulled a white box from the pocket of her skirts and shoved it into Clare's hands. "I'd forgotten about this on Tuesday, and had thought to give it to you after dinner tonight, but as I'm to be sent to my room, it seems pointless to wait."

Clare's fingers closed over the paper box.

She knew what it was and who it was from without opening it.

And this time it was her heart, rather than her stomach, that clenched in anticipation.

Lucy swept from the room, her chin held high. Such an exit would have been stunning if executed in a London ballroom. In truth, the scathing set-down Lucy had just delivered would have served her well in the fashionable gauntlet of the ton.

When had her sister become so polished?

Just as Clare thought she might actually pull it off, Lucy tripped over her heavy skirts and fell against the door frame. She regained her balance with a haughty sniff that would surely improve with practice. "And if I might be permitted to offer my opinion, it's a shame to see Geoffrey return to such boorish behavior, simply because *you* think your ankle is healed. It seemed as though he was finally making progress, thanks to Dr. Merial."

Lucy's parting words echoed the regrets that were already flooding through Clare's mind. Was she right? Were the changes they had seen in Geoffrey this past week—changes that now seemed in jeopardy—primarily due to Daniel's strong influence?

Worse, though it had not been discussed, what might his sudden dismissal mean to Lucy's future? As her sister's blond head disappeared around the corner, Clare realized for the first time all evening that Lucy's hair had been put up in a fashionable chignon.

Oh God, oh God, oh God.

She was being selfish, only thinking of herself and her dangerous reaction to the kiss that probably hadn't meant anything. In sending Daniel away, had she just removed the most important positive influence in Lucy's and Geoffrey's lives?

Her thoughts raced furiously. She couldn't fix this, not entirely. The damage had been done. But perhaps she could ensure a slower separation, a gradual easing of contact with Dr. Merial, instead of this awful, abrupt ending. And *surely* she was enough in control of her emotions to ensure that the dreadful kiss never happened again.

But if eventual separation was the goal, why did her stomach clench so enthusiastically at the thought she might see him once again?

As the servants flowed around her, removing plates, collecting cutlery, Clare opened the top of the paper box Lucy had shoved into her hands. She stared down at the beautiful sugary pieces. Today's selection included candies the size of marbles, shaped like plump berries in vivid shades of purple, red, and blue. Tiny green leaves curled around the tops. Though her own pin money was enough to accommodate the occasional purchase of such treats, she never bought them, fearing their long-term effects. She knew that Daniel could scarcely afford such an expensive confection, probably not even once a year, and certainly not twice in the space of a month.

It would be a shame to throw them away.

Clare picked one up and placed it in her mouth. It dissolved on her tongue, the danger and sweetness lingering long after the candy itself was gone.

Not unlike Daniel Merial's blasted kiss.

"I declare, I don't know what to do with either of them." Her mother's slurred voice jerked Clare's gaze from her marzipan reverie back up the length of the almost empty table.

Clare fumbled the lid back onto the box. "If it eases your mind . . . I don't think they are trying to vex you on purpose, Mother," she said, the sweetness of the candy still thick on her tongue. "Lucy seems to be turning a page for the better, at least with respect to her hair, and Geoffrey is still quite young. Dr. Merial suggested he would mature out of this phase in a year or two."

"I suppose." Her mother heaved a long suffering sigh. "But if we are speaking of the doctor . . . now that we are alone, perhaps you might tell me the real reason you've dismissed Dr. Merial? Geoffrey was correct." Her table-length gaze was bleary, but it was still direct enough to make Clare squirm. "You limped as you came into dinner. That hardly supports the miraculous recovery you've claimed."

Clare slid down in her seat. "Not *much* of a limp." She fought against the urge to fidget. "Dr. Merial does not understand the intricacies of the Season, Mother." *Or have any notion of propriety and class boundaries.* "You know as well as I that his recommendation for a month's convalescence would be disastrous for my chances for a good match this year."

"Is there a particular gentleman you are eager to see, then? A match you have in mind?" her mother pressed. She took a veritable gulp from her glass of Madeira—her third, by Clare's count. Or was it the fourth? "The world can be a harsh place, and I am eager to see your future secured. Perhaps Mr. Meeks has made a more favorable impression this year?"

"No." Clare put some emphasis behind the word, determined to thwart another bout of her mother's meddling. She could not bring herself to mention Mr. Alban.

Not yet.

It was safer to unleash Mother only after a proposal from her future duke was well in hand. "But I won't have any hope of encouraging an eligible gentleman's interest if I remain confined to our drawing room. My ankle is healed enough to walk up and down the stairs unaided. I believe I can manage a quiet musicale, as a start."

Her mother hesitated. "Well . . . I had thought to refuse Lady Austerley's invitation, as I had presumed your ankle still on the mend. But if you wish to attend, I suppose I could send her our acceptance." She sighed, swirling a finger along the crystal rim of her glass. "Perhaps we should ask if your father might want to attend as well. He has always enjoyed music, though he claims dancing is painful for his knees. But a musicale might sway him, don't you think?"

Clare slid the box of marzipan into her pocket. Was she hearing correctly? Not once this Season had Father accompanied them on a social outing. She'd imagined her father's absence was due to Mother's preference on the matter. But tonight's conversation suggested things might be more complicated than she'd imagined.

He's always with her. As Clare stood up, her mother's earlier words turned over in her head. She no longer knew what to believe, but if Father was engaged in some sort of disreputable conduct, it would sting every bit as much as Mother's indiscretion. She helped her mother to her feet, then turned herself over to the question that would not leave her mind, though she silently cursed Daniel Merial for planting the seed of doubt in her head.

"Mother . . . are you unhappy?"

Her mother froze, one hand on the back of her chair. "What an odd question to ask."

"Is it?" Clare asked quietly. "You didn't strike me as being particularly happy the night of Lady Austerley's ball." She looked pointedly at her mother's soiled bodice. "Or tonight, for that matter."

Her mother glanced down, and Clare thought she could see her blanch beneath her rice powder veil. She motioned a dismissal to the servants clearing the table, then grabbed a napkin from the table and began to dab at the stain on her bodice. "Did you . . . ah . . . mention the events of that night to your father?"

"No." Clare shook her head. "I would not betray your confidence, or purposefully damage Father's trust. In truth, I initially agreed to Dr. Merial's care that night only as a means of procuring his silence. It is part of the oath they take that a doctor cannot indulge in gossip regarding his clients." She studied her mother's blue eyes, expecting to see fear. Or possibly confusion, given the unholy amount of wine she had consumed tonight.

Instead, she saw mainly pain.

"I don't remember all the events of that evening," her mother admitted, her words slightly slurred. "Or the gentleman in question."

Clare blinked. How could her mother not *remember*? Clare only wished her own memory wasn't quite so sharp. She didn't know precisely what had occurred between her mother and that gentleman in Lady Austerley's library, but she was quite sure it involved something more damning than staring into each other's eyes.

That ought to require an exchange of names.

Preferably *given* names.

"You've not said . . . why would you do such a thing?" Clare choked out. "To Father?"

To me?

Her mother smiled, but it was a smile so brittle Clare feared she might shatter. "There are things that you do not understand. There are things that even *I* do not understand, and this is hardly an appropriate conversation to have with one's daughter." She lifted a hand to her temple, wincing. "Now, I would like to go lie down a moment. I . . . I've a headache coming on."

Clare wanted to ask more, but instead she offered her mother an arm. Clearly, a headache was not the primary cause of her mother's unbalance, and it soon became obvious reinforcements were required. She called for Wilson, and the kindly butler sprang to attention, assuring her he would assist Lady Cardwell to her suite.

With the marzipan tucked safely in her pocket, Clare made her way to her own room through the silent house. Her mind screamed for answers, but with her mother off to bed, there were none to be found beyond those she might conjure in her head.

Whatever the motive behind her mother's indiscretion, it had been a terrible risk to take, especially if she still cared even a bit for Father. A daughter's instincts—and the course of the evening's conversation—told her such feelings still lingered in her parents' stilted marriage, at least on her mother's side.

What did it all mean? Her parents had never been openly warm toward each other, but they had once at least been civil. During last year's Season, Mother had been far more attentive, carefully counting the number of dances claimed by Mr. Meeks and forming her own misguided conclusions regarding Clare's interest in the man. This year, though Clare had danced three waltzes with Mr. Alban, her mother seemed largely oblivious.

What had changed?

Was the negligence and indiscretion her mother was showing this Season an anomaly?

Clare turned over that thought as she lit the candle at her desk. She sat down, putting pen to paper. She hoped, given the conflicting evidence at hand, her mother's actions of late did not define the course of her parents' entire marriage.

And perhaps, if she were fortunate, the direction of her parents' marriage would not predict the course of her own future.

aniel made his way through the darkened streets of Smithfield with his mind fractured around a series of distinct problems, none of which he could solve tonight.

After the debacle with Tuesday's kiss—which could be blamed on none other than his own idiocy—his week had gone anything but smoothly. His experiments were not progressing to satisfaction. While his regulator was certainly safer than administering liquid chloroform, he still killed one out of five frogs, a record of success that might earn him a visit to Newgate if attempted on humans.

Worse, he'd arrived at St. Bartholomew's yesterday morning to find a letter of rejection for a paper he had written on the preliminary findings of his experiments. The editors had felt the piece was unfinished, the conclusions too poorly formed, to "merit publication in a journal as prestigious as the *Lancet*." Not an inaccurate sentiment, given that he had not progressed beyond experimentation on frogs at the moment, but the editors had also roundly questioned his experience as a physician and his commitment to the advancement of science. It was a scathing rejection, not only of his ideas, but of his very soul.

Perhaps on a footing with the one he'd suffered at Clare's hands.

Then, following this evening's rounds at St. Bartholomew's—and still simmering from the sting of his week's personal and professional failures—he'd checked in on Lady Austerley. He'd done little more than take her heart rate and respirations, which were thankfully stable. But it was hard to deny that her attacks of syncope appeared to be organizing themselves into something more sinister than the occasional swoon, and this evening her skin had displayed a yellowish cast, as if her liver was now in agreement with her heart and was close to giving up the ghost. Not even the most experienced physician could make a body live forever.

But that didn't mean it was easy to accept the inevitable march of time.

His mind occupied with these disturbing thoughts and the necessity of digging his key from his pocket, Daniel almost missed the prone body slumped in the alley next to the boardinghouse. Some sixth sense slowed his feet for a closer look. He tensed in case the setup was a ruse to relieve him of his none-too-full pockets.

In the faint glow of the overhead gas lamp, he recognized the woman as a local prostitute who plied her trade from darkened shadows. Meg, her name was. "Handsome Meg," she'd proclaimed last week, sitting up on the examining bed at St. Bart's, though her sallow skin had suggested the name was more a hopeful wish than fact. He'd treated her for syphilis and counseled her against her profession in the name of the public's health.

But judging by the smell of gin and vomit that clung to

her, it seemed like the venereal infection was the least of her immediate worries.

Though he risked exposure to footpads to linger after dark in this part of Smithfield, he knelt and took the woman's pulse, which pumped steadily beneath his fingers.

Right then. Not dead. Just dead drunk.

A month ago, when there had still been a risk for frost, she might have risked dying from exposure. It was warmer now, the season marching toward summer. But frost was not the only danger in Smithfield. He couldn't leave her here, exposed to all manner of ill intent. It was a miracle he'd discovered her before she'd been gutted or worse.

Though, worse was a stretch, given what he suspected was the nature of her usual clientele.

Daniel hefted the woman in his arms and staggered under the surprising weight of her. His rooms were only a few steps away, but before he could insert the key in the lock, a woman's voice struck from behind, like a bludgeon out of the darkness.

"Oh, Dr. Merial. *There* you are. I waited up for you."

Daniel jumped beneath his skin, nearly dropping his burden. "Mrs. Calbert!" He waited for his breath to catch up with his pulse. "What a . . . ah . . . surprise."

A light fell on him from the lantern his landlady raised in her hand. "I've a letter for you, delivered with some urgency from the hospital."

"The hospital?" Daniel turned around to face Mrs. Calbert. It was past midnight, and she should have been sound asleep. Instead, she was wearing a dressing gown that must have once been the centerpiece of her wedding trousseau, and her hair showed signs of being freshly— and thoroughly—brushed.

The hopeful smile on Mrs. Calbert's lips vanished as she took in the woman lying limp in his arms. She held the lantern closer, sending ghostly shadows dancing across the drunk prostitute's features. "Who is this?" she demanded.

"Er . . . Meg. At least, that was the name she provided at the hospital last week."

Mrs. Calbert's white gown and the unbraided hair made him feel every bit as uneasy as her resulting scowl. He tried to look anywhere but at the near-transparent front of the dressing gown, and finally landed on a cross-stitched sampler hanging on Mrs. Calbert's wall, just over her shoulder in the depths of her foyer. *Place Your Trust in God.*

Judging by the suspicious glint in her eyes, God was clearly the only entity for whom Mrs. Calbert employed such a sentiment.

"I found her in your alley," he tried to explain. "She appears to have encountered a bit of an accident." *With a bottle of gin.* But that sort of truth would only muddy matters for the passed-out prostitute, and so Daniel wisely withheld his opinion.

"I recognize her." Mrs. Calbert sniffed her disapproval. "The tenant who last rented your flat invited her in one night. That was why I finally had to turn him out." Her voice lowered, the warning clear. "I had thought you a more discerning sort of gentleman, Dr. Merial, but it seems I was mistaken."

Daniel choked back a cough of surprise. If his landlady thought he might consider doing anything but counsel a syphilis-afflicted prostitute, it was clear she didn't know him very well at all. "Come now, Mrs. Calbert, I'd only intended to help her. I'm a physician, and she's clearly in need of assistance. She'll need someone responsible to watch over her until she wakes."

"Then take her to the hospital."

He shifted the dead-to-the-world woman in his arms

and prayed that the lice which no doubt hovered beneath Meg's tattered clothes stayed on their side of the street. "Normally I would take her to the charity ward at St. Bart's, but it's already closed for the night. I would prefer not to have her in my rooms, as I know your rules are intended to ensure both the safety and propriety of your guests." Daniel smiled as winningly as he could, given the woman's heavy weight in his arms. "Could I leave her with you?"

Mrs. Calbert hesitated, clearly torn between wanting to believe the best of him and the evidence unveiled by the light of her lantern. "Well, I can allow it's a decent thing to want to help a body in need, but if you ask me, you should return her to where she fell. She reeks of gin. I'll not have her in my house."

She was unsure, though. Daniel could tell by the way her lower lip gaped, showing the recently acquired gap in her teeth. "Surely it is too dangerous to leave her passed out cold in the alley so close to where your own husband was attacked," he coaxed.

Her frown grew troubled. She crossed her arms on her chest, as if remembering the flimsiness of her wrapper. "What sort of an example would I be setting for my tenants if I took her in?"

He seized on her own argument—and her cross-stitched sampler—and turned both against her. "Surely a Christian one." He gifted her with a slow slide of a smile, the one that never failed to make women melt, though he scarcely thought it a defensible response. What man couldn't smile, should the situation call for it? It scarcely declared a man a fit partner.

For example, Alban had smiled while he sat on Clare's couch.

Too damned much.

"Surely a bit of charity could only be a positive example

for us all," he cajoled, all too ready to dump Handsome Meg on the stoop if it meant he could regain feeling in his arms. "Perhaps you might even convince her of the error of her ways. And I would be more than happy to check in on her—and you—in the morning. For breakfast."

"Morning?" Mrs. Calbert's hand crept up to smooth her hair. "With me?" Her smile returned. "Well, I suppose I might permit her to sleep on the hearth. Just for tonight, though. I wouldn't want to make a habit of it."

"You're a paragon of virtue, Mrs. Calbert. The rock of the neighborhood."

She blushed like a schoolgirl who'd been complimented on her catechism, then turned and beckoned for him to follow. Daniel staggered into the warm, bread-scented house, eager to relieve himself of the prostitute and seek the solace of his own room. He laid Meg down on the hearth and rolled her on her side to ensure any vomit that might make an appearance during the night would not asphyxiate her. Then he thanked Mrs. Calbert again and turned to leave.

"Wait."

Daniel turned back, his shoulders tense.

Mrs. Calbert reached toward the front of her dressing gown. Daniel braced himself against the horror, then exhaled in relief when she did no more than pull out a letter from its filmy depths. "I've not yet delivered your note," she exclaimed. She handed it to him, the paper still warm from being held against her skin. "From the hospital. I can only presume it is urgent, if they delivered it here so late at night."

Daniel accepted it, grimly wishing it had been lodged in a pocket instead. Or better still, shoved in a drawer. Not that there was anything all that objectionable about Mrs. Calbert, or her dressing gown, for that matter. She was perfectly nice. Perfectly available, albeit a decade too old and good deal less hygienic than he preferred. He'd availed himself of offers from occasional youngish widows in the past, when his biologic urges became too great and he had the patience to deliver a bit of pleasure to someone else as well.

But lately any needs, any urges, seemed focused far too squarely on an inappropriate and presumably virginal Society miss, one with chestnut hair and snapping hazel eyes and the most delectable smile known to man. She'd been inexperienced in the kiss he had stolen. That alone should have been an effective means of dissuading the direction of his thoughts, a dash of cold water against the heat of lust.

Instead, it had honed his interest until desire was as sharp as the blade of a scalpel.

No matter how impossible the scenario, he'd fallen under Clare Westmore's spell long before the kiss. He'd been caught in her web from the moment she'd called him a fishmonger.

"You didn't have to wait up to deliver it to me." He forced a smile in Mrs. Calbert's direction, distracted by his intruding thoughts. "I hate to think you've been put out on my account."

"Oh, 'tis no trouble. As you can see, I was just readying myself for bed." She smiled, almost shyly, though she placed an unnatural emphasis on the word "bed." "I'm glad I shouldn't have to turn you out after all, Dr. Merial. And I look forward to seeing you in the morning."

Daniel waited in the dim gaslight on her stoop to hear that she had turned the key in the lock. Only when he was sure both women were locked inside did he trudge wearily to his own room, several doors down.

He inserted the key into the lock and shoved the door open, hard. Bloody hell. Mrs. Calbert was becoming a problem he didn't know how to manage. He'd chosen this boarding house with care, presuming his flat's separate entrance onto the street would ensure some measure of privacy. But he'd not counted on having a landlady who waited up for him every night with her ear to her door.

He struck a match and lit his single lamp. The crickets chirped a welcome at the intrusion of light, but the frogs leaped for the safety of their water dishes, splashing their objections.

A bloody cold welcome for a man, all things considered.

Daniel sat down at his desk, scrubbed a hand across his face, and—with a good deal of suspicion—regarded the letter Mrs. Calbert had been so keen to deliver. While this note may have come via hospital messenger, it had not originated from within the walls of St. Bart's. For one, it was addressed to him *at* the hospital. It was not from Lady Austerley, that much he knew. Her staff knew by now to deliver a summons directly to his door—bypassing his prying landlady in the process. Besides, he had just come from Lady Austerley's house and knew all was fine there.

He turned the letter over in his hand. There was no stamp, suggesting it had been delivered to St. Bart's by courier, rather than penny post.

But far more telling, and far more hopeful, the paper was fine, the handwriting feminine.

And the weight of it smacked of Mayfair.

May 18, 1848

Dear Dr. Merial,

Circumstances being what they are, I am sure you will agree it is not a good idea to continue our association any longer than is necessary. Still, I may have been hasty in executing your abrupt dismissal. These regrets do not stem from any concern over my ankle, you understand, which is healing quite satisfactorily without further interference on your part. Nor do they spring from any measure of misplaced trust. I am now quite morbidly aware of your shortcomings, and will keep a suitable ten foot distance between us at all times.

But in the matter of my brother and sister's behavior, you may have made more of a positive impact than I previously understood. A slower disassociation might benefit their continued progress. If you are free and would accept this request, you might stop by our home tomorrow morning. Geoffrey and Lucy would enjoy seeing you, and I suspect their future disappointment will be tempered by paying you a proper good-bye.

Yrs truly,
Miss Clare Westmore

P.S. Lucy claims you owe her an outing of some sort. I am sure you can agree that it is most impossible, she being an unmarried young woman and you being of dubious moral character.

Yrs again,
Miss Westmore

Chapter 15

Daniel had never been a man plagued by unsteady nerves. In fact, he could count on three fingers the things that made uncertainty flutter in his stomach. Editors from prestigious medical journals. Mrs. Calbert's midnight inquiries. Failure. Such stoicism lent him a strong hand during autopsies, and gave him the ability to stand before an amphitheater of bored medical students and command at least a negligible amount of respect.

But as he stepped into the Cardwells' drawing room at ten o'clock the next morning, he was surprised to realize he might need to add a fourth finger to that small list. His stomach churned in anticipation of seeing Clare again, and his collar was damp with the sort of perspiration that had nothing to do with the day's mild warmth, and everything to do with the pressure in his chest.

How to apologize for a kiss he couldn't regret?

And how to say good-bye to a woman he didn't want to forget?

Clare was standing by the window, her back to the door,

staring out at the sunshine. He had expected to see Geoffrey and Lucy, their blond heads bent over a chessboard, but the room was otherwise empty, save a mob-capped maid who was dusting the Oriental vases and other useless curiosities on the mantel. As he stepped into the room, the servant looked up from her duties and promptly dropped her feather duster.

Daniel tried to ignore the invitation the girl's flash of a smile offered, as well as the generous backside she displayed as she bent over to retrieve the item she'd dropped. Without a doubt, a pretty, fresh-cheeked maid was a suitable candidate for courtship for a man like him, someone who might never—if the editors at the *Lancet* had their say—progress to be anything more influential than a provincial doctor. And the maid certainly appeared interested, if her dimpled smile was interpreted of a fashion.

But Daniel's stubborn eyes insisted on pulling back to the rigid, chestnut-haired siren at the window. "Good morning, Clare." It was startling to discover his voice still worked.

She turned her head. "Dr. Merial. I see you received my letter." She made no move toward him. Ten feet, her letter had said.

It might as well have been ten miles.

"I am here to offer an apology." He hesitated, wishing it wasn't so hot in the room. But stripping down to his jacket and necktie would send a poor message, all things considered. The attraction that simmered between Clare and himself could go nowhere. But knowing it and facing it were two different things, and today could not end without some final agreement on that point. "And a good-bye, as you requested," he added softly.

She stared at him an inscrutable second, then turned in the maid's direction. "Maggie, would you please tell

Geoffrey and Lucy about Dr. Merial's arrival? They will want to see him."

"Yes, miss." The servant tucked her duster under one arm and tossed one last, inviting smile in Daniel's direction as she quit the room.

The door to the hallway remained very properly open, but they were alone. Clare began to move through the room —never closer than ten feet—and trailed a finger over the recently dusted items on the mantel. Her gait was quite steady—no sign of a limp now—but her chest rose and fell too rapidly for the pace she set.

Apparently he wasn't the only one who was nervous.

The realization cheered him more than it ought.

"I expected Geoffrey and Lucy would be here to greet me," he said, "given your letter implied that was the express purpose of my visit."

A furrow appeared between her brows. "I didn't tell them about the invitation because I didn't want to buoy their hopes. In truth, I wasn't sure you would come."

"And ignore such a delightful summons?"

She rounded to face him. "You must admit, I have reason to be less than delightful where you are concerned."

"Clare." He said her name gently, ignoring, for the moment, how she stiffened at his use of it. She'd set the stage by calling him Dr. Merial instead of Daniel this morning. But she'd once afforded him permission to use her given name, and despite all else that had passed between them, she'd not retracted her offer. He spread his hands in supplication, wanting to somehow return her association to someone he could tease, if not touch. "Permit me to say that I am sorry."

"You may tell Geoffrey and Lucy when they arrive."

"No, I am apologizing. To *you*. It was not my intention to cause you any distress, and I regret having done so."

"I am not distressed." She lifted a hand to her lips, though Daniel doubted if she realized she did it. "I just think it would be best if we forget it happened." She nodded, as if to convince herself. "And ensure it doesn't happen again."

Daniel had come prepared to apologize, and he had. But *forget* was rather a strong word. Given that the woman herself was forbidden to him, he had at least ensured a heated memory to warm him during the cold, coming months.

And when she married her future duke, well then, he had at least given her something to think about during her passionless marriage, hadn't he?

She began to move again, walking more gracefully than he would have thought possible given her recent injury. "Your ankle has healed well," he remarked, seeking a safer topic to settle on than the kiss she was insisting he forget.

"And in only two weeks," she offered, a hint of smugness in her voice. "I believe I originally predicted as much, that night in Lady Austerley's library. Perhaps *I* should go to medical school."

Daniel grinned in spite of himself. "Perhaps you should. You are more clever than most of the students I currently lecture." He cocked his head as she looked down, clearly discomfited by his praise. Time to lighten the conversation. "Although, it seems as though the daily lectures would be an inconvenience for your social calendar. And in my own defense, four weeks was not an imprudent guess when I wasn't sure whether any bones had been broken. You'll find that in clinical matters, I prefer to err on the side of caution."

He caught the hesitant flash of her smile. "No wonder Lady Austerley doesn't listen to you either."

"Lady Austerley listens well enough," he chuckled. "She simply does whatever she wants, regardless of my recommendation."

She pivoted on her heel at the edge of the room and began to move in the opposite direction. "Lady Austerley sounds like an intelligent woman."

"I suspect she would say the same of you." Satisfied that Clare's ankle was no longer a pressing medical concern, and relieved that her animosity toward him seemed to be weakening, Daniel let his gaze drift to where it wanted.

It wanted her.

Today she was wearing a walking gown of vivid moss green, accented with a delicate gold braid trim. As he enjoyed what he presumed would be this last, aching sight of her, he realized that today, of all days, she had elected to *not* wear a corset. His body responded to the lack of it —and the soft, natural flare of her hips—with predictable enthusiasm.

Christ. That's all he needed, a raging erection to convince her he'd come in peace.

He shifted uncomfortably. He'd thought he could do this, could come and apologize and escape without further insult or injury. He'd imagined he could *behave.* But he'd held her in his arms, and knew what her body felt like beneath those scant layers of silk and cotton.

He was not a gentleman prone to envy, but God above, he envied the gentleman whose privilege it would be to eventually kiss her without repudiation.

"Your . . . er . . . gown is lovely," he offered, lifting his eyes to the ceiling and wishing the younger Westmores would emerge from the depths of the house a bit more apace.

Because at this rate he'd have their sister ravished in a heartbeat.

THOUGH SHE STILL felt restless, his words pulled Clare to a stop.

She eyed Daniel warily across the ten feet she'd threatened to keep between them. She'd called him Dr. Merial, and quite pointedly, too, but her mind—opinionated thing that it was—refused to revert to the required formality. She suspected he would always be Daniel now in her head, no matter how she tried to school her thoughts otherwise.

And no matter her hopes to pretend the kiss had never happened, her own body was proving an unruly partner in the ruse. Every time she looked at him, her eyes flew straight to his mouth, remembering the feel and the taste of him.

"That, sir, only proves you have no sense of fashion." She gestured to her gown. "I am wearing a dress that is at least two years old, as I find I can no longer fit into my current wardrobe, thanks to a mysterious bit of marzipan that keeps finding its way to my lips. I would die if Mr. Alban or my friends saw me in this."

"Surely not literally." His lips twitched. "Unless it possesses the magical ability to burst into flames?"

Clare felt her own face stretch in response. This was a return to comfortable banter, the same easiness they had once shared before that messy business with the kiss. Perhaps she was overanalyzing the significance of Tuesday's mistake. He'd apologized, she'd accepted, and Geoffrey and Lucy would be here any moment to save her.

She stepped toward him, and was startled to realize it felt as though she were finally moving in the right direction. She risked another step, and then another. "If you brought more marzipan," she warned, "you should be prepared to receive it back, shoved in a most uncomfortable place."

His chuckle smoothed over her like warm brandy. "You've been enjoying it, then?"

"I wouldn't say 'enjoying' it, precisely." Clare forced herself to stop two feet away, but the distance proved too meager for safety in the end. Her nose filled with the heated, sharp scent of him, soap and medicine and things that made her stomach stir pleasantly.

Blast it all, but it was hard to ignore the energy that simmered between them.

She'd danced with plenty of handsome men over the course of her one-and-a-half Seasons, including Mr. Alban, whose broad shoulders and pleasant features made more than one woman's heart trip faster. But she was beginning to realize that what she felt when dancing with Mr. Alban was something far less exhilarating.

Apparently, interest and attraction were entirely different reflexes.

And unfortunately, *this* man's smile engendered a powerful dose of both.

"If I were pressed for a medical opinion," he said, "I would say the candy has lingered in all the right places." He lifted a hand, his fingers reaching toward her cheek but hovering too far away to pose any danger. Yet her skin burned, as if she could feel the scorching warmth of his touch. "Your face has begun to lose that hollowed appearance you had when I first met you," he added. "I think it does you better credit."

Clare blinked. If Sophie or Rose had said such a thing, she'd have taken offense in a heartbeat. Odd, how such an insult made her heart twist in an eager direction, merely because it came from him. Was it the smooth tenor of the voice, delivering the words in such a way that she shivered in anticipation rather than anger?

Or was it the man himself, his gaze warmly appreciative on her skin?

"I thank you for your generosity," she said softly. "I know the price of the candy must have been dear."

Geoffrey chose that moment to bound into the room, his broad face lit up with pleasure. "Dr. Merial!" he crowed. "I'd thought I wouldn't see you again!"

Clare cringed. It was clear, in her brother's excited greeting, that Dr. Merial provided something he was otherwise missing in his life. And it was equally clear, now that she had witnessed the reunion, saying a final goodbye would be harder than she thought.

Lucy strolled in next, dressed in a walking gown of a color blue that matched her eyes. Clare blinked in surprise. Had that particular ensemble always been in Lucy's wardrobe? Her sister also had a pair of gloves clutched in her hands, and a suspicious smile on her lips. "Ah, there you are, Dr. Merial. Just in time."

"Just in time for what, exactly?" Clare demanded, apprehension fluttering in her stomach.

Lucy ignored her and beamed up at Daniel. "I've the perfect outing picked out for us. If we hurry, we should just be able to have you back to St. Bart's by noon, especially if we take the omnibus."

"What are you talking about?" Clare looked between her siblings.

Both looked smug.

"We're going out," Lucy replied. "With Dr. Merial."

Daniel spread his hands, and for a second Clare thought with relief that he was going to provide his regrets, as any sensible man must. But then he smiled, and it was not an apologetic sort of expression. "Though your consideration is appreciated, Miss Westmore," he said to Lucy, "you may be pleased to know I do not lecture today. I am not expected at the hospital before evening rounds." He bowed from the waist. "It seems I am at your disposal."

Clare gasped. "Absolutely not. There will be no outing." There would be no *thoughts* of an outing.

And there would be no disposal, lest it was of the doctor's own body.

Lucy lifted her chin. "I want to see Madame Sylvie. The *Times* says she's attempting a walk today across the Thames, a distance of over six hundred yards from Battersea to Cremorne Gardens. I, for one, plan to be there to see her make history."

Clare questioned the functioning of her ears, though her eyes had seen the newspaper article her sister referenced. "Lucy," she said firmly, shaking her head. "You are *not* traveling to Chelsea as an unmarried and unchaperoned young lady, to see a woman break her neck attempting to walk a high wire." She turned to Daniel, livid. "Tell her. I invited you here this morning to say good-bye. Nothing more."

But the blasted man was stroking his chin as if in thought. "Madame Sylvie, hmm? She's a patient of mine, you know. I treated her after her last failed attempt, when she got a ducking in the Thames and two cracked ribs for her trouble."

"You treated Madame Sylvie?" Geoffrey breathed in awe. "She's very pretty." He blushed. "At least, the drawing in the paper suggests she is."

"I can probably secure you an introduction." Daniel cuffed Geoffrey on the shoulder. "After she is finished with her walk, of course. She will be quite focused at the moment on the coming attempt. I wouldn't want you to distract her."

"It is decided, then." Lucy sounded pleased. She motioned toward the open drawing room door. "We'll need to hurry if we're to procure a spot near the front of the crowd. By my calculations, the bus will be here in ten minutes."

Bus? Calculations? *Crowd?*

Time to launch a battle to regain some measure of control. "Lucy, Dr. Merial isn't going with you on an outing," she said firmly. "It would be improper."

Lucy's eyes narrowed. "I am not sure it is a matter that requires your approval. He promised me an adventure. He has established he is not expected anywhere else." She pulled on her right glove. "Ergo . . ."

"Ergo?" Clare's hands clenched to fists. Wonderful. Now both her siblings were spouting Latin, courtesy of one abominably handsome doctor. "You are but seventeen," she ground out. "Unmarried. *Unchaperoned.*"

"Plenty of young women are permitted advanced studies with tutors or even colleges at my age, so it scarcely seems a relevant argument against a simple, educational outing. I'll even acknowledge I'm unmarried," Lucy said. Shaded by the brim of her bonnet, her face looked surprisingly mature—and, for a change, quite feminine. But then she smiled impishly. "And I confess I have no intention of ever changing that status. A wise person once told me the most important thing was to be myself, so that is what I intend to be. I want to go on this outing."

"But it wouldn't be *proper*," Clare objected. And what was this nonsense about Lucy needing to be herself? If ever there was a piece of advice sure to ruin a girl's chance for a proper Season, it was that.

"Lucy, I'm afraid she is right," Daniel broke in. "You would need a chaperone." But then his eyes slid toward Clare, accompanied by a grin that made her insides flop. "Which is why your sister should come with us."

Oh God, oh God, oh God.

He was deranged.

"No need. It is already arranged." Lucy stepped to one side, revealing a woman who had apparently been standing behind her in the open doorway. "Because Maggie has agreed to come along as chaperone. Haven't you, Maggie?"

Clare stared in disbelief as the pretty, brown-haired servant she had sent to find her siblings stepped forward, her reticule in hand. The maid's apron had been dispatched to parts unknown and her white lace cap was replaced by a serviceable bonnet.

It seemed Lucy had thought of every argument, and planned her attack accordingly.

The servant darted a telling glance in Daniel's direction, and her lips curved upward in a marked invitation. "Indeed, miss, I am looking forward to a spot of fresh air."

"I see," Clare said tartly, feeling suddenly and inexplicably left out. She couldn't help but wonder who would chaperone the maid, because given the mooning glances the girl was offering Daniel, it seemed *someone* ought to.

"You could still come with us." Daniel's voice felt like fingers, trailing up her spine, daring her in this direction, making her lose all common sense.

"How can I go with an injured ankle?" Clare protested, though her heart thumped an eager response.

"You said just last night your ankle was healed," Geoffrey pointed out.

"And we are taking the omnibus," Lucy added. "Cremorne Gardens is but a short walk from King's Road. If you are truly as healed as you claim you are, you should be able to manage it with nary a limp."

Clare searched their faces. Did they really want her to go? She cast about for a way to defuse this terrible, tempting idea, and found none at the ready.

"Perhaps, you might consider this a test, of sorts." Daniel took a step toward her. "It would prove you are well enough for Lady Austerley's musicale." He leaned in until his voice tickled the fine hairs along her cheek. "Which I can unfortunately confirm the countess is insisting will go on as scheduled tomorrow, despite my advice to the contrary."

The change in proximity between them scrambled Clare's senses. Of course, he would not try anything untoward with a drawing room audience. In fact, she could probably go on this outing and remain perfectly safe, given the mob that would no doubt be flocking to Chelsea. Was there anything more public than a London spectacle?

And was there any safer way to be in the company of a rake than surrounded by throngs of people?

Clare bit her lip. "I believe I have proved my recovery well enough, given the mile I've paced on the drawing room carpet today." But she didn't say no. She *couldn't* say no.

Her tongue quite refused to consider it.

"Come with us," he coaxed. "You have my promise I won't accompany them without your permission, which should make you happy, at the least. But we've a chaperone, and a destination, and a glorious afternoon waiting for us. What would it take for you to enjoy the day, and possibly even the company?"

Clare felt as though the breath had been knocked from her lungs. She was wearing her oldest gown. Without a corset. He was asking her to ride an omnibus. He was supposed to be ten feet away from her, and yet here he was, close enough to touch.

Close enough to tempt.

"People might see us," she mumbled, but the protest sounded vague and hollow to her own ears. "You have no idea what it is like to be someone in my position."

"No, but *I* do." Lucy stepped forward, gloved hands outstretched, her blue eyes softening. "I'll understand it even better next year, I imagine. But it seems to me that Dr. Merial is right. No one will judge you—they'll be too busy judging Madame Sylvie's performance. For once, can't you just take a chance without calculating the risks to your reputation, or the damage to your gown, or the cost to your schedule? We miss our sister, Clare. At least, we miss the sister you used to be."

Clare blinked, shaken by Lucy's claims.

Had she really altered herself so much?

She'd faced difficult choices, of course, since the start of her first Season. Tolerating Sophie and Rose's snide remarks and snubbing young men like Mr. Meeks were only part of the daily dilemmas she faced. But what young woman who dreamed of being a duchess didn't need to make a few concessions?

Somehow, though, she'd not realized the changes were so noticeable.

Geoffrey nodded his agreement. But unlike Lucy, he offered her a frankly mischievous grin. "What will it be, sis? And if you stay here, I should point out *you'll* have to be the one to explain to Mother where we've gone when she finally hauls herself from bed."

Clare dried her perspiring palms on her skirts and glanced again toward the window. Mother was still abed, no doubt sleeping off the ill effects of her prior evening's overindulgence. But eventually she would wake, and given the discomfort of last night's revelations, the thought of being elsewhere when their mother stumbled downstairs had some appeal.

Moreover, Daniel hadn't been exaggerating: the sun outside the window *was* glorious. She hadn't ventured farther afield than the drawing room in two long weeks, and she had never felt the loss of fresh air more acutely than she did in this moment.

Perhaps she should count the past two weeks as a brief diversion in her quest to secure her future, a moment's anomaly in the continuum of a well-planned life. Perhaps she could relax and truly enjoy herself, just once, before returning to the fray.

And perhaps an outing—if it was brief and controlled—wouldn't hurt anyone.

"Are you sure you wouldn't rather just go for a nice, sedate walk in Hyde Park?" she asked, making one final bid for sanity.

"No!" came the chorus of her siblings' voices.

"No," Daniel added, a grin splitting his handsome face. "I *did* promise Lucy an outing of her choice." His dark gaze met hers, warm and approving down the slope of his perfect nose. Clare felt herself slipping into the fast-moving current of his smile. "And then I will go my own way," he said, his voice lowering. "All contracts fulfilled, all parties duly satisfied."

Clare was no longer sure such an outcome would leave *her* satisfied, but she nodded. "All right," she said, "to Chelsea, then," causing Geoffrey to erupt in cheers and Lucy to clap her gloved hands. Apparently by omnibus, though she wasn't convinced which was the greater spectacle here: public transportation or a female exhibition-ist, flashing her petticoats above the crowd. Clare prayed Madame Sylvie was properly bracing herself for impact, because it seemed quite clear the world was coming to an end.

And if the high-wire line above her own future was any indication, it was going to be devilishly difficult to navigate the next few hours safely.

Chapter 16

From the moment they stepped off the omnibus, it was clear to Daniel that the spectacle at Cremorne Gardens might be best defined as a "riot."

Set between the river and King's Road, the venue was always known to be colorful and loud, though it lacked the flair and reputation of Vauxhall. From the top of the Cremorne pier, colorful banners streamed on the steady, foul wind pushing in off the Thames. Juxtaposed against the stench off the river came the stomach-pleasing scents from vendors selling every type of food imaginable: sticky buns, meat pies, and roasted chestnuts—though surely, by now, they were down to the moldy dregs of last year's crop.

But the contrary scents and jumbled sights appeared not to have deterred anyone from attendance today, because more than anything else, there were people. Bodies pressed in on four sides. It was a remarkable slice of the British populace. Young and old. Wealthy and poor.

Washed and unwashed.

All here to see a woman walk a high wire across the Thames

Competing for space and scent with no less enthusiasm were the flowers. Late spring azaleas blossomed on every bush, red and white and coral, choking the air with their heavy fragrance. Closer to the ground, precious tulips that had no doubt been planted by some well-meaning philanthropic organization were being trampled as the crush spilled over into the cultivated beds.

"What a mob!" Geoffrey exclaimed in excitement. "We've a quarter hour, do you think, before Madame Sylvie starts?" He breathed in deeply. "I think I smell gooseberry tarts."

Daniel was rather used to such crowds himself, but he glanced over at Clare with concern, in case she was finding the experience overwhelming. Her eyes were wide, but there was a marvelous flush on her fair cheeks. She was pointing her finger at her brother. "No tarts. These vendors are filthy, Geoffrey, have you seen their hands? I want you to stick tight to Maggie's side. Loop arms. If we lose you in this crush, we'll never find you."

"An excellent idea," Daniel agreed, sidestepping a dog that had broken its lead and was tearing about, tongue hanging out. The dog's owner charged through soon after, scattering the crowd for no more than a moment before the bodies pressed back in, shoulder-to-shoulder. "We must strive to not become separated." Christ, but it was crowded, and growing more so with every passing second. "But we should agree on a meeting point, in the event one of us becomes lost." He pointed to the iron gate they had just come through. "There." It was impossible to miss, rising eight feet tall, with ornate molding and gilded lions' heads that reflected the sun like small mirrors. "Anyone who is separated should come here to the north gate and wait for the others."

Fingers clutched at his sleeve. He grabbed the hand, imagining it was a pickpocket. The crowd would no doubt be full of them. But it was Clare, her gloves soft beneath his fingers and her eyes wide now with something other than excitement.

He loosened his grip slowly, but she didn't pull her hand away.

"Daniel," she breathed, and the panic in her voice was unmistakable. "Where is Lucy? I thought she was right with us, off the bus."

He turned in a circle, searching for light blue skirts. He caught sight of her standing on the wrong side of the gate, near the omnibus that should have by now pulled away from the curb. Lucy had one hand on the horse's bridle and was arguing with the red-faced driver, who looked nearly ready to use his whip.

Unfortunately, not on the horse.

Clare spied her at nearly the same time. "Oh, God," she gasped, then clapped a hand over her mouth, as if such blasphemy was on par with her sister's idiocy.

Daniel was already in motion. "Stay here. And for heaven's sake, don't move."

He dodged his way through the milling crowd and pulled a belligerent Lucy back to their little group. Clare grabbed her sister's arm and shook her, hard. "I swear, you just took a year off my life! What were you thinking? If we become separated in this crowd, we'd never find each other again. We were supposed to meet by the gate if one of us is lost, and there you were, clear on the other side of it, wrestling with a horse."

"Well, *someone* needed to do something," Lucy protested, throwing her hands up in exasperation. "It was starving! You could see the poor horse's withers!"

"Er . . . its withers?" Daniel asked, perplexed.

"On its *neck*, Dr. Merial." She pointed an accusing

finger in the direction of the disappearing bus. "You could see its bones. It's the same on the other buses, too. You can see *all* of their bones. The poor animals need to be fed better, and I intend to organize a movement to see that it happens."

Daniel stifled a laugh. "Lucy, visible withers are not a sign of malnutrition. In fact, it is rather a desirable trait in a horse."

She blinked. "Surely not."

He studied her face, trying to see if she was joking, but she remained red-faced and earnest. *Bloody hell.* Was she honestly so invested in a cause she knew little about?

"Horses lack a clavicle," he explained, realizing too late that the resulting quartet of blank faces meant his audience probably didn't know what a clavicle was. He motioned to his jacket, outlining the area of his own collarbone. "So, unlike humans, the muscles of a horse's front leg attach to the vertebrae."

"What is a vertebrae?" Geoffrey interjected.

Daniel sorted through the jumble of medical and equine knowledge in his head and tried again. "Vertebrae are the pieces of the backbone, and in horses the top of those pieces form the withers." He thought back to his childhood, and could almost hear his father's patient voice explaining how to pick apart a horse's conformation and predict its future use and value. "Withers are an important predictor of a horse's athletic ability. Longer withers predict an increased length of stride." Daniel paused at Lucy's slightly stricken look. "I take it you've not spent much time in the company of horses?"

She worried her lower lip. "Our mews boast only the two horses that pull the coach, and Father's intemperate stallion that never gets exercised because he spends all his time at his club. I lectured the grooms about increasing their oats, but they've done little more than laugh at me."

"Ah." This time he couldn't hide the amused smile that claimed him. "Well, increasing oats for a stallion who is not regularly exercised is a poor idea all around. Makes them hot and ill-tempered. And if you would but take a careful look around, you'll realize you never see a horse without withers. It's a feature of their conformation that has little to do with the nutritional status of the beast. I suspect you want to look at the ribs for that."

"And that horse's ribs were just fine," Clare broke in dryly. "Honestly, Lucy, before you embark on your *next* crazed quest for justice, would you please consider researching your subject first?"

Lucy looked chagrined, but before she could say another word, a minor scuffle broke out among two young men standing just to their right. A stray elbow caught Clare just below her diaphragm and she pitched forward, off-balance. Daniel reacted on instinct, catching her up and holding her safely. The young men were immediately off and away, shoving their way through the crowd, no doubt fearing the thunderous look he suspected was strung on his face.

"Are you all right?" He frowned down at her.

"I . . . I think so," she said, though she made no move to extract herself.

Catching her had been a reflex, and a powerfully protective one at that, but other instincts were now starting to take over. His arms tightened around her, instead of letting her go. She was pressed against him, silk to wool, heart to heart.

"Easy now," he murmured, quite unable to control a single piece of his anatomy, including his mouth. "You don't want to reinjure your ankle." He bent low, to the space below her bonnet where one pert earlobe, with its diamond ear bob, could just be seen. "Or is it that I'm to be *your* next crazed quest?" he whispered. "In which case, carry on."

She wrenched herself away and shot him a dirty look, but at least it wasn't the sort of affronted anger she'd supplied him on Tuesday. She did, however, spend a good deal of time brushing down her skirts, as if those were the primary injured party.

Daniel's fingers itched to tuck an errant lock of chestnut hair back into her bonnet, but he wisely kept them clenched by his sides instead.

"Dr. Merial!" A woman's voice cut through the crowd.

He turned to see Handsome Meg grinning up at him, and his smile was automatic in response. When he'd checked in on her this morning, his landlady hovering like a persistent gnat, Meg had still been snoring on the hearth. He'd left some money for her in Mrs. Calbert's hands, in the hopes that the aging prostitute might use it to turn herself around.

Last night she'd looked rather the worse for wear, sacked out in the alley as she had been, but if forced to lodge an honest opinion, Daniel would say this morning she didn't look much better. In daylight it was far easier to see the syphilitic ulcers on her upper lip. Her hair hadn't been combed and she was wearing the same torn gown as last night. But she was upright—if still smelling of gin— and awake—if somewhat stooped and unsteady.

"Meg," he said warmly. "You're up and about."

"Oh, aye, nothing like a Chelsea crowd to make a few pennies."

Daniel glanced uneasily toward his audience. Geoffrey looked curious. The maid looked aghast. Lucy, however, looked enthralled. She stepped forward. "Are you a lady of the night?" she asked in a hushed voice.

Meg waved a cheery hand. "Night, day, breakfast, lunch. Any time, and anywhere at all."

"Anywhere?" Lucy echoed. Daniel could see the wheels turning in those blue eyes, and suspected that Miss Lucy may have just found her next crazed quest. "And how much do you charge a gentleman like Dr. Merial for . . . er . . . lunch?"

"Lucy," Clare hissed, looking mortified. "Leave the poor woman alone. And I scarcely think Dr. Merial needs to know how much she charges." Her gaze shifted to him, and he was surprised to see those hazel eyes soften. "Can't you see they are friends?"

Daniel stared at her in surprise. Of all of them, he'd expected the most judgment from her. Last night his landlady had leaped to an unsavory conclusion, just because he'd picked an unconscious Meg up off the street. Given outward appearances, he wouldn't have blamed Clare if she'd done the same today. After all, he'd taken a rather indecent liberty with *her*, and he was now the opposite of trustworthy in her mind.

But the look she was giving him was the opposite of accusing.

"Miss Westmore," he said, feeling uncertain. "May I present Meg."

"*Handsome* Meg," the prostitute corrected cheerfully. "I'm a patient of the good doctor's."

"Pleased to meet you, Handsome Meg." Clare smiled, and he caught a rare but gratifying glimpse of that slightly crooked cuspid she took such pains to hide from the world.

Shaken by the impact of that smile, he took Meg by the arm and pulled her to the most private spot he could manage, which, given the crowd, turned out to be no more than a step or two away. Certainly not far enough to be out of earshot of the now-fascinated Lucy. He tried to sort out how to issue a warning without violating the confidentiality he owed the woman, given his status as her treating doctor. "You'll remember what we discussed? About finding a different way to . . . er . . . make those pennies?"

Meg reached into a basket she had looped over one arm and pulled out a bunch of posies. "Oh, I'm here on a different mission, aye? I came into some money this morning. That landlady of yours, she's a regular gem. Gave me a whole five shillings. So I went to a flower seller I know and he set me here with some stock. Only a farthing, and they're right fresh, too. Perhaps you'd like to buy one for your lady in green?"

"That is very sweet of you, but I'm not his lady," Clare broke in from over his shoulder. But she did it kindly, and Daniel was grateful for the warmth in her voice. Not everyone of Clare's stature would treat a prostitute so well.

Daniel dug a penny from his pocket. "I'll take three," he said, then handed the purchased bouquets to Lucy, Maggie, and Clare. Clare accepted hers more hesitantly than the others, her eyes slightly narrowed. But then a reluctant smile broke through and she buried her nose in them.

He refused the change of a farthing, knowing Meg needed it more than he did, which was saying something, given the increasing emptiness of his pockets. Last night's charity and this morning's omnibus fare had lightened his pockets considerably.

"Thank you, Meg." Daniel found he was glad to see the aging prostitute put to a safer industry, and not only because it meant there would be less cases of syphilis to treat in Smithfield. It was because Meg herself would be safer.

"Ach, it's *you* I should be thanking," Meg replied. Bony fingers reached out to scratch at his coat sleeve. "Yer landlady says ye plucked me off the street last night and deposited me on her hearth like a sack of potatoes."

"Well." He grinned down at her. "A sack of potatoes left untended in Smithfield won't last very long, will it? You need to have more of a care with yourself, Meg. I'd hate to see anything happen to you."

"Have a care yourself," she cackled. "And good luck. I can tell yer going to need more than posies with that one in green." With one last grin, Meg shuffled off, basket in one hand.

WAS IT POSSIBLE to have the time of your life, standing shoulder-to-shoulder with the dregs of London, your nose filled with the dueling scents of posies and the rotten-fish smell of the Thames? Yesterday, Clare would have never imagined the answer could be yes.

But today her mind was quickly changing.

Reading about such things in the *Times*, cloistered in the safety of her Grosvenor Square drawing room, paled in comparison to being physically surrounded by thousands of other pounding hearts. The memory of how strenuously she'd argued against this outing came close to shaming her now. What had she been afraid of?

And why wasn't she afraid anymore?

The overhead sun laughed down on her warmed skin in delight. The wind was almost preternaturally still. Or perhaps it was so many bodies in motion, blocking the breeze like a great human wall. But despite the heat and the noise and the energy from the crowd swelling in her ears, it was glorious.

And then, of course, there was Daniel himself. She risked a look in his direction, over the tops of her posies. "Did your landlady really give that woman five shillings?" she asked. "Or did you leave it for her?"

He squinted up at the sky, his dark eyes reflecting the sun like molten chocolate. "I left her twenty." His lips firmed. "It seems like Mrs. Calbert decided to take a week's extra rent for her own pockets. Then again, I can't begrudge it of her. God knows she probably needs it, too."

Clare turned that over in her head. Daniel lived on fifteen shillings a week for rent? Her pin money alone was three pounds, doled out by Father's secretary the first of each month, to be spent on ribbons and lace and expensive stationary. It made her feel ill to think of the difference in their stations, and their lives. Yet, despite his meager finances, he had given away close to an entire pound last night. *To a prostitute*. He'd also bought these flowers and purchased the omnibus fare for all of them. The challenge of sorting him out made her heart simultaneously pulse faster and skip the odd beat.

"It's getting even more crowded now. How many souls were there, do you think?" Lucy asked no one in particular.

"Twenty thousand, I should say," Daniel answered.

"Gor!" Geoffrey exclaimed. "I thought they'd done away with large public assemblies."

"Not if they are organized *by* the government, instead of in opposition to it," Daniel said. "And this isn't anything close to the crowd I saw at Kennington."

"You were at Kennington?" Clare asked, fascinated by the thought. She'd never seen a crowd as dense as this one, though she'd certainly read of the mob that had marched to Parliament.

He shrugged. "I thought they'd have need of a doctor, but fortunately, the crowd did not turn violent."

Somehow, she didn't quite believe that was the only reason. His presence at Kennington established his political leanings better than any oath, and she realized with a start that she now knew more about Daniel's views on such things than she knew about Mr. Alban's, though Alban would arguably soon be in the thick of Parliament's decisions on the matter.

Clare glanced out at the ragged crowd, considering his words. Perhaps Daniel was right. Perhaps today's exhibition *was* meant as a distraction, an approved outlet for the crowd's anger and energy, in the form of one Madame Sylvie. "Bread and circuses," she muttered.

"Precisely." Daniel shot her a thoughtful glance. "What else, but a diversion intended to titillate and amuse and, ultimately, silence the people?" His brow furrowed. "You are rather perceptive, Miss Westmore."

For the daughter of a viscount.

He did not say it, but he almost certainly thought it, because Clare's mind tripped there herself. And could she blame him? It was the men with titles—men who could claim little by way of character or skill beyond an ancestral lineage to someone long dead—who demanded the entire spectrum of political power, and who jealously guarded it against all interlopers. She might be a viscount's daughter, raised in an environment of privilege and wealth, but even she could see such ideology would not work forever. Nor did she think it should.

Eventually, the world would change.

According to the *Times*, it was changing now.

But Daniel, apparently, was not content to read about those changes. He was wading into the fray, and she could not help but feel a frisson of respect at the thought.

A great shout went up across the river, from Battersea, if she had to lodge a guess. Clare looked up. Sure enough, the wire stretched above them was vibrating. "I think," she mused, "that perhaps we should go in farther, toward the pier. I predict the crowd will open up closer to the river. And the pennants are flying there, which suggests a breeze exists, if only we seek it out."

"I don't know." Geoffrey sounded skeptical as he tilted his head back. "Madame Sylvie will walk this way and it looks like she will exit just there." He pointed to some scaffolding that had been erected about twenty feet away. Beneath it, a crowd of enthusiastic young men waited, no doubt anxious to welcome the pretty acrobat down.

Clare winced as yet another elbow caught her in her unprotected ribs. "Well, the crowd is growing unruly," she gasped. She could scarcely imagine how wild it would be when Madame Sylvie passed overhead.

Daniel motioned with his hand. "This way, then."

They began to walk. Or rather, they began to crawl upright, elbowing their way through the mass of people, the overhead wire their guide. As Daniel pushed through the crowd, making a space for them to follow, Clare was struck by how many heads turned to track his progress. *Female* heads. He did not appear to notice.

Or, if he noticed, he did not appear to encourage them.

It occurred to her, in a flash of unwelcome insight, she couldn't say the same thing about Mr. Alban. With respect to appearance and confidence, the two men were nearly on equal footing. But Mr. Alban was a man determined to cultivate his appeal, making the rounds at every ball, smiling here and flirting there.

Daniel turned heads without effort.

He could probably smile at any woman here and have them melting in a puddle on the trampled grass. And yet, here he was, task in hand, focused only on her and her family. She tried to imagine going on such an outing with Mr. Alban, her siblings bouncing along in tow.

She failed miserably.

Finally, they tumbled onto the pier, the breeze better now, though it was stiff and sour in her face. She pushed tendrils of damp hair from her heated face. While the breeze was certainly improved, the mob here proved just as thick as it had been by the front gate. She was left with no choice but to press herself tightly against Daniel's side. His hand was gentle and reassuring against her back, but still her heart was like a drum her in chest, and not only due to the raucous cries going up around them.

"There she is!" someone shouted.

Clare craned her neck. There on the wire, high above the oily, swirling water, a figure in indecently short skirts was walking, one foot carefully placed in the front of the other. A long pole swayed like a drunken pendulum in her hands. The woman's unbound hair blew out behind her, free as the gulls that dipped on either side of her, jeering her on with their harsh cries.

Clare sucked in a breath as Madame Sylvie's pole slowly, slowly, began to tip in the opposite direction. "Surely she will fall, holding a pole like that!" she gasped, clutching at Daniel's arm.

"No, the length of the pole helps her balance." Daniel pointed. "It's physics, really. See how she is subtly shifting her weight? You can tell by the line of her shoulders. She uses it as a fulcrum, to adjust for changes in the wind and her own balance."

"Oh." Yes, she could see it now. The pole began to tip opposite again, and the woman's shoulders tilted with it. In fact, if she focused on the beautiful figure, instead of the terrifying height, she could admit the woman looked as poised as the most accomplished debutante. There was an artistry in Madame Sylvie's posture, and in her careful but determined progress toward shore. "Geoffrey, can you see her?" she asked.

When she received no response, she looked around.

"Oh, God." This time she didn't even try to hide the fact she'd said such a blasphemous thing out loud.

Because Geoffrey and Lucy were gone.

Chapter 17

*P*anic ripped through her. The rest of the crowd fell away, and Clare felt only the choking absence of her family. "Where do you think they are?"

Daniel peered up at the wire, his eyes crinkling in thought. "Young Geoffrey looked rather determined to meet Madame Sylvie," he mused.

"Surely he wouldn't have," Clare protested, her fingers curling around the wilted posies. Her heart tumbled in her chest, seeking traction and finding none. "Surely *Lucy* wouldn't have. We instructed them to stay together."

"True. And I imagine they have—just not with you. Your sister and brother strike me as the sort of souls who might twist those instructions to suit their own advantage, especially when there's a bit of adventure at the ready. Geoffrey wandered off for a bit at St. Bart's, too. I found him knee-deep in the morgue."

"That doesn't make me feel better," Clare retorted, nausea being the natural response to the thought of Geoffrey anywhere near a morgue—be it as voyeur or victim.

"If it eases your mind, I don't think he intends any offense. He's still possessed of a boy's curiosity. They will have turned back to the scaffolding, I suspect."

"But . . . they'll be alone!"

"Hardly. They've each other. And they are with your maid, who seems worldly enough."

Clare emitted a strangled gasp, thinking of the looks the maid Maggie had been dropping toward Daniel all morning, and the way the servant had winked at Geoffrey when she looped her arm through his. "Is that supposed to *reassure* me?"

She pivoted on her heel, determined to plunge back the way they had come.

But in the moments since their feet had found the pier, the crowd had closed in behind them, thick and jostling. She dropped the posies and pushed ineffectively against the wall of bodies with her hands, then began to pound on shoulders and backs and bellies alike, but it was like kicking a bare foot against Hadrian's Wall.

Not that she wouldn't sacrifice a phalange or two for her brother.

Toes. She'd meant toes.

Oh, *curse* Daniel Merial and his maddening interference in her life!

"Clare." A touch on her shoulder froze her frenzy. Daniel's voice reached down to her, distinct through the throbbing pulse of the crowd. "It will stay too tight to navigate until Madame Sylvie passes. You may trust me on this, after my experience at Kennington. The mob is like an animal. You can coax it, but you cannot change it. There is naught to do but wait."

She whirled back around to face him, her fists clenched, ready to fight. But the look on his face trapped her objections in her throat. He looked . . . determined. The realization that he wanted to find Geoffrey and Lucy, too, calmed her somewhat.

Daniel stretched out his hand and beckoned to her. She numbly placed hers in it, not knowing what else to do. "They will be fine," he told her. "I promise."

But his promise felt a bit like that pole in Madame Sylvie's hand, swaying in the breeze.

He squeezed her hand, and the strength in his touch made her want to believe him. They couldn't go back yet, that much was clear. They were trapped on the pier until Madame Sylvie made her overhead pass, at least.

"We made a plan, if you remember," he pointed out. "The gate?"

She breathed in through her nose. They *had* made a plan. She could almost feel her heartbeat slow as she considered it. But in the space left, worry sank its determined teeth. "I am sure you are right," she said, willing herself to believe it. "I am sure that nothing has happened to them physically. But their reputations—"

"There's not a soul here looking at the body next to them as an individual at the moment. No one is watching, Clare." Daniel's hand tightened around hers. "Besides. It seems to me that a reputation is a body's own. They will have made this decision for themselves. Lucy is old enough to know her own mind, and Geoffrey seems rather young to have a reputation to worry about."

"Tell that to his headmaster at Eton," Clare muttered darkly.

He chuckled, and his easy laugh eased the last remnants of her worry to only a lingering irritation. "Don't you trust them to know their own conscience? To make their own decisions?"

That sounded suspiciously like a reprimand. She opened her mouth. Shut it again as she realized her hand was still trapped in his.

That was a problem.

He'd touched her in myriad ways during the course of

their two week association. With clinical fingers, probing her ankle, testing its soundness with the confidence of a doctor. He'd touched her in other ways, too, lips to lips, as bruising in their promise as the threat of discovery. But this touch felt different. His fingers lay warm and strong beneath the soft calfskin of her gloves. The significance of the crowd and the day and even her errant siblings seemed very far away in comparison to the significance of this simple, benign touch.

"But . . . they are my family," she protested weakly, trying to remember why she was worried. "I am the eldest. It is my responsibility to protect them."

"They ought to be capable of looking to themselves for ten minutes. You need to give them a chance to prove it." Those handsome lips curved in the slightest of smiles. "And all this talk of protection." The fingers of his free hand reached out and brushed a strand of hair from her face. "Who protects *you*, Clare?"

She stilled.

His head dipped low, toward her ear. "After all, *they* are in the company of a chaperone. At the risk of pointing out the obvious, you are not."

Had she imagined the day was so hot? How to explain the shiver that swam its way up her spine, then? She had thought such a public venue would provide a measure of safety. That so many eyes and ears would keep hands in place, and thoughts of kisses and the like tightly harnessed. But Daniel was right. No one was watching them with the slightest bit of interest. They were naught but anonymous leaves, floating on currents of noise and energy in this pulsating river of bodies. Anything could happen in a crowd such as this.

Anything at all.

Her pulse shifted direction, charting a new course. She was out of her element, in over her head. But she was also entranced by the possibilities. Here there were no snide comments from Sophie to deal with, no eager young men to sidestep. To stand in the middle of a mob and not worry whether friends and rivals were analyzing your every move was strangely freeing, as though she had been gifted with invisibility and then been invited to explore.

The crowd had eyes for no one but the woman on the wire, but Clare found she could no longer look up, for fear of missing what came next. Drat it all, did the man who accompanied her have to be so *attractive*? There was something about him that could only be described as potent, and it had little to do with the arrangement of his features or the expanse of his shoulders. It was like staring into the sun, and no manner of spectacle—save Madame Sylvie dropping on top of them in a flail of arms and skirts—could have pulled her attention away in that moment.

She imagined he would take some advantage now. After all, he'd already proven he had a scoundrel's heart, that day in her drawing room. But he did not move.

Perhaps he was more of a gentleman than she had credited him.

A cheer went up all around them, signaling Madame Sylvie's imminent approach. Soon the crowd would loosen, and they would return to the scaffolding to scold her siblings. But for now Clare let herself be jostled by nearby elbows, moved and pinched and prodded by the crowd until she was pressed tight against Daniel's chest. Fate was pushing her toward him, and it seemed not to matter a whit whether she was determined to fight it or not. The panic she felt earlier over her siblings' misbehavior shifted to something more dangerous, and the hard thump of her heart confirmed she was about to do something no well-bred girl would do.

But she had come here today to make a memory, hadn't she?

It seemed the choice was now firmly in her own hands.

She pulled her hand free of Daniel's grip and stripped off her gloves—gloves she had bought thoughtlessly with her exorbitant pin money at the most expensive shop on Bond Street—and let them drop to the filthy, weathered wood of the Cremorne pier. Later, when she looked back on the moment, reliving it in her head, she'd question her lack of judgment. Later, she would blame her decision on the heat of the day, the press of the crowd, the subdued panic she still felt to have her siblings out of sight and out of reach.

Anything to avoid the truth.

But now, in this moment, she could see nothing but this man, could feel nothing but her own desire, pushing her further down this forbidden—if temporary—path.

She framed Daniel's face with her bare hands and rose on her toes. The wide, face-shading brim of her bonnet proved a moment's distraction, until she sorted out how to tilt her chin up to meet him. Daniel's own hat tumbled to the ground, knocked off by her restless fingers.

She pressed her lips against his, almost experimentally, to see if her memory was anything close to accurate. Once again she was jolted back to that place in her drawing room, a moment of surprise that an act so simple could be at once so complicated and unforgettable. Three days ago he'd left her dreadfully aware of what a kiss could do, and she'd thought about it all too frequently. Their first kiss had caught her off guard, delivered, as it had been, in the heat of an argument. But this kiss was her own, taken in the heat of the moment.

And unfortunately, it knocked her every bit as far afield. Her knees threatened to buckle at the sweeping invasion of his tongue, but then his arms settled around her waist, drawing her even closer, until her body settled flush against his, belly to hip. She felt an answering tug in intimate places, a softening of her core that made her only want to burrow closer. She felt . . . wicked. *Daring.*

Safe.

Standing in the bright sunshine, surrounded by the roar of the crowd, Clare closed her eyes and simply kissed this man who was so wrong for her. She ran her fingers over the angled planes of his jaw, then reached farther, behind his neck, her fingers tangling in the length of his hair. The locks were damp where they had rested beneath his hat, but higher up the strands flowed like silk across her fingers. She marveled that a man at once so hard, so capable, should have such soft hair.

A shadow passed overhead. The crowd began to turn.

And with them, Clare's conscience began to turn as well. Dimly, she knew this was wrong, no matter that the kiss could be laid squarely at her own feet this time. He'd made no improper advance, taken no liberty she hadn't offered.

She had no one to blame but herself for the molten want coursing through her.

She pulled away, breathing hard, though she was gratified to see she had stripped the composure from him as well. Sanity slid fitfully back into place, a final puzzle piece she'd been pretending was missing during the last few minutes.

This had not been wise. Anyone could have seen them. But a cautious glance around told her no one was paying them the slightest bit of attention.

She smoothed her hands down the front of her skirts before risking a peek at the man she had just brazenly kissed in a public place. His hair was newly rumpled, and sunlight glinted like quicksilver as it flashed off the dark strands.

He frowned down at her. "What are you thinking, Clare?"

"Your . . . er . . . hat." She took a step backward. "It will be crushed."

He stooped and retrieved his hat, then tried to shake it back into shape with a series of quick slaps against his thigh. It was an exercise bound for failure: she could see it was now bound for the rubbish bin. It's a sacrilege to cover such hair with a hat anyway, she thought, then realized how dangerous it was to have a thought like that.

Gentlemen wore hats. Ladies wore gloves. Ladies also wore corsets. But hers no longer fit, and her gloves were now lost in the mass of milling feet.

Heavens above, what was this man doing to her life?

Daniel dropped the hat back to the pier floor with a sheepish shake of his head. "That will hurt my pocket to replace, I am afraid." He glanced back at her. "What else are you thinking?"

Clare laced her bare fingers together. The crowd seemed to be loosening, but for the life of her she couldn't remember why that was a good thing. "I am not thinking of anything."

"You forget my life's profession. I see every sign, you know. Every symptom you think you hide." He motioned between her eyes. "A small furrow appears just here when you are focused on something that bothers you."

Clare ducked her head, her cheeks warming. Did she really have a furrow?

It seemed a frightful thing for a girl to possess.

And it seemed an even more frightful thing for a gentleman to notice.

She tried to school her expression to neutrality, and

turned in the direction of the black iron gate rising above the heads of the thinning mob some hundred yards distant. Oh, yes. Now she remembered. *Geoffrey and Lucy.* It shamed her to have so neatly forgotten her missing siblings, but then, Daniel's kiss had a way of stealing her wits along with her breath. "We should return now and make sure Geoffrey and Lucy are safe."

He fell into step beside her and helped part the remaining crowd with a forward-stretched hand. "Your furrow has deepened."

She offered a sideways glare. "It has not."

His grin was sudden and jarring, those perfect teeth flashing as though he could read her mind. "Are you meaning to slap me again?"

Mortification swam through her—whether due more to the memory of her reaction to their first kiss or the inadvisability of their second, it was difficult to be sure.

"I'm the one who took the advantage this time," she admitted tersely. "It scarcely seems fair to reprimand you for that."

"And what was *that*, exactly?" he asked, his voice warmer even than the insistent beat of the sun.

She breathed in, the forbidden taste of him still sharp and poignant on her tongue. But Daniel, very much like the marzipan he had once so injudiciously pressed upon her, posed a hazard to her future—a future she had been raised to expect, and was determined to acquire. "It was good-bye," she admitted. "Out of sight of my family, where I could offer it properly."

He stopped and pulled her around to face him. "That didn't feel like a good-bye."

She shook his hand away from her sleeve, her heart thumping inexpertly. She'd let down any number of men, poor Mr. Meeks included. Why, then, did this feel so different?

So wrong?

"Daniel, I am grateful for everything you have done for my family." She licked her lips, and looked away toward the gate, still too far away for reassurance. "For everything you have done for me."

"It didn't feel like gratitude either," he growled.

Her gaze swung back to his face. "That isn't what I meant."

"Damn it, you kissed *me* this time, Clare. What was that about, if not an expression of your regard?"

"I wanted . . ." She searched her thoughts for an explanation that would both appease his lengthening scowl and explain her brash behavior. He was a curiosity, she supposed, and she was the cat. "I wanted to know. If it would feel the same if *I* initiated it."

"Today's kiss was an experiment, then?" At her nod, his eyes narrowed. "And what were your observations, if I might ask?"

"My observations?"

"Experimentation requires a faithful weighing of facts." He chased his words with a harsh laugh. "I should know. I sacrifice a good many hours of sleep at its altar." He raised a brow. "I would know your conclusions on this matter."

She touched a bare finger to her lips, startled by the notion he was pressing her for a scientific analysis. "I suppose it felt the same." She hesitated, knowing she wasn't expressing the experience faithfully. "Actually, that isn't true. It felt . . . more."

His expression darkened. "More than *Alban's* kiss, I presume?"

Irritation pricked at her. "Not that it's any of your business, but I haven't kissed Mr. Alban yet." At his deepening scowl, she threw up her hands, her reticule flopping on her wrist. "I don't know what else you want me to say! I've experienced precisely two kisses in my life, and both of them felt *more*."

There was a beat of silence where Clare was quite sure she could hear her lungs contract, no matter the dull roar of the crowd.

"Then why must it be good-bye?" His eyes were dark pools, but she could see the question lurking in their depths.

"It *must* be, Daniel. You know as well as I this can go no further. We've shared a pair of kisses, nothing more. If you care for me at all, you will accept this good-bye in the spirit in which it is intended and let us part as friends."

"Friendship is a pale description of what lies between us," he pointed out ominously. "And I think you know it well. You cannot convince me you do not feel this. That you do not *want* this every bit as much as I."

Her eyes fell to his clenched hands, to the callused ridge of his thumb and the scar that lingered there. No gentleman would have such hands.

And no lady should feel such things, looking upon those hands.

"Wanting and having are not the same thing." She said it as much to convince herself as the man standing before her. "I am the daughter of a viscount," she said, proud that if her knees were going to shake, at least her voice sounded steady. "You are a doctor, and a poor one at that." She lifted her chin and forced herself to meet the gathering storm in his eyes. "My path is set, Daniel."

"So that is to be it, then?" A muscle twitched along his jaw. "You would ignore this thing between us?"

"Yes," she said firmly. "I have never given you reason to believe otherwise."

They could not hide from this truth. She might hate the words, but she would not hesitate to confirm them.

Because being confused about the state of one's feelings was not the same as being confused about the state of one's future.

And she needed to guard her emotions—and her reputation—if she was to have any hope of winning Mr. Alban back.

She turned away, toward the looming iron gate, seeking fresh air and family and escape—not necessarily in that order. She pitched through the dwindling crowd, searching for the bright yellow flash of her siblings' hair. *There.* She could see the miscreants standing in the shade of the scaffolding, happily eating fruit tarts with Maggie the maid. She raised her hand just as Daniel caught up to her side, his face an uninterpretable mask.

"Geoffrey!" she shouted in desperation, though she knew such an unladylike sound should never be permitted in public. She breathed a sigh of relief as her brother waved vigorously in return.

A cowardly way to end the conversation perhaps, but at least it was done.

Geoffrey hopped from foot to foot as they drew closer. If the boy was feeling apologetic for his disappearance, he'd buried it somewhere at the bottom of his enthusiasm. "I talked to her, Dr. Merial! I spoke to Madame Sylvie! She told me to tell you hullo."

Lucy's shrewd gaze seemed to probe beneath Clare's skin. "Now, where did you two get off to?" she asked, her voice tinged with suspicion.

Her sister's question—and the insinuation that Clare was the one who had become separated from the group—caught her off guard. "I . . . er . . . that is . . ."

"We went to the pier," Daniel answered, "and then became trapped in the crowd on the return."

"No harm done." Clare forced a close-lipped smile to her lips. "Though we should probably thank Dr. Merial for having the good sense to agree on a meeting place in case we became separated."

"Hmmph." Lucy wiped a corner of her mouth with the delicate tip of her glove, then looked from Clare's ungloved hands to Daniel's bare head, back to Clare again. "I suppose. I just didn't expect your *clothes* to become separated as well."

THEIR RETURN TO the quiet streets of Grosvenor Square seemed to have different effects on each of them. Lucy and Geoffrey chattered like magpies, carrying a piece of the boisterous day home with them. Clare was quiet, though to Daniel's eye the furrow between her brows had deepened into more of a trough.

Daniel himself had plunged into a brooding silence, the sort he usually reserved for scathing rejections from editors of medical journals.

I have never given you reason to believe otherwise, she had told him.

Perhaps she hadn't.

But she *had* given him hope, damn her kissable lips.

And then crushed it beneath the paper-thin sole of her very fashionable shoe.

As the gleaming white walls of Cardwell House rounded into sight, the maid proved the one member of their party who was moved to decisive action. Maggie looped her arm through Daniel's and pulled him against her generous curves. "I've a free afternoon tomorrow, if you'd like to come and call on me." She took no pains to lower her voice. "I know a lovely private spot we could go."

Beside them, Clare's slim shoulders stiffened.

He wasn't surprised by Maggie's offer. She had been tossing him none-too-subtle smiles all afternoon. Worse, with Clare's rejection so firmly felt, it was hard to remember why he ought to avoid such an invitation. Still, he was not quite the scoundrel she had once accused him of being, and he would not use one woman for the purpose of inspiring envy in another.

He unpried the maid's fingers. "I'm afraid I promised to spend tomorrow afternoon visiting with Lady Austerley."

"Isn't tomorrow her musicale?" Clare asked sharply.

Daniel gritted his teeth. "I suppose. But I always read to her Saturday afternoons." And he was determined to keep this appointment and try one last time to talk the dowager countess out of her folly.

Maggie's face fell. "Oh." She chewed on her lower lip, which *was* rather full and inviting, though he perversely preferred the pair just beyond, which at the moment were firmed in stern disapproval. "Perhaps next week, then?" the maid countered.

"Dr. Merial will not be returning next week, Maggie." Clare's eyes met Daniel's over the maid's head. "I believe I've proven my ankle is healed enough now to no longer require a doctor's care. That was always the agreement, wasn't it?"

"But . . . *we* can see him again." Geoffrey's voice rang out, hurt and petulant. "Can't we?"

"Geoffrey and I were just saying we ought to take Dr. Merial to Ascot," Lucy added. "He clearly knows a great deal about horses. Why, with his expertise, I've no doubt we can finally pick a winner this year."

Daniel's chest tightened to hear of their plan. Hadn't he known it would come to this? They were trying to side-step their sister's wishes, and so *he* would have to be the strong one here and insist on a permanent good-bye.

"I am afraid it is impossible. My duties call, and I've neglected them enough as it is." He shook his head. "And you know as well as I they would not permit someone like me at Ascot."

"But you'd be with us," Geoffrey protested. "Attending

as our guest. They'd never need know you're not a proper gentleman."

"At least, they needn't if you would wear a hat," Lucy added.

Daniel tugged a hand through his hair. "They would know." Hat or no, the strands were too dark and thick to pass for anything but exotic. His features might be pleasing to most women's eyes, but they were not *aristocratic* features. "Do you want to know why I know something of horses, Geoffrey?" At the boy's eager nod, he tossed himself over the edge of this cliff he'd been pretending he could scale. It scarcely mattered anymore whether Clare thought well of him or not, after all. And this bit of truth could only hurry along the necessary good-bye. "My father was a horse trader, and Roma at that."

Geoffrey's eyes widened. "Gor! A Gypsy horse trader?"

"Yes." Daniel knew the boy meant no insult, and so he didn't react as he might have if one of his peers had muttered the words. "He was well-respected, and dealt with gentlemen of means, but he was a horse trader nonetheless."

Lucy's expression was suddenly sympathetic. "You said your father *was* a horse trader?"

"He died ten years ago," Daniel admitted, "after suffering a crushed leg in a fall from a horse."

"But . . . a crushed leg doesn't usually kill someone, does it?" Geoffrey interjected, a puzzled frown on his face.

"It does if the attempt to remove it goes awry," Daniel answered quietly.

They stared at him in a harsh mixture of horror and sympathy. In fact, his father had died during a hastily attempted surgery to remove said crushed leg. Daniel had only been eighteen, untrained and unschooled, his fingers shaking with dread as he helped hold his father down beneath the bone saw. But the damned doctor who was called in—if indeed the man had ever been credentialed by a licensing board—had proven too inexperienced and far too slow. In the end the blood loss and pain had proven too much for his father's aging heart.

"I blamed myself, of course. If the surgery could have gone faster, or my father had been rendered insensible first—" He broke off the thought in mid-sentence.

Surprisingly, it was Clare who spoke first. "You sound as though you miss him."

He wanted to grab hold of the sympathy in her voice and shake it. *Hard*. Rattle her bones and show her that she might be the daughter of a viscount, but the same emotions, the same universal needs, ran through their veins.

Instead, he nodded. "I do. His death left me . . . unsettled." He hesitated, but it was a story only partially told, and Geoffrey and Lucy were staring upon him as if they had no idea who he was. Indeed, they hadn't the faintest notion.

"Though I was supposed to take over my father's business, I decided to study medicine instead. I initially established a practice in Yorkshire," he explained, "but I had always wondered if my father might have lived if there had been a way to safely administer an anesthetic. And so I came to London six months ago, determined to create a device that could deliver drugs like ether and chloroform safely."

"So you're not just a doctor?" Geoffrey exclaimed. "You're a Gypsy tinker, too?"

Daniel smiled grimly. "I suppose that's one way of looking at it." He could not deny his upbringing, his *heritage*, had given him a certain set of skills and an innate understanding of how things worked. Most doctors were incapable of possessing the knowledge of how to assemble a device as complicated as his anesthetic regulator. He ran a hand over his hair once more, forcing the midnight black strands he'd inherited from his father back into proper place. "So you see, I am my father's son. Dressing me in a top hat and sneaking me into Ascot won't change that."

Maggie clutched at his arm. "Well I, for one, think you're very handsome for a Gypsy."

"You misunderstand me." He once again disentangled himself from the maid's tenacious grasp. "I don't resent my father's physical influence or my place in life. My father taught me to work hard for the respect I intend to earn, and there is no shame in that. But such things are not accepted among the ton."

Clare's face had gone pink beneath the shade of her bonnet. Perhaps she'd been comforting herself that if she'd sunk so low, she'd at least committed her sin with a gentleman physician, someone from a respectable stratum of Society. No doubt the horror of kissing the son of a Gypsy horse trader was only now beginning to sink in.

"But no one objected to us coming with you to Chelsea today," Geoffrey protested, though he sounded less sure of himself.

"You were able to come to Chelsea with me today because your presence in *my* world raises far fewer eyebrows than my presence does in yours." Daniel thought back on that moment at Lady Austerley's ball when he'd acknowledged Lord Hastings and was roundly snubbed for the effort. "It would be another matter entirely at Ascot," he finished.

A small, discontented silence fell across their group as they ground to a halt in front of the town house. The dead quiet of the street felt as rough as glass paper to his already bruised ego. It wasn't as though he had ever had any right to entertain the thought this could proceed beyond a heady flirtation, or a stolen kiss. She was a viscount's daughter, and he was naught but her doctor. He was supposed to be logical, methodical, *practical*. His head and his heart should never have been turned by a fashionable—if swollen—ankle.

But somehow these heady weeks of seeing her had stripped the sense from him, and he needed to find his way back to sanity now.

Daniel glanced at Clare, seeking some small sign of encouragement that he was doing the right thing. But as his eyes met hers, she looked away.

Clearly, her good-byes had already been made.

"I won't forget any of you," he told them. "But your sister is correct. This must be good-bye." He turned to Lucy. "Next year you are going to give the gentlemen in London something to think about. I think you are going to do brilliantly."

She inclined her head, a sad smile playing about lips. "As a wise man once encouraged me, I shall endeavor to be myself, Dr. Merial."

He turned to Geoffrey next. "You, my young friend, are bound for great things. Never forget that. But make your future count. Find one thing you are passionate about and pursue it, head on. And keep up with your Latin." He grinned down at the lad. "You're doing remarkably well."

Geoffrey scowled a long second, and then stretched out a hand. *"Amicitiae nostrae memoriam spero sempiternam fore."*

I hope the memory of our friendship will be everlasting.

Daniel clasped it and forced himself to smile. "As do I."

But unfortunately a memory was all he could be.

May 19, 1848

Dear Diary,

It seems important to tell the truth to oneself.

Or, barring that, to tell the truth to one's diary.

As glorious—and dreadful—as today was, I cannot permit myself to dally any longer. Tomorrow's musicale marks my return to the Season, and my receipt there will set the stage for the remainder of the year. There can be no acceptable outcome but to turn Mr. Alban's head squarely back in my direction, and if I can coax him into a kiss, preferably one as stirring as the one I shared with Daniel, it would probably bode well for an immediate proposal.

But if I am being honest (and what is a diary for, but a time for abject truth?), the musicale—or, God help me, kisses from future dukes—are not foremost on my mind.

I've been raised to believe that finding a husband was a matter of title and fortune, and any decision to be made on the matter centered mainly on the pattern of seed pearls to be used on my gown. I was led to believe that choosing well would ensure my future happiness.

But Mother and Father do not seem very happy.

And I can't help but fear that a proposal from Alban might win me a similar fate.

Chapter 18

"Where do you think Father is?" Geoffrey scowled up from his breakfast plate. It was the second time he'd asked the question since sitting down to the table, and he'd gone from worried to angry over the course of buttering his bread.

"I don't know." Clare lifted her coffee cup to her lips, wishing she knew some way to improve the boy's mood. Since Dr. Merial's departure yesterday, Geoffrey had descended into a self-absorbed sulk. "As I've already said."

Lucy swallowed a bite of sausage, having noticeably moved on from her obsession with saving the blameless animals of London. "Perhaps," she said, waving her fork in the air, "he is visiting a brothel or some such establishment. According to Maggie and some of the other maids I have spoken with, the nicer ones offer overnight accommodations."

Clare choked on her mouthful of coffee.

Even Geoffrey—usually a fount of offensive phrases—gasped.

Lucy, however, took another bite of sausage.

"It would be highly inappropriate for us to speculate." Clare glared at her sister. Ever since their encounter with Handsome Meg, Lucy had been asking the most outrageous questions imaginable. The animals of London might now be safe, but it was clear the prostitutes needed to have a care. But despite her resolve to follow her own sage advice, Clare's thoughts pulled insistently in a similar direction. "And do not let Mother hear you say such things," she warned, gripping the handle of her cup.

"As if she would ever rise from bed in time to listen." Lucy shrugged. "Wherever he is, it isn't like Father to miss breakfast. Should we be worried?"

Clare stared down at her cup. It admittedly *wasn't* like their father to be gone from breakfast. He was already missing from much of their day—and much of their lives—but mornings were a time that had always seemed sacred. Today was the first she could recall where Father had not made an appearance, and a whisper of hurt curled around her heart.

They had so little of him as it was.

But their father's whereabouts were not at the top of her list of worries. She felt wrung out, exhausted and heart sick. Last night had been rendered almost sleepless, her dreams chased by intrusions that involved a dangerous degree of kissing. She'd told Daniel goodbye, as any girl in her precarious position must. But her subconscious was proving more difficult to convince than she'd imagined, and this morning she'd awakened in twisted, damp sheets, her heart pounding with the echo of loss.

"Lucy, I . . . I can't think about Father right now." Clare wrapped her fingers around her cup and wondered if she ought to try to eat something more substantial to settle her jumping stomach. "Not with the musicale looming."

A small lie that hurt no one. She *should* be thinking

about tonight's musicale and the need to turn Alban's head thoroughly in her direction.

"You aren't looking forward to tonight?" Lucy asked, cocking her head. "I thought you were excited. You even had a new gown made for the occasion, didn't you?"

Clare hid the retort that sprang to mind behind another robust sip of coffee—which she had liberally and rebelliously sweetened this morning. Yes, she had a beautiful new gown. The modiste had delivered it last night, and it cost twice what it should have, on account of the rush. But despite its beauty and extravagance, she couldn't even find the wherewithal to be glad it was hanging upstairs in her room.

"I don't know what to expect," she decided on as the safest and truest answer. She studied the swirl of drink in the bottom of her cup. Perhaps she should have had tea this morning. Then, at least, there would have been leaves she could pretend to read. "I have missed two weeks of the Season. Much can happen in that space of time, and I am not sure everyone will welcome my return."

Or indeed whether she wished to go back herself. How had two weeks of gnashing her teeth over her injury turned into this feeling of dread?

"You refer to your friends, I presume?" Lucy frowned. "They don't strike me as being very kind. I overheard them talking the day they came to visit. I think you need to have a care where they are concerned."

Clare straightened in her chair, her chest feeling tight. "What did they say?" She was more than willing to overlook the fact Lucy had been eavesdropping if it could give her some insight into what she faced this evening.

Lucy shrugged. "Oh, just the usual mean-spirited sort of things. They sounded envious of Mr. Alban's interest in you. But it was *how* they said it that bothered me. Harpish shrews, if you ask me."

Clare tried to relax against the back of her chair, though her muscles still felt coiled tight. This was nothing new, nothing she hadn't already considered. "Thank you for telling me," she said tightly. "It is always helpful to know if people are talking about you, and to sort out if there could be ill-feelings behind the gossip. You cannot imagine what a gauntlet it is, to walk into a room and have everyone stare at you. You suspect your hair is coming down or you've something stuck in your teeth."

Lucy grimaced. "If you are trying to convince me that next year is something I should look forward to, you might want to change your tactics."

Clare hid a smile. It was good to hear her sister had shifted from the idea of "if" she had a Season to "when" she had one.

"It isn't *that* terrible," she offered in what she hoped was a reassuring tone.

Except, of course, it was.

She ran her tongue over the slight crookedness of her tooth, recalling the fresh fear she had felt at the start of her first Season as she'd stepped into the ballroom and a hundred heads turned in her direction. She'd felt almost paralyzed, wondering whether her smile would reveal something that might spell her social downfall.

She'd survived it, even triumphed, of a fashion, once she aligned herself with the likes of Sophie and Rose. But it took a good deal of fortitude to be so aware of what you stood to lose, meanwhile pretending you didn't care a whit.

Clare lifted her coffee cup again, then stilled as she realized Geoffrey had quite an odd expression on his face, as if his milk had gone sour. "Don't worry." She smiled reassuringly at him. "You've some years yet. And it isn't nearly as difficult for the gentlemen."

"I don't care about what may happen to me." He

frowned. "But did you mean it? About *needing* to know if someone was speaking poorly of you?"

Clare felt a sudden shift in her pulse. "Yes. You cannot plan a competent defense against an unheard and unknown enemy."

"And you would want to know? If someone said something about our family?"

Her senses prickled in alarm. "If you've heard something, then yes."

He met her gaze hesitantly. "Then you should know there is talk in other corners as well."

Clare's immediate instinct was to dismiss her brother's words and his notion of "corners." Whatever talk Geoffrey thought he was privy to, he was only thirteen years old. How much could he have heard in the isolated halls of Eton? But something in his expression made her stomach tilt sideways. He was neither making his usual kind of joke nor seeking to ruffle her ire. In fact, he looked close to tossing his breakfast back onto his plate.

"Go on," she said tightly.

"Well, there's this boy at school, you see. Peter. He's an insufferable snob. *Lord* Peter, he makes us call him, even though we'll all be bloody lords eventually." Geoffrey shifted in his seat. "Anyway, he said some terrible things about our family. I was angry with him for spreading such lies, so that's why I did it."

Lucy leaned forward. "Does this have anything to do with your expulsion?"

He nodded, the tips of his ears turning pink. "I knew I couldn't call him out on it, because that would only make the rumor spread faster and I just wanted it to go away. And I can admit I'm not the most accomplished person when it comes to swords and knives and such."

Foreboding rippled through Clare's stomach. *Call someone out? Swords and knives?* She'd wanted the details of Geoffrey's hijinks, to be sure, but this was far more alarming than she'd imagined.

Geoffrey fidgeted with his napkin. "So I electrified his doorknob."

"What?" Clare and Lucy exclaimed in perfect, horrified synchrony.

"His doorknob. I electrified it." He looked up, and something akin to pride shone in his eyes. "It was a copper doorknob, you see. A near perfect conductor. We were studying batteries in science, and so I made a ripping good one. Good enough to knock Lord Peter on his nobbish arse." He grimaced. "But the headmaster touched the knob first. Got knocked on *his* arse instead, and didn't come around for ten minutes." He looked at Lucy, his expression sheepish now. *"That* was why I got expelled."

"But . . . why would you do such a thing?" Clare demanded.

Geoffrey swallowed. "Because the rumors are about you."

"Me?" Clare gripped the delicate handle of her cup. She couldn't make sense of it. After all, it was her family that was the embarrassment here. Lucy, with her mannish shoes, and Geoffrey with his pranks.

And Mother's indiscretions . . . she could scarcely bring herself to think of it.

But she had always guarded her own image amongst the ton. She had cultivated her reputation and chosen her friends with the sole purpose of engendering the *right* sort of gossip. Ever since her first ball, of her first Season, she had ensured that if anything was to be said of her, it should be of the vein that her taste in fashion was immaculate, and that her heart floated well above the reach of those gentlemen of less exacting pedigrees.

"You," Geoffrey offered in quiet confirmation. "And

Father. Or rather, the rumor is that Father isn't your real father."

Clare slumped back in her chair, breakfast now forgotten. The room seemed to spin on a broken axis. She'd seen whispers about things far less calamitous inspire the slow social downfalls of any number of girls. But this was not a nameless, faceless bit of malice, bandied about the retiring room at some obscure ball and easily dispelled with a laugh.

Oh no, nothing that simple.

This was a rumor generated by a future peer, a classmate of Geoffrey's and likely the son or brother of someone she knew.

And her heart was not slapping against her ribs because of outrage.

It was because she couldn't help but wonder if it might be true.

Lucy had gone quiet but she was staring at her, no doubt looking for evidence. There was plenty to be had. Because even if the rumor wasn't true—even if someone had conjured this bit of gossip for no reason other than their own sordid entertainment—Clare was the dark-haired daughter. The brown-eyed sibling. A notable anomaly in a towheaded, blue-eyed family. She was the ambitious Westmore, the *athletic* child, everything her siblings and her father were not.

"Does Father know about this?" she whispered.

"He knows why I was expelled, of course. The headmaster was most explicit in his descriptions. At least I've escaped any official charges. There are *some* benefits to being only thirteen." Geoffrey began to look worried. "But I couldn't tell Father why I did such a thing. It *can't* be true." He hesitated. "Can it?"

Clare wished she could be as confident. Uncharacteristically, she found herself without words, without reassurances. It wasn't even the first time she had considered such a possibility, that she was somehow different than her siblings.

But it was the first time she had encountered that question posed by someone else.

And worse, it was the first time she had considered it with the recent evidence of her parents' presumed faithlessness in hand.

A flurry of activity and the quick shuffling of servants pulled Clare's attention away from such a distasteful thought. She turned in her chair, only to battle a jolt of surprise as Father walked in, looking disheveled and exhausted. He was wearing the same clothing he'd worn yesterday—albeit far more rumpled than before.

"Good morning," he told them, stifling a yawn.

Lucy, thank God, managed to keep all mention of brothels to herself. But as Father shuffled to the sideboard and began filling his plate, she leaned in over the table, her blue eyes filled with worry and suspicion. "Do you think it could be true?" she asked, the stark urgency in her voice shaking Clare from her stupor. She shot a worried glance toward their father's hunched shoulders. "Not the bit about the overnight accommodations, but the other?"

Clare straightened her shoulders. "It isn't true," she said firmly.

And even if it was, she couldn't imagine ever asking their mother the question.

Truly, there wasn't enough Madeira in the world.

Chapter 19

The imported soprano was already running through her scales when Daniel stepped through Lady Austerley's front door. By the sounds of things, the singer was in possession of a set of vocal cords that implied a future danger to even the most stoic of tympanic membranes. The noise followed him up the stairs and into the dowager countess's bedroom—an impressive feat, given that Lady Austerley's rooms occupied a suite on the third floor.

He set his bag down on the bedside table, wondering if a bit of the cotton batting he used for packing wounds could be repurposed for ear protection. He'd never been one for music, the cost of an opera ticket and his evening hours being too dear to waste.

His ears now told him such frugality had been an excellent decision.

The dowager countess greeted him with a smile. He greeted *her* with a frown and a frankly clinical eye. The old dragon was wearing rouge tonight, for Christ's sake.

And a corset again, if the stiffness of her posture was any indication.

"Lady Austerley," he sighed, "need I remind you that you are technically an invalid?"

"Oh, posh and nonsense. 'Tis only a little musicale, Dr. Merial. Hardly an event worth worrying over." She struggled to rise from her prone position on the bed, her skirts a froth of netting and lace that would hardly have been appropriate on a woman even fifty years her junior. The maid rushed to help her, putting her shoulder beneath the older woman's arm and heaving up. The effort left them both panting and disheveled, and Daniel found it difficult to watch. After all, he knew what this evening would cost her, even if she refused to acknowledge it herself.

"All right, then," she said crossly and waved the maid away. "I can manage myself now."

The servant began to fuss about her own hair, several strands of which had come down in her struggle to help her mistress sit up. Her efforts made Lady Austerley roll her eyes. "No need to try so hard to impress him, child," she scolded. "He's not shown the slightest bit of interest in you to date. Tidying your hair isn't going to suddenly convince him you're a raging beauty."

The poor, put-upon maid flushed the sort of red that normally made Daniel think of a high fever. His lips twitched in sympathy. The dowager countess was an outspoken old woman, and there was no getting around her tongue when it lashed out. But despite her sharp words, he knew Lady Austerley cared deeply for her servants, even if she occasionally harangued them. They wouldn't have been so concerned for her health otherwise.

And the maid *did* have a habit of forgetting her duties whenever he came into the room.

"Now then, Dr. Merial." The countess's eyes held a lively gleam, and she placed a hand on her chest, the gnarled fingers splayed as if in promise. "As always, I appreciate your medical opinion, but I'll only be sitting downstairs, enjoying my guests and listening to a bit of music. And I am feeling as healthy as a horse tonight." She eyed his bag. "Or at least I will be, once I've had the draught you've brought."

"Not all horses are healthy." Daniel unsnapped the top of his leather bag. "In fact," he added, "a good many of them are bound for the knackers." He thought of Lucy Westmore's obsession with London's cart horses. Maybe he should toss Lady Austerley into the girl's path. He could think of less worthy crazed quests, and *someone* needed to take the dowager countess on as a project. He glanced toward the door as the soprano began to run through a new scale.

A little boredom was clearly a dangerous thing in an old, wealthy, dying woman's hands.

The laugh that seized Lady Austerley seemed to squeeze from her chest, like air from a bellows, and he glanced back at her sharply. Her sense of humor—grown pinched with age and experience—was one of the reasons he enjoyed visiting with her so much. She not only welcomed such cheek from him, she gave it back, tenfold. But tonight her laugh sounded moist and suspicious, and he knew that if he placed his auscultating device to her chest he would hear the sounds of congestion typical of a failing heart.

Daniel reached into his bag and pulled out a bottle. "This may help with the difficulty you are experiencing drawing a proper breath." He winced as the soprano downstairs hit a particularly offensive note. "I doubt it will help with *that*, however."

"You've no ear for music, Dr. Merial," she chided. "This particular soprano was very expensive. And I have it on authority that the cost of the entertainment is all that matters to my guests." She looked sideways at the maid, who was fluttering at the window, closing the drapes.

"But in the interest of safety," she whispered behind a cupped hand, "I'll admit I've instructed my housekeeper to put away the crystal."

"An excellent idea." Daniel poured her a careful dose. Then, considering the slight wheezing he could still hear on the edge of the dowager countess's exhalations, he added a finger more. She dutifully drank the draught, then sat a quiet moment on the bed, eyes closed and age-splotched hands gripping the coverlet.

"Now then," she said. "Is everything quite ready for my guests downstairs?"

The maid drew aside the curtains she had just closed and peered out at the darkening streetscape. "I certainly hope so, my lady. The first carriages are starting to arrive."

"Heavens, child, do you think that will make my nerves settle any faster?" She flicked an impatient hand at the servant, though her eyes remained squeezed shut. "Could you please go downstairs and tell our soprano she can stop her preparatory squawking now? And make sure everything is properly prepared on the refreshment table. I am worried about the punch."

"The punch?" The maid blinked. "But . . . it has been made according to your explicit specifications."

"I know. I've changed my mind."

"Less wine, then?" The girl looked a tad relieved. "Oh, I am so glad you think so, because it seemed that the four bottles you instructed me to tell the housekeeper was a bit much—"

"It needs more gin." Lady Austerley cracked open an eye and impaled the poor girl with the force of her gaze. "A good deal more gin. And possibly some rum, too."

In spite of himself, Daniel chuckled as the exasperated maid left to do her mistress's bidding. "Lady Austerley, it sounds as if that punch is going to be rather strong. I must caution you not to drink it yourself. The effects of liquor and atropine can be unpredictable when combined."

Both eyes opened, and she gazed up at him "Oh, 'tis not for me. I suspect, given the sound of that soprano, my guests will need some additional fortification. And my poor maid needs a task to keep her busy. She's a sweet thing, but good heavens, she makes me nervous, the way she hovers about and moons in your direction." Her hand crept out to brush his, found his fingers, and squeezed. "Plus, you have a way of calming me that she doesn't. Will you stay with me a moment, Dr. Merial?"

"Of course." Daniel helped her settle back against her mound of pillows, arranging her until she was nearly horizontal. He hoped it would help her breathe easier against the constricting corset, at least until the drug began to work its magic.

"Ah, that is better." She closed her eyes again and clasped her hands over her chest.

Daniel sank down in the overstuffed chair beside Lady Austerley's bed, where he usually sat when he came to read to her. History told him the medicine would take effect quickly, but until it did, she often felt worse. "Would you like me to read? It is Saturday, after all."

"No, I am too excited over my musicale. Tonight I need a better distraction than a sordid novel read by a handsome man." Her hand waved about, though her eyes did not open. "Tell me about your experiment."

"Which one?" he asked, though they'd been over this particular course of inquiry enough that he knew precisely what held her interest.

"You know very well which one." One eye cracked open again, and he could see with relief the pupil was beginning to dilate. "The one with the frogs. Is it going better than the last time, when the creatures kept flinging themselves out of their bowl?"

"Much better." He leaned back in the chair and placed one foot over his knee. Though his concentration had floundered a bit since becoming entangled with the Westmores, he'd thrown yesterday's frustration into an all-night binge, and his focus had paid off. Last night he finally had the breakthrough he'd been hoping for. It was not yet complete—there were several more variables to test, and he still needed to write a formal summary of his findings to present to the *Lancet*. He knew his arguments must be irrefutable after the last rejection they'd delivered.

His first instinct this morning had been to tell Clare of his findings. His second had been the mind-numbing realization that he couldn't.

Not anymore.

"In fact," he admitted to Lady Austerley, "I've had a bit of a revelation."

"You've decided to put a cover on the bowl?" the dowager countess asked, too innocently. This time both eyes cracked open, and he could see her pupils were dilated— but not *too* dilated. He exhaled in relief. Getting the dose right was tricky, especially when her worsening condition required constant recalculations. "I would have thought you intelligent enough to think of that weeks ago, Dr. Merial. In fact, I recall telling you that very thing."

He grinned. There was nothing wrong with the woman's memory. "No, actually I've moved on from the frogs. I am convinced that as subjects, they lack some important characteristics to model the effects in humans. This time I tried the device on myself."

She blinked at him in alarm. "Is that safe? I had thought you would employ someone when you were ready for that sort of thing. I have offered to invest in this grand device no less than ten times, so lack of funding is no excuse for such callous disregard of your person." She harrumphed.

"And I assure you, the world would suffer greatly from your premature loss."

"As I've told you before, Lady Austerley, I cannot accept your generous offer. You know as well as I that financial payoffs are not my primary motivation." He frowned. "Whether I fail or succeed, I won't invest someone else's funds when disappointment is the more distinct possibility."

"But I thought you said you'd had a revelation," she huffed. "And how on earth can you record your findings if you are . . . if you are . . ."

"Unconscious?"

"If you are dead!"

He smiled to hear the concern in her voice. As far as distractions went, he supposed this qualified rather well. Better than the current novel they were meandering their way through, at any rate. She'd even forgotten to worry about the guests downstairs. "I used small doses of chloroform, so I was guaranteed a quick recovery. And I carefully noted the start of each dose, and again the time I was sentient enough to look back at my watch."

"*Each* dose?" Her lips thinned. "You've done this more than once?"

"Four times." At her strangled objection he added, "My conscience won't permit me to risk it on another human— even a paid human—without trying it on myself first. I had a sense that my limited success with the frogs was distracting me from the real purpose, which was to use the drug properly on a human. I was correct." He leaned in conspiratorially. "It turns out that frogs are *too* easy to render insensible. I suspect it is the surface area of their skin."

She snorted. "Or else the thickness of your own head."

Daniel laughed out loud, glad he'd been able to tell *someone*. He stood up and pulled out the auscultating device he kept in his coat pocket. Leaning over the countess's bed, he said, "Let's have a listen now, shall we?" He helped her sit back up, then placed the flared end of the wooden device against her chest. Long used to the request, she inhaled slowly, as if testing the air and finding it to her liking. "Good," he murmured, readjusting the piece. "Again?"

When he again nodded his approval, she gingerly inched her legs over the side of the bed. Her respirations were now much steadier than a few minutes ago, when she'd struggled to draw a proper breath. She waved his offer of an outstretched palm away with an annoyed hand, as if she was brushing away a gnat.

"Now then," she said, pushing herself to standing without any assistance at all. "I'm feeling much better, and the guests have already started to arrive." She shook out her bunched skirts. "Will you walk me down?"

"Of course." He offered her his arm. As they began the slow, shuffling process of getting Lady Austerley down to the stairs without taking a tumble, he gave in to the urge to finally ask the question that had chased him here. "And would you . . . ah . . . would you like me to stay for the musicale? Just to be safe?"

A sharp bark of a laugh shook her thin frame. "Have a mind to expand your musical horizons, do you?" She cast him a shrewd, sideways glance as they walked. "I don't think the soprano would hold much interest for you, Dr. Merial. My maid is far prettier, and you've scarcely looked in *her* direction, though she's more than made her hopes for it clear." Her lips tipped into a wrinkled smile. "Or is it, I wonder, someone else? The girl. What is her name? Miss Westmore. The one who inspired you to borrow *Cousin Bette*."

"She's coming tonight?" he asked, praying he sounded surprised. His eagerness to stay here at number 36 Berkeley Square tonight had nothing to do with the fact he knew Clare would be in attendance. Nothing at all.

Perhaps if he said it out loud, it might even make it true.

"I was quite pleased when I saw her mother had accepted my invitation." Lady Austerley chuckled. "I suspect you are as well. Not that I blame you. She's a delectable thing."

Though he was supposed to be the steady one, Daniel tripped over his feet at the countess's words. He had not realized his inner thoughts regarding the inarguably delectable Miss Westmore had been so obvious. "I am only interested in her as her recent physician," he protested. "This is Miss Westmore's first formal event since she sprained her ankle."

"Oh come now," Lady Austerley chided, patting his arm with her free hand. "There's no need for such subterfuge. You've done nothing but talk about this girl for the space of the last two weeks. You can't deny you've shown far more interest in this particular patient than any of my maids who've been flinging themselves at your feet."

Beneath the weight of the dowager countess's smug stare, Daniel felt like fidgeting.

Either that or bolting.

But his arm stayed curved around Lady Austerley's gnarled hand, and his shoes stayed planted on the Persian stair runner. He was hard pressed to deny it. He'd even come prepared, worn his good jacket and taken the time to shave.

At his uncomfortable silence, Lady Austerley leaned in. "And of course, I would like nothing more than to have you stay, Daniel. But not as my physician. As my friend. This is to be my last event, and I want you to enjoy yourself."

"Your last event, hmmm? I'll admit it's good to hear you've finally decided to take my advice," he teased, but something in her voice plucked at his worries. "But please, try to avoid any overexcitement tonight. And stay away from the punch. I've already picked out a Christmas gift for you, and I refuse to accept that your time is to be shorter than that."

"Oh, I think you know very well I'd host another occasion if I could, and probably another after that. I am determined to make the most of the time I have left. But my bones feel heavy tonight, as if they've settled into an irrefutable conclusion." She squeezed his arm, and he imagined he could feel the strength draining out of what must have once been a formidable grip. "So I will enjoy tonight, and when it is over and the punch has all been drunk, I will be grateful for the memory and count my remaining breaths as gifts I do not expect."

A lump rose in Daniel's throat. They had reached the bottom of the stairs now, and the sound of her arriving guests' voices washed over them. The very *loud* sound of her guests.

Had she invited all of London this time?

He wanted to bundle her back to her bedroom and tuck her into bed. Instead, he leaned over, kissed the paper-thin surface of one cheek, and turned her over to a waiting footman.

He couldn't be so callous to deny a dying woman an opportunity to say good-bye on her own terms . . . even if those terms involved importing an expensive soprano from France and wasting her last precious breath on social niceties delivered to people who didn't deserve them.

No matter Lady Austerley's continued decline, and his own complicity in it, he wanted her last days to be happy. He could well imagine a person with so little time left wanting to make the most of it.

If nothing else, his brief time with Clare showed him that.

Chapter 20

*I*t should have been the night that marked Clare's triumphant return to her Season, her ankle almost fully healed and her future firmly in sight. Instead, with the day's revelations so fresh in her mind, she felt as though she were stumbling into an adder's nest.

Had the faces of acquaintances and friends always been such vague masks, their eyes so hot on her skin? Or was it only that she was more aware of the scrutiny now?

"It's dreadfully warm this evening, isn't it?" Her mother fanned herself. "Shall we start with a glass of punch?"

Clare eyed the refreshment table on the far side of the room and shifted her weight, testing the strength of her ankle. It still gave her twinges on occasion. No matter her claims of complete recovery, it had ached dreadfully following yesterday's excursion to see Madame Sylvie. But with no dancing on the schedule tonight, she felt confident enough in its performance for the next few hours.

Her emotional performance, however, was another matter entirely.

Her palms felt clammy beneath her gloves, and her

stomach was already objecting to the noise and mayhem of the milling crowd. "No, thank you." She forced herself to smile at her mother. "But do go on ahead."

As her mother slipped away, Clare scanned the room, scouting for friend and foe alike. An entire herd of butterflies had taken up residence in her stomach. Had it really only been two weeks since she'd been here? The room looked completely different.

Or perhaps it was more that she *felt* completely different.

Tonight, the chandeliers had been lowered to provide a more intimate setting, and the scent of beeswax candles hung thick in the air. The high-ceilinged ballroom she remembered from her last visit had been repurposed, with row after row of chairs marching their way across the parquet floor. Experience suggested that Sophie and Rose would choose seats near the front, where they could best share the spotlight intended for the evening's entertainment.

The question at hand was where should *she* sit? At least there was no designated wallflower line to contend with tonight. Everyone would be seated.

And everyone would be watching.

Clare finally spied Sophie and Rose, holding court over a cluster of fawning gentlemen in one corner of the room. But tonight her feet hesitated to carry her into the thick of it. She could not credit her reluctance for anything but cowardice. After all, her friends had shown her nothing beyond the usual degree of friendly banter in the days before her injury, given her no indication they'd heard or believed a rumor such as the one Geoffrey had revealed so disastrously over this morning's breakfast table.

She collected herself in small degrees and pasted a close-mouthed smile on her lips. There was nothing for it but to test the waters, however dark and foreboding they might be.

Rose saw her first, and whispered in Sophie's ear. Sophie glanced over.

And then both friends very clearly and very deliberately turned their backs on her.

Clare detected a shift in the undercurrent of voices around her, and she knew she was not the only one who had seen it. Her feet froze fast to the parquet floor.

How could they? They were supposed to be her friends.

But of course, she knew precisely how they could. She'd watched them do it on any number of occasions. She'd even joined them at times, though the realization of what her victims must have felt shamed her now.

Her gaze fell upon Sophie's gaggle of male admirers, wishing naively, perhaps, that one of them would come to her rescue to save her from such a public cut.

No such rescue came.

But it was the seeming ambivalence of one very particular gentleman in the group that made the air still in her lungs. Tall and familiar, his chestnut head stood several inches above the nearest competitor, though he was facing away from her and she could not see his face.

Mr. Alban. He seemed firmly under Sophie's spell. Anxiety and dismay curled through her stomach. It seemed to have been a busy two weeks.

She studied her friends' backs, looking for some flaw she could turn to her advantage. Drat it all, why couldn't Sophie have worn pink tonight? Instead, she wore a gown in a flattering hue of green, the silk glowing warmly against her olive skin.

Clare turned away, her cheeks burning. She supposed she ought to be grateful it was only a cut. Sophie, in particular, could be rather brutal in her verbal engagements.

Still, the evening was young yet. There was still time for hurtful words.

She headed in the opposite direction, fumbling her way

through the crowd, seeking fresher air and kinder smiles. But as she stumbled onto the edge of the ballroom, she nearly tripped over the terrifying visage of Lady Austerley, seated in a chair and holding a vigil over her circus of a musicale.

"Running from something, my dear?" The dowager countess raised a wrinkled brow.

Clare's feet slowed. Tonight Lady Austerley didn't much resemble the cantankerous patient Daniel so warmly recounted. Her skin was sallow, her eyes sunken into the already deep planes of her face. Her gray hair had been curled and arranged with care, but she could see through the thin strands to the pale, dull skull shining beneath.

"Er . . . I was hoping to find *you*." A white lie that hurt no one, and one that apparently pleased the older woman enough to kindle a smile. Clare sank into a curtsy, but faltered on the nadir, her ankle threatening to twist from under her. Belatedly, she realized she hadn't practiced this particular motion with her still-healing ankle.

It could have used another week of rest, her conscience whispered as she struggled to rise, but she squashed that traitorous thought. She would not let Daniel Merial creep into her thoughts tonight, no matter how difficult the exercise.

"Thank you for inviting me."

"I am pleased you could come, Miss Westmore." The older woman squinted up at her. "You look well recovered."

"I am, thank you." After a moment's hesitation, Clare dug into her reticule and pulled out the copy of *Cousin Bette* she'd brought with her tonight. She'd meant to leave it somewhere inconspicuous but could now see how cowardly that impulse had been. Daniel had implied the dowager countess was lonely and that she would welcome a visit from friends.

Even returning it by penny post with a brief note of thanks would have been kinder.

"I wanted to thank you for loaning the book to me." She held the book out, her fingers sweating in her gloves. "Daniel—I mean, Dr. *Merial*—mentioned it was one of your favorites." She held her breath in horror at her disastrous mistake. Had Lady Austerley caught the slip?

But the countess showed no signs of having registered the use of her personal physician's given name, and Clare comforted herself with the presumption that perhaps the older woman was a little hard of hearing. "It helped me pass the long, lonely days during my recent injury," she added, raising her voice, just in case. "I appreciate your kindness more than you know."

"It was my pleasure, child." Lady Austerley winced, and raised a gnarled hand to one ear. "Although given the way my soprano is shaping up, you might have been better off keeping it for another half hour or so. Having something to read during the performance may save your sanity in the end."

Clare choked back a surprised laugh. She was beginning to see why Daniel enjoyed this woman.

The dowager countess smiled up at her. "Tell me, did you enjoy it?"

Normally, Clare would have avoided any conversation about books in a venue that might be considered public. But for some reason, tonight she did not hesitate. "I found it interesting," she admitted. "De Balzac is certainly an engaging writer. But I found the degree of drama inside its pages painful to wade through."

"Oh?" Lady Austerley lifted the quizzing glass from the shelf of her bosom and peered up at Clare in undisguised interest. "Did you find the scheming of the female characters distasteful, then? Pray don't tell me you are one of these brainless females who believes women incapable of such strategic maneuvering."

Clare bit her lip to hide a smile. "No. I found it neither distasteful nor unbelievable." She glanced out at the room, with its clusters of whispering and tittering young ladies. Her gaze settled on Lady Sophie, who was leaning toward Mr. Alban with a coquettish smile on her traitorous lips. "A little too close to life, perhaps. After all, one reads to escape their life's troubles, rather than dwell upon its more disturbing realities."

Lady Austerley chuckled, though her bemusement ended on more of a hacking cough. "A bit of a gauntlet, is it tonight? I was always more of a wallflower myself. Of course, that was over a thousand years ago." The quizzing glass lowered to reveal pupils like black oracles, rimmed in a thin strip of blue. "When our *Dr. Merial* told me about you, I felt as though I knew you. Something of a kindred spirit, hmmm?"

Clare cringed to hear the woman's slight emphasis on Daniel's name.

His proper name.

Clearly, her earlier mistake had not gone unnoticed.

Worse, the supposition that she could be a kindred spirit with someone who had once been a self-admitted wallflower made her feel off-balance. She'd clawed her way to her position at the top of the social rankings. It had taken a sprained ankle to get her anywhere close to the wallflower line this Season. And yet . . . she couldn't deny she did indeed feel a sort of kindred spirit in Lady Austerley.

"Dr. Merial speaks very warmly of you and your family," the countess went on.

"Does he?" Clare asked, startled. After the way they had parted yesterday, she might have imagined he had some rather choice words to use when speaking of her. "He has been kind to my family as well."

"He is here tonight, you know," Lady Austerley craned her neck. "Ah, there he is. Helping your mother with the punch. Handsome devil, isn't he? Easy to pick out in a crowd."

Clare whirled around just in time to see Daniel extract a glass from her mother's hand. Her eyes took him in like a greedy gulp, no matter that she had been the one to so firmly establish the limits of their continued association. In his serviceable coat and necktie, he looked nothing like the fops who were hanging on Sophie's every word, nothing like the sort of gentleman she was *supposed* to want. Even Mr. Alban—who was admittedly a bit grander than most, and who should have claimed her immediate and undivided attention—faded into the background.

"He's . . . ah . . . that is . . ." Clare floundered, searching for words that could describe what he was to her without giving her emotions away. She hadn't considered that he might be here. A naive presumption, perhaps, given that she'd met him in this very room, but hadn't she proven she wasn't thinking clearly where this man was concerned?

"It seems he's appointed himself guardian of my punch bowl." The older woman sighed. "I suspect he's a teetotaler, you know. He always refuses my offer of brandy when he comes to read on Saturday afternoons. He claims he needs to remain clear-headed for his experiments and his patients, though it isn't as if a single glass would fell such a strapping young man." She chuckled. "Although I suppose I *did* order the punch to be made a bit strongly tonight."

"The punch is laced with spirits?" Clare asked, turning back to the countess. She prayed her mother had limited herself to a glass or two. "Is that really a good idea?"

Lady Austerley rolled her eyes. "Not you, too, Miss Westmore. I refuse to let you and Dr. Merial conspire against my fun." She motioned to the footman who was standing at attention behind her chair. "Do go and relieve the doctor of his post, or he will ensure my guests will never have a chance to enjoy the performance tonight."

Clare risked another look toward the refreshment table as the footman stepped out, and cringed as she saw her mother stare at the bowl, clearly hesitating.

"You don't look much like your mother, do you?" Lady Austerley mused. Clare's startled gaze swung back just as the older woman asked, not unkindly, "Perhaps you take after your father?"

"I . . ." Clare felt a rising panic. No, she didn't take after her father. And there was clearly nothing wrong with the dowager countess's hearing *or* her eyesight.

"Has something upset you, child?" Lady Austerley asked. "You've gone quite pale." She cocked her head. "Should I call Dr. Merial over?"

Clare swallowed the objection building in her throat. Had she imagined she could do this? The eyes of the crowd, the cut from Sophie and Rose . . . those things she could survive. Even Daniel's unexpected appearance and her mother's obsession with the punch were distractions she could overcome.

But this . . . she wanted to sink to the floor and hug her knees tight against her chest.

She tried to breathe deeply through her nose, recognizing the symptoms she was experiencing now as remarkably similar to those that had sent her pitching from the ballroom two weeks ago.

You are panicking, nothing more. It is not the end of the world.

But it was potentially the end of *her* world.

She began inching away, determined not to add a public

display of hysteria to her expanding list of catastrophes. "No," she gasped. "I . . . I suppose I just need a bit of quiet." She lifted a hand to her forehead, and didn't have to feign its tremor. "Might I beg the direction of the retiring room?"

The dowager countess clucked in sympathy. "I could probably use a little lie-down myself, but don't tell Dr. Merial such a thing. I refuse to let him think he is right. 'Tis the first hallway, third door on the right." She held out the book. "And when you are feeling better, the library is just beyond the next hallway beyond. It is a nice quiet spot, with a settee you can lie down on if you are feeling faint. Perhaps you might return the book there?"

"Of course. I know it well," Clare managed to choke out, clasping the book against her chest, as if it might help steady the slamming beat of her heart.

Too late, she realized that perhaps she had confessed too much.

Chapter 21

It was too early in the evening for calamities like ripped hems and spilled glasses of punch, and the retiring room was mercifully empty save a single maid, sitting bored in one corner. Clare shook her head at the servant's inquiry of assistance and aimed instead for a large oval mirror that had been propped on a table.

She laid down the book and pulled off her gloves, breathing in the blessed silence in great, needy draughts. But though her physical reaction began to calm, her self-doubts only clamored louder. The silence in the retiring room and the desire to avoid the dangers lurking outside engendered too much in the way of self-reflection.

What had Lady Austerley seen in the contours of her face?

What did *everyone* see in her face?

She looked into the mirror with distrust. Yesterday, her life had still seemed her own. Her features—while different from Geoffrey's and Lucy's, perhaps—had been *hers*, functional and familiar. It was a face she had once imagined might carry her all the way to a ducal mansion, if only she would remember to hide her teeth behind a half-checked smile.

Tonight it seemed more the face of a stranger staring back at her.

She turned her head from left to right, critically examining her skin, her eyes, her hair. She found nothing lacking. Nothing, that was, except the obviousness of family.

Clare breathed in deeply. Who *was* she? Why *didn't* she have blond hair and blue eyes? Why were her features small and delicate, her chin heart-shaped, whereas Geoffrey and Lucy had broad faces and upturned noses, like Father? She supposed there might be something of Mother in her chin, in the slope of her brow, but of Father there was nary a trace.

She felt ill to consider the possibilities. Her future, which had once seemed a brilliantly drawn still life, now felt smeared and stained.

Outside, she could just hear the opening strains of *Le Nozze di Figaro*. She should probably return to the ballroom and find a proper seat, or else locate her mother and haul her away from the punch bowl. But just as she had almost convinced herself of the need to move, the sound of excited whispers pulled her attention to the doorway. She had barely enough presence of mind to slide her reticule over the cover of the book before Sophie and Rose glided in.

The maid rose from her chair. "Do you need assistance, miss?"

"Could you run and fetch me a cool cloth for my head?" Sophie purred to the servant, her voice as sweet as treacle. "And please, take your time about it."

"A quarter hour, at least," Rose added.

Clare stayed silent as the maid hurried out. She was still unsure of her former friends' intentions. Perhaps they were simply in need of a quiet moment themselves.

But then Sophie moved forward, a cat stalking its wounded prey. "You appear to be spending a good deal of time in the retiring room this evening," she observed, stepping to Clare's left in a puff of perfume-scented air. "We used to laugh about the wallflowers retreating here, their tails tucked between their legs. Have your opinions on such things changed?" Sophie preened in the mirror, lifting a gloved hand to her dark, perfectly arranged curls. "Or perhaps it is more that you have become a wallflower yourself?"

Clare's first instinct was to leave. An easy enough solution, and one most young women would have seized, facing the wrath of Sophie's chameleon smile.

But she knew a retreat now would only seal her fate. "I have no reason to hide."

Sophie raised a dark brow. "Haven't you?"

Rose leaned in on Clare's right. "We thought perhaps you were in here because of the rumor." Both girls paused in their preening to stare at expectantly at Clare.

"Which rumor would that be?" Clare asked through the sudden lurch of her heart.

Her mother's indiscretion in the library?
Her unhealthy obsession with a lowly doctor?
Her questionable parentage?

Truly, there were so many that could apply. Just two weeks ago she'd floated through life in a haze of cautious surety, her life and her future mapped out, her image cultivated beyond reproach. And yet here she was, cornered in a retiring room by her former best friends, frozen in fear over which terrible, life-altering secret might impale her first.

Sophie's lips curved upward. "The rumor about you and Mr. Alban, of course."

Clare felt a surge relief to hear the hinted rumor was not, in fact, one of her more significant unvoiced fears. In fact, it came closer to the sort of whispers that had once comprised her hopes and dreams. "Oh?"

"Is it true he's come to call on you twice this month?" Rose asked.

"Yes," Clare admitted, seeing no cause to deny it. Presumably Alban had even mentioned it himself, when he'd spoken with them earlier this evening.

"And he hasn't spoken to your father about an arrangement yet?" Sophie leaned closer to the mirror and ran a practiced finger over an already immaculate brow. "That seems a bit suspicious, don't you think? Most gentlemen would have asked for an audience by now."

Clare glanced toward the room's door. The soprano sounded as though she could hit her stride at any moment. She should be out there with everyone else, eyes lifted to the makeshift stage. "The Season is still early yet," she said, wanting only to escape this nightmare.

"Not *so* early," Rose pointed out. "We are nearly four weeks in now." She tittered into her glove. "Of course, I keep forgetting you've missed two of them. So much has happened during your absence, you know."

Clare's irritation flared. She wished they'd just get on with whatever this was. She had enough experience with this pair to sense they were leading her down a dark and twisting pathway, at the end of which probably awaited her own personal bogeyman. "Well, do either of *you* have a proposal in hand yet?" she retorted, though she knew they did not. The *Times* would have announced any significant betrothals, and she'd been sure to keep up on the news on that front. At their silence, she snatched up her gloves and reticule, keeping the book carefully hidden beneath. She was more than ready to quit the room and this fiasco of a friendship. "I didn't imagine so," she muttered.

Sophie placed a firm hand on her arm. "We only tell you this because you're our friend."

"*Are* you my friend?" Clare shook off Sophie's hand. "Because I was given the distinct impression earlier this evening that you cared little enough for that history when you gave me the direct cut."

For a moment Clare felt like cheering at their shocked expressions. After all, the value of the cut was the refusal to speak of it. Most girls suffered the humiliation in silence. By calling them out, she had snatched away a degree of the power they had tried to claim.

But then Sophie's lips firmed. "It wouldn't have done to have you join our little group and be hurt by what Mr. Alban was saying."

"How," Clare asked, incredulous now, "would Mr. Alban saying he had called on me be something that would hurt me?"

"Because it made it obvious to everyone," Rose piped up.

"Made *what* obvious?" Clare snapped.

Sophie shrugged. "He doesn't want you as a wife."

"Then what is his interest?" Clare wondered if she ought to bring out *Cousin Bette* after all and slam it down over both their heads. "Why would he have come to call on me, not once, but twice?"

Sophie's laugh held the stamp of authority. "That *is* the question, isn't it?"

Clare glared at her. Sophie's particular brand of battle specialized in the long, drawn-out siege, and this one had all the makings of a blockade to rival even Carthage. Something dark and feral loosened in her chest as she contemplated Sophie's motives. This was nothing close to a little petty jealousy. Sophie knew she had her sights set on Alban, and had apparently decided to thwart her. The odd thing was, Clare wasn't even sure she *wanted* to marry Mr Alban anymore.

But she was quite sure she didn't want Sophie to have him either.

"I am beginning to suspect," she said slowly, "your obsession with this topic has less to do with Alban's interest in me and more his *lack* of interest in you."

Sophie smiled, making the fine hairs on the back of Clare's neck prick to attention. "Honestly, Clare, are you really that naive? So sweetly innocent of what is being said about you in halls more hallowed than Eton?" Her eyes sparkled. "Oh yes, I've known since the start of the Season, but it seemed a secret worth keeping until the right time."

The floor felt uneven beneath Clare's feet, and the pulse she had worked so hard to calm began to thump in her ears. "Peter . . . is your brother, I presume?"

At her friend's triumphant nod, she finally realized the full truth. Sophie had known about this rumor. Possibly even started it herself.

Worse, Sophie had enthusiastically encouraged her interest in Mr. Alban—the ton's most exciting and eligible new bachelor—since the first event of the Season, no doubt because the higher Clare aimed, the more entertaining her fall.

It was unfathomable.

And it was pure, vintage Sophie.

"You may as well accept your lot in life, Clare." Her upper lip curled, and Clare recognized the gesture well. It was the smile Sophie used exclusively for cringing wallflowers and sons of marquesses—a category in which Clare could see she now fit, thanks to the malicious gossip.

"What lot?" she choked out, though in truth she had a fair idea.

"Alban could only be interested in you for less honorable reasons than a betrothal now." Sophie gathered her skirts and motioned for Rose to follow with a sharp tilt of her chin. "After all, for a girl with your questionable origins, being offered a position as a wealthy man's mistress *might* even be considered a boon."

Chapter 22

aniel nearly collided with two young ladies pouring from the retiring room door. Choked as they were with unbecoming laughter, he didn't immediately recognize them, but then again, most of the women in attendance at these events seemed to blur into a big colorful knot, one he had no hope of unraveling.

Clare, it seemed, was the notable exception.

When he'd first met her, he considered her plumage to be identical to these preening birds. Now he found himself unable to even stand at a refreshment table and see anything or anyone but her.

The girls froze in mid-flight, staring up at him in surprise. The slighter blonde gave an admiring squeak that kindled a faint sense of recognition. The brunette tilted her head, and he couldn't help but feel she was calculating the perfect angle to best display the column of her neck. But he felt not even a flicker of interest in the girl.

How could he, when his thoughts were so squarely focused on Clare?

"Dr. Merial, I believe?" the brunette said, her voice like rich cream.

"Have we been introduced?" he asked distractedly.

A pout claimed the girl's full lips. "Never say you don't recall. We were introduced at Lord Cardwell's house."

He searched his memory. "Ah, yes." Though their names escaped him, these were Clare's so-called friends. The ones who'd thought him a footman.

He inclined his head in a slight acknowledgment. "I am, in fact, looking for Miss Westmore. Lady Austerley said she wasn't feeling well and might require medical assistance. Is she perchance in the retiring room?"

The two girls exchanged glances. "She is . . . ah . . . just inside," the blonde said.

The brunette smiled, the gesture all the more suspicious for its lack of warmth. "I am sure it would be all right if you went inside." She tugged on her friend's arm. "Come, Rose."

They clipped down the hallway without speaking further, but he could hear the staccato burst of giggles that followed them as they turned the corner. He frowned and took a step toward the retiring room door. No matter the taller girl's assurance it would be all right, such places were forbidden to the male members of the species. He had a bone-deep certainty Clare's friends had been up to no good, but he was less certain what to do about it.

Should he call out to her? Step inside?

In the end his deliberations proved unnecessary. Clare emerged from the room of her own accord, her head down and a book clutched tightly in her hands.

She stopped dead still when she saw him, her breath a faint hiccup in her throat. "Dr. Merial." She looked from right to left down the empty hallway, as if searching for co-conspirators or onlookers, but all souls save themselves were firmly in the hands of the soprano. "What are you doing here?"

"Lady Austerley said you seemed ill and suggested I check on you in the retiring room. And if not there, the library." His gaze fell to the book. "By the looks of things, I must presume you've not yet made it to the library."

"I am fine." She tried on a smile, but to Daniel's eye, it didn't quite fit. "Although how *thoughtful* of Lady Austerley to tell you not only of my discomposure, but also so specifically where you might find me. I am beginning to suspect the countess has meddlesome thoughts where we are concerned."

He did not disagree—but that did not mean he hadn't seized the opportunity.

"I must go." She swept by him, her skirts rustling with the threat of her imminent departure.

"There is no need to hurry back," Daniel said, just loud enough to be heard over the muted noise from the distant ballroom. "As you can hear, the music has already started, and the guests' attention will be firmly anchored elsewhere."

"Nonetheless, Mother will be looking for me."

"Your mother was with me when Lady Austerley asked me to check in on you. She trusts you will be safe with me."

She paused in mid-step, her shoulders stiff with disbelief. "Safe. With *you*?" Her harsh laugh bounced off the hallway's high ceiling, and the candles seemed to flicker their agreement.

She swung around to face him.

"Clare—"

She flinched. "Please," she whispered. "Don't call me that. Not in public."

He took a step toward her, and then another, until he

was close enough to trail a finger along the ridge of those pale, stiff shoulders, should he want to. No matter the overwhelming urge to touch her, to comfort her, he kept his fingers sensibly harnessed by his side. Now that he was closer, he could see how pale she was—paler, even, than she'd been the night of Lady Austerley's ball, and he'd thought her anemic then. "Is your ankle bothering you again?"

She shook her head mutely.

He studied her a moment, this girl he could not have, but could neither forget. She was wearing a gown of gold lace that hugged new, softer curves he couldn't help but notice a little *too* well. She was still slim, still exquisitely wrought.

It just didn't hurt his clinical sensibilities to stare at her angles anymore.

Outwardly, she seemed composed. Her chin was up, her eyes focused. But by now he knew this woman well enough that her usual physical reaction to emotion or embarrassment was a lovely high color, and her current pallor bespoke a deeper concern. But even with that evidence, it was the wrinkle between her brows that really gave her away.

She was anything but fine.

"You look as though you may still need a moment to compose yourself," he said, still trying to dissect the source of her discomfort. "Do you wish to return to the retiring room?"

She shook her head. "I'd prefer to not be cornered in there again, thank you very much."

Ah. So her friends *had* been up to mischief. Daniel felt a simmering anger toward the two young ladies, though he had little idea what had been said. He could imagine, though, recalling the barbed undercurrents of conversation he'd heard during the ball two weeks ago. Still, Clare had a spine of steel, no matter that she sometimes covered it with witless giggles and expensive gowns. Surely she could withstand a bit of mean-spirited banter from her friends.

"The library, then?" He gestured to the second hallway, a journey he well remembered from the night of Lady Austerley's ball. "It has a door with a lock, if I recall."

She looked pensively in the direction he indicated.

"And you *do* have a book," he pointed out. "You do not have to worry about your friends returning to bother you. I will wait here for you, and stand guard in the hallway until you feel well enough to return to the musicale."

She shook her head. "I would not force you to miss the music, Daniel."

He chuckled as the soprano reached for—and just missed—a high C note. "I assure you, it is a price I am willing to pay."

The groove between her brows deepened. "Why must you always be so kind?" she whispered, her voice barely audible. "So *perfect*."

Daniel winced. "I am neither of those things." He knew full well it was neither kindness nor perfection that engendered these protective feelings when he was around her. Kindness was a mild emotion. And a perfect gentleman would limit himself to its banality and acknowledge this simmering attraction between them for the danger it was.

The hazel eyes that haunted his dreams lifted to meet his, hanging on a beat of hesitation. "What if . . . I don't want you to wait in the hallway?"

Ah. So this was it. "Is it to be good-bye, then?" he asked softly. *Again.*

She swayed in place, and Daniel reflexively stretched out a hand to steady her arm. At that single touch, need arced through him and every good intention he possessed disintegrated in a cloud of greedy want.

"What if I don't wish you to say good-bye, either?" she said softly.

Daniel sucked in a surprised breath. If not good-bye, what was she asking for? But he couldn't bring himself to ask her to redefine the question, because she was turning away from him and taking a first hesitant step toward the waiting library.

"Clare," he began, "I don't think—"

But any objection he might have summoned became silenced by her second step.

He followed her, of course. He didn't just follow, he bloody well *chased* her, his heart jumping with an eagerness that ought to have scared them both.

And as they stepped through the open library door, he barely had enough sense to kick it closed and turn the key before she threw herself in his arms.

Chapter 23

Clare pressed her face against the cheap wool of Daniel's coat and simply breathed.

It was dark as sin in the library, no more than a few embers burning in the fireplace to illuminate their folly. As his arms tightened around her, the monsters outside the door began to recede. He didn't speak, just stood like the rock he had somehow become in her life, holding her. His fingers cupped the back of her head, and she shuddered into the gratifying feel of his hands. No doubt he was loosening a legion of hairpins, destroying the efforts of her maid.

She found she didn't care.

She blindly lifted her chin, seeking . . . *something.*

And then his lips met hers, warm and reassuring and—astonishingly—lacking any immediate demand. It was a far different kind of kiss than the others they had shared, and she nearly sagged in relief at how right it felt.

How long they stood that way, she couldn't have said. Ten seconds . . . ten minutes. Gently giving, sweetly taking.

But all too soon something shifted in her womb, unfurling like a flag on the wind. She was consumed by a restless stirring, a want she could not define. She squeezed her eyes shut and told herself she probably would have flung herself at poor Mr. Meeks if he'd appeared out of nowhere and smiled at her in such an understanding fashion. But it wasn't the uninspiring Mr. Meeks with his arms around her, in a darkened library, out of sight of anyone who might object.

It was Daniel.

And her initial desire for comfort was rapidly shifting to something far more potent.

With the alteration in her awareness came an alteration in the kiss itself. As if by mutual decree, it became more demanding. She felt as though she couldn't catch her breath, as if his lips had somehow stolen the air from her very lungs. Something unyielding pressed between them. Dimly, she became aware she was still clutching the book.

She flung it and her reticule to the floor, then fisted her freed hands in his coat, pulling him closer still, and then finally she was assured of the hard, delicious press of his body against hers. She parted her lips at the feel of him, and his tongue dove in, dancing against hers in a sensual sweep. There was a rhythm to his movements, a wicked promise, and she felt herself tipping greedily toward a place where things like ducal mansions and titles and gossip didn't matter.

She bit his lip, *hard*, and he pulled away with a guttural oath that stirred her nearly as much as his kiss. The knowledge that she could strip his composure formed its own sort of pleasure. Emboldened, she ran an incautious hand down the front of his waistcoat, past the hard, flat abdomen that no gentlemen of the ton should possess, and cupped her hand around him.

His indrawn hiss of breath told her she had surprised him, but perhaps no more than she was surprising herself. Two weeks ago, in this very library, she had cringed at the idea of her mother seeking comfort in the arms of someone she should not.

Tonight she was well proving herself her mother's daughter.

His hands shot downward to grip her wrists. "For Christ's sake." His voice was hoarse, broken. He pulled her fingers away, bruising the vulnerable skin of her wrists. "I am beginning to question whether you are thinking clearly enough tonight to be trusted with me."

She stilled. "But . . . don't you want me?"

"I want you more than the air I breathe." His fingers loosened, but the loss of his touch somehow felt more painful than his grip. "But as you pointed out just yesterday, wanting and having are not the same thing."

Clare's eyes were adjusting now to the meager light. She could see his jaw was an objectionable, hard line. She reached a hand up to trace the edge of it, and the feel of his skin through the delicate fabric of her glove seemed as unyielding as his words. She was surrounded by the scent of him, soap and starch and that undefinable scent she could not name but that was so firmly associated with him. There was a roaring in her ears, and she could focus on nothing beyond the immediacy of these feelings.

She had no idea who she truly was in this moment, what mysteries of birth floated in her veins. No idea if tomorrow she would wake to regret this, or if she was doomed to wake again in lonely, tangled sheets, wanting more of this man. She felt as though she was groping her way along a darkened, unfamiliar corridor with nothing but a guttering match to guide her.

"What did you follow me for, if not this?" she asked. She knew he wanted her as well. She'd held the proof in her hand, had felt the wild leap of his pulse in that most intimate part of his body as her fingers had circled him so boldly.

"I followed you to make sure you were going to be all right."

Her eyes narrowed. Lowered. No matter the room's shadows, it was not so dark she could not see the impressive tent of his trousers. She knew an uncharacteristic— and unladylike—flash of relief that he could not deny it. "Your body suggests otherwise."

He shifted uncomfortably. "Your heart needs comfort tonight, Clare, not ruin. I am enough of a gentleman to offer you one without the other."

Clare felt knocked off-balance by the absurdity of it. He was nothing close to a proper gentleman, and they both knew it. And yet . . . she was quite sure none of the polished dandies locked outside the door would have turned down what she offered.

She stepped forward, intending to kiss him again, test his mettle, change his mind.

But his hands snaked out to grasp her arms, just above where her elbow-length gloves ended. His grip tightened, a cautious warning. "Remember the man you tempt, Clare. The son of a Roma horse trader. A man who will never enjoy a seat in the House of Lords."

She felt her anger stir at his unholy restraint. Couldn't he just hold her tonight?

Kiss her again?

"Just yesterday you tried to convince me it didn't matter that I was the daughter of a viscount," she said, her voice shaking. "Is this a game to you now? A punishment for my refusal of you then?"

"A game would be far more pleasurable, don't you think?" He released her, then tugged a hand through his hair, as if he could somehow extract the truth from his roots "The damned thing is, you were right. You lay your head on a Mayfair feather bed every night, while I spend my evenings alone, hunched over my desk in a god damned hovel on Aldersgate Street. You live in a gilded cage. I live in a part of Smithfield I wouldn't wish you to visit in your nightmares."

Clare realized then, with a clarity that could only come from the most profound sort of embarrassment, that he was rejecting her. *Refusing* her. It was a scalding realization. Her cheeks burned as she considered how she had just touched him.

"I see," she said bitterly.

Daniel muttered an incoherent oath. "No, damn your eyes, I can see you *don't* see." He pulled her once again into the makeshift shelter of his arms. "I'll not have you thinking your touch or your regard means so little to me. I care for you, Clare." She could feel his chin resting against the top of her head and the shudder of breath releasing from his lungs. "Probably *too* much."

"Then . . . why?" she asked miserably into his coat.

Or rather, why not?

"Because I don't only want a moment." He pulled back and glared down at her, looking for all the world as though he could not decide whether to ravish her or shake her. "As tempted as I am, I refuse to do something I would be forced to disavow come morning. I cannot in good conscience take what you have offered and then turn you over to your bloody future duke. If a night— a moment—is all you have to give, there is too much at stake here, for both of us."

In the dim light his explanation felt almost too intimate to bear. She felt numb—but not so numb that his words couldn't kindle *some* irritation. After all, he had no capital in this fight. She was the one teetering on the edge of ruin, so desperate for the comfort to be found in his arms she'd been blind to the fact that if nothing else she at least still had a choice.

Pride, though, was a sticky thing. "I can well see how my own reputation would be in tatters if you were not the gentleman you've proven yourself to be," she said, shaking now with the knowledge of just how close she had come to that very disaster. Because while Daniel's was the face she saw in her dreams, she could still not quite envision it as the face she saw in her future. "But you are a man. Impervious to ruin, by design. What is at stake for *you*?"

He scoffed, a rueful sound she felt beneath her very skin. "Do you think an instructor's salary at a charity hospital pays so well? My experiments—be they successes or failures—are paid out of my own pockets, and I depend on my reputation as a physician to find outside clients in order to secure more funding. But if any hint of impropriety leaks out, I promise you, no one will trust me with their families." He swallowed. "With their *daughters*."

His words stirred her muted conscience. Until this moment she had been pursuing only her own admittedly selfish needs, and she suddenly felt ashamed by the oversight.

But he was not yet through tormenting her. "A decision like this could not be undone. Think of your dowry," he said, his tone softening now. "The almost certain loss of it if you marry a man outside your family's approval. Think of your future. Your *children's* futures."

She did. And took a step away.

"YOU ARE SAYING it is impossible. That no one would be that brave."

"Not impossible." Daniel hesitated. When she'd first touched him so boldly, he'd experienced an understandable surge of lustful anger. He'd wondered whether she, too, saw him as nothing more than a handsome face, someone who might fulfill her needs without the attachment of emotions or strings. But that initial anger was fading. She was hurting. Confused. He needed to be honest with her, and push his own misgivings to one side.

But would the truth tempt her or terrify her?

"I've seen the example, in my own parents," he admitted. "You know my father was a horse trader."

"Yes," came her confused whisper. "But I do not see—"

"My mother's family was landed gentry, and her father objected to her choice. So they went to Gretna." Despite Clare's indrawn breath, he plowed on, committed to this course. "Her family refused to see her anymore, refused, even, to acknowledge me as their grandson. She was denied her dowry of five hundred pounds, cut off, isolated. But she never regretted marrying my father. She was happy, while she lived."

"She . . . died?"

"When I was ten. In childbirth, the babe along with her."

Her eyes flew wide in the dim light. "That doesn't *sound* very happy."

"I suppose it depends on your perspective." Daniel reached out, his hands relieved to finally have permission to touch her again, if only to lift her reluctant chin. "What I remember most about her was her smile. She was always laughing, always smiling. She loved my father enough to be that brave. I've seen a handful of other souls who share this feeling as well, couples standing hand-in-hand in the casualty ward, refusing to leave the other's side, risking illness and contagion even when an infection might take them both, in the end."

Clare shuddered. "That sounds dreadful."

"Yes. I suppose it does." His hand fell away and he smiled grimly. "And yet that's what I feel when I look at you. I could love you, Clare. So easily."

If he had imagined she would instantly echo a similar depth of emotion, her frozen silence told him he may have yet misjudged the moment. Whatever she had thought might happen here—and whatever she had imagined he might say—he could tell that this rending of his soul went beyond her comprehension. Worse, he'd taken this moment and turned it squarely back around on her. He wanted her. Desired her. Would be willing to marry her.

Which meant this was her refusal. *Her* impossibility.

"My dowry is not five hundred pounds, Daniel." She exhaled slowly, then shook her head. "'Tis five *thousand*. And what you're asking for . . . what you are suggesting . . . I can't," she whispered.

Daniel unclenched his fists. "I know," he said, hoping it came out more kindly than it felt. He had seen it in the wild flare of her eyes, the unconscious step back she'd taken when he'd spoken of her dowry and her future. He should be grateful for that clap of awareness. He was a bounder and a fool, and if nothing else, she was proving intelligent enough to recognize the danger he posed.

He never should have followed her in here. The thought of what had almost happened—the taste of her kiss, the feel of her slim hand as it had wrapped around his body—made him feel ashamed. Not of her. No matter that first flash of anger, he knew she was too innocent to know the path she'd been tripping blithely down. She'd been curious, perhaps, but far too injured tonight to know her own mind. He, on the other hand, had been too greedy, too blinded by hope and lust, to see where she intended to go. He should have seen the disaster unfolding and flung them both out of its barreling, unrepentant path.

Instead, he'd been caught off guard, bracing for impact several seconds too late.

At least tonight he had redeemed the spot in heaven

he'd endangered by kissing her to begin with. Probably an ivory pedestal with a seat of nails, reserved for martyrs, fools, and virgins. Not that he believed in a celestial version of heaven at the moment.

Or put much stock in virginity.

In fact, that was the real problem here. If she had been a lonely widow, perhaps they could have somehow found an accord. Found a way to help—and love—each other. But Clare was a well-bred innocent, and her future was a diamond-paved path stretching before her.

He was not well-bred, and his intentions were the furthest thing from innocent. He could offer her nothing but a bleak promise of happiness.

Ergo . . .

He stepped toward the library door. Turned the key. Pulled it open and looked from right to left. The hallway was empty, and he knew a moment's relief that fate would finally be kind. Beyond the open door he could still hear the god-awful soprano, warbling to the crowd.

There was time yet. Time to slip back unnoticed.

Untouched.

He turned back and met Clare's troubled gaze, illuminated by the slant of light from the hallway. His eyes lingered on the deep wrinkle between her brows, and a dark regret brewed in his gut to know he was responsible for placing it there. "And that is why you are going to leave this room now. Alone. No danger to your future. No harm done."

He could see her grappling with the decision, saw the exact moment she came to the correct one. He watched the change steal over her, the positioning of her bones for what was to come. She straightened her shoulders and walked toward the open door.

He watched her go, those gold skirts twitching about

her ankles. As she stepped into the light of the hallway, he could see her color had returned in spades. Whatever demons had chased her into his arms had been temporarily banished, at least. She did not look back.

And why would she? Her future lay before her.

And he was always meant to be left behind.

Chapter 24

Clare spent several unsettled minutes pacing outside the ballroom door, only finding the courage to step back into the thick, bright lights when the soprano ended her reign of terror.

She felt shattered by Daniel's confession.

Rearranged by her awareness of it.

She was returning to the musicale a changed person, and Sophie's waiting claws seemed a kinder punishment, somehow, than the look on Daniel's face when she had walked away.

He'd spoken of love. Of *marriage*.

She felt speared by the sheer impossibility of it, that he could envision it, much less speak of it. She might have doubts about who she was, but that did not mean she could so easily give up her hopes for her future. Had she once imagined a perfect marriage to be a casual conversation with a handsome duke, sitting across the breakfast table?

How naive, how silly, how *stupid* she had been.

Tonight Daniel had described the imposter, the thief, the poor cousin to her grand dreams. And yet, a part of her soul mourned the loss of the sort of idyll he had described.

The crowd broke into a smattering of not-quite-enthusiastic applause and began stirring. Clare stirred as well. She needed to find her mother, though she cringed to consider the condition she would likely find her in. At least with the evening's primary entertainment at an end, no one would question their decision to leave now.

But her search was arrested by Sophie and Rose, who stepped in close to flank her on either side. Oddly, they seemed to come from behind. "I wonder . . ." Sophie said, purring in her delicate, feline way, "where could you have you been for so long?"

"And who could you have been with?" Rose added nastily.

Clare clenched her fists and faced the pair, remembering Sophie's parting words. "Not with Mr. Alban, if that is what you are implying."

Sophie's laughter felt hollow at its core. "Oh, I don't think there's any question of that." She leaned in conversationally, and for a moment Clare could almost—*almost*—believe things were normal between them, that she wasn't Sophie's latest diversion to be toyed with and discarded once she stopped squeaking in protest. "I am not sure you should hold out hope he might consider you for his mistress now. He's been in the front row slavering over the soprano, you see."

A hint of jealousy rang faintly through Sophie's contempt, but Clare could not summon the energy for such an emotion herself. Two weeks ago the thought of Alban dancing with someone else—much less slavering over them—would have been worrisome. In this moment, she felt only a vague relief at the evidence that perhaps he was no longer interested in her. "That doesn't seem surprising," she managed to say, "given that it's a musicale."

"A musicale you've missed in its entirety," Rose pointed out.

Clare clenched her teeth. "I was in the library. Reading."

"An odd excuse for someone who has always claimed to dislike reading as much as you do," Sophie prodded. "Surely you can do better that."

Clare stared at the friends with whom she had once spent an entire Season but who didn't know her at all. But could she blame their ignorance? They, like everyone else, only knew the face she had put to the ton, the smiling girl who pretended to be dimwitted and unread.

At her silence, Sophie smiled. "There is no need to sidestep the issue. We know Dr. Merial was looking for you. In fact, we helped deliver him to your arms." She tossed something through the air. Clare caught it reflexively, only to realize with horror it was her beaded reticule.

The one she had left in the library.

Oh God, oh God, oh God.

Had they been hovering outside the entire time, waiting to pounce?

"By the looks of things, it seems as though he found you," Sophie said smugly. She reached out a hand and lifted the coil of hair lying across Clare's shoulder—hair she hadn't even realized had come down. "I wonder if Lady Austerley will still think so highly of her lauded doctor when she is told what mischief he has been up to with her guests?"

A memory stabbed at Clare then, of Daniel's hand, cupping the back of her head, hairpins flying. She jerked away from Sophie's hand and tried in vain to tuck her hair back in place.

"Perhaps someone should tell your mother," Sophie said next.

"Or the authorities," Rose added gleefully.

Clare's gut clenched. Because now they weren't just threatening to destroy *her*.

They were threatening to ruin Daniel as well.

She somehow found the courage to laugh as though she didn't care. "Feel free to tell my mother and Lady Austerley whatever you wish. Dr. Merial is naught but my family's physician, and he was only checking on my ankle's progress tonight, with both of their blessings."

"Progress?" Sophie scoffed. "Is *that* what you would call it?"

Clare schooled her smile into the sort of sneer Sophie herself would have been proud to claim. She had learned a great deal during her first Season as she had stood in the shadow cast by her friend's brilliance. And this moment called for her finest performance.

"It occurs to me that neither of *you* have such a handy excuse as a sprained ankle to have sought him out in the library. Perchance you harbor such an interest in Dr. Merial's activities because you fancy him yourself?" She tapped a glove finger against her lips, as if thinking of the most delicious secret imaginable. "I wonder what your parents would think—and what your many besotted admirers would imagine—if they knew how you followed him about?"

"But . . . we *don't* follow him about!" Rose protested.

"All that matters is whether they believe you might." Clare paused, letting the tension settle between them. "That is the thing about rumors, after all. They do not have to be true, as long as someone believes them."

Rose grew even paler than usual. "You wouldn't dare."

"Wouldn't I?" Clare stepped closer, enjoying the turnabout more than she should. She had never lied so well, but the beauty of this performance lay not in the details of the lie, but in pieces she could claim as truth. "To my recollection, you were both quite besotted with him that day in my drawing room."

"No one would believe such a thing, not coming from someone like you," Sophie sneered. "Your reputation is not what it was last Season."

No, it wasn't. They'd made sure of it, hadn't they? "You think no one would believe the rumors I would spin?" Clare smiled slowly, as if their ruin mattered not a whit to her. And in this moment she wasn't sure it did. She felt powerful, holding their burgeoning fear in her hands.

This is what it feels like, she willed them to understand. She could ruin them, so easily.

And some small meanness inside her whispered it would be only fair.

She recalled how Sophie and Rose had emerged from the hallway behind her, intent on mischief. They'd missed the spotlight and the music in order to do their worst. But in their desire to ruin her, they had neglected an important fact, and Clare found she was not above exploiting it. She turned Sophie's classic smile back on her now. "Have you considered that *your* absence from the musicale has likely been noticed by most of the guests in attendance?"

Sophie frowned, but Clare was not yet through. "I, at least, have a medical reason to see Dr. Merial. Lady Austerley and my mother even asked him to check in on me. But you both lack such an excuse, and your obsession with the man suggests perhaps some *personal* interest." She offered a soft, calculated laugh. "Although, I suppose I can understand why. Dr. Merial is quite handsome, handsome enough to tempt even the most wellborn of ladies to seek a bit of higher learning in a library. But the thing you fail to realize is that he's nothing but the son of a Gypsy horse trader." She let her false smile stretch wider, not even caring if her crooked tooth showed. "I am appalled you would set your sights so low, simply out of sordid curiosity."

She steeled herself for the expected denials. Waited, too, for her own regrets to settle. It didn't feel good to demean Daniel in such a way, but surely it was all justified, if only his reputation as a proper and trustworthy physician could be preserved. She'd felt the passion in his voice when he'd spoken of his experiments. His work was important, not only for him, but for the world. If she'd destroyed that tonight with her carelessness, she'd never forgive herself.

But the expected protests never came, and Clare became aware that perhaps her former friend's wide, worry-filled eyes were not even focused on her.

She turned slowly, to see Daniel standing not ten feet away.

Gone was the easy laugh that had so often greeted her in the drawing room. Gone, too, was the stark look of need that had chased her from the library not ten minutes ago. In that moment, he looked a handsome stranger, the chiseled planes of his jaw edged by some mysterious sculptor's hands.

There was no doubt he'd seen her, and not only the physical pieces of her person. She'd just given him a glimpse into her soul, shown him what she was capable of. She could be every bit as brutal as Sophie. She'd proven it, on any number of past occasions, through her withheld objections to their cruelty, if not her outright agreement with their antics.

I am not like them, her conscience wanted to scream.

But of course she was.

The scramble of slippers on the floor behind her told her Sophie and Rose were executing a hasty retreat. She exhaled in relief. She had silenced them—for now.

Called their bluff. Won Daniel a temporary reprieve from the mean-spirited gossip they had planned to distribute amidst the crowd like alms to the poor.

But at what cost to them both?

She opened her mouth, prepared to apologize to him now that their audience had flown, unsure of how much he had heard. But before she could, he turned from her.

Oh, God. What had she done?

And more to the point, what else *could* she have done?

She watched him walk away, the rigid line of his shoulders conveying a message more powerful than any words. She held herself in check as the distance between them widened, her hands clenched in her skirts. It was the only way to keep from to sinking to the floor and weeping in frustration as his departure became utterly clear.

"Is everything . . . all right?"

Clare looked up, and her heart shrank in her chest. *"Oh,"* she gasped. "Mr. Alban."

She looked around wildly. The crowd was thinning, drifting, leaving. It occurred to her that perhaps the future Duke of Harrington had come to drive the point home, to finish what Sophie and Rose had started but were now too frightened to finish. An attack dog, summoned to do their bidding. He'd certainly seemed held captive by their smiles earlier this evening, when he'd refused to save her from their cut. "I am just . . . just . . ." She clapped a gloved hand over her quivering, blabbering mouth.

And then tears started to fall in earnest.

"Come now," he said, his voice gruff. "You'll have them saying I've made you cry next."

"Next?" Clare peered up at him through tear-clogged eyes.

The handsome jaw she had once admired from across the space of a waltz hardened. "Your friends have been stirring mischief, I'm afraid. I can't abide gossip, and those two are among the most polished professionals I've ever had the misfortune to encounter."

Clare swiped at her eyes. "You mean . . . you don't believe them?"

He reached inside his coat, pulled out a handkerchief and handed it to her. "It is more that I am sorry others do. I did not realize my interest would be so obvious. Or that their response would be so vicious."

Interest? *Obvious?* If he believed them—which she couldn't help but notice he'd neither confirmed nor refuted—how could either of those things still be reasonably true?

Clare took the square of fabric he offered, scarcely knowing what else to do. It was plain white, embroidered about the edges in a scalloped blue thread. She lifted it to her nose and sniffed. No matter her running nose, she couldn't blow her nose in it.

It was a future *duke's* handkerchief.

She could scarcely bring herself to touch it wearing elbow-length gloves.

It hit her then, the impossibility of this dream she had harbored since the start of the Season. Even should her origins prove more definable than Sophie's rumors implied, the hint of them was the death knell for any chance of a match between her and someone like Mr. Alban.

Whether or not *he* believed them, others might. The wife of a duke must be beyond question. She couldn't in good conscience marry him knowing she would be naught but a liability about Alban's handsome, titled neck.

But if she was honest, that was not the only reason for this impossibility. The handkerchief he'd given her smelled of bay rum and leather, echoes of a life of privilege. They were scents she should be dreaming of, but which gave her no shivers at all.

In contrast, her glove—the one she had earlier clapped to her mouth—had smelled of soap and starch and Daniel.

And she wanted only to raise it to her nose again.

She held the handkerchief back out. "Mr. Alban, I appreciate your kindness. But I am afraid, in the matter of your stated interest, I cannot—"

"Clare!" Her mother's screech prematurely struck down that thought.

Clare turned to see her mother staggering toward her. She was dragging Mr. Meeks by the arm, and with a last, final lurch, deposited the bewildered man squarely in between Clare and Alban. "Have you heard the glorious news, Mr. Alban?" she wheezed. "Mr. Meeks has asked for my daughter's hand in marriage. Her father and I have every hope for a splendid match."

Alban looked between Clare and her mother. "I . . . er . . . no, I had not heard."

Clare glared at her mother. "That was *last* Season," she hissed, her cheeks as hot as a branding iron. Was her mother so drunk she'd forgotten? But no . . . Mother didn't look as she had on either of the two prior occasions when Clare had seen her in her cups. In fact, she looked steadier—and more determined—than she had in months.

"But she . . . ah . . . did not accept, by my recollection." Poor Meeks looked as though he wanted to shrink into the floor. Clearly, he'd not been privy to her mother's script. He mopped the top of his balding head with his hand, then darted a nervous glance toward Clare's mother. "Perhaps I should ask again?"

Mother flapped her hands with enthusiasm, as if it was now just a matter of drawing up the contract. "Yes, yes, of course. Come along, Mr. Alban, and let us leave them to their very important discussion."

"No." Clare snarled the word.

Everyone froze, looking at her.

She shook her head, and that coil of hair that had proven so damning earlier flopped down on her shoulder. It had given up, it seemed.

She refused to do the same.

No matter her prior plotting, Clare understood now that a future with Mr. Alban was impossible. Indeed, it was close to an unconscionable thought. He was kind, even familiar. But he engendered nothing by way of a romantic interest, and she could see now that he never had. But that did not mean she thought Mr. Meeks engendered it, either.

"I've a better idea," she ground out, even as she turned toward the door. "I am going home." And perhaps, if she were lucky, she would sprain both ankles climbing up into the coach, and might never have to come out again.

DANIEL PAID THE cab driver with his last few pennies and stepped into the sullen silence of his rooms. Even the crickets were quiet, perhaps sensing his black mood. He removed his hat and dragged both hands through his hair, but something felt wrong.

Christ. He was still wearing his evening gloves.

He ripped them off and flung them against a wall, and the slap of noise caused the frogs to splash awkwardly in their bowls. No matter Lady Austerley's meddling, he was through attending balls and musicales. He was beginning to wonder if the dowager countess's condition didn't possibly tip over into derangement, because she appeared to harbor a faith in him that went far beyond that of her more lucid peers. It wasn't as though wearing gloves had ever made a difference or turned him into a gentleman in the eyes of the ton.

He had been pretending to be something—someone—he was not.

Tonight, finally, he'd seen the futility in it. How stupid he had been in hoping for more. In hoping for *her*. The words he'd overheard Clare tell her friends might have merely been echoes of his own stated reservations, but they held a far different significance coming from her own lips. He thought back to the library, to the way she had touched him. He was a fool to even think she might respect him as a man, rather than a handsome toy to be brought out, played with, and then put away for another day.

His skin itched with resentment beneath the trappings of his best clothes, which still fell so short of her expectations. He felt desperate to expend his anger and energy into something productive. But if that something was not Clare—as he had imprudently, briefly hoped tonight— then what else was there?

He began to bump about in the darkness, feeling for the lantern he'd left on the table. He struck a match, but a sudden knock on the door sent him jumping before he could set it to the wick. He burned his finger and nearly dropped the thing.

"Dr. Merial." A soft scratch trailed against the door. "Are you awake?"

"Oh, damn it all to hell," he snarled beneath his breath, letting the match gutter out.

Mrs. Calbert.

He stood silent in the darkness, willing her to move on. It was after midnight. She should be asleep in bed. Her *own* bed.

And he was far too irritated to deal with her tonight.

The scratching came again, but he ruthlessly ignored it. If Mrs. Calbert was in need of a physician for some legitimate medical complaint, she ought to have enough sense to knock louder. And if she was in need of something *else*, she was going to have to bloody well knock on another tenant's door.

Finally, the shuffling outside his door ceased and he dared to light the lamp. His amorous landlady was becoming a problem he didn't want to think about, and he wondered if a firm word—or a well-placed suggestion of venereal disease—might dissuade her. He placed the lamp on the table, and the light fell over an array of papers, scribbled notes and haphazardly organized thoughts. He sat down heavily in his chair and thumbed through the mess of last night's frenzied experiments—prophetic, he supposed, for the mess of his life. There was hope there, to be sure.

But there was also regret. Missed starts and wasted potential.

He tossed the notes aside. *Ah, God, Clare.*

He lowered his head into his hands. What a muck of an evening it had been. Was it possible to want someone so much, when the wanting itself had the power to destroy them both? He'd been raised to believe love was possible. Important, even. He'd found it by chance, and lost it tonight by design. In his heart, he understood it was the right thing for Clare.

But that didn't mean he was bound to enjoy the process.

The anesthetic regulator lay on its side, mocking him. He reached out and picked up the brass mask, running a finger along its velvet lining. Too finely made for frogs, but then, it had been fashioned to use on humans. He was so close to proving his theories correct . . .

And yet tonight he'd neglected to finish the experiment, choosing to go to a bloody musicale instead. Not at the request of a dying countess, but because of the mere *hope* of encountering a pair of hazel eyes and damnably kissable lips.

More fool he.

He turned the mask over in his hand, remembering the excitement he'd felt describing his findings to Lady Austerley. What in the hell was he *doing*, gallivanting about London, stealing kisses from a woman who thought herself far above him? Six months ago he'd left behind a dependable practice, people he cared about. He'd been possessed of a grand idea, and he'd taken the miserable position at St. Bart's because the Royal College would never give credence to a paper written by a poor country doctor.

He'd sacrificed everything to see this through.

And now he needed to complete his damned experiment.

Daniel picked up his notes again, running over his prior observations, sorting out the last necessary steps. He could see it unfold before him, a few hours of work, at most. Grimly, he picked up his pen. His father had died, and there was no changing it.

But others could still be saved, if he could only get his head refocused.

Chapter 25

One would think an advantage of lying wide-awake, staring at the ceiling and mentally reliving the terrible events of the prior evening, would at least ensure some punctuality for breakfast. But Clare had drifted off to a fitful sleep just before dawn, and barely managed to pull herself from bed when she heard the clock in the hallway strike nine.

As she trudged into the dining room, her siblings' banter and the scents of toast and herring washed over her. Geoffrey and Lucy were leaning over their plates, arguing industriously with Father, who—perhaps in a bid to make up for yesterday's shortcomings—looked clean-shaven and neat this morning.

Everything was back to normal, it seemed.

Everything, that was, except her.

Clare sank into her chair and numbly accepted the cup of coffee a servant pressed into her hand. Out the dining room window she could see a gray, dreary morning brewing. It was the sort of weather that prompted one to wear a cloak over their summer walking dress.

Not that she was brave enough to walk about Hyde Park today, weather or no.

Not after the damage Sophie had wrought last night.

She took a long sip from her cup, then looked up to realize three pairs of eyes—each markedly and agonizingly different from her own—were staring at her.

Geoffrey spoke first. "Good God, sis. Did you sleep in a gutter?"

Lucy smacked him on one shoulder. "Be kind, Geoffrey." But then an impish smile claimed her lips. "Because gutter or no, she clearly didn't sleep *at all*." Her smile trailed away as Clare glared at her. "Was the musicale truly so awful?"

Clare gripped her cup. "Why would you presume it was awful?"

Was it somehow written on her skin? Stamped upon her forehead?

Father cleared his throat over the lowered edge of his paper. "You . . . ah . . . look to have not brushed your hair."

Clare lifted her hand, and cringed to discover her hair was indeed a wild snarl about her face. Breakfasts at home might be informal, but—with, perhaps, the exception of Lucy—its preparations usually involved at least a hairbrush.

"I do not wish to talk about it," she whispered.

Indeed, she didn't wish to so much as *think* about it.

But unfortunately, her thoughts could not be as easily schooled as her tongue.

Lucy gave her a sympathetic grimace, then turned back to their father. "As I was just saying, the entire business of hunting up a husband is barbaric. Why, look at how miserable Clare is! Why shouldn't a woman's dowry be given directly to her, in the event she does not marry? It hardly seems fair that a gentleman's inheritance is given to him outright on the occasion of his majority, but a woman's is given only to her husband on the occasion of her enslavement."

Geoffrey snorted. "Who would take you, unless Father paid them for the displeasure?"

"It's fortunate you're not a woman, then, because I can't envision a scenario in which someone would take *you* without fair recompense," Lucy snapped in return. She leaned forward. "I am serious, Father. The practice is positively medieval."

"How appropriate, given you are like the plague," Geoffrey quipped.

"Oh, do shut *up!*" Lucy threw up her hands. "It nearly guarantees a woman is saddled with someone who views her as little more than property."

Father took off his spectacles and cleaned them with the edge of a napkin. "This talk of dowries and enslavement seems premature, given you've not even had your Season. As we have already discussed, your dowry will be delivered into the hands of the gentleman you marry, provided he meets with my approval." He looked almost longingly toward the door. "And really, shouldn't you be speaking of this to your mother? She should be here, answering your questions about husbands and the like. Instead she's always . . ." His voice faltered. " . . . in *bed.*"

Through the weight of her own misery, Clare's gaze lifted in surprise. It was the first indication she'd ever had that perhaps Father regretted their mother's absence as much as she appeared to object to his. But even as she tried to reconcile his words with any kind of logic, her thoughts were already tripping down a different path. This talk of dowries was alarming, and worse, converged squarely with yesterday's terrible argument with Daniel. She'd known from the moment she'd understood the implications of her gender that she was a marketable, five thousand pound boon to a future husband. It was a security she'd never questioned before now.

But if Father *wasn't* her real father—as anyone with eyes in their head must surely question—would it even be ethical to accept it?

He began to fold the *Times*, a signal he was about to be off to his club, though Clare herself was beginning to have doubts about the nature of this mythical "club." A waiting mistress seemed increasingly more likely. But if it was a mistress who claimed his attention each day, why had he indicated a wish this morning that Mother would join them for breakfast?

"Take this Alban chap, for example," Father continued as he laid the folded paper down in front of him. "He's the sort I would have no concerns with. Should Clare marry him, I would have no objections to honoring the terms of her dowry."

"Well, of course not. He's going to be a blasted duke," Lucy muttered to no one in particular. "It makes *perfect* sense to give the money to someone who doesn't even need it."

Their father started to rise, and Clare's anger began to poke through the gray shell of the morning. "Father, can you put off your club for five minutes?" she demanded. "One would think you had another family to run off to."

Her father's eyes widened through his spectacles. "I did not realize . . . that is . . ." He lowered himself slowly back into his chair, looking shocked by her outburst. "I suppose I could spare a few more minutes. Did you have something you wished to discuss?"

Clare gripped her cup of coffee as if it could save her. If she couldn't outright probe the details of her legitimacy, what other pieces of this puzzle could she explore? She thought back on the stir Mr. Alban had created upon his arrival at the start of the Season, a freshly minted temptation. He'd not been born to the promise of the title, and was named Harrington's heir only through a series of unforeseen misfortunes. It had been easy for everyone— male and female alike—to overlook the shadows of his birth when his future burned so brightly.

But what if it hadn't been so easy?

"What if Mr. Alban wasn't the Duke of Harrington's presumptive heir?" she pressed. "Would he still meet your approval then?"

"It's rather a moot point. He *is* Harrington's heir." Her father took off his spectacles and rubbed his eyes. "I have no worries he will make you a fine husband, should your conscience lead you in that direction."

Clare lifted her chin. "And if my conscience led me in the direction of another gentleman?"

Father shifted in his chair. "I want you to be happy, Clare. If someone else has caught your eye, I could be persuaded to give consent. Provided, of course, I felt assured he would make you a good husband."

"What if he is not a peer?" Clare breathed, knowing her question ran deeper than that.

Father replaced his glasses. "If you have set your sights on a second or third son, I could give my consent if I believed you truly loved the man." He stared at her a long moment down the bridge of his nose. "But do not forget, you are the daughter of a viscount. There are certain expectations in your position. I should not have to remind you of that."

A terse silence descended.

"At the risk of pointing out the obvious," Lucy finally said, her voice small and pinched, "we can marry whomever we want when we reach our majority."

"Not if you expect your dowry," Father answered with an irritated sigh.

Clare felt as though a veil were being pulled slowly from her eyes. The world had well and truly shifted into something unrecognizable if Lucy was suddenly defending a woman's right *to* marry.

But Father did not seem to notice. He stood up again. "It is the way things are done," he frowned, "and I assure you both, I've made as many sacrifices in that area as anyone." He tugged at his waistcoat. "So I suggest you both refocus your heads. Lucy, you *will* have a Season next year, and your mother and I both expect you to make a proper go of it." His eyes shifted to Clare and gentled a bit behind the glare of his spectacles. "And Mr. Alban is interested, hmm? Why muddy this up any further?"

Her mother's gasp echoed from the doorway. "Mr. Alban has asked you to marry him?"

Clare turned in her seat. The gray light filtering in from the window fell across Mother's face and landed in every faint line, making her look every inch of her forty years. But despite her frank exhaustion—and despite the fact Clare couldn't remember the last time she'd arisen before noon—very much awake.

Father began to sidle toward the door, his head down, eyes averted.

Mother stepped aside to let him go, though her gaze followed her husband's retreating figure. "Geoffrey, Lucy," she murmured. "I would like a moment to speak with Clare about last night."

"Does this have something to do with her hair?" Geoffrey asked, too cheerfully for the weight of the morning.

Mother turned back to face them, sparing Clare's hair scarcely a glance. "And I would speak to her *alone*."

"But I haven't finished my plate," Lucy protested.

"Then take it with you to your room." Mother frowned, stepping inside and pointing toward the waiting hallway.

Her siblings scrambled to their feet. Lucy tossed Clare

a worried look as she made her exit, clutching her plate. Clare watched them go broodingly, mentally shoring herself up for a lecture on her behavior last night. As Mother dismissed the servants and closed the dining room door behind them, unease rippled through Clare. The silence was far too grave for just after nine o'clock in the morning.

Worse, Mother said not a word about the coffee in Clare's hand.

"I must speak to you about last night." Her mother sat down heavily in the chair beside Clare, the words sounding methodical.

"Yes, I believe you mentioned that," she answered coolly.

"I can admit I've been a bit . . . *distracted* this Season." Her mother's eyes drifted hazily toward the picture window, as though she were trying to recall the words she wished to say. "Too distracted, unfortunately, to realize Mr. Alban's growing interest in you. I should have paid more mind, should have watched you more carefully. But now that the damage is done, I must insist you do nothing to further encourage his interests. Mr. Meeks is a far better choice."

Clare's chair seemed to twitch beneath her. *Not this again.* "I do not wish to marry Meeks, as I've already said." She was growing irritated by her mother's lack of logic on the matter. In truth, she harbored no wish to marry Alban either, but shouldn't her mother be thrilled her daughter might set her sights on a duke? "Why are you so insistent on this match with Meeks? It has always felt as though you were pushing me toward him, when I've never expressed an interest in the gentleman beyond polite regard."

Her mother's gaze swung back to Clare, pleading now. "I felt he was . . . suitable."

"Suitable?" Clare said harshly, shocked by her moth-

er's simplistic view of the process. "Surely there are more important things about finding a husband than his suitability. What about respect? Mutual interests? Affection?"

Her mind tripped further, thanks to Daniel's confession last night. *What about love?*

"You must trust me on this." Her mother's lips firmed. "I had hoped you would quickly find a good match your first Season, but you seemed determined to stretch it out. Can't you see how dangerous that is? It is important to see you settled, as soon as possible. And a suitable husband is better than a disastrous mistake."

Clare slowly drew her hands away from her cup of coffee. There was a troubling undercurrent to her mother's anxiety on the topic. "Nonetheless," she said slowly, her fingers bunching in her skirts, "I will not marry Mr. Meeks."

"Someone else, then." Her mother's voice hitched. "Anyone but Mr. Alban."

Clare dwelled on that an uncomfortable moment. This was not only about making the best match possible, then. There was no sane world in which her mother would look at the handsome, winning heir to the Duke of Harrington and think he was an unsuitable choice.

Unless it was morally wrong.

Years of childhood musings, the recent rumors, and Mother's strange behavior distilled down to a single, gasping suspicion. "What is Alban to me?" Clare hesitated, afraid of her mother's answer, and yet increasingly sure her life and her future depended on ferreting out the truth. "And what is he to *you*?"

To her credit, this time her mother did not look away toward the temptation of the nearby window. "Alban is your uncle."

Clare's cheeks burned with embarrassment, but not, unfortunately, disbelief. *Her uncle.* Could it be true? She conjured an image of him in her mind, focusing on the familiar slope of his nose, the color of his eyes.

Arguably more similar to her own features than her own siblings'.

"I never thought to have to tell you," her mother continued, her voice sounding far less rehearsed now. "Really, to tell *anyone*. But it is clear my selfishness has put you in danger."

"How?" Clare demanded, scooting her chair closer. She leaned in, as if proximity could somehow extract the facts with greater efficiency and less pain. "And I would know *all* of it, Mother. I think you owe me the truth, at least."

Beads of unladylike perspiration shone against her mother's forehead. "My desire to see you quickly married and settled is complicated." She took up a napkin from the table and blotted her temple. "I know something of disastrous mistakes, you see. Too impulsive, I suppose, and prone to rash mistakes. We are not unalike in temperament, you and I, and that is why I have always felt it important to see you settled quickly."

Clare privately disagreed with her mother's assessment of her personality, given that her every move during both Seasons had been carefully orchestrated—right up to the point she had sprained her ankle. Only then had her carefully constructed plans been turned on end. But instead of contradicting her, she reached out her hand and covered her mother's fingers with her own, squeezing gently. "Go on."

Her mother unleashed a tremulous sigh. "When I was nineteen, I fell in love with a young man named Benjamin Alban—Mr. Alban's older brother, though at the time their family's connection to Harrington was so distant there was never a thought of possible succession. He was neither wealthy nor titled, but I loved him fiercely. Against my wishes—or perhaps because of them—my parents entered me into a betrothal with someone else, someone who *was* wealthy and soon to be titled."

"Father," Clare choked out.

Her mother nodded, looking down at their joined hands. "I was young and impetuous and determined to have my own way in this." Tears welled up in her eyes. "Benjamin and I left for Gretna, and I . . . that is, *we* were in a dreadful carriage accident, just over the border." The anguish on her face appeared fresh, and perhaps, in this moment, it was. "He was killed when the carriage rolled over."

Clare gasped. She didn't know this man being described to her, but she was, after all, hearing about the death of the man she had just been told was her father.

"My parents spirited me away and insisted I breathe nary a word of it, to anyone. As my injuries were healing, they cleaned up my mess in the most expedient way possible. Within a few weeks I found myself married to your father by special license."

"But . . . you didn't *want* to marry Father," Clare said, her heart pounding. Her mind flew inexplicably to Lucy's claims of enslavement. "You could have refused, after all."

"Could I have?" Her mother's smile seemed breakable. "I was too numb to protest. Injured and hurting. Possibly not even in my right mind." Finally, there came a hesitation in the story tumbling out of her. "And you were born seven months later."

Clare was stunned. Not only from the shock of it, but her mother's confession that she had done something so . . . so . . . unlikely. *So brave.* And she could see, quite clearly now that the pieces had been fit into place, that her mother had done it for her.

"Does . . . Father know?" she asked, torn between relief to finally know and dread over what this meant to the people she loved. "That I am not his true daughter?"

"How could he not suspect, given the timing of your

birth and the stark physical differences between you and Lucy and Geoffrey?" A tear rolled down her mother's cheek. "The truth is, your father is a good man. Though we've never spoken of it, I don't think it matters to him whose blood runs in your veins. He loves you very much. You must know that."

Clare hesitated, still trying to sort through it all. In this moment, she couldn't even begin to wrap her head around what these revelations meant for her or her future.

She was too consumed by these details of her past.

"Did you ever love Father?" she asked, pulling her hand away. She was shocked to realize she might no longer even be able to call him that, and an angry hurt burrowed beneath her skin at the unfairness of that fact. "I mean, Lord Cardwell?"

"There is no need for that." Her mother sighed. "He is still your father, Clare, in every way that matters." She smiled grimly. "I cannot deny we have had our difficulties. And I am sure much of it was my fault. I did not tell him about any of it before we married—it was important my reputation be unblemished, my parents said, or it could be considered a breach of promise. But even after we married, I could not bring myself to speak of it."

"So you have lied to him all these years," Clare said bitterly.

"You have much to learn about matters between a husband and wife, Clare." Her mother shook her head sadly. "How could I tell him I loved someone else? He was a good man, and he deserved a wife who would give him a chance. But it turns out I was not the only one who lied. Your father was none too happy to marry me either. He had a mistress when we married, someone he apparently loved but who was unsuitable in character and breeding to be the wife of a future viscount. He never told me about her, and he eventually ceased all contact with the woman. But two months ago he received a letter. It seems his former mistress bore him a daughter, and that young woman reached out to him after her mother's death."

The room spun, and Clare clapped a hand over her mouth to capture the gasp that insisted on escaping her lips.

Oh God, oh God, oh God. How many hidden relatives would be uncovered here today?

"I have objected to the association, of course," Mother went on, her voice growing hard now. "But since we arrived in London for the start of the Season, he has insisted on spending all of his time with her."

Clare closed her eyes as she considered her father's recent absences. *He is going to her,* Mother had said, that night over dinner.

Not a mistress, as they had all suspected.

A daughter.

She opened her eyes, stunned to her core. "What . . . what is she like?"

"What is she *like*?" Her mother's voice cracked. "She is *younger* than you, Clare. Which means he was unfaithful to me, at least at the first. And now he is proposing bringing her here, to Cardwell House." She drew a deep breath. "A bastard child, living under our roof . . . I cannot bring myself to agree. How can he ask it of me?"

Clare hesitated, unable to see the cause for panic. After all, *she* was a bastard child living under this roof. And if disastrous mistakes had been made on both sides, it seemed a little compassion was going to be necessary to set things to rights. "I would imagine," she said softly, "if Father just learned of her existence, he would want to make amends for being absent in her life."

But Mother stubbornly shook her head. "It is too much. We would not be received."

Clare raised a brow. "I am not sure I mind, truth be

told. The Season holds less interest for me this year than I had hoped." She thought back to last night's whispers. The stares.

The cut.

"Oh, I am not so worried for you." Mother waved a dismissive hand. "You've friends enough among the ton to survive it. But Lucy has not even had the benefit of a chance at a Season yet. This could very well destroy her meager chances for a suitable match, before she has a chance to even come out. We must be careful of appearances, for *her* sake."

Given that Lucy had just this morning loudly bemoaned the very idea of marriage, Clare wasn't sure the argument held water. And to hear the word "suitable" again grated every bit as much upon her nerves as the last time her mother had uttered it.

"If you are so worried about appearances," she pointed out, "why did you risk an indiscretion in Lady Austerley's library? If someone had discovered you, it would have been every bit as damaging as this."

Her mother raised a hand to her temple, and Clare could see that it trembled. "Please . . . try to understand. No matter our rocky start, your father and I had finally reached an accord in our marriage. Possibly, even, found a measure of strong affection. But the appearance of this girl has destroyed all of that. He was clearly unfaithful to me, at least in the beginning, and my vanity was wounded by his confession. I . . . I am afraid that night at the ball I sought the wrong sort of comfort. I admit, there was a part of me that felt justified in hurting your father, but my mind had been muddled by the champagne I had consumed. I did not think of how I might also be hurting you." She winced. "And for what it's worth, I have already apologized to your father. I realize, now, that discretion is paramount to preserve our family's reputation."

Though it was gratifying to hear that this, at least, was no longer a secret she needed to guard from Father, Clare remained worried. Her mother had good reason to be concerned about the damage that could be done by gossip, but Lucy's reputation was largely a *future* concern. In contrast, Sophie's malicious gossip had already spread, and the knowledge of what people already knew—or thought they knew—tilted in.

"I am afraid," Clare said slowly, "that discretion in matters of our family's private affairs is now out of our hands. There are already rumors circulating on the matter of my legitimacy." She swallowed. "Or rather, my illegitimacy. And it is a stretch to imagine my 'friends' might carry me through it, when they are the ones who have fueled the gossip from the start."

"But, *how*?" her mother gasped. "How would they know? I've never told a soul."

"I don't know," Clare admitted. "But Lady Sophie is at the center of it, and she did her worst last night, I am afraid."

There was a moment of silence, and then her mother stood up and began to pace in a small circle. "Then you are truly out of time, Clare. Can't you see?" She threw up her hands. "You *must* seize the opportunities you have, before they disappear. Mr. Meeks will have you, I think, even with the rumors."

Clare shook her head, more sure of this than anything else. "I can understand wanting to see me settled, but how could you think to force me to the same unhappy circumstance of a marriage that you and Father have had? How could you force me to repeat your mistakes?" She rose slowly, straightening to her full height. "I do not want to merely reach an accord in my own marriage, Mother. I do not want to settle for the worst and hope for something tolerable. How could you encourage me to marry a man

I do not love, when that very thing has caused so many problems in your own life?"

Her mother stopped her pacing and frowned. "Do you love someone, then?"

For Clare, the pieces settled into place, a perfect, terrifying fit. She didn't know if she loved Daniel, but she at least knew that what she felt for him was different. Perhaps not yet different enough to toss her on a coach to Gretna. Perhaps not yet even enough to give up the promise of five thousand pounds a year.

But different enough to at least say no to the easy answer Mr. Meeks presented.

In suffering this fall from grace, it occurred to Clare that *she* now had a choice. She had been thrown to the bottom of this well, but she was gamely treading water, refusing to drown. Surely fate was by now wrung out with trying—and failing—to shove her under. She needn't marry anyone she didn't wish, her future and her dowry be damned.

Moreover she had a new sister, one whose blood was not of her own, but one who deserved to know the love of a father.

"I cannot yet say if what I feel is love." Clare took a deep breath. "But I intend to find out."

"But . . . who is it?" her mother pressed, looking stricken. "Is it someone I know?"

But Clare only shook her head. Her mother wasn't the only one who could keep secrets. "I am not yet ready to say. But if I were asked my opinion on the matter of this girl, the one who has caused so much discord between you and Father, I would say let Father bring the young woman here. Let her know her family."

There was already one bastard child living under the roof of Cardwell House.

What was one more, in the grand scheme of things?

Dear Diary,

Dicere quae puduit, scribere jussit amor.

What I am ashamed to say, love compels me to write.

It sounds like something Daniel would say, and I cannot tell whether the fact brings me more comfort or distress. The difficulty is that I am not entirely certain I understand what love is. It is clear my parents have not provided the example, and in truth, I cannot think of a single member of the ton whose marriage does. Last night Daniel told me I was someone he believed he could come to love, and I was too afraid to accept the gift of such regard.

But if love is a puzzle I need to unravel, I suspect simply scratching down words in my diary is not going to suffice.

Chapter 26

As Clare knocked on what seemed like her hundredth Smithfield door, it occurred to her that evening was beginning to settle in with earnest. The thought sent a frisson of fear through her. She pulled her wet cloak tighter about her shoulders and held her breath to avoid breathing in the sour ammonia smell wafting from the nearby alley. The wet wool—a byproduct of an unfortunate late afternoon thundershower—did little to ward off the encroaching chill of night. Worse, the shadows stretched around her, taunting her with long fingers.

She'd naively imagined that when Daniel said he lived in Smithfield, she had a navigable point of reference. But the rookeries of Aldersgate Street were a complicated tangle of tenement houses and side streets that had apparently escaped the notice of London's cartographers. Her walking map, purchased on Bond Street and no doubt intended for wealthy foreign tourists, held little sway amidst these twisted alleys, if indeed she still had it to consult.

But it had unfortunately disappeared along with her reticule, neatly nipped within the first quarter hour of her arrival in Smithfield. The dainty ribbon handle—so fashionable in Mayfair—had proven an astonishingly easy mark here. Gone, too, was the fifteen shillings the bag had held, insurance for a return hackney should she be unsuccessful in finding Daniel.

Which was looking more and more like a distinct possibility.

After no luck searching for him at St. Bartholomew's hospital, she'd spent the past few hours knocking on random doors. More often than not the doors that opened sheltered haggard young women with squalling babies on their hips, or grizzled souls too bent and haggard to venture out onto the streets. None did more than crack open the door and peer out with suspicion.

Her latest attempt appeared to be faring little better. She knocked again, growing desperate enough to consider trying the latch on the door, if need be. But the door—which appeared to have once been painted a cheerful red but had long since faded to a nauseating pink—finally opened. A woman of middling years peered out, and with her, a puff of air escaped, liberally laced with the smell of rising bread. She dusted her flour-covered hands on her skirt. "May I help you?"

Clare breathed a sigh of relief, and not only because the homey scents provided a welcome counterbalance to the stench from the nearby alley.

Here, at last, was someone reasonable, offering her a proper greeting.

"Oh yes, thank you. I am ever so glad you opened the door."

"Well, I don't have any rooms to let at the present, and I don't take on female boarders," the woman said. "Too much trouble."

"You mistake my inquiry, Mrs. . . . ?"

"Calbert."

"Ah. Well, good evening, Mrs. Calbert, I am looking for someone who told me he rents a room in this area. His name is Dr. Daniel Merial, and he told me he lives on Aldersgate Street. I've tried nearly every other door, with no luck." Clare smiled in what she hoped was a trustworthy fashion. "Does he perchance live here?"

The woman's gaze narrowed, skating over Clare's sodden cloak to her bedraggled hem, hovering a moment on her muddied silk slippers. She frowned. "What business does someone like *you* have with Dr. Merial?"

Clare's smile faltered. "It is a private matter."

"Well, the charity ward is three blocks east." The door began to inch closed.

Clare abandoned her Society smile—which was clearly not serving her well in this neighborhood—and shoved her left foot into the jam. "I am not his patient, if that is your worry," she gasped as the door connected with her thin-soled slipper.

Although, perhaps a broken foot would return her to that blessed state.

Ironically, St. Bartholomew's was the one landmark in Smithfield she was sure of, given that it rose like a fortress above the squalid neighborhood, and given that she'd started her search for Daniel there this very afternoon. But according to the authorities she'd spoken to, he didn't work on Sundays. And that meant she had no idea where he might be.

The offending door began to open again. "I cannot say that I know him," Mrs. Calbert snarled. Before Clare could protest further, the churlish woman brought her heel down on the top of her foot. As Clare reared back in pain and surprise, she added nastily, "And if I did, you can bet I wouldn't approve of visiting ladies, either."

The door slammed closed

Clare stood in the gathering twilight, her mouth open, toes curled in agony.

"*Psssssst.*"

She whirled around, her heart crawling up her throat. She saw naught but an empty sidewalk, but nonetheless edged away from the unseen voice, the crumbling mortar of the building's wall at her back. The gas lamps had not yet been lit, if indeed there was a lamplighter in London brave enough to walk these streets. She peered from side to side, searching for danger.

Why would a footpad be trying to catch her attention? Surely they could just brain her over the head, drag her into the shadows, and—

"*Here.* In the alley, miss."

Clare closed her eyes and shook her head. No matter how nicely a footpad asked—no matter, even, if said footpad was female, as this one clearly was—she was not about to blindly follow their invitation to a dark, murderous rendezvous.

"I know the man you seek."

Clare's eyes opened to see a woman shuffle ghostlike from the alley, her hand raised in greeting. She blinked in surprise through the twilight. "Meg!"

The apparition cackled. "Oh, aye. You remember me, eh?"

"Of course. I met you with Dr. Merial, in Chelsea." Clare smiled nervously, though she still kept close to the wall, as if it might offer her some security against the unknown dangers of Smithfield—which apparently included slamming doors and ghosts in alleys. "*Handsome* Meg, isn't it?"

Meg smiled, revealing a large gap where teeth ought to have gone. "A spanking good memory, to go along with such a pretty face. No wonder Dr. Merial's smitten."

Clare stepped forward at his name. "Do you know where he lives?"

"He lets a room from Mrs. Calbert." Meg pointed behind Clare's shoulder with a gnarled hands. "Second door to the left."

Clare looked behind her suspiciously. Several closed doors waited, a bit further down the street. She'd overlooked them at first, thinking them little more than side doors to sculleries and such. But then, she'd presumed this building was a single home. Now that Meg had pointed it out, she could see the rooms had been subdivided as individual living quarters.

"But . . . Mrs. Calbert said she didn't know him," she said in confusion.

"It's more that she doesn't want *you* to know him. Catch my drift, dearie?" Meg turned and began to amble down the street. "Just don't let her find you out, hear?" the woman called over her shoulder. "There's a woman I wouldn't want to cross."

As Meg turned a corner and disappeared from view, Clare shook off her surprise. She knocked on the indicated door, then waited with her heart in her throat. It seemed like only seconds before it swung open. The wave of air that reached out to greet her this time did not smell of freshly baked bread, or worse, a fetid alley. Instead, the strong, sweet scent she'd always identified with Daniel greeted her like an old friend.

He looked tired and disheveled, as though he'd been up for days, but he was still so impossibly perfect she wanted to collapse in relief.

THE SIGHT OF Clare on his doorstep was like an old wound, freshly torn open. The last time Daniel had seen her, she'd been standing beneath the bright lights of Lady Austerley's ballroom, regaling her friends with tales of his Roma heritage, her voice smug and confident as she delivered the damning words. But in her bedraggled bonnet and soaked dress, tonight she looked as much a Gypsy as he.

"May I come in?" Even her voice seemed sharp as a scalpel.

He nodded, stepping aside for her entry, then turned around just in time to see Clare's cloak hit the floor in a sodden heap. Her gloves were peeled off next, followed by her bonnet. The frogs announced their approval of the disrobing process by splashing about in their bowls, but then fell uncharacteristically still as she began to unpin her hair.

No doubt they were as awed as he.

She squeezed the water from the released tresses, and drops fell onto his floor with a soft patter. The sound finally brought him around. He disentangled his frozen limbs and shut the door, then pulled a blanket off his bed, as much for his sanity as her health.

"For God's sake, Clare." He held it out. "You are soaked through."

"I was caught out in the rainstorm." She took the blanket from him, and as her cold hand brushed against his, a curl of heat unfolded in his gut. But he ruthlessly ignored the urge to take her in his arms and warm her up the fastest way possible. Because the storm had come through around six o'clock. It was now closer to eight. His mind clacked through the math and arrived at an unpalatable conclusion.

"You've been wandering about Smithfield for two hours?" he asked, incredulous.

"Four. The rainstorm hit about two hours into my search for you, I should think. That was after my purse was stolen, of course." She tossed her still-damp hair over one shoulder, and he tried very, very hard not to notice it fell to her waist. Her very *damp* waist, the fabric of her wet dress plastered against her curves. "I tried to wait out the rain in the coffeehouse on Giltspur Steet, but they turned me away." She held the blanket back to him. "They insisted I buy something, you see, and I was quite unable to do so without any money."

Daniel took the blanket back with numb fingers. *Bloody hell.* She'd spent four hours in Smithfield? Six months ago a man had been gutted in broad daylight, not two blocks away from that very coffeehouse. Mrs. Calbert's husband had known the streets—and the dangers—as well as anyone, and it had still not been enough to keep him safe.

How was a woman so delicately fashioned still standing? Still *breathing?*

But of course, he knew by now she was stronger than she seemed.

"Why do something so foolish?" he demanded gruffly. His fingers gripped the coarse wool of the blanket, now damp from its brush with her body. "I would have come to you, if you'd only sent a note."

She hesitated. "I wasn't sure. Not after the way things ended between us last night."

Daniel's heart contracted around her explanation. He felt like smashing something. She'd been robbed, on account of him. Refused entry to a common coffeehouse. Soaked to the bone. It was a wonder she wasn't bleeding to death in an alley somewhere.

Instead, she was here. Dripping wet and beginning to shiver—though whether from cold or residual shock, it was difficult to tell.

Fighting back a snarl of anger, he tossed the blanket back onto the bed, then snatched a cup from his sideboard—unfortunately chipped, though it was ostensibly the finest piece of china he owned—and poured her a finger from the bottle he kept there. He held it out to her. "As I said last night, Smithfield is no place for a lady."

"I had hoped that perhaps you at least lived on a safe street." She accepted the cup with both hands, and when he saw her fingers were shaking, he cursed his haste in not warming the drink up first. "I have discovered, however, you are not prone to exaggeration." She took a cautious sip, then wrinkled her nose. "This is terrible brandy."

"That is because it is whisky."

Her eyes widened. "Lady Austerley told me you were a teetotaler."

He dragged a hand through his hair, though he really wanted to drag it through hers. He'd never seen it unbound before, and even with its dampness, it glowed with life and vitality.

"Not a teetotaler." *Not tonight, at any rate.* "I am just careful."

Daniel poured himself a glass, this time in a cup with a broken handle. "Even a glass or two can impair a man's judgment, and I need my wits about me to do my work." He took a long swallow. "But as I've just completed the last of my experiments with my anesthetic regulator today, I believe I've earned a celebratory glass myself."

"You've finished it?" she asked, and he could imagine— perhaps naively—that he could see a flush of excitement steal across her cheeks.

His stomach churned—whether from the burn of the whisky or the burn of her presence, it was difficult to be sure. What was she *doing* here, asking questions, as if she had a right to be interested in his work? She'd made his position in her life damnably clear last night. He wiped a sleeve across his mouth. "I stayed up all night to finish it," he admitted, though he did not add he was driven, in part, by frustration over their parting. "I wrote the manuscript this morning, and sent it on to the editors at the *Lancet* this afternoon."

"You must be relieved."

"Relieved?" He snorted. "Not bloody likely. The fate of six months of work now rests in the hands of an editor who likely doesn't know his arse from his elbow."

"But . . . if it works, surely they will have to publish it."

"If history is any judge, the editors will have their own opinion on what constitutes a publishable finding. And they've viewed my ideas none too favorably in the past."

He could see her fingers tighten around her chipped cup. After a moment she raised her glass. "Well then, we should drink to your hopeful success. If anyone deserves it, it is you."

He raised his own glass, though he harbored doubts about his ability to swallow it properly, after such a pretty speech. "To success," he echoed, then tossed it back. The whisky slid down his throat like fire. He savored the burn. If nothing else it was reminder that he was not dreaming—an important fact to remember, given that he was drinking a fine Scottish whisky in the presence of one very forbidden Miss Clare Westmore.

She set her cup down and then circled his dining table. Her fingers trailed over the bowl with the frogs, then lingered over the chaotic profusion of papers that still littered the table's surface. "This is where you work in the evenings?"

"Yes. I am sorry for the . . . er . . . mess," he offered, lacking a better description for the tangle of papers and pests. "I use amphibians in my experiments." He stepped closer and reached out to straighten his notes. "I was not expecting you."

Damn it, why was he apologizing?

This was *his* flat. *His* frogs. She had not been invited,

and the condition of his things did not sit in wait of her approval.

"No, I imagine not. Not after last night." She sighed, and the sound seemed to echo through him like a cold wind. "I know you are angry. I can see it in the way you look at me."

He stayed silent. Not to be cruel, but because he didn't know how to answer her.

Her fingers brushed against the regulator, where it lay on its side in an inconspicuous heap. By appearances, it looked little more than a jumble of parts, he knew. The sort of thing a blacksmith might put together on a lark. Or a dare.

Somehow, though, she seemed to know. "Do you mind if I touch it?"

Her innocent question took his thoughts in a decidedly *not* innocent direction. If she'd asked that exact question last night, they might have had a different ending to the evening. Instead, he'd reacted to protect her, and ended up embarrassing them both.

He shoved such an incongruent thought from his head and tried to focus on the present. He wasn't sure what she wanted, but at the moment it didn't seem to be a return to last night's argument. He'd never shown his work to anyone before, aside from writing the details of its performance down on paper, and he wasn't sure he wanted to show it to her now.

But all it took was her hesitant smile, and as if on the cusp of a dream, he lifted the regulator and placed it in her hands.

"The chloroform rests here." He pointed to the machine's tin body. "As it evaporates, it mixes with air and creates a vaporous mixture that can be inhaled."

"I'm not familiar with chloroform, although I've read

about the uses of ether in surgery in the *Times*," she said, turning it over and inspecting the tubing. "The article I read claimed it was dangerous. Is this safe to use?"

"Chloroform and ether can be dangerous, especially in the hands of someone lacking the proper experience," he admitted, thinking of the handful of anesthetic deaths he had observed at the hands of ether just in his six months at St. Bart's. "One advantage of chloroform over ether seems to be its more agreeable effects on the body. A Scottish physician published a pamphlet on it last November, and when I read it, I was seized with the idea for a regulator that might deliver the vapor of the drug more safely. I left my practice in Yorkshire to come to London and work on it."

She turned it over in her hands, and he could tell she was studying how the pieces fit together. "It is a miraculous invention," she said simply.

A tremor of what may have been pride arced through him. Not only pride in himself, or even in his hard-fought accomplishment. Pride in *her*, in her innate curiosity, her ability to see things others did not.

"Not miraculous," he said, shaking his head. "A simple concept, really. Chloroform vapor is heavier than air, and I simply took advantage of the fact to collect it in a precise manner. I can envision its use in surgeries. Midwifery. Even extracting a tooth could be done far more safely." His pulse sped up, as it always did when he considered how the future of medicine could be shaped by such a device. "The possibilities are limitless."

Her eyes reached out to him, probing. "The potential income as well."

Daniel stiffened. "I do not intend to patent this invention, Clare. Fate is blind in its brutality. The lower classes are already discriminated against in every other aspect of their lives. I would not invent a means of relief for their suffering, only to deny it to them by selling it at auction to the highest bidder."

She caught her lower lip between her teeth, worrying it a moment. "But even if you do not patent it, surely there is some income that might be anticipated, however small."

Daniel shook his head. Did she see this as some future financial security for him, then? A potential replacement for the loss of her dowry, should she be foolish enough to be actually considering his mention of marriage? Hope flared wildly in his chest, but in the end he mercilessly tamped it down. Even if given a choice to do it over, he wouldn't. He might cut off his right arm to keep her, but he could not sell others' souls in the hopes of acquiring hers.

"The paper I submitted to the *Lancet* explains how to make it. How to replicate it. Details, diagrams, everything. I always intended it to be accessible to everyone." He shook his head. "There will be no money for me in this discovery."

Her gaze scraped against his skin. "This is what drives you, isn't it?" she whispered. "'Tis not money, or even fame. It's the potential in this discovery. The desire to help those who need it." She paused. "Men like your father."

"Yes." He ground his teeth together. "If the physician who'd treated my father had access to a safer anesthetic and a precise way to deliver it, perhaps the outcome would have been different." Daniel held his breath, waiting for her reaction. For some reason he didn't care to examine, her opinion mattered to him.

A terrifyingly good deal.

"Would you show me how it all works?" she asked, holding it out.

And he knew that he was done for.

Chapter 27

lare surprised herself by the audacity of her question. On the table, crickets jeered at her from a pail. It seemed as though they were laughing at her.

The question remained . . . would he?

She'd wanted only to see him this evening. To apologize for last night, and to tell him of the astonishing revelations of the morning.

And—if she were honest with herself—to rest a quiet moment in the comfort of his arms.

But the residual wariness in his eyes when she'd stepped across his threshold had held back the more pertinent questions that wanted to tumble from her. Somehow, this one had dared to take their place.

"All right." He began to work on his necktie. She watched, her breath in her throat as he pulled it free from his collar in a long, sensual slide. He picked up the lamp and walked toward his bed, with its damp blanket and heart-stopping possibilities. For a moment she stood still, shivering in her wet clothes, wondering if perhaps he'd misinterpreted her question.

"Show me" could mean a good many things.

"Bring the regulator over here," he called out. He placed the lamp down on the bedside table, then sat down on the bed and rolled up first one sleeve, then the other. "And the brown bottle on the table as well. Take care not to drop it, though." A hint of bemusement infused his voice. "That is a mistake I am not eager to repeat. The scent has lingered for weeks from the last time I dropped it."

Clare fetched the requested items. So *that* explained the fragrance she so associated with him, that sweet, cloying scent that made her want to bury her nose in his jacket and never come up for air. She wondered what he would think if she admitted such a thing.

"Are you limping?" he asked, distracting her from the task at hand.

At the unexpected question, the bottle almost slipped out of her fingers. She pulled it close against her chest, her heart pounding. "My ankle is feeling fine."

"I should hope so, given that it is your *other* foot you are favoring tonight."

The thought that he noticed such a small, insignificant thing startled her nearly as much as the near-miss with the chloroform bottle. "I had a door slammed on my foot," she admitted, "but it does not hurt overmuch." She set the bottle down gingerly on the bedside table. "Smithfield's residents are not the friendliest of souls."

He began unbuttoning the first few buttons of his shirt. "Considering the reception I have received at your Society functions, I think I should prefer Smithfield. Aside from Lady Austerley, the citizens of Mayfair haven't exactly flung their doors open in welcome for me, either." He pointed behind her. "There's a chair, just there. You will want to sit for this, I think."

She took the indicated seat and watched as he pulled the stopper from the bottle and poured a small amount of chloroform into the tin's port. The sweet, cloying scent grew stronger, and she held her breath.

As if he could sense her unease, he smiled at her. "There is no need to worry here. Outside the device, the mixture of air is too strong for the chloroform to have much of an effect." His smile turned grim as he replaced the stopper. "There are several stages to the effects of anesthesia, and I want you to be prepared."

"You mean, you don't just fall asleep?"

"No. It renders a body unconscious, but not asleep. You can wake a sleeping person, but a patient under the effects of chloroform cannot be roused." He placed the stopper back in the bottle and set it down on the table. "Now, in the first minute or so after placing the mask, I may seem highly agreeable. There is a sense of euphoria that comes with the first degree of anesthesia, but then my thoughts will become more disordered. Possibly even delusional. I need you to count to one hundred. Timing is crucial, otherwise it can be dangerous."

"Dangerous?" Clare straightened in alarm, her fingers curling in protest around the hard edge of the chair seat. "I thought you said it was safer than ether. I do not think—"

His hand reached out to touch hers. "Safer, yes. But not entirely without risk. The danger will be assuaged by having someone sensible monitoring the effects, I should think. Afterward, the sequence occurs much in reverse." He squeezed her hand. "You can do this, Clare. I trust you."

She breathed out. Nodded.

He lay back on the bed, though he did not yet fit the mask to his face. "I will hold it in place, but remember, it is vital you remove the mask after I am unconscious, or else I will continue breathing the vapor and can suffer too heavy a dose."

Clare shivered beneath her skin, and not only because of the cold seeping through her wet clothes. How on earth would she have the courage to wait until she reached one hundred, chased by a dire warning like that? The thought of putting him at risk made her feel more than a little ill.

But he believed in this machine, and in the strength of his own experiments.

The least she could do was believe in him.

He held the mask over his nose. Clare held her own breath as the faint, pungent scent of vaporized chloroform filled the air. It is far more concentrated in the mask, she reminded herself, but that only made her stomach turn over in fear for him.

"One, two, three." She frowned, concentrating on the numbers. "Four, five, six."

She made it to fifteen without seeing what she considered any change in Daniel's behavior, but then, just as she reached twenty, his muffled voice rang out.

"God, you are beautiful."

She forgot, for the moment, to count properly. Dark, serious eyes met hers above the bit of brass and tubing, and for a moment she felt as though *she* were the one going under, flailing against the undertow of that hypnotic gaze. She shook her head in denial. "You are deranged. I look like a drowned rat." She paused, sorting out where she had been before his words had pulled her from her task. "Thirty, thirty-one, thirty-two."

"Miss Westmore." Was it just her imagination, or did his voice sound more slurred than affronted? "Did you just call me deranged?"

"Thirty-five, thirty-six."

"I am a fellow of the Royal Medical and Chirurgical Society."

In spite of herself, Clare smiled. "Yes, I recall you mentioned that, once upon a time."

"It means I am sworn to honesty in all matters personal

and professional. You are beautiful, Clare. You may trust me on this."

She laughed out loud, remembering his earlier warning. *Highly agreeable, indeed.*

"Ah, an elusive sighting of Miss Westmore's crooked left cuspid." His voice seemed to be weakening now, but he was apparently still possessed enough of his faculties to reach out with his unencumbered hand to cup her cheek. "I see it in my dreams, you know."

She caught her breath, as much at his words as the touch of his hand. He'd noticed her tooth? She felt a restless stirring at the thought—not from embarrassment, or resentment that he should mention it. It was hard to resent the reminder of her physical imperfection when he also said he thought her beautiful. Although . . . perhaps this was less the agreeable phase of the experiment and more the disordered delusion he had warned her about.

By the time she hit seventy, his dark, thick lashes had begun to flutter against the stubbled arc of his cheek and his hand had fallen away. By one hundred he was well and fully unconscious, and she reached out and tugged the mask from his unprotesting fingers.

"Daniel?" she whispered. She tapped his shoulder.

Oh, God. There was no response.

It was like watching someone die before your eyes.

She felt a tremor of terror to think that he had willingly done this to himself, all because she had asked him to show her his work.

She grasped his hand, and was relieved to find it was warm beneath hers. Her finger rubbed against the tiny scar on his thumb, the one she had spied during his first visit to her drawing room, only two weeks prior but seemingly a lifetime ago. She remembered how it had proved he was human, rather than some Greek god fallen to earth. She resolved to ask him how he had acquired it, should they be fortunate enough to escape this foolish endeavor with his wits intact. At the moment she feared for the worst.

Despite her fears, she could see his chest rise and fall in a faint but steady rhythm. But the rest of his body, and that beautiful, quick mind . . . those things were utterly silent. She felt helpless in the face of such a striking vulnerability.

Gradually, she began to convince herself he was not in distress. Indeed, if she looked carefully, she could already see signs of his impending recovery: a fluttering of eyes beneath his closed lids, the purposeful curl of his fingers into his palms. The trust it must have required to put his life in her hands in this manner staggered her.

Perhaps there was a glimmer of hope here, a chance he didn't hate her after all.

She reached out and slipped a hand beneath his unbuttoned shirt, her palm resting against the firm, reassuring bump of his heart. He was startlingly hot. Or perhaps it was that she was cold. Her fingers curved into his skin, the hair there crisp and springy, and she marveled at the stark difference in its texture compared to her own. She leaned over and placed her ear against his lips, seeking audible reassurance of his breath sounds. "Brilliant man," she whispered, her face turned so she could see his fluttering eyes. "You have done it. Not only shown me, you've shown them all."

She gasped as his hand snaked up to grasp the back of her neck. The moment hovered, unscripted and unsure. He blinked in muted awareness and then his dark eyes anchored insistently to hers. "Clare?"

To her needy ears, it sounded more like a benediction than a curse.

"Yes," she gasped, though his fingers were punishing against her skin. Her hands crept up to tighten over his, telling him by touch of her presence. "I am here."

His grip slowly loosened, but as she drew his hands back down and straightened her back, her fingers lingered over his. She felt the small scar on his thumb again, and remembered her promise to herself. "Daniel," she whispered, sensing he was beginning to drift away. She felt the sharp arc of panic. He *couldn't* sleep, not now that she had finally gotten him back. "How did you get this mark?" She rubbed her finger over it. "Was it the slip of a scalpel?"

He frowned and seemed to take an hour to respond. "Have you been inspecting my thumbs while I was unconscious, Miss Westmore?"

"I thought it would be less objectionable than stealing a kiss from a man who was incapable of protest."

"Less enjoyable, though." His head lolled toward her. "I'll have you know I prize my thumb's privacy."

Clare stifled a laugh, relieved he appeared to be regaining the capacity for banter. "Perhaps your thumb *wants* me to know."

"Very well, then." His smile was weak but gratifyingly real. "Hoof knife," he croaked.

It was a somewhat less heroic injury than she'd imagined. "Tell me how it happened," she pressed gently, sensing it was somehow important to keep him talking.

"I was nine," he said, his voice fainter now. "Father showed me how to trim a horse's hoof. The horse objected. Ergo . . ."

A giggle escaped her lips. She had to imagine he was well on his way to a full recovery if he was lucid enough to quote Latin.

"He always wanted me to be a horseman like him." His eyes swayed drunkenly over her face. "I didn't have the heart for it, though. I kept wanting to fix the ones bound for the knackers."

She squeezed his hand, wishing she had known him as

that nine-year-old trying to please his father. But it would have been impossible to know that boy. It *ought* to be impossible for her to know the man. Without the miracle of a turned ankle, she would not be here now.

"I cannot imagine he would not be immensely proud of who you have become," she told him solemnly, all amusement falling away. She knew *she* was proud of him, and more than a little in awe of his accomplishment. She remembered the words he had once tossed in her face, during the heat of their first argument.

I promise you, there are more rewarding and scintillating aspects to my life than wrapping the ankles of spoiled, fashionable young ladies.

He'd not been lying.

He'd not even been exaggerating.

He drew a deep, shuddering breath, as though trying to purify the residual chloroform vapor from his lungs. For a minute or so he lay quiet, as though resting again in the arms of the drug. But then he cracked open an eye. "I am not dreaming, then. You are still here."

She hid a smile. "Yes."

Both eyes opened. *"Why?"* He turned his head slowly toward her, as though his body had not yet caught up with the recovery of his thoughts. "Why did you even come here tonight?"

Clare bit her lip. No longer delusional, then. He had returned to lucidity—and apparently, mistrust—with remarkable speed. "I came to talk to you," she admitted.

"What of your future duke?" he asked, his voice hoarse.

Clare looked down at her hands. How quickly they came to the heart of it. Perhaps chloroform was a sort of truth serum. She imagined she could use a bit of it now.

"Alban is not my duke, Daniel. He never was." She hesitated, but he deserved the truth, and the version he knew still held too many hidden layers. She lifted her chin and met his impenetrable gaze. "He is my uncle, if you must know. I am illegitimate, and rumors to that effect are already spreading, thanks to Lady Sophie. And I imagine that changes things a bit where my future is concerned, doesn't it?"

He studied her a long moment, as though he could dissect her thoughts down to the marrow. Or perhaps he was trying to gather his chloroform-scattered thoughts. "Christ, Clare." He scrubbed a hand over his unkempt jaw. "Is that the only reason you came to me?" His voice sounded raw. "Because you are afraid no one else will have you?"

"No!" The blood pounded in her ears, each beat its own roar of denial. "I came tonight because I needed to talk to someone who *knows* me. Not the image I project to the world, but the person I am beneath." She leaned forward on the chair, searching for the truth she suspected was still somehow buried in these brimming emotions. "I came because out of everyone—those I once considered friends, even my family—you are the only one who does. I came because I wanted to, Daniel." She swallowed. "Because I wanted *you*."

His hands snaked out once more, this time grabbing her wrists. "That is certainly highly agreeable of you," he growled.

Clare found herself pulled toward him, off the chair and onto the bed.

And then his lips met hers.

Chapter 28

Until now Daniel's recovery after each experimental bout of anesthesia had gone something like this: a slow, rising awareness, a regained capacity for movement, and finally—least predictable in terms of timing—a return to full sensation.

The final piece of the sequence had sometimes taken a quarter hour or more.

Tonight he accomplished those steps in record time.

Perhaps it was the whisky he'd consumed first, that grand remover of inhibitions and good sense. Indeed, it seemed as though some of those milestones might even have been reversed, because his body was already stirring to life. Of course, the part of his anatomy in question depended on blood flow more than muscle strength, but how, then, to describe the sensation arcing through him? Was this a biologic response to the feel of this woman in his arms, warm and eager beneath his lips? Or was it her confession, the hope of what this might yet lead to, that banished the last dregs of sluggishness from his veins?

The scientist in him wanted to take a moment, write the observation down.

The beast in him firmly objected to that plan.

And so instead he kissed her. Kissed her the way he'd wanted to for two long weeks. He cupped her head in his hands and pulled her into him, invading her whisky-sweet mouth with a single purpose in mind. Not seduction— that was too delicate a term to define what he wished to do to this woman.

He wanted to consume her.

The sounds she made deep in her throat told him she did not object, and so he gathered his muscles and shifted their bodies until she was lying beneath him on his bed. He pressed his length down over the top of her as they kissed, marveling at how perfect, how *right,* she felt there. It seemed his body had known she would be a perfect fit from the start, and he was beginning to realize that fighting the objections of his conscience had always been an exercise in futility. She tipped her head back and gasped his name, until he could think of nothing but sinking his teeth into the skin of her beautiful neck and claiming her as his own.

But he needed to know. Know she understood who she kissed, and what this meant.

That there was no going back from the precipice over which they dangled.

And so, though his body raised a strenuous objection, he somehow summoned the strength of will to end the kiss and raise himself off her. "Clare," he said, his voice hoarse and barely recognizable to his own ears. "Are you sure you want this?" He stared down at her beautiful, flushed face. "That you want *me*?"

"Yes," she gasped, arching up to meet him.

The friction between their bodies made the breath hiss

out between his teeth. He wanted her with a desperation that terrified him, but he was not so addled with lust that he couldn't see those wants were selfish, at best. She was poised to relinquish five thousand pounds, when all he could promise her in return was a modest future.

His body might try to convince him otherwise, but his heart knew it needed to be said.

"I am not a man of whom your father would ever approve, Clare," he warned. "I am only the son of a Gypsy horse trader." He summoned his memory of her words from last night, the ones that had cut to the quick. "I am appalled you would set your sights so low."

She stilled. "Daniel, I am so, so sorry you heard that."

"Why?" he said, pushing himself more completely off of her and shifting to one side. "You only spoke the truth, after all."

"But I would not have you believe it is a truth that matters to me. I am not proud of my behavior last night. I only said those things to dissuade Sophie from spreading further lies about you. She needed to feel there was greater danger in the lie I would spread about her." Her voice gentled to a whisper. "I know these things about you, and still my heart is pointing me toward you. It is *my* choice." She linked her hands behind his neck, pulling him down into her. "I want *you*, Daniel." Her voice reached into his ear, darkly seductive. "The man you are."

They were the words he had wanted—needed—to hear.

And yet he pulled at this thread, determined to unravel her resolve before they did something she would wake up to regret. "I will never be more than a doctor," he reminded her, though the gathering incoherence of his thoughts meant he was hard pressed to remember why this was a problem.

"A *brilliant* doctor," she corrected. She reached toward

him and her teeth nipped against the column of his throat, as though she was willing to take whatever pieces of him he denied her.

Christ, but he was helpless against her.

He'd never had a horse in this race for resistance.

He dipped his head down and ran his tongue in hot swirls against the inviting length of her neck. "There is also the small matter that I am Roma," he whispered against the wicked heat of her skin. "You would be turned away from drawing rooms everywhere."

She squirmed beneath him. "I do not *care*, as long as you do not stop."

He kissed her again, more tenderly this time. Unclenching his hands, he smoothed the damp hair away from her face. "I will follow your lead, then, and not stop unless you tell me to."

He waited, and when no protest seemed imminent, he trailed his palm up her abdomen, registering again the damp clothing that still lay between them. That, at least, was a problem that could be fixed. His fingers set to work on the mother-of-pearl buttons of her bodice. "Praise Hippocrates," he breathed as the fabric obligingly parted to reveal the transparent chemise beneath. "You are not wearing a corset tonight."

She shuddered—though whether due to the air on her chilled skin or his irreverent observation, he couldn't tell. "You once mentioned they promoted an unhealthy posture."

"I thought you didn't listen to me," he said, lowering his head to press a kiss to the erotic curve of one clavicle, lingering a moment in the hollow of space it created.

"I *always* listen," she sighed into his touch. "I just don't always agree."

But she was agreeing to this. He could feel her skin warming beneath his lips, knew she felt the tug of attraction every bit as much as he did. It was in the small, encouraging sound she made as he slipped the thin straps of her chemise from her shoulders and pushed the fabric down to her navel, the way she gasped in pleasure as he blew lightly across the pebbled skin of her bared breasts.

And ah, good Lord, her breasts. Hadn't he known she was an anatomist's dream?

They rounded enthusiastically in his palms, and the nipples peaked against his thumbs as they brushed across them. She felt alive in his hands, and he marveled that a woman so finely made might entrust him with her keeping. "God, Clare. Do you know what you do to me?"

"No," came her choked whisper.

"Well, from the start, you've rendered me far more insensible than chloroform."

There was a beat of silence, of held breath. And then an easy breath of laughter escaped her lips, as if she didn't quite believe him but had no choice but to take him at his word. "I am less easy to regulate, I imagine."

He chuckled in return. The sound of her laughter was like a beautiful drug, and he was firmly in its thrall. With his fingers, he traced the delicate pattern of veins visible just below the skin on her breasts, marveling with the knowledge that each one carried blood now heated by his touch. "Ah, but didn't you know? I am willing to experiment until I achieve success." He leaned over to blow a trail of warm air across one pert nipple, and as her head thrashed from side to side, he bent lower, drawing her into his mouth.

A cry wrenched from her throat, but he refused to be diverted from this path. He was more than willing to use his mouth as an implement of torture in pursuit of this pleasure. Not his own pleasure—*hers*. He wanted her to realize there was far more here to discover. And damn any regrets she might have on the morrow, he wanted to be the one to show her.

He gathered her wet skirts in his fist and dragged the fabric slowly, slowly upward.

"What are you doing?" she gasped, causing him to still.

"I will stop whenever you want," came his clenched reply. He forced his hands to still. Waited for her to catch up. To decide. He would wait forever if he had to, because her trust in this—in *him*—was too precious to squander, no matter the insistent drum of desire in his veins.

"I don't want you to stop." She squirmed beneath him, her hands busy about her waist. "I want them *off*." And then she was reaching behind her and the heavy mass of damp fabric was being unfastened, shifted. Removed. His breath caught in his throat as the clocked silk stockings that stalked his dreams slid into view, and then, above them, he was treated to the pale perfection of her thighs.

Time seemed to still.

Or perhaps it was more that she did, treating him to this first intimate glimpse of her.

Christ, but she made him feel inarticulate.

There was no word—in the English *or* the Latin—that could be applied.

He smoothed a hand across the damp cotton of her bunched chemise until his fingers met soft skin. God, but her bones intrigued him. They always had, even when she'd sat straight-backed and hostile, sniping at him from the wallflower line. But they had never tempted him more than now, the hidden lines of her laid out, quivering in wait of his personal discovery.

He lifted her leg and pressed a kiss to the delicate curve of her stocking-clad ankle, her instep, her toes, at last giving in to this urge that seemed to have possessed him since the first time he'd seen that clocked silk. He took his time, gauging her reaction, even as his teeth clenched from the strain of holding back. "You still do not wish me to stop?"

"No," she breathed. "I want you to *hurry*."

He focused his attentions now on the pale skin just above where those stockings ended, brushing his cheek across her inner thigh, deliberately scraping his day's growth of beard at this most sensitive point. "Why should we hurry?" he asked, pressing his mouth there next. She tasted sweet, of flowers and vanilla, and the merest hint of salt. "Perhaps I am content to linger here awhile."

He felt her fingers tangling in his hair, trying to pull him back to her. "Because I may die if you don't kiss me. Or I may kill you. Either way is bound to be a problem."

He shook free of her hold and then brushed a hand reverently across the dark curls that guarded her entrance. "Kiss you, hmmm?" He swept a finger against her labia, the folds delicate and pink as the inside of a shell. Her body stiffened—not in denial, but in welcome, and he knew a startling jolt of possessiveness that *he* was the one to whom she was giving this gift.

He carefully explored her with a finger, making her nearly buck up from the bed.

"Daniel—" she gasped.

"Shhhh, love." She was unbearably responsive. *Ready.* He wanted to shuck his clothing and abandon the leisurely pace he had chosen. But she was inexperienced. Innocent. She might not understand what came next, but she was trusting him to show her. His experience as a physician told him this first joining would be painful for her, and he wanted her to enjoy this part of it, if nothing else.

And so carefully, deliberately, he lowered his mouth to her and gave in to the beast.

OH GOD, OH God, oh God.
Surely no gentleman would do such a thing.

Surely no lady would *enjoy* such a thing.

And surely she would rather die than stop.

She felt pulled under by the overwhelming feel of him. Not only the sensation of his mouth, there at her core, which was vivid enough. She could still feel him elsewhere. *Everywhere*. The scrape of his chin where it had ravaged the sensitive skin of her cheek, the vivid warmth of his mouth where it had fit against hers—even his hands had left a lingering trail of sensation, her toes still tingling from his attentions. She felt as if no part of her had gone unscathed, as though he'd seen through every layer, every secret, and had methodically—expertly—stripped her bare.

And she was greedy enough to want more.

His mouth was a thing of torment, but it was a torment so sweet she could do nothing but give herself up to it. His tongue found a place along her seam that made her hips lift from the bed and her breath wind tighter and tighter. She felt a coiling deep inside, a place at once impossible to reach and impossible to ignore.

And then without warning her body pitched forward, flying, falling.

It was like nothing she had ever felt. Pleasure was far too bland a word for it. She felt unraveled, the breath spinning ruthlessly out of her, the world receding to a distant point.

And then it was gone, rolling away like ripples on water.

She lay a long moment, too stunned to move. How did one recover from a surprise like that, the realization your body held such secrets? Perhaps the sensible thing would be to gather the scattered pieces of the armor that had once held her together.

But in this boneless state of wonder, she couldn't even think of where to begin.

Dimly, she became aware that Daniel had somehow

shed his own clothes and come to lie down next to her, his arms gathering her close, her back to his bare chest. He buried his face against her neck, and she felt his own strained breathing, in and out.

"What . . . *was* that?" she found the courage to ask.

"The scientific name for it is orgasm." His breath lay hot against her neck, and she closed her eyes, reveling in the feel of it. "But the French have a far better name for it. They call it *la petit mort.*"

The small death. An apt description.

She drew a shaky breath. "I never imagined . . ."

And she'd certainly never read about it in the *Times.*

His chin tickled the sensitive skin of her ear. "Your body is fashioned for this, Clare." He demonstrated with a hard slide of his body against her vulnerable core. The motion sent heat jumping again in that hidden, mysterious place. "Fashioned for me."

His mouth blazed a trail of promise down the side of her neck, and though she might have liked to close her eyes and lean into the weight of it, she turned and wriggled in his arms until she was facing him. The crisp hair on his chest chafed against her breasts, but it was a sensation she welcomed. *Craved.* She might have liked to take a moment to look, to savor this first glimpse of his nude body. But they were far past such easy perusals now, and so she lifted a hand to his chin, reveling in the masculine texture and shape of his features.

"Only you," she whispered. *No one else.* She knew it beyond any shadowed doubt. The words had begun to assemble in her mind, even before he'd given her this gift. This was the elusive emotion he'd spoken of in the library, the hurtful, terrible thrill of it.

Love. No title, no grand mansion, could compare with this.

And she'd been a fool to fight it so long.

She tipped her forehead against his, welcoming the thin sheen of sweat she could feel there, soaking into her own skin. To her mind, the discovery was as significant as the knowledge that his mouth had just wreaked havoc on the most intimate parts of her body. It was evidence of his struggle, his care with her. His own denied release.

"Show me," she whispered.

She could feel him shudder. He was contemplating retreat, though she could see it was something his body fought. "Clare, we do not have to do this." He shook his head. "I am content to have shown you this small piece of it."

"Well I am not content." She reached down and touched him, running her fingers across the heated, velvet length of him. This time he did not pull away. Indeed, he pressed his body more firmly into her palm. "I want to know the rest of it," she whispered. "*All* of it."

For a moment she thought he would deny her.

But no . . . he was moving. Kissing her again. His stubble scraped the vulnerable skin of her jaw, but she welcomed the discomfort of it, proof of his intent. He tasted of whisky and sweet, dark heat, and she wanted more of both.

She could feel his hands shake as he dragged the damp, clinging chemise toward her head. It surprised her to realize it was still on, bunched as it had been about her waist. She lifted her arms, willingly casting any last shreds of modesty to the winds. His hands skimmed her shoulders, her ribs, her belly, raising gooseflesh in anticipation of what he might touch next. He uttered a soft groan as his hands came up to brush against her bare breasts. "God, Clare. You are so finely made."

Impossibly, she believed him. Believed that someone could find her beautiful. Desirable. *Just the way she was.* There was no pretense left, no fashionable clothing to hide her flaws. It was in the heat of his gaze, the visible pulse at the base of his throat. She believed him.

She believed in herself.

She reached a hand down to unhook her stocking from her garter, wanting only to be skin-on-skin with this man who had stolen her heart with his infinite patience, his quick mind, his refusal to be someone he wasn't. But his hand stilled her progress.

"No. Leave them on," he said hoarsely. "Give me this, and I'll show you anything you want." He followed the command with a kiss, open-mouthed and eager, his body pressing down into hers until she gasped from the sweet friction of it.

The scent of his heated skin—sharply masculine, salt and sweat—only ravaged her senses more. She lifted her stocking-clad legs over his hips and pressed up to meet him. His breathing had turned ragged now, and that sheen of sweat had transformed into droplets beading on his perfect forehead. "Last opportunity for sanity," he growled. "Do you want me to stop?"

She shook her head.

And miraculously, he obliged. The pain was fleeting, a nuisance that pulled her from the moment for the briefest of seconds. And then he was filling her completely, holding himself still above her, protecting her from his weight.

That place inside—the place that had so surprised her before—clenched in approval. She exhaled and shifted her hips experimentally beneath him. "Don't stop here, either," she warned.

"I wouldn't dream of it." He tipped his mouth to hers, cupped her face in his hands, and began to move against her. His motions were slow and controlled at first, though she could feel the leashed passion beneath his skin. She could feel herself rolling toward it again, that place where she would be undone, but his pace was not enough to tip her over the edge.

"I will not break, Daniel," she whispered, arching up against him.

The last dregs of his restraint vanished and he swept her arms over her head, pinning her wrists to the mattress. His breath was a storm in her ear, and he moved as a man possessed, his rhythm primal. She turned herself over to it, trusting him to know what she needed and to be willing to take her there.

As her world exploded in a muffled cry of relief, he found his own release, her name an anguished groan on his lips. Though the room was still spinning, she kept her eyes open, watching him fall apart with her. There was no perfect man to be seen, his features contorted in a mask of animal pleasure, sweat dripping from his body.

But he had never looked more perfect to her.

She floated back slowly, lost in the remnants of her own pleasure, floating on an insensate cloud. Dimly—though he must be every bit as tired as she—she realized he somehow still possessed the presence of mind to reach out a hand and extinguish the lamp.

He pulled the still-damp blanket over them, and Clare felt herself shifted, gathered against him. "Are you content now?" he whispered against the curve of her ear.

She nodded.

And then she slept like the dead.

Chapter 29

aniel came awake with a jolt.

For a moment he lay still, unsure where he was or what had wakened him. He blearily sorted through the habitual sounds of the crickets skittering about their pail and the clock tower striking some early morning hour in the distance. The sun had found its way through the room's single window and was poking at him with its usual insistence.

But that was where the familiarity ended.

For one thing, he was lying in his bed, not hunched over his notes at the table.

And for another, rather than a pounding head, this morning it was his muscles that ached like the very devil—a side effect, no doubt, of last night's exertions and sleeping with a warm, restless body curled around his own. He turned his head and caught his breath. Clare lay on her stomach, her bare skin dappled with beads of light. The blanket had slipped down, and he could see the elegant curve of a shoulder, the lovely bump of her vertebrae.

His attentions wanted to focus lower on her body, to areas that had brought them both such pleasure last night. It would be the work of a moment to kiss her into wakefulness. But he paused, arrested by the sight of her face as she lay sleeping. Her lashes were a sooty smudge against the pale arc of her cheek, and he could see the faint flutter of movement beneath her lids. If he was not mistaken, there was a new bruise on her throat—in the perfect shape of his teeth. He reached out a hand and smoothed a gentle finger over it, feeling both regretful and possessive of the mark. But his perusal was interrupted by a sharp rapping at the door, and he suppressed a groan as he realized what, precisely, had awakened him.

"Dr. Merial, are you awake?" Mrs. Calbert's wheedling voice reached through the wood. "I've an urgent message for you."

He cursed low beneath his breath as Clare began to stir. "I'll just bet you do," he muttered to his intrusive landlady.

And it probably involved a request to help her remove her clothing.

He scrubbed a hand across his face as another knock echoed through the air like a gunshot. Clare came fully and regrettably awake.

He lifted a finger to his lips, encouraging silence.

She sat up, eyes wide in alarm, blanket clutched to her chest. "But . . . someone is at the door," she hissed.

"If we are quiet, she will move on." He kept his voice to a low whisper, and bent to press a kiss against her bare shoulder. "Mrs. Calbert does this regularly."

"Mrs. Calbert?" She pushed a fistful of hair from her eyes. "Your landlady?"

"Have you met her?" Daniel asked, surprised.

"I've had the misfortune, yes. She's the one who

slammed the door on my foot last night." She began to pull frantic fingers through her hair.

Unconcerned himself, given the strength of the door's look, Daniel propped himself up on one elbow and lifted a hand to her thick chestnut strands, letting them sift through his fingers. Her preoccupation with her hair told him that she had not realized the blanket had slipped down beneath her breasts, but only a fool would point that out.

"Dr. Merial?" came the voice again.

"What does she *want*?" Clare moaned.

Daniel chuckled. "The same as you, I would imagine. Only you've actually found a way into my bed. And acquitted yourself well, I might add."

Her cheeks turned an enthusiastic shade of pink. "Do not make such jokes, Daniel." She swatted at his wandering hands, then tried to loop her snarled hair into a coil at the nape of her neck, only to then fumble for a way to secure it. He contented himself with watching her fitful progress, but as his eyes appreciably traced each pale, sweet curve, a thought occurred to him.

Could his landlady have seen Clare come into his rooms last night?

But no . . . Mrs. Calbert's voice outside the door sounded hopeful, not suspicious. And he knew she would never have let such a clear transgression of the rules go unimpeded.

Somehow, he found a hairpin lodged in the wrinkle of the bedclothes. He handed it to Clare like an olive branch. "You know you haven't a prayer in the world of repairing your hair and clothing to something approximating a pre-ravishment state," he whispered.

She looked down and gasped, then abandoned the effort to contain her hair and jerked the blanket up, making him regret the confession.

"Dr. Merial?" Mrs. Calbert's voice rang out again. More suspicious now.

The latch rattled once, twice.

Clare bolted from the bed, the blanket fisted in her hands. Her movements had the misfortune of pulling the bedclothes away from Daniel's own nude body, but as her eyes skittered across his bare chest, he could tell that, in spite of herself, she was admiring the view.

"This won't help return me to a preravishment state either," he teased. Indeed, beneath her hot gaze, his body was already stirring with interest, in spite of the racket at the door.

She tore her eyes away and tripped to the corner of the room like a frightened horse. "If you don't help set me to rights," she hissed, bending down to scoop her dress from its damp heap on the floor, "everyone will guess the moment I step from this room."

"Guess what, precisely?" Daniel asked softly. "That I love you?"

She whirled around to face him, the dress clasped tight in her fists.

He shrugged. "I think it's likely, yes. And I would have them know." He chased the confession with a smile. She cared for him. *She must.* Last night she had eagerly turned herself over to intimacy—indeed, she had been the one to pursue it. But even in the heat of the moment, she'd still not said the words he wanted to hear.

The hue of her cheeks deepened. "Daniel—" she began.

But the sound of the door scraping open pulled his attention away from the frightening flare of uncertainty he'd seen in her eyes.

Oh, *bloody fecking hell.*

His thoughts raced back on his actions last night, when he'd shut the door. Locking the door was an ingrained habit, but he had been so stunned to see Clare standing in his flat removing her wet things that he'd been close to paralyzed. He might trust the lock to hold, when properly engaged. It hadn't occurred to him to question his ability to remember to turn the key.

Mrs. Calbert stepped inside, clad in a flimsy wrapper and night rail. She gave the air a suspicious sniff, but then her eyes fell across his nude body and her mouth fell open.

"Ooooh, Dr. Merial," she breathed. "Are . . . are you waiting for me?"

Daniel narrowly resisted covering himself. He could think of far more pleasant things than being laid out for Mrs. Calbert's unwholesome perusal, but he knew Clare could use any bit of diversion he could provide at the moment.

For now, his landlady's attention was focused squarely on his . . . er . . . greeting.

And for a change the frogs were the least of his concerns.

"Mrs. Calbert," he coughed. "I . . . ah . . . I believe our original agreement stipulated that your tenants could expect some measure of privacy."

"It wasn't locked." Mrs. Calbert licked her lips, her gaze still focused too low for comfort. "And I *did* knock first."

In the shadowed corner of the room, he could see Clare jerk her dress over her head, and he breathed a sigh of relief she would at least be spared that indignity. Swinging his legs over the side of the bed, Daniel reached for his trousers. He shoved one leg in, then the other, fighting the urge to hop in the opposite direction as his landlady took a step toward him.

"I've brought you a letter." She held out an envelope. "The courier tried to sneak in without announcing himself." She frowned as he found his shirt, though whether her disapproval was due more to the courier's infraction or his disappearing nudity, it was difficult to say. "That is against the house rules, you know."

Daniel stifled a snarl. "Yes, Mrs. Calbert, I am well aware of the rules." He took the letter from her hand and tried to guide the persistent woman back toward the door. If he could just keep Clare shielded from view, they might yet escape this mess. "I shall endeavor to make sure it does not happen again. Now, if that is all—"

But Mrs. Calbert was twisting in his grasp, her eyes narrowed on something just beyond his shoulder. She stepped around him and headed for the table. "Are those . . . frogs?" She tapped a finger against the glass bowl and the amphibians exploded to life, splashing their objections.

She shrieked and jumped back a foot. "Dr. Merial!" Her voice ascended a hysterical notch. "There is a firm policy against pets!"

Daniel's hand tightened against the edge of the door. "They are not pets, Mrs. Calbert, they are part of an important scientific experiment."

"Experiment?" She whirled to face him, one stern finger already wagging in the air. "Has this anything to do with the opium?"

"There is no opium, Mrs. Calbert, as I have already—"

"Dr. Merial." Her voice raised in a screech. "I have overlooked a good deal these past six months, distracted as I've been with poor Mr. Calbert's passing. You've a fine face to recommend you, and I'd hoped your character followed suit. But you cannot just—" Her objections choked off as her eyes darted somewhere to Daniel's left. Her cheeks, always ruddy, even under the best of circumstances, turned scarlet. "You've brought in a *girl*?"

Daniel felt a bolt of protective anger. His first instinct was to defend Clare, but as he reached for an appropriate descriptor for what she was to him, he realized he wasn't sure. No matter what he hoped for—no matter, even, after all that had passed between them last night—she had not yet consented to marry him. "Not the sort of girl you are thinking," he ground out. "Miss Westmore is a respectable young lady."

"*Respectable?*" Indignation flared in Mrs. Calbert's voice. "I saw her last night. A respectable young lady does not skulk about Smithfield after dark. A respectable young lady does not sleep in a room with an unmarried gentleman. A respectable young lady does *not*—"

"Need to hear anymore." Clare stepped forward. With her hair a wild tangle about her face, she admittedly looked the furthest thing from a proper lady. The furthest thing, too, from a wallflower. She lifted her chin, those hazel eyes flashing. "Especially not from someone who sneaks into her tenants' rooms clad in her nightclothes."

"How *dare* you!" Mrs. Calbert's eyes bulged. "Why, I ought to call the copper. Have you arrested for trespassing."

Clare raised a perfectly arched brow. "An excellent idea. And when he comes, perhaps you can explain what became of the twenty shillings Dr. Merial left in your charge, when only five made it into Meg's hands."

"That's ridiculous," Mrs. Calbert sputtered, though she looked less sure of herself. "Any reasonable body would have considered that payment for taking such a terrible woman in. Why, it's a wonder I'm not in the poorhouse, the piddling income I get for my trouble." She began to edge toward the door. "But I am done with *your* sort of trouble, Dr. Merial. Frogs and whores and God knows what else, going on behind locked doors. I won't have it in my house. I expect you to be gone by noon."

The door slammed shut behind her.

"Bloody hell." Daniel rubbed a hand across his temple. "God, I am sorry, Clare. She should not have said those things about you."

"There is no need to be sorry." She released a shaky breath. "Truly, I've suffered far worse at the hands of friends this week." She bit her lip. "I am sorry for what I have done to *you*, though. I have gotten you tossed out of your rooms. Where will you go?"

Daniel hesitated. "I am sure Lady Austerley will put me up for a night or two." Though the thought of accepting such charity made his throat tighten. "And there is nothing to apologize for. You were correct to point out the hypocrisy. Mrs. Calbert has fifteen extra shillings lining her pockets, a week's rent paid in advance, and she'll probably have a new tenant installed here by dinner." He looked down at the letter in his hand. As its significance began to register in his addled brain, it occurred to him that only one client ever sent messages directly to him here, at his Smithfield address.

Urgent, Mrs. Calbert had said.

He tore open the envelope, and as he skimmed the hastily penned note, the floor seemed to tilt out from beneath him. It took a tentative touch on his arm to jerk him back to reality.

"Daniel . . . is something wrong?"

"Lady Austerley . . ." He held the letter out. "She's gone."

Chapter 30

Of all the ways Clare had imagined returning home, being left alone on the front steps of Cardwell House might have once required the furthest stretch of her imagination. But now that it was real, it seemed her imagination had left out a few additional important facts.

Such as how bruised she felt by the notion of this hurried good-bye.

And how on earth she was going to explain the bowl of frogs in her arms.

Daniel pressed a quick kiss to her forehead. "I could spare a few minutes if you want. Come in and speak to your father." But in the gruff tenor of his voice, it was clear his mind was focused on other things. Not that she blamed him. She had been nearly as shaken by the letter bearing news of Lady Austerley's passing as he, and she'd spent the long bus ride to Mayfair immersed in her own thoughts, contemplating life and death and everything in between.

"We already discussed this." She hugged the bowl tighter against her chest. "You are needed at Berkeley Square, and I . . . I would prefer to speak to my family alone."

"Shall I come later, then? Perhaps for dinner? There is still much we need to discuss."

Clare nodded, feeling a bit dizzy as she stared up at this man she'd chosen to entrust with her heart. After the violence of last night's storm, the morning had dawned clear, and the sun was bright and unforgiving against his unshaven face. He'd not put on a hat during their hasty departure, and in this moment, his face drawn in lines of grief, he looked much as he had that day in Chelsea, frowning down at her but so impossibly handsome her eyes hurt at the sight of him.

But today his anguish had not been caused by her. His pain was for another kind of loss, and she felt helpless to comfort him. He'd told her he loved her, just before it all began to unravel. She felt needy, wanting to hear it again, wanting to whisper it back in his ear.

But he was clearly hurting, and she would not be an added burden to him now.

She kissed his cheek, then turned and began to walk slowly up the gleaming white steps of Cardwell House, the bowl of frogs wobbling in her arms. On the top step she paused and pulled in a lungful of fresh air, imagining it was courage. She needed a bit at the moment, her slippers hesitating to take the last step. She'd made her choice last night with eyes wide-open, and she did not regret a moment she'd spent in Daniel's arms. But there was more to discuss this morning with her family than *her* feelings on the matter.

Clare stood on the top step and stared at the door she had known her entire life, as though seeing it for the first time. She dreaded the thought of the coming conversation. She could accept these circumstances in her own life. Indeed, she even knew a welcome twinge of relief. Hers was a fresh start, a chance to shed the false coat of Society that had never felt right, a future with Daniel smiling at her across the breakfast table, the *Times* spread out between them.

But she hated to think of what this could mean for Lucy and her debut next year.

Was she being too selfish, to want a chance for her own happiness, when it meant someone else must sacrifice theirs? It seemed patently unfair that Lucy should suffer a fate not of her own making, merely on account of a sister's ruin. Perhaps she could suggest that Father double Lucy's dowry, take the five thousand pounds that had never been rightfully hers and bolster Lucy's chance for success, in the hopes it would help overcome the stigma that would almost certainly come with this decision. She wished she had an answer, a magic solution that would make it all go away, but she knew as well as anyone the harsh realities of the ton.

And standing frozen on the front steps was not bringing her any closer to a solution.

She kicked at the door with her slipper, but when no one came, she somehow managed to open the door with the bowl of frogs balanced precariously against her chest. She stepped inside just as a flustered-looking Wilson tore into the foyer. He skidded to a halt, gaping at the frogs, then panted, "Miss Clare, *there* you are! I've been looking everywhere for you."

She tried to smile, though her heart thumped nervously at his obvious panic. It seemed her absence had been noted. "Good morning, Wilson," she said with false brightness. "Is everyone at breakfast?"

"Everyone?" The butler's voice sounded strangled. "That is one way to put it."

She cocked her head, taking a closer look at this man who kept her family running in top order. The servant's normally combed-over hair was disheveled, his waistcoat askew. "Has Mother come down for breakfast this morning, then?" Clare asked sympathetically.

"Er . . . yes. Your mother has joined the family for breakfast." He looked from right to left, and his voice dropped to a haggard whisper. "They asked for you, but then Mr. Alban came to call." Wilson mopped his brow with a kerchief pulled from one pocket. "I did not tell Lady Cardwell, per your previous instructions, and it seemed Lord Cardwell would also not be a good choice, given that the morning is already in upheaval. And I could not find you anywhere, and that was when I feared you had—"

"It's all right," Clare soothed, fearing for the poor man's health. *Poor Wilson.* They each had their secrets, and he was charged with the keeping of all of them. "All that matters is I am here now." She handed him the bowl of frogs. "Where is Mr. Alban?"

"I have installed him in the drawing room, my lady, but made sure not to mention anything to Lady Cardwell. I hope that meets with your approval?"

"Yes, of course. You may tell my family I will be in shortly." She offered an apologetic smile. "And you no longer need to hide word of Mr. Alban's visit from Mother. I should not have asked you to keep that secret from the start." Indeed, if she had been more honest, none of this would have progressed to the point at which she now found herself.

He looked relieved. "Very good, Miss Clare."

She set off toward the drawing room, resolved to tell Mr. Alban once and for all why he must no longer come to call.

"Miss Clare!"

Clare looked over her shoulder.

Wilson held out the bowl. "Are these to be taken in to breakfast then?" He looked stricken, as if perhaps they were intended to *be* breakfast.

"No." She stifled a smile. "The frogs are for Geoffrey, a gift from Dr. Merial. You may put them in his room."

Mr. Alban was pacing by the picture window, his hat in his hands, looking very much like a man with an important question on his mind. She stepped inside, smoothing a hand down the front of her wrinkled skirts. It was odd, but for this coming audience her feet were not inclined to hesitate. Her ruin was already assured, thanks to the rumors Sophie had circulated. There was no thought of denial or of sweeping it aside. For once, she was determined to face the ton and their judgments head on. For now, though, she would start with the future Duke of Harrington.

She put on a smile. "You are up early today, Mr. Alban."

He turned. "My apologies, Miss Westmore. I had a matter of some urgency to discuss with you."

It was startling to see him now, and, with more educated eyes, see the strong resemblance to her own features. He was the only connection she had to the gentleman who had sired her, and she imagined now she might see some of that man in Alban's face.

"I know my timing must be very inconvenient," he went on, "but I must beg a moment to explain something, and ask you a question."

Clare felt a jolt of worry. "There is no need to apologize. In truth, there is a vital matter I must discuss with you as well."

"If I might be permitted to speak first." He twisted the brim of his hat in his hands. "At the musicale, I wanted to ask you an important question, but you left before it could be said."

She shook her head, trying to dislodge the thought. "Please, Mr. Alban, I beg you not say anything more." Bile crept up the back of her throat. "I cannot marry you, under any circumstances."

"*Marry* you?" His mouth opened in astonishment. "Miss Westmore, I must assure you, that is not the nature of my interest in you."

"It isn't?" Clare stared at him in surprise. "But . . . all those waltzes. The times you came to call—"

"I wanted to know you." He walked toward her, hazel eyes searching her own. "Since I met you, I've been struck by the oddest sense of familiarity. I called on you in the hopes of meeting your family, sorting out whether my thoughts might be true."

"Thoughts?" Clare echoed, taking a cautious step backward, until the wall met the stiffened blades of her shoulders. He took another step toward her, and she froze. She didn't know what to think, and permitting him to come too close was something she was not yet prepared to do. But he didn't look dangerous or deranged.

He looked nervous, the absolute opposite of how a future duke should look.

"Miss Westmore . . . I must beg that you forgive this presumptive question. I assure you, I mean no harm." He spread his hands, his hat loosely clutched between his left fingers. "But is it possible . . . is it conceivable . . . that you might be my niece?"

Clare gasped in surprise. "You know?"

"I suspected." His gaze softened. "Hoped, I suppose."

Her mind raced backward, over all the conversations they had shared. She could see it now, of course. During his visits he'd dwelled upon on the weather. *Her lack of resemblance to her family.* Painful, ordinary things. She had naively presumed his strong interest lay in a particular

direction—namely, whether she would make an appropriate duchess. But with the veil of self-absorption finally
lifted, she could envision a different interpretation.

He'd suspected their family connection.

He pulled a miniature from his pocket, and this time
Clare let him approach. She was tempted to close her
eyes, but then she looked down and caught her breath. A
young man was painted on the small canvas. Her greedy
gaze fell upon starkly familiar features. The pert chin,
brown hair, hazel eyes . . .

Her father.

"You look just like him, you see." Alban held it out,
and after a moment Clare dared to pick it up, though her
fingers shook with the effort. "I worshipped him when I
was a child. I was still a small boy when he died, and I
was devastated by his death, as were my parents. But in
you, a piece of him clearly lives on." He smiled gently. "I
am so glad to have uncovered the truth."

Clare's palm curled possessively around the miniature.
"But why?" she somehow managed to say. "My illegitimacy hardly does either of us credit."

"Illegitimate?" He sounded shocked. "Why would you
presume that? Benjamin had married your mother, before
he died."

"But my mother said he was killed in a carriage accident en route to Gretna." She lifted a hand to her mouth,
catching the gasp of uncertainty. Actually, that wasn't entirely true. Her mother had not actually specified on *which*
side of the journey the accident had occurred. Moreover,
Mother had confessed a need to guard her reputation, in
order to marry quickly.

A confessed elopement might have destroyed her
chance at such security.

"Last week, I sent my steward to Gretna," Alban said.

"I told him to search every blacksmith shop, every parish register he could find."

Her lungs felt heavy, bruised. "Why would you do such a thing?" she choked out. "Why confirm such a scandal?"

"Because the scandal you speak of is my fault."

"*You* started the rumor?"

He looked uncomfortable. "It was more that I made the mistake of posing the question of your parentage to your friend, Lady Sophie, at the start of the Season, and she proved more malicious than I had imagined. Once the rumors began to circulate, I knew I needed to move quickly. My steward returned last night with proof of my brother's marriage in hand. You are his daughter, Clare. His *legitimate* daughter. And far less a scandal to know their union was lawful, I should think."

Clare leaned back against the wall, not trusting her knees to hold. She couldn't quite wrap her head around the legitimate part.

Alban spread his hands. "'Tis not as grand as being recognized as a viscount's daughter, but my family is respectable enough, particularly now that circumstances have made me the duke's heir. My brother died without much, but what little bit of money he had set aside was properly invested. In the twenty years since his death, it has turned a handsome profit. About six thousand pounds now, I should think. That money should go to my brother's child. I cannot undo what Lady Sophie has done, but perhaps, in this small way, I can make some amends."

Oh God, oh God, oh God. Surely he was not serious.

But if he was joking, he was a better thespian than even Sophie.

A clatter of shoes and voices at the drawing room door pulled Clare's attention beyond the immediate conundrum of her birth and the money she was apparently to inherit. Without warning, her family began to pour into the drawing room.

Mr. Alban watched them come with a raised brow. He bent his head to her ear. "They really don't look anything like you, do they?" he chuckled.

"No." Clare shook her head, her lips twitching as she watched them come, chattering in their familiar, comfortable way. "But that doesn't mean I do not love them." It would have once been her worst nightmare, Alban's exposure to her family's boisterous and eccentric nature. But in this moment she wanted only to introduce them all.

"Ah, Clare, there you are." Her father beamed. "I've an important introduction to make."

"As do I." She turned to Alban. "Mr. Alban, you've met my mother last night, and Lucy during your last visit, but may I present my father, Lord Cardwell, and my brother, Geoffrey?"

Her father's gaze moved from Alban to Clare, then back again. Clare could see a flare of understanding—or perhaps, more correctly, suspicion—in the hardening of his jaw. "I've heard a lot about you, Mr. Alban." He hesitated. "But this first sight of you is something of a surprise to me, and I am sure you understand why."

Alban inclined his head. "Yes. The resemblance is striking, isn't it?"

Her father rubbed the back of his palm across his forehead. "Well, Harrington's heir or no, you must know I cannot give my blessing for you to marry my daughter."

Alban lifted his hands in assurance. "I have come as a matter of family, not matrimony."

As Clare exhaled in abject relief at the lack of histrionics, it occurred to her there seemed to be too many people in the room. She counted in her head. Lucy, Geoffrey, Lucy . . .

Her eyes pulled back to the doorway. Two Lucys?

But no . . . there was a stranger who looked like Lucy, hesitating just outside the door. And perhaps not a stranger, either. Because the young woman had fly-away blond hair. Westmore blue eyes. And—as she finally tripped forward—a tendency to fall over her feet.

"I followed your advice." Clare was startled to hear her mother's voice close to her ear. "I told your father he could bring Lydia here. You were correct, it was the right thing to do. And perhaps now we can all heal, as a family."

Understanding dawned. At last it all made sense. Wilson's distress, and his declaration that *everyone* was awaiting her at breakfast.

"But . . . what about Lucy's Season?" she whispered back, her mind stumbling over all the reasons Mother had initially objected to having the girl come to Cardwell House.

"We may need to postpone Lucy's debut for a few years," Mother confirmed in a low voice. "But then we'll just have to make it so grand she rises above the gossip."

Clare turned her mother's words over in her mind. Could it really be so simple? Her own reputation no longer mattered, but she was still worried what this all might mean for Lucy. But maybe Mother was right. Time had a way of easing the worst sort of gossip, and in a few years Sophie and Rose would hopefully be married and moldering away in their husbands' country estates, unable to damage Lucy's reputation with their snide remarks and misplaced wit.

And perhaps—gossip or no—it wouldn't be a terrible thing to give Lucy a few more years to grow into her skin and out of her crazy ideas.

Clare pressed the miniature she still held into her mother's hand, then stepped toward the young woman who was looking shyly in her direction. As she contemplated what the future might hold for all of them, her heart felt a stone lighter.

Or perhaps that it was finally full.

She smiled. "And Mr. Alban, may I also present my sister, Miss Lydia Westmore," she said, and then folded her newest sibling in her arms.

Chapter 31

Sighing in pleasure, Clare set down her fork on top of her empty plate.

Her corset was now groaning against its seams, but tonight the discomfort was easy to overlook. Far from being a formal affair, the meal carried the ring of laughter and the hum of enthusiastic conversation. She'd finished her entire plate before she realized it.

And her heart was every bit as full as her stomach.

Lydia and Lucy were seated side by side, blond heads bent close, giggling over the plans they were making to feed the ducks in Hyde Park tomorrow. Geoffrey was explaining the principles of electrifying a doorknob to a much-bemused Mr. Alban, demonstrating the manner of twisting the wires around the knob by wrapping his napkin around his fork.

And by the warm look her parents were exchanging down the dining room table, it seemed clear that dyspepsia had been banished from Father's menu tonight.

There was only one person missing to make the meal perfect. And while he had not yet come, as he'd said he would, Clare could see that it was long past time to introduce her family to the idea that she planned to spend the rest of her life as Mrs. Daniel Merial.

She felt suddenly breathless. Not out of fear, but out of anticipation. No matter their reaction to what she was about to say, this was the choice she *wished* to make. She would not be swayed by her mother's remonstrations or tears. Neither would she be swayed by Father's talk of dowries or peers. She was no longer interested in making a proper match.

Why would she be? She was no longer a proper young woman. She'd been freed from the yoke of that responsibility, and had no intention of shouldering it again.

She raised her glass. "Mother, Father, I have some news I want to share while everyone is sitting down." She delivered the words with what she thought was an admirable steadiness, but her voice must have held a secret tremor. Or perhaps it was that today, of all days, the promise of *more* news was impossible for her family to ignore.

Whatever the cause, the table fell silent.

Clare looked out over her family's expectant faces, considering how to begin this necessary speech. "If I have learned nothing else today, it is that secrets have no place among family. We should be open and honest with each other, even if we fear the news might disappoint someone we love. After all, it is better to tell the truth than live a lie."

"Hear, hear!" Geoffrey crowed, raising the half glass of wine he'd been permitted tonight, on account of it being a special occasion.

She glared at her brother until he settled, then lowered her glass and drew a deep breath. "Even though I know that what I am about to say may come as a shock, I will not keep this a secret anymore. I have made my choice for a husband."

There was a moment of strained silence, and then Mother lifted a trembling hand to her throat. "Never say you've finally decided on Mr. Meeks," she said in a choked voice. "I know I had pushed you in that direction, but I must say, I have my doubts as to the suitability of the match."

Clare bit her lip, trying not to laugh. How could Mother think she would choose Meeks, after everything they had discussed?

"I know the revelations of the day are a lot to take in," Mother went on, "but surely there is no need for panic."

"I am not panicking, Mother." In fact, Clare felt the oddest sense of calm, as though the air in the room and the blood in her veins had stilled in anticipation of her announcement. "It is just that given the importance of my decision, I do not want to wait a second longer to tell you."

Her mother's brow wrinkled. "There is no need to be hasty."

"I am not being hasty either," Clare protested, the sense of calm slipping toward irritation now. This was *her* news to share. And she'd not yet had chance to share the most important bits.

"I didn't know you were interested in Mr. Meeks," Alban said, turning in his chair to face Clare. "I can't fault your choice, though. He's a capital fellow. Handy with a cricket bat. I went to school with him at Harrow."

"I like a good game of cricket myself," Geoffrey exclaimed. He straightened in his chair. "I say, Father, maybe *I* should go to Harrow." A grin washed over his face. "And it would be lovely to trounce those Eton dandies in next year's match at Lord's field."

"Harrow, hmm?" Father scratched his head. "That is not such a bad idea."

"I can speak with the headmaster, if you like," Alban offered. "I've kept in touch with him through the years."

"Now, who exactly is Mr. Meeks?" Lucy broke in, her eyes narrowed, as if trying to remember. "I do not recall spying on someone by that name."

Clare sighed. Good heavens, there were five different trains of thought happening, and nary a one involved her intention to marry Daniel. When had the conversation been so thoroughly wrestled from her hands?

And how could she wrestle it back?

"About my news," she huffed. "If you would just let me explain—"

"Yes, we were talking about your choice of husband," Mother interrupted, her voice now contorted into a shrill knot. "I *know* I had been encouraging you to marry quickly, but I am quite regretting it now."

"There is no need to regret—" Clare started, only to be cut off once more.

"And you must think of poor Mr. Meeks as well. The man is admittedly fond of you, but with the details of your birth to be made public now, he could hardly be blamed if he cries off." Mother broke off her tirade, then tilted her head, staring quizzically down the table toward Clare's father. "Unless we doubled your dowry," she mused. "*That* might tempt Mr. Meeks to overlook it all."

Clare almost choked on her snort of laughter. "Er . . . no." She hesitated, realizing how ungrateful she probably sounded. "That is, thank you, but I am not interested in doubling my dowry. In fact, I am not interested in *any* part of my dowry."

Father's brows bunched. "Clare, you must know I would gladly double your dowry if it brings you happiness."

Her throat clogged with tears, and the room seemed to swim before her eyes. "Thank you, Father. Your offer means more to me than you can imagine." She shook her head, trying to clear her vision. "But with the inheritance provided by Mr. Alban, it seems I no longer have need of a dowry." She glanced at her sisters—one familiar, one new. "You might consider doubling Lucy's, though, or providing one for Lydia."

Her father rubbed a surreptitious finger along the bridge of his nose, and though he was some ten feet away, Clare could see that his eyes were suspiciously moist. "You were always my most sensible child," he said, his voiced graveled with emotion. "It should not surprise me you would be sensible in this as well."

The tears fell in earnest now from Clare's own eyes, splashing on her empty plate. She still considered him her father, and always would. He was the man who had raised her, after all, the father she loved.

But to hear he still considered her *his* child closed the last tiny hole in her heart.

She swiped a hand across her eyes and met her mother's still-worried gaze. "I am not interested in Mr. Meeks in that way, Mother. I would not pretend I might make a suitable viscountess, not anymore."

"But with the right dowry," her mother protested, "you might still aim for a baron."

"Or a second son," Geoffrey supplied helpfully. When all the women at the table stared at him, he shrugged. "You cannot deny that second sons can afford to be less fastidious in their choice of a wife, the lucky bastards. I live in terror of the thought of the shrew-faced heiress I will probably be forced to marry when I come of age." He grinned. "Maybe the trick is to be so incorrigible no one respectable will have me."

Clare winced. There was a terrifying logic at play in her brother's mind. And there was no doubt he was well on his way to earning the title of such an adjective. But she didn't want to talk about Geoffrey's future. She wanted to talk about *hers*.

It was time to end this circus of a confession, in the only way she knew how.

She placed two hands on the table and pushed herself to standing. Unfortunately, this made the gentleman at the table gain their feet as well, which rather lessened the effect. She had to fight the urge to roll her eyes at the absurdity of manners at a time like this.

"I do not want to marry Mr. Meeks!" she all but shouted. "I want to marry the man I love, and the man I love is Daniel Merial."

She looked around the silent table, taking in her family's stunned faces.

"He makes me happy. He makes me *beyond* happy. He challenges me, even as he accepts my flaws. And it really doesn't matter if you object or not. If you will not grant your consent now, Father, I will simply wait until I am of age."

"Why would I refuse my consent?" Father asked slowly.

Of all the things she had expected her father to say, this was furthest from what she had constructed in her head. "Well . . . because he is my doctor," Clare admitted.

"Because he is poor," Mother said, though she sounded unsure of herself.

"Because he's a Chartist?" Lucy said, her tone more of a question than a fact. But there was no surprise in the echo of her voice. Indeed, a smile was stealing across her face, one that quite cried *I told you so*, and she nudged Lydia with an elbow, nodding.

For her part, Lydia stayed wide-eyed and silent, though she sent Clare a distinctly sympathetic smile.

"Because he's a Gypsy," Geoffrey added, making Clare want to wrap her fingers around her brother's neck. He rubbed his hands together with glee. "Oh, this is rich. It is the prank to end all pranks, and I didn't even come up with it!"

"It's not a prank," Clare muttered, feeling deflated. "It's my *life*."

"And I am not saying no," Father said, pinning her with his gaze over the rims of his glasses. "Sit down, please, so we can discuss this like adults."

Clare sat.

Father stayed standing, staring down at her from his position at the head of the table. His hand stroked his chin in thought. "Dr. Merial makes you happy?" he finally asked.

Clare nodded.

"And you would relinquish your dowry to have him as your choice?"

"Without hesitation," Clare answered, her heart beating mad circles in her chest. She would wait to marry Daniel until her twenty-first birthday if she had to, but she really didn't want to delay her future happiness a moment longer than necessary. "In fact, I quite insist on it."

"I see." Father looked at Mother. "You were objecting to hasty decisions earlier. Do you have any objections to her choice of Dr. Merial, beyond the state of the man's lack of a title?"

"No." Her mother shook her head. "Not if she loves him." She smiled then, just enough, and to Clare's mind—though it was nigh on nine o'clock at night—the sun began to peek over the dim horizon of this day.

"Well then, I see no reason to withhold my consent." Father lifted his chin in Alban's direction. "And besides, if it came right down to it, you could always petition the court to recognize Mr. Alban as your guardian and have *him* offer consent." He shook his head. "No, far better to do it this way. Keep it in the family." His face grew stern, accenting the lines at the corners of his eyes. "I love you, Clare. You will always be my daughter. And though it may be hard to see sometimes, the happiness of his daughters is a father's primary concern."

Clare flew from her chair and launched herself down the long length of table into her father's arms. As his arms closed around her, she breathed in his pipe tobacco and peppermint scent, utterly swamped with happiness.

It was going to be all right.

If only Daniel would come.

May 24, 1848

Dear Diary,

My happiness seems assured, but for one important fact.

Daniel has not come, as he promised he would.

It has been two days. Two days full of new family, but missing the one man I most want to see. I have so much to tell him, so much to explain. But he has not responded to the letter I sent to St. Bartholomew's, and I've no notion of where he might be staying now that he has been turned out of his rooms.

I am trying to be patient, truly I am. But if there is one thing I have learned over the past month it is that I am not a patient sort of woman.

And I would have thought Daniel knew that as well.

Chapter 32

*L*ydia, what is the difference between a courtesan and a mistress?" Lucy asked as they crowded into the hot, busy vestibule of St. Paul's Cathedral.

Geoffrey leered at a woman to his left. "And do you think I might meet one here today?" he asked.

Clare glared daggers at Geoffrey's back—not that the imp seemed to notice or care. Dressed as he was in respectable black, he gave an initial impression of maturity, but he had quite ruined the gentlemanly effect by tugging at his necktie until it tilted in a raffish fashion.

"For heaven's sake," she warned. "Show a little respect. We are in a *church*."

And by the looks of things, they were not the only ones.

It felt as though the entire city had turned out for the dowager countess's funeral. Everywhere Clare looked, she saw somber black crepe and gray wool, despite the swelter of May. Perhaps, she thought peevishly, if a few more of these souls had turned out during the woman's life, without a lavish ball or musicale to draw them to her side, Lady Austerley might have kept her health a bit longer.

"Presumably courtesans go to church as well." Geoffrey shrugged, glancing back over one shoulder with a devilish grin. "They've more sins to atone. And it seems like it's time for me to begin thinking about these things if I am to begin cultivating a reputation as a proper rake."

"Oh, stuff it Geoffrey," Lucy interrupted. "*I* was asking because I intend to help save them from scoundrels like you." She arched a fair brow in Clare's direction. "And you needn't look as though I've said something blasphemous. I am only asking about them because of your suggestion."

"My suggestion?" Clare echoed, thoroughly confused.

"You told me to properly research my topics, after the disaster with the horses."

Clare closed her eyes and prayed she might find a modicum of patience. Did Geoffrey really think there was such a thing as a *proper* rake? And leave it to Lucy to decide fallen women were her latest obsession, with Lydia so recently joined the family. Given that Mother and Father had gone on ahead and were already waiting in the family box, it was her responsibility to keep them all in line. She tried to bolster the energy to deliver a lecture worthy of an older sister.

But when she opened her eyes, instead of landing on her siblings, her gaze insisted on scanning the milling crowd instead.

Speaking of prayers . . .

She knew Daniel was here somewhere, paying his respects.

Her pulse kicked up a notch.

"It is all right." Lydia's quiet response pulled Clare's attention reluctantly back to the conversation. "I don't mind the questions. The truth is, I don't know much about the subject." She shrugged her thin shoulders. "My mother was simply my mother."

Lucy looked momentarily chagrined. "Oh, I am so sorry, Lydia. You mustn't take offense to my rambling. I do not mean any disrespect, you know. It is just that I had hoped you might know more of these things than I do."

Lydia shook her head. "I never even realized my mother had been your father's mistress until I found her letters after she died. From what I read, I suspect their arrangement was based as much on love as necessity."

Lucy stepped closer and slid her arm around Lydia's shoulders. The sight of their growing closeness sent a pang through Clare's heart. There was no doubt that out of all of them, Lucy had the most to lose in this new family arrangement. And yet, she'd welcomed their long-lost sister as though she were a veritable pardon.

Perhaps to Lucy's mind she was.

But Clare knew that Mother was already plotting a spectacular launch for Lucy in a few years, something the ton would remember, in order to quell the inevitable whispers. Perhaps, when enough time had passed, they might even eventually give Lydia a Season of her own. She only hoped *both* her sisters were prepared for Mother's meddling.

Despite the assurance being offered by Lucy's arm, Lydia's feet seemed to hesitate. She looked miserably over at the rows of pews marching to either side of the cathedral, where those without the money to rent a box sat. "You have all been so kind to me. But are you sure you wouldn't rather I sit back here? I don't mind . . . truly, I don't. I do not want to do anything that might cause people to whisper."

"They will find out eventually," Clare said firmly. "And as Mother said, it can only help matters to have your first appearance with our family be in church." She intended her words to soothe, but by the stiffening of Lydia's posture, she could tell the girl was not convinced.

"Well I, for one, cannot wait to see the expression on people's faces when you sit down in the Cardwell box," Geoffrey said, a tad too gleefully. It was clear he was every bit as excited by the stir they were about to cause as the new sister he had to torment. "It's housed five generations of Cardwell arses, you know."

"As apt a description for our brother as there ever was." Lucy squeezed Lydia's shoulder encouragingly. "But don't worry. I promise I shall sit between you and the monster. He pinches, you know. Besides, if the service goes long, I'll need you to keep me awake." As they continued their good-natured banter, Clare slowed her feet until the milling bodies quite obliterated her family from view. She might be the oldest sister, but she could see they didn't need her to hover beside them, not anymore.

She drew a deep breath, seeking courage.

Because Lydia wasn't the only one about to cause a stir.

She craned her neck, searching again for a handsome dark head. It had been four days since Daniel had left her on the Cardwell House steps. Four days since she'd told her family of her intentions, their acceptance making it easier to manage than she had feared. But despite the remarkable and unanticipated support of her family, Daniel was proving the biggest uncertainty of all, and every minute without word from him seemed to stretch to five. Whatever the cause for his absence, it felt suspiciously like a rejection. He'd said he would come, but he hadn't. Worse, the letters she had sent to St. Bartholomew's had gone unanswered. She knew of no other way to reach out to him, given that he'd been turned out of his flat.

Had he changed his mind? Begun to regret his choice?

Or was he simply lost, mourning the death of his friend? She finally caught sight of him, sitting alone in a common pew on the left side of the cathedral. With a jolt of awareness, she realized he was watching her. Everything about him—from his hair to the hands shoved in his jacket pockets—gave the impression of a dark scowl.

Clearly, he had noticed her arrival.

But he was neither standing up nor lifting a hand in greeting.

And so Clare gathered her skirts and wits in hand and started toward him. He was avoiding her, though she didn't know why. But she refused to relinquish the future she'd chosen without a fight.

As ALWAYS, THE sight of her kicked the breath from Daniel's lungs.

Like a man on borrowed time, he watched her come, wanting but wary of each torturous inch lost between them. As she settled onto the pew next to him, the floral scent he always associated with her washed over him like scalding water. He'd once presumed the fragrance to be an artifact—perfume or soap, liberally applied. After the night they'd spent together, he now knew it was something that hovered beneath her skin, impossible to wash away.

Equally impossible to forget.

She stared straight ahead, toward the front of the cathedral, but he sensed she hovered on the edge of some very choice words. Her cheeks were already awash in color, though they'd exchanged nothing more potent than a glance across the vestibule. God knew he deserved whatever bit of anger she had brought with her, given that he'd been too busy to see her.

No, that wasn't quite right. He'd been too cowardly to see her.

He was brave enough to admit that, if nothing else.

From the start she had always swayed his resolve to be

sensible, and the only solution at his disposal these four days past had been distance.

God, he'd made so many mistakes. He'd been desperate to believe her. That the stark differences in their stations didn't matter if love bound them together. She'd seemed to believe it herself, that night in his flat. After all, she'd come to *him*, knowing the risks. There was no duress, no reason for her to have been here other than her own want.

But she'd not spoken of love the following morning, or even of marriage.

All during that long omnibus ride to Mayfair, after the disaster of the morning and the terrible letter bearing news of Lady Austerley's death, she'd sat beside him, pinched and silent. It had startled him to realize that perhaps he did not care if she was not able to return the sentiment, if only she would consent to tolerate him.

But then he'd seen her hesitate, there on her family's front steps, and he'd known she was dreading speaking with her family. *About him.* He had imagined, in the slowing of her feet, that she must finally see it all clearly. He was a burden she had shouldered, a mistake she would now be forced to live with.

And he'd known only that he didn't want to be the man who ruined her life.

He was too weak to resist watching her now, though, and his head turned toward her of its own volition. She smoothed black gloves down the front of her skirts but did not look at him. Like the rest of the crowd, she was dressed in somber clothing, but unlike the others, she seemed to shine like a beacon, blinding him to his resolve to keep a firm distance.

"It seems congratulations are in order," she said crisply.

Out of all the things he might have expected her to say, this fell somewhat short. "Congratulations?" he echoed, staring at her profile. "For what, precisely?" Was she con-

gratulating him on his pressing grief over Lady Austerley's passing?

Or, perhaps his idiocy in all things related to her?

"Your manuscript was published yesterday in the
Lancet."

He exhaled. "I was not aware you regularly read the
Lancet."

"I do not." She shot him a sideways glance, and in the
sudden purse of her lips he was reminded of how she had
looked that evening in the wallflower line, so many weeks
ago. "But the *Times* ran a feature on it this morning. They
are calling your anesthetic regulator a miraculous invention. There is even talk of a potential knighthood. You
must have been so pleased with your success you forgot
to come and call." Her gaze more fully met his, and he
thought he saw a challenge in those hazel depths. "As you
promised."

Daniel felt mired in the absurdity of this conversation.

Pleased with his success? How could he be, when he
could think of nothing but her?

Once upon a time he had dreamed of the very sort of
success that had been delivered into his hands these past
few days—the acknowledgment from the editors who had
once given him naught but scathing rejections, the admiration and respect of his peers at St. Bartholomew's. But
now that his grand idea had been published, it was pain-
fully clear that without someone to share it with, those
accolades—those triumphs—were hollow, at best.

He settled on a response that held echoes of the truth,
but avoided the more pertinent part of her question. "I am
pleased it will benefit those who need it, yes."

He could see the clench of her jaw. "Why didn't you
come?" Her voice dropped to a whisper, and this, finally,
snapped him out of his daze. Whispers implied secrets.

And secrets implied shame.

In the end, *this* was why he'd stayed away, despite the almost overwhelming need he'd felt to see her. *"Why?"* He laughed, and it was a harsh, regrettable sound. "Because you deserve better, Clare. Better than me, and better than the life I can give you." And if she refused to see it herself, he would make this sacrifice to protect her.

She stiffened. "Are you telling me you regret that night?"

"No. But *you* should." He tugged a hand through his hair. "I've not a spare farthing to my name, nor a home to offer you. I've spent every shred of my savings, designing and testing the regulator. Now, with Lady Austerley's passing, I've lost one of my primary sources of income."

He closed his eyes, as if that could somehow extinguish the fact that Lady Austerley's coffin waited at the front of the cathedral. Knowing the old dragon as he did, she had probably arranged to be buried in a corset and ball gown. He felt numbed by the loss of her, and the fact that he had not been able to save her, even from herself. Worse, he felt embarrassed by his grief. Lady Austerley would have laughed at such histrionics.

He opened his eyes to find Clare watching him, her eyes wide with something that might have been sympathy. "You miss her." She did not phrase it as a question.

He nodded. "Not that financial matters lay at the core of my friendship with the countess," he added, more gently now, "but I am in no position to support you now that she is gone. *That* is why I did not come to Cardwell House." He breathed in the resulting silence, trying to quell the hemorrhaging of his heart. Because it was a half-truth, at best.

He would live in a hovel with Clare, if only he could believe that she loved him.

Her hand settled on his arm, and he could see her throat working above the black lace of her collar. "Daniel . . .

you spent your savings for the betterment of the world, and you haven't a spare farthing because you've spent them all on marzipan and reformed prostitutes. And you've been turned out of your flat because of me. Now you are mourning the loss of a good friend, and there is honor in that—in *you*—whether you see it or not."

Christ. He was so tempted to believe her, to sink into the acceptance she offered. But he feared his instincts were the opposite of trustworthy, mired as they were in selfish hope. Why in the devil was she saying these things, and making these arguments, when he had *seen* her warring with the enormity of the decision she faced?

"If you believe those things," he said miserably, "then why did you hesitate?"

She blinked in confusion. "Hesitate?"

"You hesitated, the day I took you back to Cardwell House. I saw you, there on the steps." He exhaled, the truth at last laid at her feet. "It was clear you were thinking of all you might lose. Your family, your dowry. And you were right to think of those things. *That* is why I didn't come."

A look of surprise, then horror, crossed her face. "You don't understand." She shook her head. "I admit, I *did* hesitate that day, but not for the reasons you think. I was worried about Lucy, and what my illegitimacy might mean for her future. I swear, my dowry—*you*—never impacted my decision. You are worth more than five thousand pounds to me." Her fingers tightened over his arm. "Or is it that you will not have *me* without it?"

"*No.*" Daniel nearly choked on the word. "I would marry you if you hadn't a penny to your name. But I will not trap you in a marriage with a man you cannot love, simply out of my own selfish needs."

"*That* is what this is about?" she demanded in an astonished whisper. "You think I don't love you?" She slid closer, until her skirts brushed against his trousers and he had to brace himself against the feel of her. "For all your ability to see my crooked teeth, the furrow between my eyes . . . how can you not see this, too?"

Daniel stared down at her, at the tears swimming in her eyes. For the first time in days hope shifted in his chest. Was it possible he had so misread the situation?

And then hard, feminine laughter jerked Daniel's focus clean over Clare's shoulder.

"Well, well, well, what do we have here? The ton's newest disgrace and her doctor."

Oh, bloody hell. Lady Sophie Barnes was standing at the edge of their row. And she looked far too delighted to see them.

Chapter 33

Clare stood up, her heart pounding. She was grateful to feel Daniel rise with her. The hum of the busy cathedral seemed to recede to a whisper. Or perhaps it was that every sense she possessed was trained on the man standing beside her. The man who loved her so much he had been willing to let her go, simply because he thought her unsure of her own feelings.

And the man she prayed had been convinced she loved him in return.

"What do you want, Sophie?" Clare was proud to hear her voice did not tremble.

Sophie tapped the edge of her black silk fan against one hand and leaned toward Rose, who stood eagerly at her elbow. "What do you think, Rose? Has our dear friend been keeping secrets from us? Were all those threats the night of the musicale just a ruse to throw us off her own trail?"

"Indeed." Rose giggled. "It appears she suffers a sordid curiosity in the doctor herself. Perhaps we should tell someone."

Sophie smiled unkindly. "Perhaps we should tell *everyone*." Her smile shifted into more of a sneer. "Then again, given her origins, perhaps such low standards make perfect sense."

Clare breathed in deeply, anchoring herself in the dry, dusty air of the cathedral and the faint scent of chloroform that still clung to Daniel's coat. She met the gaze of her former friend head-on. "I am as legitimate as you, Sophie. My mother and my real father were married. And if you don't believe me, you can ask Mr. Alban. My *uncle*."

There was a moment of dumbstruck silence before a mean, ugly smile claimed Sophie's face. "You can't be Alban's niece," she sneered. "Surely I would have heard such a thing."

"Can't I?" Clare lifted her chin. "You don't know everything, Sophie. For example, I would wager you have no idea I am something of an heiress as well."

Sophie's sneer faltered, ever so slightly. A less caring soul would take pride in such an impossible feat, tuck it away to savor later, or else plot how to twist it to her advantage. That was, in fact, what Sophie herself would have done. But Clare was a changed person.

And besting Sophie and Rose was not her primary goal.

"It cannot be true." Sophie's cheeks washed with unbecoming color. *Pink*. The most hideous shade possible, given her olive complexion. But rather than taking pleasure in the unbecoming transformation, Clare discovered she only felt sorry for her. Because *she* had the love of a brilliant man, and a future worth holding in her hands.

Sophie had her mean-spirited gossip and little else to sustain her.

"I imagine learning the news in this manner must come as a bit of a shock," Clare went on, as if her heart weren't twisting in her chest. "But I am not surprised you haven't heard any of it, given that Mr. Alban no longer trusts your judgment. So do your best, Sophie. Gossip to your heart's content. Tell whoever you want, *whatever* you want. I am not ashamed of my past or who I am. And I refuse to let your vain and empty threats hurt me anymore."

Sophie's green-eyed gaze raised to Daniel. "Oh really?" Her lips curved upward once more. "And how does Dr. Merial fit into this charming little picture? I've asked my father about him, you know. It seems he is known to be something of a Chartist sympathizer." Her eyes narrowed back toward Clare. "And if you *are* the future duke's niece, surely you realize an association with someone of that reputation is ruinous."

Clare tensed. She didn't mind so much when Sophie was spewing her venom toward her, but now she was shifting her sights to Daniel. It was difficult to believe she had once lived and breathed for this girl's approval. What a fool she had been, to believe her life rested so precariously on the opinions of Lady Sophie Barnes and the upper ten thousand.

"According to whose definition of ruin?" Clare demanded. "Unlike you, my future is no longer dependent on marriage to a proper peer. My life is my own, to do as I please, and I'll have you know I sympathize with the Chartists as well. If either of you ever took the time to read a newspaper, you might discover there's a revolution occurring that is far bigger than Mayfair, and certainly bigger than the likes of you."

Clare took a determined step backward. Not in retreat. *Toward the man she loved.*

"So I will gladly tell you how Daniel fits into my life," she went on, her voice raised so high it turned heads several pews over, "because I am not ashamed for you to know." Her hand fumbled behind her and she breathed a sigh of relief as she felt his fingers curve over hers.

Sophie's lip curled. " 'Daniel,' is it?"

"Yes." Clare drew a deep breath. "Daniel Merial. The son of a Gypsy horse trader, and the most brilliant man I know." She turned and looked up at his darkly handsome face, knowing she would never hesitate again where this man was concerned. "The man I love."

IT OCCURRED TO Daniel that in this moment, with her hand squeezed tight in his and her heart so publicly bared, she was neither a lady nor a wallflower.

She was simply Clare.

A woman who had just told half of London she loved him.

"You . . . *love* me?" he asked hoarsely.

"Yes." Her eyes met his, so achingly beautiful he had to think to breathe. "I love you," she said again, her fingers curling into his. "And I would marry you tomorrow, if you would but ask me properly."

Daniel studied the features he knew as well as his own, cataloging the signs. Her color was excellent, her respirations even. Even more telling, her brow was smooth, no furrow to speak of. She had not had to think overly hard on this decision, and with that knowledge, his past four days of uncertainty and the eyes of the crowd fell away.

"Miss Clare Westmore," he said, lifting her gloved hand to his lips. "It would be my greatest pleasure if you would do me the honor of becoming my wife."

"That isn't exactly framed as a question," she said, her voice thick with emotion.

He chuckled. "That is because I no longer harbor any doubts as to your intentions, my love." He whispered the endearment, and as a tear spilled down her cheek, he brushed it away with the pad of his thumb. "Will you marry me, Clare?"

"Yes," she whispered, and then she was in his arms.

He caught her cry of gladness against his lips, and as his arms closed around her, he knew a moment's astonishment that she had done such a thing, in such a place.

It was nothing like that day in Chelsea.

For one thing, he could tell she kissed him out of love, not out of curiosity. He could tell this kiss was different, too, by the way she trembled against him, and by the way his own heart shifted in his chest, leaning toward her.

And for another, *everyone* was watching. From the frankly disapproving faces five pews over to the red-faced Lady Sophie, still glaring at them from the end of the pew. He had no doubt that even Lady Austerley was watching, and smiling from somewhere beyond the grave.

They broke off, gasping for air, and that was when Lady Sophie's outraged hiss reached them. "Have you no shame? Kissing someone in public?"

"And worse, marrying someone like him?" Rose echoed, though she looked green with envy.

Daniel was sure he had never wanted to strangle two people so much. It occurred to him that Lady Sophie and Miss Evans would make two striking additions to St. Bartholomew's morgue, and not only because female cadavers were few and far between.

It was because he had a sneaking suspicion the pair lacked beating hearts.

But Clare only smiled up at him, and he felt his future unfurl beneath his feet. "On the contrary. I will be proud to be Mrs. Daniel Merial," she said.

And then she kissed him again.

Chapter 34

As transcribed by Bros. William and Thompson of London, this 19th Day of May, 1848

I, Lady Eugenia Austerley, being of sound mind and enduring memory, make this my last will and testament. First, I revoke and make void all former Wills and Testaments. Lord Harold, the 8th Earl of Austerley, may have inherited my husband's title, but as he could not be bestirred to come and visit a lonely old woman in her final weeks, he deserves little more than my contempt.

Enjoy the poorhouse, Harry. You have earned it.

To each of my loyal household staff, I leave a sum of one thousand pounds, in the hopes they might find themselves well settled. They have always done their best to ensure my comfort and there is no doubt their efforts extended my final days.

While I have considered bequeathing the remainder of my estate—encompassing some three hundred thousand pounds, a town house at 36 Berkeley

*Square, and various and sundry household ar-
tifacts —to Dr. Daniel Merial, who, in my final
months, showed me not only the compassion of an
knowledgeable doctor but the tolerance of faithful
friend, I know Dr. Merial would not appreciate the
gesture. Truly, I've never seen a man so averse to
accepting a bit of well-meant charity.*

*And so, I hereby bequeath these items to St. Bar-
tholomew's Teaching Hospital, to be sold or managed for the purposes of establishing a new surgery
wing. Said wing shall be named in Dr. Merial's
honor and dedicated to the betterment of all who
pass through its walls. I further declare that from
this sum, an annual salary of five hundred pounds be
provided to the hospital's newly established Chair
of the Board of Surgery and Anesthesiology—and
further, that this entire bequest be honored only
under the stipulation that Dr. Merial be named
to—and accept—the position in permanence.*

*On this I set my hand and seal, on the day and
year first written above.*

Daniel sat back in his hard-backed chair in the office of
Bros. William and Thompson, glaring at the dour-faced
lawyer sitting on the other side of the desk. "The old
dragon," he muttered. "She always did insist on having
her own way."

Beside him, her hand tightly clasped in his, Clare shook
with suppressed laughter.

"I will just give you a moment to absorb the news," said
the lawyer, standing up and straightening his waistcoat.
As he made his retreat, Clare devolved into an audible
snicker.

"I suppose you think this is amusing?" Daniel scowled
down at his wife of two weeks, but there was no heat in his

words. He could not, however, say the same for his gaze, and he could see she noticed by the way her own eyes darkened. A marvelous flush spread across her cheeks, as though anticipating what he might do to her later for her insolence, when they found a private moment.

"Well." Clare pursed her lips. "She claims she is of sound mind. And you *did* refuse to have anything to do with my inheritance when we drew up our marriage contract."

"Because I earned no part of it," he protested. "That money is yours, to do with as you would."

"And this is yours, Daniel. Apparently whether you like it or not." She smiled, and he caught a glimpse of that slight crooked tooth. As always, the sight sent pleasure spreading through him. "Truly," she said, "did you expect anything less? Lady Austerley orchestrated our lives from the moment we met. Do you remember the night of her musicale, when she practically tossed us into the library?"

This time it was his turn to smile. "Yes." Christ, how he remembered. And he was grateful for the old woman's foresight, nearly every day. He went to bed every night eager to make love to the woman whose hand was now clasped in his.

And each morning, he awakened to the glorious improbability of Clare in his arms.

She reached out a hand and picked up the damning bit of paper that would decide his future. "Look at the date." She pointed to the top of the page. "Lady Austerley drafted this will the day before her musicale. She knew then, you see, that we were meant to be. So in my mind, the main question here is do you plan to reject an old lady's last will and testament, when she was clearly so right about us?"

"No. I will not reject it." Daniel exhaled, already thinking of the possibilities, damn Lady Austerley's sweet, meddling heart. In truth, it was a position he would be quite honored to have . . . under less questionable circumstances. "But I *do* object to being manipulated from the grave."

"She understood what drove you, and she's found a way to make not only *our* dreams come true, but the dreams of thousands. Think of how many people you could help with this bequest. How many surgeries your anesthetic regulator could assist, how many lives might be saved. People like Handsome Meg would have a place to be healed, with no regard to income or class. *Think* on it a moment. Think of what she's done." The smile spread more widely across her face. "Why, if I didn't know better, I'd be tempted to suspect Lady Austerley was a Chartist."

In spite of himself, Daniel laughed. "I would not be surprised." He sobered. "She always did choose the most cantankerous path possible." He still missed the dowager countess, but more and more he found himself remembering her spirit with a smile, rather than with sorrow. "You are right," he admitted. "And although it pains me to say it, it seems Lady Austerley is right as well. It is a perfect opportunity, and I will not squander it for pride." He frowned. "But I can't quite wrap my head around the sum. Will three hundred thousand be enough to establish the sort of ward that could help thousands of people?"

"Perhaps." Clare's hand squeezed his. "But if it isn't, then we will have to seek additional donors." Her hazel eyes sparkled. "Now . . . who do you know with poise and grace, someone who was once widely acknowledged to be one of the most sought-after women in London?"

He grinned. "Lady Austerley?"

The grip of her hand turned to more of a warning pinch. "Someone who is still with us, and who is still accepted in at least *some* drawing rooms across London, thanks to her familial connection to a future duke?"

Daniel's lips quirked upward. "You, of course." He leaned over to press a kiss to the top of her head. "My wife." He breathed in the floral scent of her, so grateful for her quiet strength. "My love."

"Well then, Dr. Merial. Best get started." She beamed up at him. "We shall do this together, whether Lady Austerley approves or not."

*Next month, don't miss those exciting
new love stories only from
Avon Books*

Broken by Cynthia Eden
Amnesia victim Eve Gray seeks out ex-SEAL, Gabe
Spencer, and the LOST team to help uncover the
truth about her past. Eve is a dead ringer for the
heiress thought to be the latest prey of the serial
killer who goes by the name Lady Killer. When
another Eve lookalike disappears, Gabe vows to
protect her at all costs, even as their explosive attraction becomes irresistible.

It Started with a Scandal by Julie Anne Long
Lord Philippe Lavay took to the high seas to restore
his family's fortune and honor, but a brutal attack
lands him in Pennyroyal Green. Ruined, Elise Foun-
tain's survival means taking on a position no woman
has been able to keep: housekeeper to the frighten-
ingly formidable prince. Elise sees past Philippe's
battered body into his barricaded heart . . . and her
sensuality ignites his blood.

When It's Right by Jennifer Ryan
Warily accepting an invitation to her grandfather's
Montana ranch—a man she's never met—Gillian
Tucker hopes to find a haven from the violence of
San Francisco. Ranch co-owner Blake Bowden's
reckless past is over, and he knows his partner's
granddaughter is off limits. But she ignites a desire
in him he can't deny, and when danger surfaces,
Blake will do anything to keep her safe.

REL 0315

Available wherever books are sold or please call 1-800-331-3761 to order.

TEN THINGS I LOVE ABOUT YOU

978-0-06-149189-4

If the elderly Earl of Newbury dies without an heir, his detested nephew Sebastian inherits everything. Newbury decides that Annabel Winslow is the answer to his problems. But the thought of marrying the earl makes Annabel's skin crawl, even though the union would save her family from ruin. Perhaps the earl's machinations will leave him out in the cold and spur a love match instead?

JUST LIKE HEAVEN

978-0-06-149190-0

Marcus Holroyd has promised his best friend, David Smythe-Smith, that he'll look out for David's sister, Honoria. Not an easy task when Honoria sets off for Cambridge determined to marry by the end of the season. When her advances are spurned can Marcus swoop in and steal her heart?

A NIGHT LIKE THIS

978-0-06-207290-0

Daniel Smythe-Smith vows to pursue the mysterious young governess Anne Wynter, even if that means spending his days with a ten-year-old who thinks she's a unicorn. And after years of dodging unwanted advances, the oh-so-dashing Earl of Winstead is the first man to truly tempt Anne.

At Avon Books, we know your passion for romance—once you finish one of our novels, you find yourself wanting more.

May we tempt you with . . .

- **Excerpts** from our upcoming releases.
- Entertaining **extras**, including authors' personal photo albums and book lists.
- Behind-the-scenes **scoop** on your favorite characters and series.
- **Sweepstakes** for the chance to win free books, romantic getaways, and other fun prizes.
- Writing **tips** from our authors and editors.
- **Blog** with our authors and find out why they love to write romance.
- **Exclusive content** that's not contained within the pages of our novels.

Join us at
www.avonbooks.com

AVON
An Imprint of HarperCollins*Publishers*
www.avonromance.com